The PURLOINED PORTRAIT

BOOK FIVE
THE HAPGOODS OF BRAMLEIGH

CHRISTINA DUDLEY

Cover design: Kathy Campbell,

ISBN: 978-1-963408-04-1

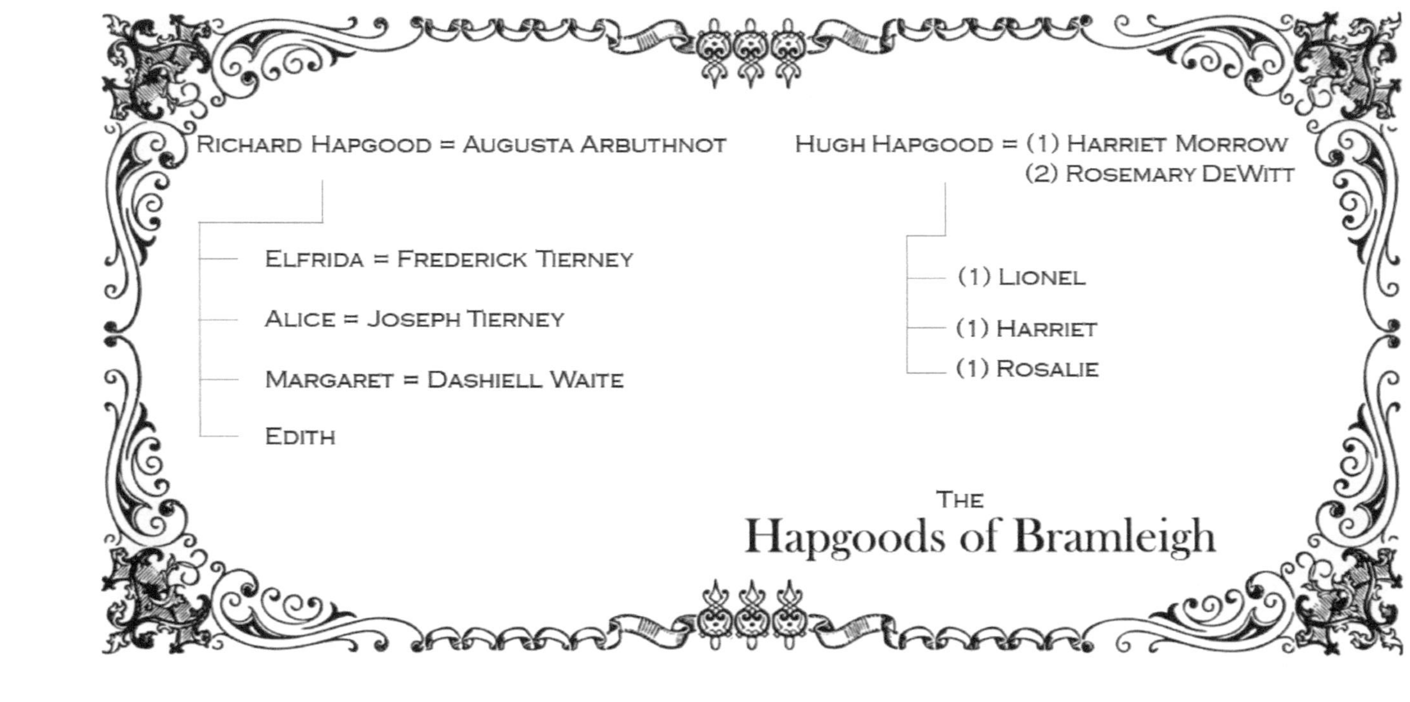

RICHARD HAPGOOD = AUGUSTA ARBUTHNOT

ELFRIDA = FREDERICK TIERNEY

ALICE = JOSEPH TIERNEY

MARGARET = DASHIELL WAITE

EDITH

HUGH HAPGOOD = (1) HARRIET MORROW
(2) ROSEMARY DEWITT

(1) LIONEL

(1) HARRIET

(1) ROSALIE

THE
Hapgoods of Bramleigh

PROLOGUE

June 1814

**"Persons desirous of becoming Purchasers, are request-
ed to apply to the respective Artists."
—*The Exhibition of the Royal Academy: The
Forty-Sixth* (1814)**

"I tell you, Lionel, it is you to the life! You must see it."

"I already know what I look like," Lionel Hapgood yawned, crossing his booted ankles on the deal table of their spartan lodging in Marylebone. "Therefore, why should I inspect some coincidental likeness?"

Trinity term was ended, and he had accepted Clinker and Clunker's invitation to join them in town for general mischief and mayhem. Well, Clinker (christened Jason by his parents) must supply the mischief and mayhem, for his twin Clunker (termed by the family "Edward") was far more interested in the arts and the composition of turgid poetry. In appearance the Clinkett brothers were far more alike, being both lanky and dark-haired, with prominent joints and eyes and Adam's apples.

"You must see it because it is remarkable," Clunker insisted. "If you were not the sitter for it, there is some young man in the kingdom who might very well impersonate you."

"What's so distinctive about Lion?" drawled Clinker. He had a damp towel wrapped about his head and was sprawled across one of the unmade beds. "There must be thousands of auburn-haired young men in London alone. And, pray, Clunk, don't speak so loudly. Lord, how my head aches."

"Lionel's isn't just *auburn*. It's a particular shade. A distinctive shade. With gold and red in it."

"I suppose. And a little orange," conceded Clinker.

"Yes, and orange, of sorts, though there's something so unpoetic about the word 'orange.' When I tried to paint him myself, I couldn't capture his hair."

"That's because you can't paint a whitewashed wall, much less a person," said his brother.

Clunker sputtered, offended. "I'll have you know, white isn't simply white. A dozen shades are required to depict something so plain as a whitewashed wall. You couldn't do it either. You're simply cross because you drank too much last night."

Clinker groaned, rolling his long frame to face the wall.

"And it wasn't only that the subject shared your hair coloring," Clunker resumed to Lionel. "There was something about the eyes. I stood there and thought, 'Bless me, if that isn't Lionel Hapgood to the inch!' There was a crowd gathered around the picture, even though the exhibit this year seems almost entirely portraits. Yours drew nearly as many spectators as Phillips' of Lord Byron in Albanian dress."

"Don't," complained Clinker again, from the depths of the bedclothes. "Don't tell Hapgood such things, or he'll bore the common room with tales of how he's more famous than Byron. And handsomer."

"Too late," Lionel said. "If the thing's truly such a wonder, I'll purchase it to hang beside Cardinal Wolsey in the Hall, right above the high table. Or perhaps I will hang it *in place of* Wolsey. What was the name of the piece, Clunker?"

"*Portrait of a young gentleman.* Does this mean you will come see it?"

"I had better, or how will I buy it? That is—how will Clinker buy it, since he owes me...what is the tally now, Clink? Twenty-five guineas?"

The only response was another groan, and Clinker pulled a pillow over his head. "I will never play cards or dice again, Lion. Nor drink anything stronger than barley water. Go away, the both of you. Do."

It was a gloomy, smoky afternoon, more like November than June, and the two young men did not reach the Royal Academy of Art in Somerset House until nearly closing time, having first inspected horses at Tattersall's near Hyde Park Corner, before wandering into the park itself, in search of inspiration for Clunker's poetry. But the air was too thick for any young beauties to be abroad, and Clunker could think of no rhymes for "smoke" apart from "choke" and "croak," so eventually they proceeded along Pall Mall and the Strand to the exhibition.

Portrait of a young gentleman hung near the door in the anti-room of the Royal Academy, flanked by such companions as *Portrait of the late Earl of Uxbridge* and *View on the Clyde, with the rock of Dunbarton.* The young gentleman in question was captured in an unconventional pose. He was out of doors, seated atop a stile, his face alight and intent, as if he were about to say something quite reckless to the artist and debating whether he dared.

"What did I tell you?" said Clunker, standing beneath the portrait and gesturing like a showman. "You, to the life. You are fortunate there is no one about, for once, or I imagine there would be quite a stir. Everyone might rush at you, thinking you had walked right out of the canvas."

Clunker had not exaggerated. Lionel gaped at the portrait a full minute, speechless, before sinking onto the nearest bench. For it was indeed himself, to the life.

That is, the subject did not merely resemble Lionel Hapgood, it *was* Lionel Hapgood. He, himself! For he himself had sat for a sketch on that very stile in that very place only the summer before. There was no mistaking the matter and no forgetting it.

Absolutely no forgetting it. Not that Lionel had not tried. Tried for an entire year. Even this mild London debauch in company of his class-fellows Clinker and Clunker formed part of that forgetting strategy, putting off, as it did, the inevitable return to Somerset for the long vacation.

Nor could that moment be more permanently captured in paint than it was in his memory. For that was the day he had declared himself. And she—

"I say—are you unwell?" Clunker asked.

"No. Yes. That is—"

Clunker frowned at his companion, but it was a frown of contemplation, rather than concern. "You are ashen, Hapgood. No—grey. 'Gris,' as Chaucer would say. A face gone gris. A phiz all gris..." Plumping down beside him, Clunker removed a tiny pencil and notebook from his pocket and began scribbling away, chewing his lip thoughtfully. "'Alack for this! His face gone gris.' No, no—'He stood amazed, his face gone grey.'" When such fits of inspiration took him, Clunker was lost to the world, and Lionel knew, with relief and gratitude, that his friend would not trouble him with more questions at present.

He rose, not very steadily, to draw closer, peering in vain to pick out her signed initials on the painting or to read the little placard below the work. It was no good. Turning, he plucked the exhibition catalogue from Clunker's other pocket. His friend didn't even glance up.

Struggling not to tear the pages in his haste, Lionel skimmed the catalogue. The frontispiece. A list of more than two hundred works. The Inner Room. The Anti-Room. 290, 291...296! *Portrait of a young gentleman*. And the artist?

A. J. Morris.

A. J. Morris? Who on earth was A. J. Morris? How utterly useless! Unless—

He tapped his fingers on the catalogue cover. Could she have entered the work under an assumed name, so that the Academicians would not guess she was a young lady? But why "A. J. Morris"? Did the name "A. J. Morris" have any significance to her that he could think of?

He continued turning the pages and was gratified to find a more detailed list of exhibitors "with their places of abode." This would make things clear. If A. J. Morris lived in Somerset or at any address in London belonging to her family members, then that would mean she had submitted the painting herself to the Academy for consideration.

But no. The entry read: "A. J. Morris. 63 Jermyn Street. 296, 574." Lionel knew her oldest sisters Elfrida and Alice both used the Tierney townhouse in Portman Square when they came up with their husbands. And her third sister Margaret would stay at her mother-in-law's townhouse on Bruton Street, now also the home of their uncle Alwyn Arbuthnot, who had married Margaret's mother-in-law.

So who could live in Jermyn Street?

It must wait. First, he must see the other accepted work of this so-called A. J. Morris. He riffled back through the catalogue to number 574, which was listed among the works hung in the Antique Academy. 574: *Portrait of Sir C. Nightingale, Bart.* Lionel could not think of anyone in his acquaintance with that name, but who knew how her fame as an artist might have spread? Perhaps this baronet was known to Viscount Marlton's family.

Without sparing a glance at Clunker (who was still hunched over his notebook muttering, in any case), Lionel set off in search of the Antique Academy. If number 574 by A. J. Morris was another of her—of Edith's—paintings, Lionel would know.

The Antique Room was much smaller than the other exhibition spaces. It might almost have been called out of the way. Here it was more difficult to view the paintings because sculptures in the classical style cluttered the room. Torsos, legs, figures speechifying or throwing things. Lionel took no notice of them except as obstacles, circling and dodging the marble statuary until he found Sir C. Nightingale, Baronet.

And though he was no art expert, it did not take him long to dismiss it.

It was not hers.

She—*Edith*—did not favor stiff formality or wooden expressions or backgrounds of ruined masonry. And even if this Sir C. Nightingale was, in truth, a stiff, wooden block of a man who insisted on ruined-masonry backgrounds, the portrait entirely lacked that particular quality found in everything Edith drew or painted. That life in the eyes and insight into the sitter's character. The sympathy that came from her own heart and was conferred upon her subjects by her pencil or her brush.

Sir C. Nightingale, Baronet was an inferior work, and Lionel was gratified to think the Royal Academy agreed with him, hiding it away in the Antique Room behind all the marble scrap, as one might stow a broom in a closet when guests were expected.

But what then could it mean? Who was this A. J. Morris, inferior artist, and how did he come by Edith's painting? Did she press Morris to enter her work as one of his own, too shy to submit it herself? Or did Morris, realizing her superior skill, beg her to let him do so? In either case, how did she know him? And, far more importantly, what did he mean to her? And what could it mean that, of all her works, she chose to submit her painting of Lionel? Not to mention, how had it even come to be a painting, when he had only known it as a sketch?

It was a marvelous portrait, of course—and Lionel knew without extraordinary vanity that his personal appearance was pleasing—but having seen a countless number of Edith's works, he knew as well that it was only one among many she might have ventured to submit.

There were no more answers to be found in the Antique Room, and Lionel hastened to rejoin Clunker, who was now surrounded by discarded wads of notepaper as he stared unseeingly at the Cipriani medallions adorning the anti-room ceiling. Though Lionel was impatient to visit Jermyn Street and learn more about this Morris fellow, it would only be a few minutes more before the closing of the gallery put an end to Clunker's compositional reverie.

In the meantime, Lionel's gaze returned to his portrait. And though he did not want to remember—and had spent an entire year trying not to—the vividness of the painting took him back, whether he would or not.

Back to her.

The original sketch had been done in charcoal pencil. And quickly. Because Lionel had been hurrying from Patterton to Bramleigh, and when he spied Edith in the meadow, perched on a little canvas camp chair with her sketchbook, he called to her, his heart lifting to see her for the first time in months.

"Lionel!" she cried, rising and waving. "You've come back! Oh! Stop right there—on the stile—just for a moment—"

He obeyed, of course, despite his eagerness. Even from this distance he could see she was grown prettier than ever. She had removed her bonnet, leaving the breeze to loosen some of her dark curls, and he wanted to kiss the furrow of concentration on her brow. And he was glad that she wanted to capture him because it gave him an excuse to stare at her.

"What is it?" Edith asked, her pencil flying over the page as she glanced at him. "You look as if you were ready to burst with something."

He reached for the teasing tone she would expect. "I can't wait to spread the news that I am back in Somerset, having covered myself in glory at my first year of university."

She grinned, not taking her eyes from her sketch. "That's not what your sister Hetty says. She said you were nearly sent down for your escapades."

"Sent down? I'll send her down! She's just envious. She says she doesn't see why she still has to have a governess when you no longer do."

Edith laughed, making a little curtsey. "Because my education is complete—apart from more lessons in drawing and painting. I'm afraid I now dance and play, read French and Italian, sew, and work sums as well as I ever will."

Then you must be perfection itself, he wanted to say. But instead he said, "If your drawing and painting still need improvement, you had better let me see what a muddle you've made of me. May I have a look yet?"

"One minute more..." She made a series of sweeping strokes, and Lionel knew she was roughing the background. "There. Behold—the Lion of Somerset! Hetty says that's the nickname you've been given, at any rate. Is it for your hair, which is so long? She thinks the name ridiculous, but I think it's far better than 'Clinker' or 'Clunker.'"

He was beside her before she finished speaking, wondering if he could get away with hugging her, but she was holding up the sketch, her grey eyes glowing at him and her smile radiant and unclouded.

Reluctantly he tore his own eyes from her to give the drawing a cursory glance, only to inhale sharply. The sketch was alive and arresting and—and his secret was written all over his face. Could she not see it? Could she not interpret what she had captured there for all to see?

"Edith—"

There would be no going back from this moment.

But he was only seventeen at the time. Young enough to think that, surely she must already have guessed, and if he did not speak his secret now, it would burn its way out of him. Burn its way out of him, or he would die of it.

And so he did speak.

And brought his world down around his ears.

Part One
1808 - 1814

CHAPTER ONE

What is this Relation called? Is it third Cousins?
—Benjamin Franklin, Letter dated 17 July (1768)

Miss Edith Hapgood's young life fell into two parts, the first spanning her birth to the summer of 1808, when she was eleven, and the second being all that came after.

Until that eventful summer, as the fourth and youngest daughter of Squire Richard Hapgood of Bramleigh, Somerset, Edith lived quietly at home among her immediate family. There was little money and few servants, which meant the house and grounds, though large and extensive, were rather dilapidated, and the family glory considerably diminished. When her father was not riding to hounds, he stamped about, roaring harmlessly (and never at her), while her mother kept to her chamber, nursing imaginary ailments. Edith never had a regular governess, though her two eldest sisters Elfrida and Alice did, at one point, before the money ran out. There were occasional spells with a dancing master or a drawing master in her childhood, but most education she received had been scrambled into—learned from Elfrida or from books in the family library, collected by a more scholarly forebear and frequently stuffed with plant samples Alice collected. As for friendship, while Edith's two eldest sisters petted and made much of her, it was the sister closest in age to her who provided the most company, though Margaret never forgot her four years of seniority and took care that Edith should not either.

Because the Hapgoods hadn't the means to live on a grand scale, each of the daughters found occupation at home. Collectively they read aloud and played cards and occasionally danced, played, and sang. Individually, Elfrida sewed and embroidered; Alice was forever out of doors, catching creatures and insects; Margaret practiced on the spinet or sewed with Elfie or drew with Edith, being more interested in companionship than any particular activity. But Edith—Edith could never remember a time when she was not trying to capture the world and the people around her. In pencil, in charcoal, in paint. On a slate, on paper, on a frosted windowpane, on the end pages or in the margins of books. Nor did anyone in the family reprimand her for defacing their meager library. Alice only said, "Why, Edie, your illustrations are better than the original!" and Elfie only asked her to sketch scenes of shepherds and shepherdesses, that she might use them as embroidery designs. Even the squire, who had no eye for art or, indeed, for anything that did not bark or gallop or fly—even the squire recognized his youngest daughter's gift and took pride in it. He might grumble and curse when his good-for-nothing brothers-in-law requested loans; he might roll his eyes heavenward when the quarterly doctor's bill from Mr. Lewis came; but if Margaret mentioned that little Edie's charcoal pencils were worn to nubs or that everyone had better be satisfied to be painted all in red or brown, for Edie was running low on other colors, the squire was sure to find the money somewhere.

Thus, indulged by all and encouraged to pursue what she loved best, Edith Hapgood passed her first eleven years with little to trouble her, and she was surprisingly unspoiled in spite of it.

But the summer of 1808 transformed her small world.

The first great change was that Alice married a clergyman naturalist and removed with him to Buckinghamshire.

The second was that the brother of Alice's husband began courting Elfrida. Before autumn arrived, Elfrida too would be married and gone into Buckinghamshire.

And between those two marriages, that same summer saw the death of Harriet Hapgood, wife to the heir of Bramleigh, the squire's cousin Mr. Hugh Hapgood. The bereaved widower soon descended on them for his first visit in years, his three motherless children in tow. Lionel, Hetty and Rosie were known only to Edith's older sisters, but Edith did not have to know them to pity them the loss of their mother.

And for this reason, she decided to make a gift for their arrival, bringing it to Elfrida for consultation.

"What is it, dearest?" asked Elfie, looking up from her embroidery hoop. She sat in full sunlight, the better to see her detailed work, and Edith laid her drawing on the sofa beside her.

"I thought I would make a family tree for our little cousins, Elfie. So that, even though they have lost their mother, they will see they now have us. Or—I suppose they had us all along—but now we will all know each other better."

"What a lovely idea!" The eldest Hapgood daughter, beautiful, serene, and myopic, lay aside her work to squint at the paper. "Gracious. I cannot make out your writing—it is so very minute!—but the little portraits are delightful. This is Papa to the breath! You have even made him very red, as if he has just come in from riding. I'm sure our little orphaned cousins will be much comforted."

"Yes, I have put Papa and Mama, and, under them, each of us: you, Alice and her Joseph, Margaret, and me. And it was easy enough to do Mama's side of the family over here, not that they might particularly care for *them*, being wholly unrelated. Her brothers Alec and Alwyn and their parents the Arbuthnots. But I was rather puzzled on Papa's side. Papa has always referred to Mr. Hugh Hapgood as his cousin, but Papa's uncle didn't have any children, I thought."

"He didn't. Hugh Hapgood is not Papa's *first* cousin. That is, they do not have the same grandparents. I believe Hugh is actually descended from Papa's great-uncle. Our grandfather's younger brother Ira. So is Hugh Hapgood Ira's son? No—the son of his son." Elfrida's fair brow creased in thought. "Which makes him...let me see...not Papa's first cousin and not his first cousin once removed—that would be Hugh's father—but rather his second cousin. Yes. They are second cousins. But Papa can hardly go around calling him 'my second cousin Hugh.'"

"I do not see why Hugh Hapgood should inherit Bramleigh, then, if he is so distantly related," Edith frowned.

"Because Bramleigh is entailed, sweeting—you know that. And Hugh, however distant he is, is Papa's closest male relative. In fact, his only remaining male relative, unless you count Hugh's son Lionel, who would be Papa's second cousin *once removed*!"

"But I was making this family tree to comfort our Hapgood cousins!" objected Edith, "And now you tell me Lionel and Hetty and Rosie are all Papa's second cousins once removed, which makes them hardly related to him at all! And, to *us*, why, they are only our—our—"

Her oldest sister was genuinely frowning now, trying to unsnarl the tangled family tree in her mind. "Let me see...if Papa and Hugh share a great-grandparent, then we share great-great-grandparents with Lionel and Hetty and Rosie. So that makes us...third cousins. I think. I am not positive. No—maybe we are second cousins once removed, because we are the same generation as Lionel, Hetty and Rosie. Or are we actually Hugh's generation? Ah, I give up. You had better check with Papa. In any case, you can see why no one bothers to be specific. It is easier all around for everyone to call everyone else 'cousin.'"

Shaking her head, Edith retrieved the family tree from her sister's grasp. "It is more complicated than I thought. What comfort will it be to them, to show them they have nobody on the Hapgood side but some very distant cousins? Perhaps I will abandon the effort."

"But your beautiful little portraits! No—don't abandon it. I am certain they will agree that very distant cousins are better than no cousins at all, and your pictures are better still."

As if to emphasize their relational remoteness, these third cousins looked nothing at all like the Richard Hapgoods. Where Edith's father was blond and stocky and ruddy, Hugh Hapgood was dark, lean, and rather forbidding. Where Edith and her sisters had hair ranging from golden (Elfrida) to nearly black (Edith), Lionel and his younger sisters were all pale with varying shades of red-gold hair and blue eyes.

Nor did this branch of the Hapgood family behave in ways Edith was accustomed to. Where her father was loud and demonstrative, Hugh Hapgood was quiet and contained. And while the four sisters might bicker from time to time, when they were in harmony, peace and quiet prevailed. But the Hugh Hapgood children were wont to stir things up in all circumstances, Lionel for the joy of it and Hetty to serve her own purposes.

Hetty settled down over the ensuing weeks, but Lionel's rumbustious spirits endured. He moved constantly, frolicking, teasing, testing. And, perhaps because he was a boy, such qualities were viewed with complacence, rather than deplored. Indeed, in his own way, Lionel was as admired and petted as Edith, and, as a result, he could not help being rather pleased with himself, a fact no one besides Hetty seemed to mind.

Certainly Edith did not mind, having no experience of brothers or indeed of any boys besides their servant Hal, who handled footman duties and out-of-door work at Bramleigh. Unknown quantities must be taken as they came; therefore it seemed natural enough to her that, the very first time she met Lionel, he should treat her as he did his younger sisters.

"You're all smudged," was effectively the first thing he ever said to her, upon his family's arrival in Somerset. "Have you been mining for coal?"

(Had Alice been there, she would have informed him that weren't any coal deposits thereabouts, but Alice was already in Buckinghamshire with her new husband.)

"I have been drawing," Edith answered, holding her notebook to her chest. She had, until the moment he addressed her, been dashing off sketches of Lionel, Hetty and Rosie to add to their family tree.

"Drawing?" he grinned at her as if this were not any odder than coalmining. "Drawing what? Give us a look, then."

She hesitated.

"Come on. How old are you anyway? Nine? Eight?"

Then her grey eyes flashed. "I'm eleven." She was small for her age—small for any age. "Older than Hetty."

"Ah, I see. But younger than I, at any rate, for I am going on thirteen. And Hetty already has the advantage of you in height." His grin softened, however, to see her pointed chin lift. He made her a little bow. "I do apologize, Cousin Edith. I am used to treating my younger sisters roughly, to keep them in order, you know. What I mean to say is, may I please see your drawing? It would be an honor."

There was no choice then but to hand him her notebook. She had little experience showing her work outside her family, and she hesitated now. If he didn't like what he found there—

But she need not have worried. His teasing expression vanished, and he gave an admiring whistle. "I say! Where'd you learn to draw like that? That's Hetty to the freckle! Even her contrary look. And yet you've done it in so few strokes!"

She colored with pleasure, which deepened as he continued to study her work, turning the pages. "Do you always draw everyone you see? If you don't, you ought to. These are marvelous."

"Thank you," she whispered.

He gave her a curious look, taking in the dark curling hair and solemn grey eyes. "You haven't done me, except this one profile."

"I've only had a minute. I was starting when you talked to me."

"Well, my family tells me I never sit still long, but I will try, for your sake." Grinning again at her, he struck a theatrical pose, as if he were Mungo Park at the Niger River—and indeed, in his coloring and his handsome features, he greatly resembled the Scottish explorer, whose *Travels in the Interior Districts of Africa* he had devoured. When Edith laughed at his antics, Lionel's chest swelled further.

It was not long before some mischief of Hetty's reclaimed the attention of all that day, but the work had been done: Lionel and Edith were friends, and she thought when she went to bed that night that she would very much like having these new cousins, however tenuous their cousinship might be.

The Hugh Hapgoods' visit stretched, after fits and starts, into a permanent residency in Somerset, with Lionel boarded at the vicar Mr. Benfield's in Patterton to complete his studies and the girls and their father taking lodgings close by. Soon the squire and Hugh arranged for Edith to share a governess with Hetty and Rosie, another plan which proceeded in fits and starts, but at last resulted in Edith beginning her formal education.

Therefore, if the first part of Edith's life was dominated by her sisters and her sheltered, irregular existence at Bramleigh, the second chapter was characterized by her cousins' presence and increased structure at home. For not only did Edith sit with Hetty and Rosie for lessons under a governess in the Bramleigh schoolroom, but Hugh's new wife Rosemary undertook to teach household management to Margaret, who proved an enthusiastic pupil. Under Margaret's governance, Bramleigh began to run more smoothly. Both the estate and the squire's finances improved, and, if Edith had thought much about it or cared, she would have realized her own marriage prospects would be brighter than her older sisters' had been.

But Edith did *not* think much about money or her future marriage prospects. Instead, what tended to preoccupy her was the thing which remained constant across both periods of her life.

Her art.

CHAPTER TWO

Those move easiest who have learned to dance.
—Pope, *An Essay on Criticism* (1711)

In addition to teaching Margaret Hapgood how to manage Bramleigh, Mrs. Rosemary Hapgood found another role given her: that of her stepson Lionel's confidante. Even before she married his father, he thought her easy to talk to, and there were some subjects better trusted to womenfolk. With his father he discussed his schooling, his situation at the Benfields, his future at Oxford. With the squire he talked sport and dogs and farming. With Mr. Benfield there was Greek and Latin, geography and history, mathematics and astronomy. His younger sister Hetty, naturally, was not to be told anything of importance, lest it become a whip in her hands, and Rosie was too young altogether for Lionel to take much notice of.

Therefore, when Lionel was only twelve and but newly come to Somerset, it was to Rosemary he first declared his intention of one day marrying Edith. It was a boyish announcement, made shortly after he met this new cousin, and Rosemary appreciated Lionel's confidence without attaching any actual importance to it, forgetting even to mention it to Hugh after they were married.

She was only reminded of it after nearly a year had gone by, when she met with the girls' new governess Miss Blenkensop to hear of their progress. Miss Blenkensop was a learned, angular, stern-looking woman of perhaps thirty-five, who was nevertheless soft as pudding. She adored children, even Hetty, who was not precisely adorable, and, though Rosemary initially feared little learning would happen under such an instructor, she came to be pleasantly surprised.

"My dear Miss Blenkensop," Rosemary began, when the tea was poured, "I am much encouraged to hear you feel at home in Somerset and that you have found your work at Bramleigh to your liking. It was no easy task to find a governess as accomplished as yourself, and we are grateful for you. Do tell me how you find your charges thus far. Hetty has been behaving, I hope?"

Miss Blenkensop gave a rueful little chuckle and her pale eyes twinkled. "Oh, Mrs. Hapgood—how spirited dear Harriet is! Were she not so interested in her studies, I would have my hands full with her because she is far too clever. She could get up to a great deal of mischief if she chose. And then my hands would not only be full with her but also with her sister, for little Rosalie follows wherever her sister leads."

"What you say is very true, Miss Blenkensop, and I hope Hetty's interest in her studies will continue to be consuming, for those very reasons. Tell me: does Hetty's influence extend to her cousin Edith?"

"Ah, Edith is quiet but certainly her own mistress," answered Miss Blenkensop. "She enjoys Harriet's liveliness, much as she enjoys Master Lionel's, but Edith has a mind of her own. And a good mind, too. Another girl with her talents and with what promise to be her *attractions* might suffer from conceit, you know."

Rosemary smiled. "Indeed. I hope none of the girls will ever suffer from conceit."

"Oh, yes," breathed the governess. "I share your hope. But with Hetty there is the *danger* of it, I am sorry to say. Because of her cleverness. And, while she is no artist, like Edith, she excels at everything else. Her French and Italian are *beautiful*, her playing quite superior, and it seems she need only read or be told something once to remember it. If she grows to be half as attractive as Master Lionel, she will be a formidable young lady indeed. Perhaps—perhaps *too* formidable to make the average young gentleman easy."

Rosemary didn't doubt that, but that was a worry for another day. For the present, it was enough that her stepdaughter succeed in her studies.

"And Rosie?" she pursued, after a minute.

Miss Blenkensop carefully finished chewing her bite of biscuit. "Rosalie is a darling. Hard-working, quiet, sweet. Not quite as clever as Harriet, of course, but her diligence compensates. No, Mrs. Hapgood, the girls are doing very well. I am delighted with their progress and think you should be very pleased. There is, in fact, only one area I wished to mention to you..."

"Please do, Miss Blenkensop," Rosemary encouraged, refilling the woman's cup. She prepared herself for a request of additional books or, perhaps, for Hetty to begin to learn the harp.

"It is the girls' dancing, Mrs. Hapgood," was her unexpected reply. "Without a dancing master, I have done the best I can with them, but you understand that the three girls and I can only form two couples—hardly adequate to practice the intricacies of many of the figures. I do not feel confident that they would be able to comport themselves as admirably as I would like, if they were to attend an assembly or ball."

"Ah! I understand your concern," said Rosemary. And she did, for she came from a family that loved to dance. "Though assemblies and balls are some years off for them."

"Once I did manage to enlist the squire and Miss Margaret, which did help, but Mr. Richard Hapgood is not often found indoors, and while Miss Margaret is willing, uneven numbers do not mend matters, you understand, so I more often put her to work accompanying us on the spinet."

"Yes, I see. Miss Blenkensop, I think I could persuade my family—the DeWitts, that is—to host a few evening events where the girls may practice. That would be...let me see...Papa and Mama, Roscoe and Constance, Hugh and I." Rosemary told them off on her fingers. "Norman, and the squire—if we can persuade him—and Lionel. With the girls and Margaret and you, that would make seven couples. Perhaps the Benfields might be prevailed upon as well, that we might form two squares. Would that work?"

"Oh, Mrs. Hapgood! That would be the very thing!" Miss Blenkensop sighed with delight. "Thank you. Master Lionel said you would be the one to talk to, and he was right."

"Miss Blenkensop," said Rosemary, amused, "you have mentioned Lionel several times during this conversation, and yet I am at a loss to understand how you have come to know him or consult him. Was it at church?"

"Oh, no, Mrs. Hapgood. Not at church, though he is always so well-mannered and unfailingly bows to me when he sees me on a Sunday. Master Lionel is a frequent visitor to our schoolroom. He has even danced once, when he found us practicing."

"Indeed! How can that be, when he has his own studies with Mr. Benfield?"

For the first time, Miss Blenkensop seemed to become aware that she may have got her favorite young man in some difficulty. She gave an uneasy titter. "I'm certain he only comes by when he has finished his own schooling, madam. Such a good lad. He often visits the squire or walks his sisters home. And he is *so* supportive of Edith's artistic gifts!"

"Yes? In what way 'supportive'?"

"Oh, so admiring and interested and patient—he sits for her sometimes, you know, which is much appreciated because she has so few male models. And, while he can be apt to drive his sisters wild with teasing—as any older brother might—he is charm itself to Edith."

For the first time since the previous autumn, when Lionel cheerfully told her in Mr. Benfield's study that he wanted to become a country gentleman and marry his young cousin, Rosemary recalled the incident. That his attachment had endured an entire year surprised her, and she considered whether this boyish impulse might grow into something more fixed. He was well over thirteen now, and, if he still admired his cousin, his admiration had lasted longer than she would have supposed likely. But perhaps it was only a function of not meeting any other girls his age in Somerset. Probably when he went to university in a few years, Edith would be forgotten, despite her artistic genius and budding beauty.

For the present, Rosemary determined to keep her own counsel. Lionel was lively and sometimes reckless, but surely he would not involve Edith in any mischief under the very eyes of her governess! Only if she thought Edith's heart might be touched would she intervene, she decided. In the meantime, she would simply observe.

The first gathering at Marchmont, home of Sir Cosmo and Lady DeWitt, took place a fortnight later. Because the DeWitts were always eager dancers, the drawing room furnishings had often been pushed against the walls to make room. In the end there were only seven couples, but Miss Blenkensop accounted herself pleased. In such a setting, surrounded by family and friends, her pupils would not be so embarrassed of mistakes, and Lady DeWitt was more than willing to pause in her play at the pianoforte, or to repeat measures when asked.

When she took the time to truly look at her, Rosemary could understand why the governess referred to the "promise" of Edith

Hapgood's attractions. The girl was twelve now—a little older than Hetty—and still diminutive, but her appearance rewarded patient observation. The eldest Hapgood daughter, now Mrs. Frederick Tierney, was always accounted the family beauty, and the next two sisters Alice and Margaret were fresh and pretty in their ways, but little Edith was something else. She put Rosemary in mind of walking through the woodlands in early spring and coming upon the first of the bluebells—natural, delicate, dainty, sweet—not garish and bold like hothouse flowers. The more one looked at her, the more one wanted to look at her. And the more one looked at her, the more one noticed. The fine shape of her grey eyes. Eyes which watched the world so thoughtfully. The soft curl of her dark hair, on which no iron was needed. Her straight small nose and pointed chin. And her quiet hands that held such skill.

The only wonder was how such a boy as Lionel had preferred her so quickly (though, again, there were not many candidates for his attention in Patterton). Rosemary loved her stepson—everyone did—but she would have imagined such a golden, playful, confident, often *loud* boy would have preferred the hothouse-flower variety of girl.

And now that she took the time to look, Rosemary saw that Lionel indeed still favored his small cousin. It was not that he kept to her side or addressed her constantly; it was not that he bragged or boasted or clowned for her. It was that he stole glances at her, when he thought no one (including Edith herself) would notice. It was that, when he did so, there was a most un-Lionel-like quietness in his gaze. And sometimes these glances were followed by the slightest of smiles, as if Edith were a secret told only to himself.

Rosemary was not dissatisfied with her findings. They were both very young, but if Lionel and Edith Hapgood eventually proved a match, there would be a pleasing symmetry to it. The eventual heir to Bramleigh marrying the scion of the displaced Richard-Hapgood branch. She even wondered if it were advisable to put the idea to her husband Hugh. Many a couple were betrothed younger than Lionel and Edith. She soon dismissed this idea, however, because of their very youth. Who knew how feelings might change as they grew? And Lionel's affection for Edith did not imply that Edith returned his feelings, of course. She seemed to like him well enough—again, who did not?—but she singled him out for no special attention and appeared as willing to dance with her father or Margaret as with Lionel.

"Miss Blenkensop tells me you are often at Bramleigh," Rosemary said to her stepson, when he partnered her for a longways dance, and Edith was paired with Norman DeWitt at the other end. "On days when the girls have lessons."

"Ah!" he laughed, "who knew Soppy was such a tale-bearer?"

"Lionel, she told no tales! She merely mentioned you a few times, and I asked how you came to be there," Rosemary chided. "And pray do not call her Soppy!"

"It was Hetty who began that."

"Now who is telling tales?"

He only grinned, and Rosemary saw her opportunity. "Please tell me you two have not been a bad influence on Rosie and Edith."

He threw one of his quick looks at Edith before saying, "You know Rosie will do whatever Hetty does. But you may rest easy with Edith—with her it's 'Blenkensop,' if it's anything."

He and his stepmother took hands to go in circle and he leaned in to whisper, "I don't call Blenkensop 'Soppy' when Edith is about because I know she wouldn't care for it, and one doesn't like to cross her. Apart from you, my dear stepmama, there is no one whose good opinion I value more."

Rosemary smiled at the compliment but also filed this in her memory for later pondering. She was pleased, on the whole, that he should respect the opinion of a modest, intelligent girl like Edith Hapgood. It spoke well for his own judgment. But then, why should Rosemary be surprised? For all his flighty charm and dash, Lionel was the son of Hugh Hapgood, and Rosemary held her husband's good sense in very high esteem.

Lionel was cleverer even than his stepmother gave him credit for, for he had never yet given Edith the least hint how far his admiration for her extended. He sensed—he guessed—such knowledge would not be welcome at this pass and would likely endanger their comfortable friendship. Thus, when that particular dance ended, he approached his cousin with a teasing, "If you have finished crushing Mr. Norman DeWitt's feet, you may have a go at mine, Edie."

"Thank you, Lionel. You are generosity itself," she replied, but she smiled at him and gave him her hand as they took their place in the line.

Lady DeWitt had been spelled by Miss Blenkensop at the pianoforte, so it was the latter who nodded approvingly at her charges and launched into Astley's Hornpipe, calling the figures loudly.

"Don't you wish you had your sketch book by, Edie?" he asked in passing.

"I do! I rarely see so many people gathered. And what delightful variety of faces and figures."

"Do you never try to draw from memory?"

"Yes, but even my memories tend to involve the same people and places." She looked about her, at the dancers flushed in the warm candlelight. At Rosie clapping her hands with joy. At Mr. Roscoe DeWitt assisting his wife to a seat while she fanned herself. At Sir Cosmo crossing with his daughter, stepping as youthfully as his sons. "But you're right. Tonight will yield some useful studies. I will attempt them."

"One day you will be a famous portrait artist and in great demand, Edie, and I will humbly remind you that you used to draw your family members before all the lords and ladies placed demands on your time and talents."

Her eyes were troubled. "Oh. I don't think I would like that."

"Which part? The fame or the commissions?"

"The fame. Or the lords and ladies."

He almost said, "I will manage it for you!" but succeeded in stifling this. Waiting until they had gone through the figure-eight, he began again. "Perhaps I will give you your first commission. What would you say to a picture of my stepmama? I would give it as a gift to my father."

Lionel made the suggestion on impulse but was handsomely rewarded by the glow of excitement on Edith's face. "Oh, really, Lionel? Or—are you just teasing me?"

"I may tease you about many things, cousin," he declared grandly, "—your youth, your mean stature, your frequently smudged state, your corkscrew hair—but not your art. I am in earnest about your art."

Clasping her hands together as she gazed at him, she positively radiated delight and completely forgot about dancing until Margaret bellowed, "Edie, cast outward, you're in my place!" Then she roused herself and scrambled back into position, but with a new bounce in her step.

"Very nice, very nice," murmured Miss Blenkensop, observing her oldest pupil's sudden improvement. For, indeed, Edith was floating on a cloud the rest of the evening, skimming lightly over the boards and beaming upon all her partners, her shyness forgotten.

"What has made you so happy?" Hetty demanded, when the lid of the pianoforte was closed, the furnishings replaced, and tea and lemonade served.

"Painting," said Edith dreamily. "Art." She didn't know if Lionel meant his commission to be a secret, that his father might be surprised, and she was glad to see him approaching, a plate of biscuits in hand.

"Budge over, Het," he ordered, prodding his sister with his foot so he could fit on the sofa on her other side. "Has Edie told you? I am her first patron."

"Whatever can you mean?"

He looked down his nose at his sister. "Just what it sounds like. I am commissioning our cousin to paint a portrait of our stepmama, which I then will present to my father."

Hetty's countenance crumpled with envy. "Why—whatever made you think of that? Perhaps I should like to give Papa a painting as well."

"Then you will have to wait, for Edith will be busy with mine first."

"Oh?" his sister scowled. "And how, precisely, do you intend to pay for this commission?"

She had the satisfaction of seeing her brother's condescension melt away. "Well, I—I have some—say, Edie, what do you suppose the painting will cost?"

Her grey eyes widened. "Oh—I haven't any idea. Papa buys all my supplies, but I have enough at present. I don't suppose it need cost you anything at all."

"No," both Lionel and Hetty said in unison.

"You cannot give him a painting *gratis*, or that would not be a gift from Lionel—it would be a gift from you," Hetty pointed out.

"You must charge me," Lionel agreed, rallying, "or it wouldn't be a commission."

Edith thought this over. "I see. Perhaps ten shillings, then? For the materials."

"And don't forget the time it will take you," Hetty reminded her. "He must also pay you for your time and labor."

Biting her lip, Edith threw Lionel a questioning glance, but he nodded valiantly, like a prisoner doomed to the scaffold.

It would take her hours, she knew, because, if it was to be her first commission, she would want to do her very best, and she would want the Hugh Hapgood family to be pleased with it. "It will take a little time," Edith began apologetically, "but some allowances must be made for the fact that I am inexperienced, and you are giving me an opportunity, for which I am very grateful."

"Better say five pounds, then," said Hetty.

"Oh, no! That's far too much! Two pounds. Let us say two pounds. And even then I feel badly."

"Well, five pounds or two pounds, the fact is, Lionel doesn't have it," Hetty continued placidly. "Otherwise, why would he have borrowed a half-crown from me a fortnight ago, to purchase his new cricket bat?"

Lionel's face flushed with anger. "Very well, Het, I will have to borrow a little more off you now, but I will pay you back when Papa gives me my next quarterly allowance."

She shrugged. "Or perhaps *I* will commission the portrait."

Edith thought Lionel would hurl his plate of biscuits against the wall. "See here, you plague of an infliction! This was my idea—"

"—Or the portrait can be from both of us, and you will only have to borrow one pound," Hetty finished.

He knew he had lost. And, while he would have liked to throw Hetty's money in the gutter (followed shortly by Hetty herself), he saw Edith's mouth twitch, and the humor of the situation struck him. Hetty was Hetty, heaven help the world, and he must suffer sharing the satisfaction of being his cousin's first patron. At least

Edith knew it was his idea, however Hetty might worm her way into the credit of it.

Sticking out his hand, Lionel and his sister shook in agreement.

Thus it was, at the age of twelve, Edith Hapgood became a professional artist.

CHAPTER THREE

**The Painter must also vary his Heads,
his Bodies, his Aptitudes.
—W. Aglionby, *Painting illustrated in three Diallogues* (1686)**

With two sisters married and gone, Bramleigh was not lacking in empty rooms, and it was not long before Margaret designated one empty chamber with east- and south-facing windows to be Edith's studio. Edith spent increasing amounts of time there, luxuriating in the space to spread her drawings and sketchbooks and paints and pencils and her few canvases. One canvas, in particular, was not stacked against the wall but hung—as a little joke. It was the unfinished *Judgment of Paris* Edith had done, using Elfie, Elfie's soon-to-be husband Frederick, and Margaret as models. When the Hugh Hapgoods had first come into Somerset, Lionel and Hetty painted a ridiculous, plumed bicorn hat on Paris' (Frederick's) head, and it still made Edith laugh to look at it. (Frederick shared his sister-in-law's amusement and had Edie paint a miniature of the hatted Paris, which he presented to Elfie on the third anniversary of their elopement—Edith's third official commission.)

It came to pass that Hugh Hapgood was so utterly delighted with Edith's portrait of his wife that he became another of her early patrons, commissioning a painting the following year of his three children for the lordly sum of six pounds. With pride, Edith used her earnings from Rosemary Hapgood's portrait to buy her own supplies, and, scarcely less proud, Squire Hapgood insisted Edith must have a drawing master.

"Miss Blenkensop!" he cried, stomping one morning into the schoolroom. "Miss Blenkensop, a word!"

The poor governess had been with her pupils over eighteen months by this juncture, but the squire's loud voice and bluff manner never failed to startle and discompose her. And when Miss Blenkensop was startled and discomposed, she grew even more stiff and angular, some of her pudding-softness hardening.

"Sir?" she asked icily, signaling to the girls that they were to continue with their sums.

"Miss Blenkensop, you have some knowledge of drawing and painting and such matters, have you not?"

"I was instructed in it," she replied in a guarded voice, "though I do not pretend to the talent of Miss Edith, naturally."

"No, no—no one like my Edie," he agreed. "Well, I have told Mrs. Hugh Hapgood that you will assist her to interview a Mr. Eldredge tomorrow afternoon. He comes in response to an advertisement I placed a month ago."

The girls forgot their sums. They were all staring at the squire, and Edith had paled.

"Advertisement, Mr. Hapgood!" cried Miss Blenkensop. "This is the first I have heard of it! Have my services not been satisfactory?"

"What? I mean—yes. Your services are fine, generally."

"'Fine, generally'?" echoed Miss Blenkensop in an awful voice. "If you do not mean to dismiss me, then, sir, for what position does Mr. Eldredge apply?"

"Dismiss you?" the squire was baffled. "Of course I don't mean to dismiss you! Who would teach the girls all their Frenchifying nonsense and sewing seat cushions? Mr. Eldredge applies for drawing master, of course. Says he belongs to some art society in Bath. If my Edie is to be a professional artist, she must have some tutelage other than her own instincts and what she finds in books—oof!" Here he broke off because Edie had flown at him to throw her arms about his neck.

"Oh, Papa! Can it be true? Thank you, Papa! You are too, too good! How did you know that I longed for formal instruction? And how can we possibly afford it?"

"Margaret says we can," he answered, swelling with complacence. He patted her and worked to undo her stranglehold. "And you know what a miser she is."

"Mr. Hapgood," the governess began again, drawing herself up to her full height, that she might hide her relief in buckram-like stiffness, "I understand your reasons for wanting to hire such a person, but with three young ladies at vulnerable ages, I must insist this Mr. Eldredge be not only qualified, but also entirely respectable, and, if he is to give lessons at Bramleigh, I must further insist on being present for all of them."

"Yes, yes," he waved these proprieties aside. "Naturally I hope he's not some handsome young buck bent on seduction, but I presume you and Rosemary have the good sense to know that. Better take some of Edie's drawings with you to surprise him with. I told Rosemary to offer £50 a year if he seems suitable—twenty-five from me and twenty-five from Hugh, since he'll have to teach Hetty and Rosie, too."

"Papa likely ought to contribute *more* than half," muttered Hetty. "For, as art pupils go, Rosie and I will test any teacher."

Over in Patterton, when Lionel heard of the coming of the drawing-master candidate, he raced through the day's lessons, that he might be on the spot when the Bristol coach arrived. It seemed Miss Blenkensop was not the only one who feared this Mr. Eldredge would prove some dashing young fellow, set loose at Bramleigh like a fox in the henhouse.

Lionel need not have feared. The only passenger who descended from the coach that day was a cadaverous, white-haired man, hunched about the shoulders and neck, wearing half-spectacles and mourning weeds. Grinning with relief, Lionel was able therefore to introduce himself cheerfully. He offered to carry the man's baggage into the Swan, and then proceeded with him to his father's cottage. Rosemary hid her surprise at seeing her stepson act as escort, but Miss Blenkensop beamed at him, murmuring, "What a pleasure—such a thoughtful young man."

Being eager to carry the news to Bramleigh, Lionel did not linger for the entire interview, only listening very hard to several minutes of it and downing one cup of tea before he slipped away unnoticed.

His sisters and Edith were taking a turn in Bramleigh's straggling grounds in the crisp autumn weather, and he hallooed to them as he ran down the slope, waving his cap. "Girls, I've seen him! I've seen Mr. Eldredge!"

They gathered around him eagerly, speaking over each other. "Is he handsome?" "Will he be our teacher?" "Did you see any of his work?"

Hoisting Rosie to carry her pick-a-back inside, he answered Edith first. "They hadn't asked to see his portfolio yet, but he had it with him and wouldn't let me carry it when I met his coach at the Swan."

"You met his coach?" asked Rosie in his ear. But Hetty was poking him insistently. "What did he look like, Lionel?"

He rolled his eyes. "Like Romeo," he told her solemnly. "He looked like Romeo. Or what you imagine Romeo looks like."

"Like Mr. Parvill, then!" cried Rosie, thinking of their previous governess's supposed brother, who had been so handsome he struck people speechless.

"Yes," said Lionel, as they marched up the staircase headed for Edith's studio. "That's it. Rather like Mr. Parvill. Only Parvill was not half as handsome."

"He's lying, Rosie," sighed Hetty. "We will have to wait and see for ourselves."

"It doesn't matter a jot what he looks like," Edith said, giving her cousins a little push so they would take up the latest positions she had assigned them for their portrait: Lionel seated and flanked by his sisters, Rosie in the loose circle of his arm, and Hetty with a hand on his shoulder (which too often lifted to pinch his ear). "It only matters that he is here. I am beside myself with anticipation."

"Then you won't mind that he's old as a mummy and already has one foot in the grave," Lionel grumbled, not better pleased with Edith's eagerness.

"Aren't mummies found altogether in their graves?" Edith replied. But she hoped it was true Mr. Eldredge was an old man because she would not feel as shy of an old man as she would a young Romeo. A young Romeo would be perfectly dreadful.

Having recently passed her thirteenth birthday, she had finally begun to grow. And while she would never be as tall as Margaret, or even Alice, she could no longer be mistaken for a child. Her face was losing some of its youthful roundness, throwing her eyes and delicate features into new prominence, which her artist's eye made due record of, as she began to add self-portraits to her exercises, if only to spare her long-suffering models.

Nor were Edith's eyes the only ones to study the changes in her appearance. Lionel saw and said nothing.

He was changing himself, having shot up past his father's chin in the last year, and the recent unreliability of his voice gave his sister Hetty plenty of fodder for amusement.

One afternoon when he had slipped back into the vicarage for his cricket bat, he overheard Miss Benfield and his stepmother discussing "Lionel's recent ungainliness."

"I always knew he would be tall," Rosemary said. "Just as one can judge a puppy's future size by the size of his paws. Once he reaches his full height and grows used to it, he will cease tripping over his own feet and the furnishings."

"I am sure of it," the vicar's sister agreed. "And I suspect his voice will be deep when it settles down, like his father's."

"In any event, I do apologize for Lionel stumbling and breaking things. If he ever becomes too much trouble, you may send him back to live with us."

"Never!" cried Miss Benfield. "And only see him at lessons? He may break everything in the vicarage, if he pleases. This phase of weed-like growth cannot last much longer. No, no—we should be lost without our handsome boy. Arthur already talks of taking on another student or two when Lionel goes to Oxford, lest we be too lonely and quiet with him gone."

Mortifying as such an analysis was—and Lionel *did* try to be more careful where he put his feet and arms after that—he was not sorry to have eavesdropped. A sister like Hetty did not tend to bolster a fellow's confidence, and Lionel could hardly ask Edith if she agreed in finding him "a gangling maypole" now, with a voice that squeaked "like an ill-tuned violin." At least Miss Benfield still thought him handsome, even if she was a hundred years old. It would not do for Lionel to grow ugly, if Edith bid fair to rival her eldest sister's beauty.

Edith was not pleased with her sketch's progress.

"What is it, Edie?" asked Rosie, bouncing on her toes. "You're frowning."

"It's you," said Hetty. "Stop fidgeting about."

"No, it's not Rosie."

"Then it's Lionel. You can't fit all his freakish limbs on one piece of paper."

"No—they fit," murmured Edith absently, causing Lionel to turn scarlet and Hetty to shriek with laughter. Realizing what she said, Edith waved apologetic hands. "Oh, do forgive me, Lionel. That isn't what I meant. It's just—"

Setting her charcoal pencil down, she crossed the room to rearrange them. "It's too stiff. Too formal. Too pyramidal. As if you were the Holy Family, instead of my young cousins. What if...?" Taking Hetty by the arm, she moved her to one side and set her in profile. "Hetty, you are looking at Lionel and Rosie—laughing, as you so like to do."

"What are we doing, that Hetty is laughing at us?" Lionel demanded.

"Not laughing *at you*," Edith corrected. "Just laughing."

"Most of Hetty's laughing is at us," said Rosie gravely.

"Well—not in this instance. Lionel, you stand *here*—" reaching for his hand, she pulled him opposite his sister. "—In three-quarter position."

"Am I looking at Hetty?" he asked, grateful his voice didn't crack and that his cousin didn't see him turn red again, to have her maneuvering him.

Edith thought about this. "Hmm...no. No—what if you were to carry Rosie pick-a-back again? Carry her and have your head turned as if she were saying something to you? I would sketch this very quickly, so you wouldn't get tired holding her."

"I can hold her," he said stoutly, gesturing for Rosie to jump up again.

Edith clapped her hands with delight. "Yes! Yes! This is perfect." Racing back to her easel, her pencil flew across the page, and it was all Lionel could do to keep his head as she had placed it, for he would much rather watch her excitement.

Hetty clowned and made Rosie laugh and wriggle, which made Lionel laugh in turn, and this was the happy scene greeting Mr. Eldredge and Miss Blenkensop and Rosemary a few minutes later, when the maid Dorcas slung the door open. For an instant, the models froze in their poses, but then they straightened hastily, Rosie sliding down from Lionel's back.

"Children, Master Lionel, allow me to present the new drawing instructor Mr. Eldredge," Miss Blenkensop announced in her loftiest tone.

While he was no mummy, Hetty later said of Mr. Eldredge that he had not only *one* foot in the grave but rather *both*, and they were firmly fixed therein, for that matter. He was indeed stooped and wizened, yet Edith noted that his white hair was thick and his eyes bright. Nor did his hands or voice shake as he made his bow and spoke with them.

"Have we interrupted?" he asked.

"Papa asked Edith to paint our portrait," said Rosie.

"I have only begun the sketches," Edith breathed, resisting the urge to block Mr. Eldredge's view of her easel. If he were to teach her, he must look, of course. She didn't mind Miss Blenkensop doing so, after all. But she knew that was because Miss Blenkensop was no artist.

Without a word, Mr. Eldredge crossed the room to investigate the work in progress, folding his arms over his chest, with one thoughtful finger at his lips.

Edith was not the only who held her breath.

As Mr. Eldredge stood before her sketch, studying it in silence, everyone else stared at him. It was a matter of longtime faith with all present that Edith Hapgood was a genius, but her work had never been subjected to the scrutiny of one deemed an expert. An expert who, if he had lived in Bath, appeared old enough to have visited Gainsborough's studio! Supposing this man were to find Edith's work wanting? Or were to pronounce it merely "very nice"? Not only would such faint praise be a blow to Edith, but it would disparage their own collective judgment.

As the silence stretched, Lionel found his hands balling in fists. What was the matter with the man? If this Mr. Eldredge was so expert, why should it take him ten times as long to make up his mind? He wanted to shake the old humbug, but it was Edith who broke first.

"I have other pieces I can show you, sir. More finished ones. Proper ones. This one I just dashed off before you entered."

Mr. Eldredge blinked at her, startled from his abstraction. "In good time, young lady. There is much to see here." This comment, though it could not be called praise, was at least not criticism, and it purchased him another minute of everyone's patience.

At last, he gave the sketch a nod and turned toward its creator. "The pose is informal."

"Yes, sir."

"Puts me in mind of Reynolds' portrait of the 4th Duke of Marlborough *en famille*."

Having never seen the painting referred to, she could not agree or disagree, but it was flattering enough that anything of her work might call the great Sir Joshua Reynolds to mind. After a pause, she said, "I did—I did try a more...orthodox pose, but I abandoned it." Removing her page from the easel, she revealed the one behind it.

"Ah," said Mr. Eldredge, while Lionel thought, *That's done it! Now he'll have to reconnoiter that one for half an hour.*

But they soon learned Mr. Eldredge was much quicker in dismissal than he was in admiration. "No, that wasn't working for you, was it?"

Edith shook her head, a tentative smile lighting her face as she realized that her new teacher only took a long time looking if he found something worth looking at. Replacing the newer sketch, she said, "This will be a painting for their father, so I thought an informal pose would capture them better. Few people will see it, I imagine, beyond their immediate family and friends."

"Perhaps. But later generations will glean an understanding of what the sitters were like from their attitudes—what they were like and what their relation was to each other. I look forward to the progress of this. Though I would like to see more of *your* relation to the subjects. No one here is meeting my eyes."

"My relation?" asked Edith. "I'm not going to be in the painting."

"My dear, you will be in every painting you do, whether you acknowledge it or not." He held out a hand, palm upraised and fingers beckoning. "Let me see something where the subject meets our eyes."

When he put it like that, Edith felt suddenly exposed. If what he said was true, she did not *want* to show him anything where the subject looked out at the viewer. At least, not with everyone else around. Who knew what pronouncement he might make then?

But his hand remained extended, and everyone watched her expectantly. She felt a flash of indignation: it was all very well for them to be curious—they would have quite a different expression were Mr. Eldredge asking them to share their own innermost thoughts! Especially if they had not known, until that very moment, that they had revealed them without meaning to.

Well, she had little to be ashamed of—she had, to her own knowledge, lived a life innocent of anything but the usual human frailties, and even those she had not yet had much opportunity to act upon.

Lifting her chin with a touch of defiance, Edith moved to her worktable. There she drew aside a sheaf of blank pages, as well as one of Alice's old horticulture books and some of the preliminary sketches for Rosemary's portrait. Underneath all these lay a slender portfolio containing her series of self-portraits in charcoal, seven in all.

Quietly, she laid them all out across the table and then stood to one side.

There was a brief hesitation among the group, followed by disguised impatience as they allowed the drawing master to take the premier position, and then they rushed forward to circle around. Not only them, but Margaret appeared in the doorway, having heard from Dorcas about the newcomer.

This time no one waited for Mr. Eldredge to gather his thoughts. "When did you do these?"

"Why, these are marvelous, poppet! I've never seen them before."

"Will you paint any of them, Edith?"

For his part, Lionel swallowed hard against a tightness in his throat. Because the studies were exactly Edith. Edith thoughtful. Edith wondering. Edith amused. Edith uncertain. In one, her chin was ducked and her eyes looked upward pensively, her curling dark hair loose about her neck and shoulders. He had never before seen her like that. Vulnerable. Haunting. The girl Edith was nearly vanished from that drawing, giving way to the woman who would come.

"I see," spoke the Oracle, tapping his fingers lightly on the worktable as he leaned over it. (He was partially obstructing Miss Blenkensop's view, but she held her tongue.) "I see." Raising his eyes, he met Edith's. "Yes, there is promise here."

She flushed, for all the world as if he had nominated her for the Royal Academy, and she was grateful for Margaret's arm snaking around her waist to give her a squeeze.

Straightening as much as his stooped posture permitted, Mr. Eldredge swiveled to pin Rosemary with his gaze. "Mrs. Hapgood, if you would please tell the squire and your husband, I will accept the position on the terms discussed."

Lionel's snort of disgust was mercifully drowned in the gasping and applause and congratulatory remarks. He would "accept the position"? This old dry-beard who had come in answer to an advertisement and who clearly had no more vaunted use for his time, art *cognoscente* as he thought himself?

Well, so be it.

Edith looked happy enough to cry, at any rate. And at least the man made no pretense of finding her work wanting. There was the further comfort, moreover, that the drawing master appeared to have forgotten he would have two other pupils, in addition to this prodigy of talent, and they were ones he could hardly plume himself about.

But best of all, in the fuss being made over the man, not a single person noticed that, when they finally quit the room, only six of the charcoal self-portraits remained.

Chapter Four

**They pursued their studies...
under the tuition of the most skilful masters.
—Edward Gibbon, *The History of the Decline and Fall
of the Roman Empire* (1781)**

Three afternoons per week, rain or shine, Mr. Eldredge appeared at Bramleigh, astride a sorry little donkey nearly as broken-down as he, which the squire observed with twitches of distaste. But Richard Hapgood made no complaint, for anyone could see that Edith lived for her drawing and painting lessons and would not have cared if her teacher were pulled on a sledge by dogs. Even Hetty and Rosie found the time worthwhile, for Mr. Eldredge, despite his focus on their cousin's gift, nevertheless determined on making the two sisters passable sketchers and watercolorists. Oil paints were not for them, but otherwise they learned alongside Edith and soon had each an easel and table of their own in the studio. And when the weather permitted, they were all to be found out of doors. "Why burn candles within, when this star burns brighter than a thousand candles on even the most wintery day?" he asked them. Not that it required much persuasion. After mornings spent in the schoolroom at their studies, the girls were more than eager to take their sketchbooks or their easels to the straggling grounds. True to her threat, Miss Blenkensop accompanied her charges at all times, and if the day was cold, she donned mittens, muffler and cape and stood sentinel without a word.

Mr. Eldredge was a stickler for proper terminology, and the girls soon learned a new vocabulary: Lines. Design. Proportion. Air. Aptitude. Contour. Chiaroscuro. Distemper. Gruppo. Fore-shortening. Schizzo. Tinto. Not only must they use appropriate words to discuss their work, but, for each time they set brush to canvas, they had already spent hours drawing, drawing, drawing. As he was fond of quoting, "All the Eminent Painters that ever were, spent more time in Designing after the Life, and after the Statues of the Antients, then ever they did in learning how to colour their Works." (To which Hetty muttered, "If the Eminent Painters had only the few of us and the overgrown shrubbery to draw over and over and over, they would have been glad soon enough to 'colour their W orks.'") And though Edith would always prefer capturing people to objects or scenes from nature, her teacher's fondness for the architectural precision of Thomas Hearne and the moody landscapes of Sir George Beaumont made her begin to take more seriously the backgrounds of her subjects.

"I prefer scenery myself," Hetty said one evening, when the Hugh Hapgoods were taking supper at Bramleigh. "The scenery never has a nose that goes all wrong or something funny about the eyes."

"And trees and shrubbery don't have hands," Rosie added. "Hands are every bit as bad as noses and eyes."

"Even better, scenery holds still," laughed Edith. "Though I am delighted to add Mr. Eldredge to my models. Mr. Eldredge can hold as still as a statue."

"Likely because he is already three-quarters petrified with age," was Lionel's comment.

"Age has nothing to do with it," returned Edith. "I discovered he is only a few years older than Papa, and Papa cannot hold still for more than thirty seconds at a time."

"Lionel is just cross because Mr. Eldredge has no interest in cricket," Hetty said.

"And cannot even catch a ball," scoffed her brother.

"But Lionel, you *threw* it at him while he was posing for Edith!"

"To catch a ball is *instinctive*, Het. For him to stand there like a great marble booby and let it hit him in the stomach was *unnatural*."

Hugh set down his fork. "Am I to understand, Lionel, that you have been pitching balls at the drawing master? While he is in the midst of giving a lesson?"

"Just the one ball, Father. To see what he would do. Which was precisely nothing."

"Demmed unnatural," muttered the squire, earning an approving nod from Lionel.

"Unnatural or not, you must not harass the man," Hugh insisted. "Especially when he is instructing the girls." He threw his wife a rueful glance. "Mr. Benfield's second pupil cannot arrive soon enough. What do you think, Lionel—will this Colin lad be a good companion for you?"

"I only met him the once," answered his son. "He was little taller than Rosie, but I suppose he will do." (By this point, Lionel was a lanky six feet in stature and could look his father in the eye in stockinged feet.) "Better than Mr. Eldredge, in any event."

As the seasons passed, Lionel did not have leisure much longer to hang about, disturbing the girls' art lessons or abusing the drawing master. His own university matriculation loomed, and it was an unwelcome shock for Hugh to hear the vicar was not satisfied with his pupil's progress. "Lately Lionel has not been applying himself as diligently as one would hope," Mr. Benfield reported (which, given his mild manner, could be translated as "hardly at all"), leaving the alarmed father to hurry home to consult his wife.

"Benfield tells me Lionel seems increasingly distracted. Interested in other things. Riding and shooting with the squire, bowling and batting with Colin, wandering the county on long walks! The vicar has even come upon the boy staring out the window, contemplating nothing in particular. What can it all mean?"

Rosemary set down the recipe-book she had been studying, as she had promised Margaret and the Bramleigh cook Button that a cream cheese would be attempted. "None of those things seems very unusual, taken individually, my dear. How long does he say he has observed this?"

"Several weeks—I did not dare ask him to be more specific. He says he would have spoken sooner, but he thought perhaps Colin's arrival accounted for some of the distraction. It might have—some. But not all. And Colin has been there a month now."

"I see. Have you tried speaking with Lionel? Asking if he has anything on his mind?"

Hugh sighed, dropping into an armchair opposite her. "I think if I opened the top of his head, held him upside down, and shook him, a cricket ball would fall out and not much else."

This made her laugh. "That isn't so. You know it isn't. Lionel has a very good brain. He has not always been terribly interested in his studies, of course, but some boys are made for schoolrooms and others not as much."

"Well, he's picked a bad time to let slip his efforts. I have no unreasonable expectations that he will be first in his class, but I do expect him to be *in* a class. Suppose he were to fail his examinations and be sent down after Michaelmas Term?" Rising restlessly, he took a few strides around the small drawing room where Rosemary could often be found, stopping before the portrait Edith Hapgood had completed of his children the year before. It charmed him, then, to see his adolescent son romping with his sisters. Now he felt impatience. What if the boy never settled into a steady young man? (It must be admitted that Hugh had long forgotten his own tendency to romp, which lasted through adolescence into his time at university and, indeed, until he married his first wife, who then crushed it out of him.)

"Have you spoken to him, Hugh?" Rosemary asked again.

From his hesitation, she knew the answer before his reluctant reply came: "I regret it, but sometimes between us my questions can make him assume a defensive posture."

"Perhaps a gentler approach would be advisable," she suggested, hiding a smile when she saw his shoulders drop in relief. "I will try to see where I get with him."

Leaning, he dropped a kiss on her hair. "My love, your worth is beyond rubies."

The Benfields' maid Betsy ushered Rosemary into the library, where she had first met Hugh Hapgood some years earlier, and Lionel, for that matter. She smiled to remember the boy perched on Mr. Benfield's desk in pursuit of a fly and the easy rapport the two of them soon discovered. Drawing off her gloves and smoothing them, she hoped that rapport would carry them through this delicate subject.

"He's out somewhere with Colin, Mrs. Hapgood," Betsy reported, "but I will send him in as soon as ever I find him."

"I hope they both finished their lessons before going out," Rosemary said, to which Betsy chuckled. "That makes two of us, ma'am, for it's certain that Colin will do whatever Lionel asks. If he told the lad to chop his own head off, it would be rolling on the floor before I could tell them to mind the carpet."

Not a very reassuring beginning, and Rosemary's confidence did not grow as the minutes passed. At length she plucked a book off Mr. Benfield's shelf and read several pages without absorbing a word, before she heard steps again in the passage.

When he banged into the room at last, bringing with him a rush of outside air and seeming to fill the space instantly with his long limbs, she thought, *We can hardly call him a boy anymore.*

But then his welcoming grin revealed the old Lionel. "Why, halloa there! To what do I owe the pleasure of this visit?"

She held out a hand to him, to pull him into a chair beside her. "Dear boy, I am sorry to call you in on such a beautiful day. What have you been up to? You must have finished your work in good time today."

He shrugged at this. "We did enough, I suppose."

"'We'? Yes, Betsy tells me Colin follows your lead in all things."

"Well, he *is* a mere twelve years old," Lionel replied, as if twelve were separated from fifteen by a geologic age.

"Even younger than Hetty, then," observed Rosemary. "Not that she has ever proven particularly biddable with you."

"No," he admitted, his mouth twisting. "To say the least. Girls are different."

"All girls, do you mean, or just sisters?"

He shrugged. "Rosie is no trouble that I can see. But come, my dear mama—you are not here today to talk about Colin or my sisters, are you?"

She folded her hands in her lap and took a deep breath. "No, I am not. Something else brings me." He said nothing, only waiting, so there was nothing left her but to plunge in. "We are concerned, your father and I, because Mr. Benfield suggests you have been distracted from your studies lately."

Still Lionel did not speak, only running a finger back and forth along the arm of his chair. Rosemary's hands tightened in her lap, but she went on. "I know you have not always been eager to attend university, but I would say you have generally seemed to enjoy your lessons with Mr. Benfield these past several years. Has anything changed?"

He raised his eyes to hers. "Did Papa ask you to come speak to me?"

"I offered, Lionel. Because we have always been able to talk to each other, have we not? But certainly if this is a matter you would prefer to discuss with him, I would understand and even be glad. As would he."

His gaze wandered to the bookshelves as he considered this. "I don't mind university," he said slowly, "or the idea of it, I mean. I only wish—that is—I have been thinking I would rather stay in Somerset. And, as I am not to be a clergyman or a professor or any such, I am not convinced that I need a degree. Not in mathematics, nor in *Literae Humaniores*."

"What would you do instead, then?"

"What I have always wanted to do: learn to be a gentleman farmer like the squire."

Her smile was tentative. "But Lionel, you have no estate to manage."

"The squire has already told me I may have the management of Bramleigh, if I like, when I return from Oxford."

"When you return from Oxford," she repeated, laying slight emphasis on *return*. Though this was news to her, and wasn't that just like Richard Hapgood, to go telling the boy this, without even consulting his parents? "When you returned, he would be willing to employ you as his steward?"

"Yes." He grimaced, then. "And, no, I have not asked him if I may be his steward if I do *not* go to university."

"A fifteen- or sixteen-year-old steward would be a novelty indeed," commented Rosemary. Tactfully she did not point out that Lionel's own father was the heir to Bramleigh—supposing something were to happen to the squire? Lionel could hardly serve as the estate steward without his father's consent.

But he was not a slow boy. He would know this already.

She fell back on honesty. "Oh, Lionel. I have often envied young men their ability to go to university. To learn and inquire and perhaps add to the knowledge of the world. Your cousin Alice would have relished such an opportunity."

"I know."

"And you would form friendships with other young men your age," she continued. "For all that you love Somerset, you must see that there are few peers for you here."

"No, I do see that." Picking up the volume she had discarded, he flipped through its pages, as indifferent to its contents as she had been. "I would like that part, I think. Friends. Peers. I have even liked having Colin come, young as he is."

"Then...if you like learning well enough, and you would like as well to broaden your acquaintance with young men your age, is it then only your fondness for the country and for...family that causes your reluctance? You would return to Somerset for every vacation, of course."

His brow darkened, and he tossed the book away. Rising, he made a circuit of the library, stopping at the window, though Rosemary suspected he saw no more of the view than he had of the book's contents.

He had confided in her at the age of twelve, but would he now, when he was nearly grown?

"What do you suppose will...happen to Edith?" he ventured at last, still turned toward the window. "While I am gone."

Her eyes widened. For a moment she was speechless, simultaneously gratified by his trust and fearful she would say the wrong thing. She could see in his reflection that he colored at her hesitation, his pale complexion darkening almost painfully.

"You see—you remember—I am very fond of her."

Nodding, more to encourage herself than to answer him (he wasn't looking at her, in any event), she said briskly, "I do remember, Lionel. You told me years ago, and we have not spoken of it since. So, it is still the case?"

He swallowed and managed his own nod in return.

"Have you...ever spoken of your feelings to her?" Rosemary proceeded gingerly.

That brought a vigorous shake of the head. "No. No. She's only fourteen, you know. And—thinks of me like a brother, I suspect. I don't mean to trouble her with it all now. I mean, even if she were thinking much about such things. Which she is not. Her mind is all on her art—not that I resent this fact—because you know how very gifted she is."

"I know," was Rosemary's gentle answer. He might not think himself resentful, but she remembered the ball thrown at Mr. Eldredge and the snappish comments about the man Lionel was wont to make.

Apparently, being able to share his feelings provided him considerable relief because the words came faster now, tumbling over each other. He drummed his fingers on the window-sill. "Yes. She quite worships that Eldredge fellow," he said, as if Rosemary had spoken her thoughts aloud. "Hangs on every word of his, the old codger. It doesn't matter. He's old as the hills. And knows what he's about, I suppose. And I am glad that painting is so important to her. Glad of it. Because if—if she *was* thinking of—of young men or marriage or any of that, nothing could induce me to leave Somerset." Abruptly he turned away from the casement to face his stepmother. "Because you've seen, haven't you? You've noticed, I mean, how lovely she has become."

"I've always thought her pretty."

"Yes, but now she's not just pretty. She's more than pretty. I can—I hardly dare look at her anymore because I'm afraid she'll see that I—well, I think she would shy off. At any rate—even with her not being interested yet in young men and marriage, you can understand why I would rather not be gone to Oxford for the next few years."

"But Lionel," remonstrated his stepmother, "just as you agreed there are no young men hereabouts for you to befriend, that also means there are no young men hereabouts to dangle after your cousin."

"Not as present there aren't," he said ominously. "But look what happened to Alice and Elfie! Some young man comes into the neighborhood, and the next thing you know, he carries off Alice, and his brother carries off Elfie!"

"Hmm. That's true, but I suppose those were unusual circumstances."

"You never know when circumstances might become unusual." He frowned. "At least she has Soppy—I mean, Miss Blenkensop—to keep an eye on her here."

"I am glad you have decided not to say anything to her now, at any rate," Rosemary rejoined. "For your own sake, as well as hers. The world is very wide, you know. For young men, even more than for young ladies. You might go to Oxford and discover a host of enchanting young women, and you would then be glad you were not—" but, seeing his jaw set, she broke off. Of course it was no use telling him he might come to prefer someone else, when he just confessed to preferring Edith. In his place, Rosemary would not have listened either.

She changed tacks. "I believe one thing you may depend on is your cousin's character. Because of her age and particular interests, as you say, she is not in any danger at present of letting some young man carry her off. I think you might safely go to university for a few years and take your chance."

"A few *years*," he repeated in a gloomy voice.

"Not any longer than it has already been," Rosemary pointed out.

He brightened a little at this, and she saw the shadow of his familiar grin. "You think if I wait a few years, I might address her then?"

"In a few years you would be done with Oxford and will know better what you are about. If you still felt then as you feel now, I don't suppose your father or the squire would have any objections to you trying your luck with Edith. And she would be seventeen or eighteen by then."

In a bound, Lionel crossed the room and seized his stepmother by the hands, pulling her to her feet and embracing her. Rosemary blushed with surprise and delight, laughing. "Good gracious!"

"Dearest, dearest Mama, I will do it. I will study hard for my remaining time with Mr. Benfield, and I will apply myself *devotedly* at university, and I will try my very best not to speak to Edith about any of it in the meantime, but you must make me a promise in return."

"What would that be?" she asked, as she detached herself. She hoped he wouldn't ask her not to talk to Hugh about it—she didn't think she could promise that. She need not mention it to him yet, but there might come a time...

"Promise me that, if some young man comes into the neighborhood and shows an interest in her, you will write to me immediately. At once. The very instant you hear of it!"

"Oh! And you would do what, if I did write to you of such a circumstance?"

"I would return the moment I got your letter," he declared. "I would have to! If some young man were going to put such thoughts in her head, she would need to know that there is—another—who cares for her. I would need to 'throw my hat in the ring,' as it were."

Rosemary considered this, her brow furrowing. "I see...but supposing a young man showed interest in her, but she did not notice, or she did not return the interest? Would you still have me write? If she were not interested, and you came barreling down to offer as well, it might be too soon. You might jeopardize matters."

He ran an agitated hand through his hair. Made an impatient movement. "I would certainly want you to write. Because I would want to know, at least. But, in that case, I would also ask you to advise me. I couldn't ask anyone but you, you understand."

"I do. I do understand," said Rosemary. "But Lionel, if you want me to be a spy of sorts, you must allow me to tell your father the general state of things. I do not think he would be troubled to learn that this was the cause of your distraction, especially since you have settled now on your course."

He took a deep breath. "Very well. It is a bargain. Only—please—if we could leave Hetty out of it, I would be grateful. Hetty could spoil everything, in addition to torturing me about it in the meanwhile."

Knowing very well how siblings could ridicule one's most tender feelings, Rosemary agreed easily to this, holding her hand out to him, that they might shake on it. And when she let herself out of the vicarage and was returning home, she felt decidedly satisfied with how matters had settled themselves. She could trust Lionel to take up his studies again, and she could assure her husband and Mr. Benfield that Lionel still intended to go to university. She knew

Hugh would be relieved, thinking a youthful *tendre* for his cousin would be sure to pass.

Yes, indeed. Whether Lionel would continue in his attachment, despite separation and the passing of several more years, remained to be seen. But at least Edith would not be harmed by knowledge of his feelings yet.

There was plenty of time.

Chapter Five

She rode triumphant o'er the vanquish'd world.
—Thomas Grey, *"Hymn to Ignorance"* (1775)

Lionel kept to his word. He applied himself once more to Latin translations and mathematical calculations, to rhetoric and geography, to history and rudiments of theology. There would never be any danger of him taking a first or being awarded a fellowship when he did go to university, but he would be able to comport himself respectably. As a reward for his diligence, Hugh and Rosemary allowed him great latitude his final summer, Hugh even purchasing a horse and stabling it at the Swan, that he and Lionel (but mostly Lionel) might ride.

After an unusually cold and wet spring, the summer of 1812 continued cool and rainy, and Lionel on horseback followed after the squire like a good steward-in-training, absorbing the lessons to be learned, such as they were.

"Bad spring, bad summer," grumbled Richard Hapgood. "Delay in sowing the seeds and delay in germination and likely a wretched harvest."

"Will the tenants be able to pay their rents, sir?" Lionel asked.

The squire only grunted in response, but his grim brow and crossness spoke more eloquently. "Sure you don't want to be a banker, boy, like your father, rather than a farmer?"

"I'm sure," said Lionel. The idea of spending most of his time within doors, hunched over ledgers held no temptation for him. Though, in fairness, his father had excellent posture and never hunched, not even figuratively. "Even when it's wretched, I would rather be out. Do you think we might bag some snipe and grouse soon?"

"Aye, that's right. And Marlton mentioned some stag hunting. I'm sure he won't object to you coming along." Taking in Lionel's surprised expression, he added, "He knows which side his bread is buttered on. That son of his wants to take over the hounds."

"Mr. Frank Birdlow does? But surely you would never give them up!" Lionel could be forgiven his incredulity, for the squire was known for fussing over his hounds more than over his own daughters.

A sigh. "Margaret says they're expensive and that, if the harvest will be bad, giving them over to Birdlow will go a long way to making up for it."

Lionel grimaced. His cousin Margaret might be right—and she probably was, for he had often heard his parents say what a good head for household management she had—but it pained him nonetheless that she could not think of some better plan for economy than cutting out her father's heart.

"You have decided, then, sir?" he asked.

The squire gazed down at his faithful Caractacus, who trotted along, tail wagging and oblivious to his fate. "Nothing has been decided, but I should keep Crack, in any case."

"Even if you didn't, sir, I'm sure he would escape home at the first opportunity."

As if they had planned it, both riders shifted their weight forward, leaning over their mounts and taking the modest slope at speed, that they might sail over the low stone wall at its summit.

"Well done, well done," said the squire, looking more cheerful. "That's a fine little filly Hugh purchased. I hope he plans to have her ridden regularly when you are gone."

Patting Mannerly, Lionel saw his chance. "The same thought occurred to me, sir. I told Papa it would be good for the girls to learn to ride, so they might exercise her in my absence. Hetty and Rosie could ride back and forth to Bramleigh when they come for their lessons, and perhaps Edith might have a go as well. Mannerly's the gentlest of horses, you know. And Edith does so much close work with her eyes—it would be good for her sight and her health to have exercise."

"Mm-hm. Don't know that Edie's ever been on a horse or wanted to be."

"Neither have Hetty or Rosie. I could—I could teach all the girls before I go."

The advantages of the offer brought a shine to the squire's eyes. Drawing up, he favored Lionel with a grin. "Teaching three girls to ride seems a steep price, to secure your horse some exercise, but, if they are willing, I am all for it. You might even throw Margaret into the bargain, while you're at it."

Fortunately for Lionel, Margaret declared she had neither time for nor interest in learning to ride, but when Edith wanted to beg off as well, Margaret wouldn't hear of it. "No, Edie, it is a splendid opportunity for you. If you are to become a professional artist, consorting with the gentry and lords and ladies, you ought to know how to ride."

Edith stared. "But I have told you a thousand times, Margaret, that I would rather not become a professional artist, if it requires 'consorting' with such elevated people."

"Gammon and spinach! (as Papa would say)," her sister retorted. "Suppose all your commissions were to come as they already have, by way of friends and family? I would not be surprised if one day Lord Marlton requests a portrait from you, and he's a viscount. Or say Mr. Eldredge were to make an introduction to a possible patron. He has kept some lofty company in his time. Would you then refuse?"

"I—suppose not," she admitted, "though I still doubt I would ever go riding with any of these imagined patrons."

"You never know. And here are riding lessons for you at very little expense to Papa. He need only feed and stable Lionel's horse for the day. So that settles it. Now, come—help me fold these linens."

Edith did insist that Lionel begin with Hetty and Rosie. "For, if they are to ride back and forth from Patterton when you are gone, you must give them priority."

He smiled down at her. "There's time enough for all of you. Tell the truth, cousin—your real reason is that you would like to sketch them."

"Well, Mannerly *is* a beautiful horse."

Setting up her camp stool beside the tree stump Lionel chose for a block, she opened her book. There was a holiday feeling to the lesson because they were accompanied by neither Mr. Eldredge nor Miss Blenkensop, the latter deeming time spent among siblings harmless, once she was assured the girls would be learning to ride aside. The squire came by to lend his approval, but then he was off again, followed by Caractacus.

Conscious of his cousin's eyes (and pencil) observing him, Lionel removed his own saddle from Mannerly, to replace it with the larger side-saddle, carefully tightening the additional point strap as the ostler at the Swan had instructed him. Before giving this first lesson, Lionel had tested the new equipment himself, slotting his right leg between the two horns of the saddle and riding Mannerly at a snail's pace a mile or two, the filly flicking her ears at the novel arrangement and Lionel scarcely less amazed. No wonder girls rarely galloped or hunted! Balanced so precariously atop even a well-behaved horse like Mannerly, Lionel did not trust himself faster than a walk.

"You first, Het."

Hastily, Hetty fastened on the modest riding skirt Rosemary had supplied to wear over her gown until proper habits could be made.

As the tallest of the three girls, she just managed to clamber atop the patient Mannerly from the height of the block, but Lionel had to clutch the far side of the saddle to keep it centered above the horse's back until she could situate her limbs and weight comfortably. But once she was up, Lionel could see from the sudden glint in his sister's eyes that new vistas were opening before her. She only suffered him to lead the horse once in a large circle before demanding that he surrender the reins to her. "I want to do it myself! And, if I wanted to set so slow a pace, what would be the use in learning to ride?"

"You must keep to a walk, Hetty," Lionel warned her, still pacing beside her. "Remember, you will have Rosie riding pillion behind you."

"Yes, yes. I could hardly forget that, could I? But this is marvelous! I could do this all day long." Leaning forward carefully, she caressed Mannerly's neck. "You darling—we will get along very well, shan't we? And when Lionel is gone away to Oxford, you and I will do whatever we please."

Lionel sighed. Hetty would be Hetty, and there wasn't much he could do about it. If she chose to gallop when no one was about, get thrown, and break her neck, she would have only herself to blame.

Rosie proved a more docile pupil, though she paled with trepidation. The riding skirt, once transferred to her, threatened to swallow her entirely, and Hetty ended up fastening it about her chest. She was far too small to mount from the block, and her brother had to lace his fingers together and lift her up. Once mounted, she managed to place her right leg between the two horns, while Hetty bombarded her with advice, and she was more than content to have Lionel lead the horse as she gripped the top pommel through her skirts.

"Excellent, Rosie," he praised her, after they had made two circuits. "Would you like to hold the reins yourself?"

"Perhaps the next time," she whispered, holding out her hands that he might assist her to dismount. "But may I give Mannerly a carrot?"

Lionel was grateful for the distraction of his sisters feeding Mannerly, as well as for the excuse to inspect Edith's sketches, for he felt the color rising in his face. It was one thing to assist his younger sister to mount and to see the flash of her skirts and limbs as she arranged herself, but another altogether to think of Edith in her place.

Fortunately for him, Edith was too occupied with her own apprehensions to notice. Despite her father being an excellent horseman, no pony had been kept for the girls since Margaret was little. And while Mannerly had shown herself patient as any saddle pony that morning, she was nevertheless a gleaming, well-sized, powerful-looking creature, accustomed to being ridden whip and spur over every field and hedge in the county, as Edith well knew from her father's tableside pronouncements on the matter.

"I suspect you will need my assistance to mount," mumbled Lionel. Or perhaps it only sounded muffled through the rush of blood in Edith's ears.

Adjusting the riding skirt, she mustered her courage and nodded, watching him drop to one knee in the grass, his fingers laced again. She placed her small, booted foot in his hands, hoping she would not weigh too much, and, after the briefest of hesitations, felt him lift her up.

"Take the upper pommel," her cousin croaked.

Scrabbling at it and fighting the urge to shut her eyes as she felt Mannerly shift beneath her, Edith saw Hetty bouncing on her toes and pointing. "Your leg! Your right leg! You've got to place it between the horns to hold you on."

Edith tried to obey, but her double layer of skirts was pinned beneath her, and she had to give a little bounce, to pluck loose the fabric, that she might shift herself.

Awarded the one glimpse of Edith's clean, pretty ankles and some length of her smooth left...limb, Lionel thought for a moment he might crumple to the earth and combust. Desperate, he jerked his head away to regard something else—anything else—and the remaining task of getting Edith secure and comfortable in the saddle was left to Hetty.

"Well, go on then," prodded Hetty, when she saw her brother staring idiotically into the distance. "Or do you want me to lead them?"

"No—no." Giving himself a shake, he took the reins from his sister and set Mannerly to a gentle walk. He could not quite bring himself to look up at Edith just yet, though his eyes soon drifted to her little left foot in the stirrup.

"Oh," breathed Edith. "My."

"Is it all right?"

"Yes."

If the circuit he led Edith on Mannerly was longer than the one Hetty and Rosie rode, it was all unconscious on his part, for Edith said nothing and Lionel was struggling inwardly. He was so rarely, rarely apart with her. Even here and now, with his sisters' eyes upon them, he could not remember when they had last been thus. They were never *alone*, of course, but even to be out of earshot felt exciting.

Felt dangerous.

He realized at once that, having kept his promise to his stepmother these past months, that he would not speak to Edith yet, he need not have congratulated himself on his self-control. What he had thought of as forbearance was in truth no more than lack of opportunity.

Should he then speak?

He ventured a sidewise glance up at her and saw a tentative smile growing. She was beginning to relax and enjoy herself.

He should speak.

No, no—he should *not* speak.

After all, if what he had to say to her were unwelcome, and it very well might be, she could hardly escape him when she was perched on Mannerly, and a girl ought to have the option to run away, if she liked. Lionel felt this was only fair.

He would wait. Stuff everything back down and be a proper brother-cousin and pretend she was no more interesting to him than Hetty. After all, he had said he would wait, and he ought at least to try to be a man of his word.

"Keep your heel down," he almost barked, startling her.

Having made his decision, Lionel did then congratulate himself, adopting an airy tone for the remainder of the lesson and even teasing Edith for turning paler than Rosie had.

It was just as well. For that first lesson was followed by others, and Lionel was glad he had done nothing to jeopardize the trust and easiness of their time together. While Edith and Rosie continued to require his assistance to mount, they grew more comfortable with the process, so that, even if he had not learned to look away when Edith adjusted her seat, there were few more revelations such as he had received that first time.

Soon the girls were riding easily by themselves, Hetty even venturing a running walk, but Edith and Rosie still preferred a slower gait, and though they increased their pace somewhat, Lionel found it did not outstrip his long strides if he trotted himself. He began to wish he had a second horse, though, for he imagined long rides through the countryside with his cousin. The exercise brought color and animation to her face, and some of her curls were always sure to come loose and stream out under her bonnet. Between the riding lessons and going shooting with the squire, Lionel could not remember a happier season in his young life. The only cloud on the horizon was his approaching departure for Oxford in October. He ignored this as best he could, but, as each blissful day flitted away, the cloud grew larger and more ominous.

And then he thought he might be altogether robbed of his remaining time with Edith, for, just as the season for shooting red grouse and snipe was expanding into partridges, ducks and geese, the squire was laid low by another of his worrisome "episodes," and there was a cessation of all lessons at Bramleigh.

"But what has happened?" Lionel demanded of his stepmother, for he had raced over to the cottage as soon as he heard Betsy mention the squire being "hit hard" to Miss Benfield.

"It is his heart again," Rosemary replied, setting aside Rosie's French composition. "As you know, he and Mr. Frank Birdlow have been in negotiations over the keeping of the hounds, and, just as Richard was recounting Mr. Birdlow's most recent letter on the matter, Augusta—Mrs. Hapgood—saw him falter and put a hand to his chest. Margaret thought he might fall and rushed to his side, which only made him angry, and then he did faint away, I hear, for some minutes."

"But what does Mr. Lewis say? Will he recover?" pursued Lionel anxiously.

Rosemary sighed. "Margaret says Mr. Lewis says what he always does—that Richard is to keep as calm as possible at all times and not to exert himself, if he can help it. One might as well ask the squire to take up embroidery."

"But he has been riding for several years now, without any harm done," Lionel pointed out. "And I think it has served him well. If the squire were to sit quietly at home for the rest of his days—even if he could be made to do so—he would soon be dead of a broken heart."

"Anyone who knows Richard Hapgood must agree with you, Lionel, but what else can Mr. Lewis say?"

Lionel ran a troubled hand through his hair. "May I go and see him, Mama? I will be very quiet."

"Perhaps in a few days, my dear. I know he is one of your favorite people. But let them have peace at Bramleigh now. We have already decided the girls will not have lessons for a period of time, so that he may recover the sooner."

There was nothing Lionel could do but submit, although his concern for the squire was not unmixed with dread that even more of the remaining days before his departure were slipping through his fingers. And if something were to happen to Richard Hapgood—! Lionel did not see how he could leave at all, in that case.

He waited an interminable five days, surviving on the bulletins his stepmother provided. And then, deciding it was better to ask forgiveness than permission, he saddled Mannerly and rode over.

There was no sign of Hal to take his horse, so Lionel stabled her himself. Nor did anyone come in response to his knocking, but this had been known to happen even when the Hapgoods were not in times of crisis, and Lionel wasn't one to stand on ceremony. He circled the house and found the drawing room windows also shut, but one of the upstairs casements was ajar and Margaret's voice drifted down to him: "Papa, do you really want me to write and tell Elfie and Alice not to come? They are only concerned for you."

"I am *not* dying!" cried the squire, in a weak echo of his usual roar. "And they were just here some weeks ago, and the last thing I need is everyone hovering about."

"It might cheer you to see baby Freddie again."

"What would cheer me would be for you and Lewis and your mother to go to the deuce, that I might escape your clutches and go on a long ride. Go away, Margaret, do."

There was a pause, and Lionel could picture Margaret with her arms crossed and her lips pursed, trying to decide how to proceed. He could also imagine the squire's great relief when her unwilling reply came: "Very well. I will be in the kitchen with Button, seeing to the preserves. Shall I send Edie or Mama to read to you?"

"No, confound it all!"

"Then, if you require anything, you may ring this bell, Papa. But you know there's a good chance no one will come in response."

"I should be so lucky."

A door opened and shut and silence fell, as Lionel debated his own next move. Much as the squire loved him, it sounded as if he would like to be left in peace for a time, and Lionel knew enough to realize a visit from him might tempt the ailing man to sneak away from the house and the doctor and the womenfolk.

Nor was Lionel eager to seek Margaret's company in the kitchen. But it would be a shame to ride back to Patterton without at least having seen Edith.

His mind made up, he walked the length of the house and peered up at the windows of his cousin's studio. The open casement was invitation enough, and he was soon scaling the rickety trellis, which slapped and banged against the wall, where it did not prickle him with ivy or give way rottenly beneath him.

The racket soon brought her to the window. "Good heavens! What on earth are you about, Lionel?" Edith called down. "That trellis must be a half-century old."

She was utterly adorable staring down at him, her dark curls only pulled back with a ribbon and her expression both exasperated and fond. He had to fight off a ridiculous urge to cry, "'But soft—what light through yonder window breaks?'"—an urge he succeeded in repressing when a branch of ivy swung back to smack him in the face.

"Did no one let you in at the door?"

"No one," he gasped, heaving himself over the sill as she backed away to allow him entrance. "I came to see how your father was."

"He is weak and cross, but Mr. Lewis is confident this spell will not prove fatal." Laughing, she reached to pluck a twig from his hair. "Don't tell Margaret, but I think, if Papa might only be allowed to sit out of doors or even go on a placid little carriage ride, he would be himself sooner."

Lionel's eyes glowed eagerly. "I could hire a carriage from the Swan and take him about."

"What a lovely idea! Thank you. Perhaps in another few days. Let me work on Margaret in the meanwhile, and I will send a note when I have her approval."

The conspirators grinned at each other, Lionel feeling again that prickle of delight and danger, to find himself alone with her. He turned away abruptly. "Well, then—what have you been working on these past few days?"

With a shriek she bounded in front of her easel. "You mustn't look! It's a surprise for you to take to university."

His heart gave its own leap in response. A portrait of her! He had only the one he had stolen earlier, from when she was younger, and it was but a charcoal sketch. He didn't know how he could manage a painting at Oxford—his quarters were sure to be cramped, and a miniature would have been easier to squirrel away—not to mention to carry always on his person—but he would do it somehow.

Covering his eyes with his hands he said, "For me? I am honored that you thought of it. Though I will not be able to hang it up, you may be sure that I will look at it every day."

"Why—why couldn't you hang it up?" asked Edith.

She sounded almost hurt, and he hastened to reassure her. "Oh, I should like to! I should be proud to. But, of course, we can't have all those other young men looking at you. I would be forced to fight any of them who made remarks."

"Looking at *me*?" Edith echoed, mystified. "Young men looking at *me*? But of course I didn't put myself in the painting, Lionel!" Pulling his hands from his eyes, she led him to the easel. Whereon was propped a half-finished, exquisite, lively, portrait of...Mannerly, his horse.

"...Oh," Lionel breathed, feeling heat flood his face. In fact, he felt as if his entire body had been plunged in boiling water.

"You don't like it."

"Of course I like it." He thought he might throw up, the differ-ence between his expectation and reality being so wide. But Edith would certainly interpret throwing up as a dislike for her work. "I like it very much." He wasn't lying, but, for once in his life, his horse could not be further from his thoughts.

A little frown creased her brow, and he dreaded any realization that might be dawning on her.

"It's just that I thought you thought I might be homesick," he blurted to forestall her, "and so I thought you—you—you thought you might give me a portrait of—of the family—including you, of course—to have."

The little frown did not vanish, but it lightened. "Would you really have preferred a family portrait? And here I thought I knew you so well! I thought surely you would miss Mannerly most of all."

"Of course I will miss Mannerly," he said gruffly. "But Mannerly is a horse. I will miss my family more." Then he did start lying. "Miss my parents and—Hetty and Rosie—and—and you—all—at Bramleigh."

"Ah." Turning, she gazed thoughtfully at the horse portrait. "You do like this one, though? Enough that I should finish it?"

"Yes. Please. Do finish it."

"But you would like to bring a picture of your family as well?" she prompted. "You know how long those other portraits took. But likely I could manage a very nice charcoal study before you leave."

He swallowed. "I would very much like that, Edith. Very much." Heaven knew he didn't particularly want a charcoal study of his parents or his sisters, but if it took their presence to get Edith to include herself, it was a price worth paying.

"Mr. and Mrs. Hugh Hapgood might be difficult. I have so many sketches already of Hetty and Rosie, though—"

"Then never mind Papa and Mama," he said hastily. "I might be mocked mercilessly if I bring their picture. Just leave it at Hetty and Rosie and—and you."

"And Margaret, surely?"

Lionel almost groaned. But he hoisted up a pleased smile. "Naturally. Hetty and Rosie and you and Margaret."

"Well, if your fellow students ever see such a picture, I doubt they will tease you any less."

"They will never see it," he declared. "I will keep it rolled up in my trunk, to take out when I am homesick."

Edith gave a silent chuckle, for, despite his words, Lionel did not strike her as the sort of young man who would moon about, homesick, when there would be so much novelty in his surroundings and his company. But even if the portrait lay at the bottom of his trunk, crushed by his cricket equipment and forgotten the entire time, she would make it for him. It would be as if his sisters and cousins could themselves attend university.

For a moment there, an uncomfortable notion had taken her: that it was a picture of *herself* that Lionel wanted. How else could his embarrassment be explained? But that was nonsense, of course. Her handsome, boisterous cousin who always treated her as another little sister. It must be that he was embarrassed to show such a weakness to one who looked up to him. In Edith's place, Hetty would have jeered at him without a doubt.

Well, Edith was happy to do this for someone she loved so well as Lionel. Even if he forgot about it—forgot about *them*—as soon as he entered his new world.

Thus, when Lionel rode home, he congratulated himself that his blind had been successful, his secret kept.

And perhaps it had.

CHAPTER SIX

Whilome in Albion's isle there dwelt a youth,
Who ne in virtue's ways did take delight;
But spent his days in riot most uncouth,
And vexed with mirth the drowsy ear of Night."
—Byron, *"Childe Harold's Pilgrimage"* (1812)

Edith fully expected to miss Lionel when he matriculated at Magdalen College, Oxford, in October of 1812. How could she not, when he had been as constant in her life as his sisters or Miss Blenkensop or Mr. Eldredge? Nor could it be expected that she would hear much of him after his departure. Any news must come through correspondence between himself and his parents, which would then be read aloud to Hetty and Rosie and passed along when the girls came for their lessons. But what boy of sixteen could be depended on for regular letters? Especially one as social and active as Lionel Hapgood?

"Papa and Mama stayed at the Angel Inn when they brought him up," Hetty reported, as they sat sewing their samplers. (Hetty loathed samplers, and hers was a tangle of knots and bulges. Neither did Edith enjoy the activity, but her conscientiousness would not allow her to make a mess of it.) "And Papa said, so constant were the coaches coming and going from every point in the kingdom that there was not an hour's peace to be had. And Mama said they would not have stayed long in any event because, once Lionel was situated in his quarters and met some of his schoolmates, he was occupied all round the clock."

"He will forget us entirely," sighed Rosie, surreptitiously sucking on her finger where she had pricked it.

Edith stifled her own sigh. "Did Mr. and Mrs. Hapgood meet any of these schoolmates?"

"They mentioned two in particular. Twins. A Jason and an Edward Clinkett, who hail from somewhere in Kent. Mama thought Jason Clinkett's roisterous spirits would likely be magnified by Lionel's own, but Papa says young men are often thus, and he trusts that Lionel has ultimately a good head on his shoulders. To which Mama said that may be so, but she still preferred Edward Clinkett to his brother, for Edward is pensive and poetical, and Papa said *heaven forbid* he should turn out to be some Childe Harold sort."

Not that the girls knew with any precision what a Childe Harold sort would be, since Miss Blenkensop thought the new and popular poem inappropriate for tender young ladies (not that she had read it either). But Hetty did catch their governess off guard one afternoon by asking, "Miss Blenkensop, pray, what is dissipation, that it should be avoided?"

The poor woman actually dropped both pencil and slate in her surprise and took her time in recovering them. When she finally lifted her countenance, her pupils were secretly amused to find her blushing. "Dissipation, Harriet, may be defined as—as frivolous, unrewarding activity or expense."

"Such as sewing samplers?" Hetty suggested innocently.

"Nonsense. Sewing is a valuable skill. No, I mean, such as...gambling or—or inebriation or...or..."

"Wenching, I suppose?"

"Harriet Hapgood!" cried Miss Blenkensop, dropping the slate again. "That is enough. Enough of this matter. Yes. We had better proceed to music. Come, girls."

As they left the schoolroom to descend to the spinet, Edith shook her head at Hetty, indicating little Rosie with her eyebrows, but Hetty only shrugged.

Having grown up with her Arbuthnot uncles, Alec and Alwyn, Edith understood too well the meaning of dissipation. For those gentlemen, at least, it included escapades with women, attendance at horse races, dressing as dandies, fathering an illegitimate child (Alec), generally living beyond their means, and dunning their brother-in-law Richard Hapgood for funds.

Oh! Supposing Lionel were ever to become an Alec or Alwyn! Edith thought it would break her heart. Then again, perhaps not.

Perhaps her opinion of him would always be rose-colored, and she would make excuses for him, as her mother did for her brothers.

Yes, Edith missed him. And thought of him as she studied, rode, drew, painted. When Hetty announced that her stepmother had given up on Lionel ever writing them and planned to write to him without hope of receiving a reply, Edith's contribution to the letter was a sketch of Mannerly grazing alongside the squire's horse. On the reverse she wrote, "Papa continues to recover slowly and has said several times that he misses your company, for, without it, he is 'surrounded by petticoats and fidgets.'" (Unknown to all the Hapgoods in Somerset—for Lionel neglected to respond—he received this picture gratefully, spending more time gazing at it and the message on the back side, than had been spent creating it in the first place. For which silliness he was much teased by Clinker and an anonymous cartoon circulated in the common room, depicting Lionel and his horse in the balcony scene from *Romeo and Juliet*, the balcony being a stable stall and the horse Juliet.)

Rather than from Oxford, however, the news that autumn came from London. Edith's dissipated uncle Alec was dead, and his demise led to the removal of her remaining uncle, Alwyn, to Bath, accompanied by Margaret and Mrs. Hapgood. This whirlwind turn of events succeeded in driving Lionel from her thoughts, drawn as she was into Margaret's flurry of preparation and excitement, and the Hapgoods were not the only ones in a flutter. The mere mention of Bath stirred eagerness in the drawing master Mr. Eldredge.

"I still have many artist friends there," he told the girls, one rainy afternoon in the studio. "If your family were to visit Mr. Plura's auction house in John Street or Mr. Evill's in Great Milsom and mention my name, they could be introduced to the leading painters and be invited to visit their studios."

The very idea made Edith breathless, but Margaret dismissed it instantly. "You know very well Papa only sends me along to prevent Mama and Uncle Alwyn from spending us into bankruptcy. Attending an auction would be too tempting altogether! Moreover, why would we want to visit other artists' studios, when we can see yours all we like?"

And that was that.

Away went Margaret, Mrs. Hapgood and Alwyn Arbuthnot to Bath, leaving Edith with a sensation of lowness, as she looked forward to an uneventful winter, punctuated only by Margaret's letters and occasional missives from her other sisters.

It was not to be that dull, however, for Hetty soon discovered something new to absorb the girls' interest. Namely, a budding romance.

On an unseasonably dry and clear day, following a fortnight confined within the house, the students and their instructors hastened to hold their art lesson out of doors, even if it meant donning cloaks and fingerless mittens. After a brief paean to nature's chiaroscuro, Mr. Eldredge set them to sketching the denuded copse, with its spiky branches and carpet of fallen, half-disintegrated leaves.

Minutes later, when Edith was lost in trying to capture the contrasts of light and dark, Hetty appeared at her side, setting her easel down right beside Edith's. "Don't look now," she muttered, waving her charcoal pencil at her page, though she had not yet drawn a stroke, "but Mr. Eldredge's attentions are divided."

Obediently, Edith finished the line of the beech tree, thinking how her sister Alice might like this study, especially if she included the litter of beech nuts surrounding the golden trunk. Then she carefully turned her head a fraction, to where Miss Blenkensop stood sentinel, as ever, but not alone this time. No—Mr. Eldredge was beside her, *fussing* over her! Apparently he was coaxing her to be seated and was brushing off a stump for her comfort.

"It is quite dry, I assure you, Miss Blenkensop."

"Thank you, Mr. Eldredge, but I prefer to stand."

"Well, if you should grow fatigued, it is ready for you."

"Again, I thank you."

Hetty waggled her eyebrows comically, and Edith repressed a giggle. "He is just being polite," she whispered.

"If you say so. But, as we know, the proprieties are a sure way to Soppy's heart."

"It would be rather sweet," said Edith, "for them to find each other at their advanced ages. Although Blenkensop does not appear particularly taken. Nor would they have much to live on. I believe their combined salaries amount to no more than £100 per annum."

"They would save by lodging together," Hetty observed. "And being very old, there might never be any additional mouths to feed. We must help him," she urged. "Otherwise what a bore things will become. No Lionel, no Margaret. Just lessons, lessons, lessons and rain, rain, rain. If this autumn and winter are to be a carnival of riotry for everyone else, I insist we have excitement of our own."

"Just what do you propose?"

"You must draw Eldredge out. You know Soppy will never flirt and converse with him when she thinks he ought to be teaching. Therefore you must give him opportunities to talk about himself in her hearing. And let us hope he has something worth saying."

"Why must I be the one drawing him out?" asked Edith. "This is your idea."

Hetty sighed in annoyance. "Because you are his *favorite*, to be sure. If I were suddenly to try to engage him in conversation, he would think I was trying to get out of my lesson. But he will never think that of you. So go to it!"

Edith went to it.

When Mr. Eldredge drew near to inspect her progress, she said, "Sir, for one so fond of scenes from nature, why did you make your residence so long in Bath? My sister Margaret writes that Bath is entirely people and buildings and noise and bustle in every direction."

"Ah," he sighed, a faraway look in his eyes. "Because many of those people your sister writes of are artists. Portrait artists, miniature artists, illustrators of newspaper cartoons and handbills. Engravers. Etchers. Sculptors. And for each sort of artist there is a viewer and a critic and sometimes even a purchaser or a patron. Auctions and exhibits were advertised frequently in the Bath Chronicle. And there is much time in Bath to fill. I not only painted, but I gave lessons to aspiring artists."

"But, sir, are there not all these things in London, as well? Why then did you pursue your vocation in Bath rather than the capital?"

He chuckled. "Oh, I tried that too, when I was a young man. But London is fearfully expensive. And...after many years I found even Bath growing so."

Biting her lip, Edith thought of the wages her father and Hugh Hapgood were paying. Bath must be dear indeed, if Mr. Eldredge chose to give up all that, to rusticate in rural Somerset at £50 per annum!

"And I was a landscape painter, Miss Edith, as you may have guessed," he went on, "but in order to gain my living, I spent much of my time painting country houses, and even then commissions were hard to come by."

This pitiable tale was trying Hetty's patience, as she doubted it would cause any heart swoons in their governess, and she jabbed her charcoal pencil at her page to draw Edith's attention. But before Edith could divert his thoughts into a more cheerful channel, Mr. Eldredge mourned on.

"All along, year after year, I applied to the Royal Academy! Each year I submitted work for the annual exhibition. Each year I maintained and flattered my connections. But only once was one of my works accepted for display—*View of Dyrham Park in rain*. How I rejoiced. But my one inclusion in the exhibition led neither to Academy admission nor to a purchaser for the work. And that, sadly, was the zenith of my career as an artist."

Edith hadn't the least notion what to do with such a tale of woe except to hope there wasn't more of it, but Hetty decided to take things upon herself.

"Mr. Eldredge, I am afraid you will make Edith regret wanting to become an artist."

His head reared back in genuine surprise. "Oh, no. That was not my intent. My history has no bearing on hers. It took me so many years, but I have long made peace with the fact that my greater gift lies with teaching and with art appreciation. I only regret that my head was so thick. Had I reconciled myself sooner..." He trailed off. Shot a glance toward Miss Blenkensop, who instantly looked away toward the house, as if something had caught her attention. "Had I reconciled myself sooner, I might have spent less time making my own art and more time in promoting others'. I might have increased and saved my income, which would have—would have made other things in life possible."

By other things, Edith supposed he meant marriage and family. Or even a permanent home.

Not wanting him to think she held similar costly illusions, Edith murmured, "I do appreciate your tuition, Mr. Eldredge. And your—history is educational as well. I myself harbor no fantasies of being accepted by the Royal Academy or exhibiting work there. I realize I will have to paint for the love of it, and hope only to be rewarded with the occasional commission from friends or family—I do not suppose—"

"But Miss Edith!" he interrupted. "I was speaking of myself. The course of my career has little to no bearing on yours."

She blinked at him. "Well, no, I suppose not. But I suppose as well that the course of your career is not at all unusual. I mean, it is very difficult to rise to the peak of one's profession. For every Sir Joshua

Reynolds or Sir Thomas Lawrence or Gainsborough, there must be scores of...of Edith Hapgoods and Mr. Eldredges."

Her white-maned instructor drew himself up as straight as his hunched shoulders allowed, suddenly resembling the angular and straight Miss Blenkensop. "No, Miss Edith, I was speaking of myself. I do not usually tell pupils this, for myriad reasons, but honesty dictates I make myself clear with you. Miss Edith, there are two distinct differences between your art career and my own. The first is that you prefer portraiture, which is, for better or worse, far more popular in our country than landscape painting. The second is that, to be completely frank, you have a native talent I have seldom seen equaled. With dedication and hard work and continued devotion to your craft, I see no reason you could not be exhibited at the Royal Academy and possibly even elected to its membership, although that is less common with lady artists, I'm afraid. But you might certainly submit some representative works of yours—I debated discussing this with you this early—and do so under either an assumed name or by representing your Christian name only with your initials, that the board would not know whether you were male or female."

Throughout this speech of his, uncharacteristic in both its length and its vehemence, Edith's eyes grew wider and wider until they became nearly as round as guineas. Her complexion, as well, flushed a brighter and brighter pink, as if she had caught fire within, and Hetty decided maybe there was some physical resemblance between pretty little Edith and her ruddy father after all.

Words did not come immediately, but Edith began to shake her head, backing a few steps from her easel, her chalk pencil falling into the dry grass at her feet. "No—oh, dear me. No, thank you. I mean—I thank you, Mr. Eldredge, for your encouraging words, but I—have no ambition to—no, thank you."

"Now, now," he said in a soothing voice, as if she were a dog threatening to bite. He held up his palms to calm her. "This is precisely why I had not mentioned anything of this matter. I see you are a modest and retiring sort, who might find the process intimidating, but I assure you it could be done with virtual anonymity."

But Edith was still shaking her head, and Hetty suppressed both a groan and a desire to shake Edith herself. What was there to be so frightened of? If Hetty had an artistic talent like her cousin's, she would never be tempted to hide it under a bushel, no indeed! She would storm the Royal Academy of Art and enter ten paintings all under her own, complete, *female* name and *dare* them to refuse her!

"No, thank you," said Edith again.

To Hetty's further disgust, Mr. Eldredge gave the call to abandon ship without further struggle. "Very well," he said, "I can see you find this prospect alarming, and, again, I did not intend to raise the subject so soon. We need not worry about such things, Miss Edith. Your joy in your work is enough for you. Let us be satisfied with that. And, speaking of which, this is enough chatter. Let me assess your progress so far. (Miss Edith, do pick up your pencil.) Miss Harriet, I see you have made no beginning at all. If you would please remedy that. I will begin with Miss Rosalie, will I? Ah, Miss Rosalie, what have I told you about the placement of your subjects...?"

CHAPTER SEVEN

What news? What news? Your tidings tell.
—Cowper, *The Diverting History of John Gilpin*
(1782)

Probably if Edith and Hetty had not been a little bored, they would not have noticed the growing attachment between Mr. Eldredge and Miss Blenkensop. Even with their continuous observation it was so difficult to spy that Edith sometimes thought they imagined it after all. Miss Blenkensop was so very proper, and Mr. Eldredge never stepped over any line which might distress her. Nor did he refer again to his sad history, which Hetty deemed a blessing: "Surely once he had time to reflect in tranquility, he understood he did himself no favors!"

Of the two girls, it was Hetty who was inclined to make jokes about the purported lovers, or to plot how they might be brought together, or to devise outlandish means by which they could afford to marry, and Edith was relieved when a new subject arose to claim her cousin's attention: the possibility of travel.

"My aunt Lavinia has written again," Hetty announced one afternoon. Rosie was at the spinet with Miss Blenkensop beside her, correcting her tempo and fingering. The other two pupils were supposed to be translating a passage from Dante's *Paradiso*, but not much progress was made. "She positively *insists* that we pay a long visit to Sussex and complains that we haven't in ever so long, which is entirely true, and now that the tenants who occupied our old cottage have declared they will not renew the lease, Papa must go and settle things."

"Will he, then?"

"He told Mama he supposed it must be done, and she is agreeable because she has only met my aunt once, shortly after she and Papa were married—while they were on their wedding journey—and she says of course Aunt Lavinia must want to see Lionel and Rosie and me again."

"Then the whole family will go? But how will Lionel?" Edith asked.

"We must go between terms, Papa says. "Instead of returning to Somerset after Michaelmas Term ends, Lionel will join us in town for a while!" Hetty's eyes danced. Neither she nor Edith had ever been to London. "Lionel has over a month before Hilary Term, so there will be time for both London and a few weeks in Crawley with our Sidney and Morrow relations before he must go back to school."

"Oh," breathed Edith. "Then I won't see him. I did so want to hear about his time at university." She felt her spirits sink, to think both of missing him and of how every last person she knew would be gone somewhere exciting, while she remained behind. But she tried to affect enthusiasm, for Hetty's sake. "It will be very fun for you."

"When I return, I will tell you every last little thing he tells us," Hetty assured her, with the generosity of the blessed. "And every detail of our trip. It will be as if you were present yourself. And, in return, you must report on whether Mr. E makes any progress at all with Soppy."

As it happened that winter, after the Hugh Hapgoods were gone, and almost before Edith had time to feel well and truly sorry for herself, Elfrida wrote to announce that she was expecting her second child and Alice her first, delightful tidings which renewed Edith's interest in sewing, if it meant making gowns for new nephews or nieces. On the heels of this news, a genuine baronet appeared at Bramleigh one afternoon, asking the squire for his daughter Margaret's hand in marriage! What had Margaret been up to in Bath, they wondered, when she was sent there specifically to find her *uncle* a spouse, not herself? And, if these developments were not enough, as soon as Edith could write to Margaret to demand an explanation, Margaret was writing herself to say that she had done it: Uncle Alwyn was married at last, and to a wealthy woman.

Edith feared so many thunderbolts in quick succession would be too much for her papa's weakened heart, but they had rather the opposite effect. "What a bundle of news—what a bundle of news," he cried gleefully, rubbing his hands together and nearly breaking the bell-rope summoning Dorcas. When the raw-boned maid-of-all-work scrambled through the door of the breakfast room, Richard Hapgood declared, "Tell Button she must make a feast and bake a cake! We must celebrate our deliverance from Mrs. Hapgood's brother."

"Mr. Alwyn Arbuthnot is married," explained Edith to the gawping servant. And to her father she added, "Papa, is a feast truly necessary for just the two of us?"

"Of course it is! I have had the support of your shiftless uncles for decades, and now, in the space of a few months, I have been miraculously delivered of both of them! We will have our cake and our feast and be on our way."

"On our way?"

"On our way," he repeated. "Edith, you and I are for Bath. If Alwyn has hopped the twig, we will join your mother and your sister in Henrietta Street for the remainder of the lease."

Edith screeched and began bounding up and down, clapping her hands, stopping only to throw her arms about her father, while he laughed and patted her on the back. "Oh, Papa! Bath! Oh, Papa! Do you suppose we might visit some of the artists' workshops? Mr. Eldredge says he still knows many there."

"Yes, yes. My own little artist must see the world. Now that's enough of that. If we are to be gone, I must see about stabling my horse at the Swan and sending Crack to Birdlow's."

"It is too much!" whispered Edith to herself, when she found herself squeezed against her father in the long and uncomfortable coach journey from Taunton to Wells to Bath. "Too much altogether."

But her grey eyes sparkled, and she felt again in her reticule for the two precious letters of introduction Mr. Eldredge had written for her. She was going to see the world! She was going to meet genuine, professional artists!

Even the final shock that awaited them upon their arrival—that another gentleman named Dashiell Waite wanted to marry Margaret and she him—could not make Edith entirely forget that this was to be her first exposure to the greater world of art. Her *entrée*. Even if she had no longing to place herself among its gloried members, she nevertheless yearned to move amongst them, learning and respectful and unobserved.

"Certainly I know where these artists may be found," said Margaret, when Edith showed her the addresses on the letters of introduction, "and we will call on both of them, that you might mingle with these sorts, but first you must meet my Dashiell. And he you. You did bring samples of your work, didn't you? I would dearly like to brag about you and show him I have some creditable relations. Mama and Uncle Alwyn are very dear, of course, but I suspect Dashiell had to begin to be in love with me before he could best appreciate their qualities."

Edith very much wanted to be a credit to Margaret, but making Mr. Dashiell Waite's acquaintance required all her growing self-possession and more than one self-talk because she found him quite intimidating. It was not merely Mr. Waite's handsomeness (if anything, Elfie's husband Frederick was handsomer—but Frederick was also an inveterate joker who teased Edith until she couldn't be shy of him), or Mr. Waite's cane or habitual almost-scowl, but rather that he was completely unknown to the Hapgoods, and Edith had not the chance to meet him before knowing he would be her brother-in-law.

But her fears turned out to be unnecessary. For one thing, Mr. Waite—*Dashiell,* rather—did not have a scowling personality, for all his daunting looks, and, for another, he was so enamored of Margaret and so pleased with their coming union, that Edith suspected little could upset him at present.

"I see why Margaret praises your artwork to the skies," he said after supper one evening in Henrietta Street shortly after her arrival. At Margaret's insistence, Edith had fetched the pieces Mr. Eldredge selected for her to bring to Bath and set them out on the tables in the drawing room, the corners weighted by books from the circulating library. There were ink, chalk, and charcoal drawings of family members alone or in combination. Dashiell looked longest at the sketches of Margaret, but he did manage to tear his eyes away to ask after a few others.

"Who is this young man?" he asked.

"Our cousin Lionel, and those are his sisters Hetty and Rosie. This was a study I did for a family portrait for their parents."

"You have captured them marvelously. They appear to be having a good time."

"Lionel is *always* having a good time," put in Margaret. "He's at Oxford now and, I'll warrant, having an even better time. But that portrait was one of Edie's first official commissions."

Dashiell turned to regard his soon-to-be sister-in-law. "Might I join your early patrons, Edith? I should very much like a bridal portrait of Margaret."

Margaret looked fit to burst with joy at this request, and she beamed upon her intended. She was not the only one, for, if he hoped to find his way to the Hapgoods' hearts, the best strategy was to admire their Edith. ("So obliging," fluttered Mrs. Hapgood, while pride swelled her husband like a Montgolfier balloon.)

"How kind of you," said Edith, "but, if you are to be my brother, you may have any one of these sketches of her. I have a thousand pictures of Margaret, if I have one."

"That may be," was his answer, "but I would like to commission something to capture her as she is now. A person looks different—when she is to be married."

When she is in love, Edith supposed he meant.

Edith thought Margaret appeared pretty much as she ever had, but, no, maybe when she looked at her intended there was an uncharacteristic softness and warmth in her hazel eyes. She lost some of that *managing* air which was wont to drive her family mad. So perhaps Dashiell was right. And, in any case, if the masterful side of Margaret proved to be only temporarily suppressed by the experience of falling in love, Edith couldn't blame Dashiell for wanting a record of it. To remind himself it had existed, as it were.

The bargain was struck, and sittings with Margaret must be fitted into the itinerary, amidst shopping for Margaret's trousseau and Margaret wanting to take Edith all over Bath to share in her experiences of the past months. "Yes, yes, and yes," said Edith. "All good things and all things I look forward to—only please, Margaret, may we begin with a visit to an artist?"

The very next morning the two sisters set out, Mrs. Hapgood having no interest in braving the cold, and the squire heading for Sydney Gardens to purchase his subscription to the Ride. Edith thought perhaps Dashiell might join them, but Margaret told her matter-of-factly that Dashiell always spent his mornings at the King's Bath, followed by a rubbing down. "It does such wonders for him, you know, that I suspect wherever we choose to settle, we will spend considerable time in Bath or another spa."

Of the two artists whom Mr. Eldredge proposed to introduce, the first was Mr. Liggett, a painter of portrait miniatures in Old Bond Street. He was a diminutive man, hardly taller than Edith, with a hairline in retreat and tiny spectacles perched on his blade of a nose. Because Mr. Eldredge warned her the man was timid, the girls were prepared for it and succeeded in drawing him out by abundant admiration of his work and Edith's many gentle questions on his methods and preferred materials and suppliers. Enamel versus ivory; oil versus watercolor.

"This is a very fine portrait of the Marquess of Wellington," Margaret declared, peering at the tiny oval in its glass case.

"Thank you, thank you. It is actually a copy," he demurred. "A copy of Richard Cosway's portrait of the great man. You will have heard of Richard Cosway? Member of the Royal Academy. He lives in London, naturally. I have never been so honored as to have Wellington sit for me. If you see over here, I have some copies of Gainsborough and Reynolds as well."

When Mr. Liggett excused himself to attend to a customer, Margaret waved Edith over, whispering, "My dear, look at the cost of the marquess! Forty guineas! Perhaps you should become a painter of portrait miniatures."

But Edith shuddered at the thought of keeping a store and currying favor with whoever might be lured inside. When the Hapgoods of Bramleigh had been considerably poorer, she had once thought of making her painting pay, but now, with her three older sisters married (or almost married) very well, and her two financially burdensome uncles now either dead (Alec) or advantageously married (Alwyn), might she not just paint for the love of it? Accepting commissions when she pleased, but otherwise merely working for the sheer pleasure? And her idea of pleasure did not include painting the Marquess of Wellington!

The two young ladies waved their farewells to Mr. Liggett and made their way leisurely down Union Street to Westgate, stealing into a shop or two for Margaret's items. Both the facades and the displays in the bow windows grew plainer as they proceeded, and when they turned south into Westgate Buildings, Margaret admitted she had never yet had cause to explore this area of town.

"You are sure this is the address?"

"45 Westgate Buildings," Edith answered, inspecting the envelope again. "Mr. Alexandre Olivier."

"What a French name! Did you ask Mr. Eldredge if he was French?"

"He is. Mr. Eldredge said he is an *emigré*. I do hope I don't have to try to speak French to him. Mine isn't nearly so good as Hetty's.

But Mr. Eldredge said I must be sure to meet him and that he is a good old kindly fellow. In any event, if he is anything like little Mr. Liggett, he will not be very frightening."

Eyeing the narrowness of the windows and the multiplication of nurses and wheeled chairs and walking sticks, Margaret said dryly, "One thing is clear: this Mr. Olivier is not nearly as prosperous as Mr. Liggett. He had better beware, or he will find himself buried in the country like Mr. Eldredge, paid a pittance to teach young ladies."

"It would not be so terrible," Edith replied, as their noses wrinkled, some stench of drains wafting their way. "At least in the country the air is fresh and healthy. This poor old man! To be driven first from his homeland, and then to struggle to support himself where he knows no one and must learn the language and the culture. I pity him already."

Edith's pity did not trouble her long, however. For when they gained the steps of Number 45 and plied the knocker, taking each other's hands, they heard the rapid drum of approaching footsteps, whoever it was hurrying down a staircase. The two girls unconsciously drew closer together in response just before the chipped door was flung wide. There in the doorway, to their astonishment, stood a young man clad in an open-necked, loose shirt which was untucked from his breeches, his black hair wild and rumpled, his eyes equally dark, his skin pale, and his features strongly cut.

"Yes?" Both his tone and manner were imperious, and Edith drew back. This could not be Mr. Alexandre Olivier, harmless counterpart to Mr. Liggett, or Mr. Eldredge would have warned her! Nor could he be a servant of Mr. Olivier, for what servant would perform his duties in such a state of undress?

Swallowing, she held her letter of introduction out in a trembling hand. "Pardon us. We are here to call on Mr. Alexandre Olivier. I am Miss Edith Hapgood, and this is my sister Miss Margaret Hapgood, and we are recommended by Mr. Judah Eldredge."

"Ah...Judah!" the black eyes glinted in recognition, and a thin smile twisted his mouth. Retreating a step, he gestured for them to enter. "You must forgive my *deshabille*. I am posed."

Before they could decide whether to accept his invitation, a voice bellowed down the staircase in such rapid French that neither Margaret nor Edith caught anything but the name "Jean-André."

The young man so denominated called back in a torrent of equal rapidity, but this time they caught "*Mesdemoiselles* 'Apgood" and "Judah." Then Jean-André turned to them again, smiling more fully. "You see, you must come now. He will be curious."

Had Margaret not been with her, Edith would have turned and fled, letter of introduction or no letter of introduction. As it was, she returned the squeeze of her sister's hand, and they followed the young man inside.

CHAPTER EIGHT

Without light..each parcell of the worlds fabrick lie buried in black obscuritie, & dismall squalour.
—John Swan, *Speculum mundi* (1635)

Both the ground-floor passage and the staircase were narrow and close, with odors of uncirculated air and stale food, and it was a relief to climb upward several flights, past the first floor and onward to the second, where there was a breath of freshness and increased light. In fact, the second floor was simply one large room—a studio. Canvases, finished and unfinished, were stacked against one wall. Against another a drape was tacked up, with an easel set before it. A long deal table occupied the third wall, upon which were scattered pigment powders and oils, brushes soaking in a jar, a tray of pencils and chalks and charcoals, stacks of papers, and heaps of discarded clothing, hats, feathers, wigs, and paste jewelry.

In the midst of all this stood a plump man, hands on hips, with hair and whiskers as dark as Jean-André's. This man was fully dressed, over which he wore a spattered apron.

"Welcome!" he exclaimed. "Welcome to all friends of Judah Eldredge. He has written me to expect you. I am Alexandre Olivier, and you have met my nephew Jean-André." Mr. Olivier spoke in thick, accented English, but naturally he must have been older when he emigrated. As the girls curtsied, the uncle snapped his fingers at his nephew. "But you must make yourself presentable. We will continue later."

He turned to Margaret and Edith, throwing his arms wide. "I rejoice that you visit me! Please, you must look at everything. Which one is the artist? I know it is you, tiny *mademoiselle*. Judah told me, 'she is slight and dark as a Frenchwoman.'"

Edith nodded uncertainly. Mr. Olivier might be genial as Father Christmas, but she would have preferred to find another Mr. Liggett.

Seeing her hesitation, Mr. Olivier boomed, "You want to have tea first? We can go below, and I will send Jean-André to fetch some. Our charwoman will not return until much later, I am afraid."

"Oh, please, no," piped Edith. "Do not trouble yourselves."

"Then look, look," he urged. "Look at everything. And, when you have done so, then you will show me your work. You have brought samples, yes?" Indicating the portfolio Edith had set down beside the table.

"Yes."

Like a madman, Mr. Olivier began spinning about the room, unstacking the canvases and lining them against the walls or placing them upon any available surface. He dug in his stack of papers for studies and sketches and drafts, shaking his head over some and tossing them aside or propping them up against other things. All the while, Jean-André, having buttoned on a waistcoat and knotted a length of fabric about his throat in lieu of a neckcloth, leaned idly against the rail of the staircase, observing them beneath lowered lids.

Obediently, Edith and Margaret circled the room, inspecting the works displayed. They were nearly entirely portraits, many of the subjects recognizable as Jean-André, though he appeared in various costumes and even wigs, which made Margaret press her lips together to prevent a smile. But there were other sitters, both male and female, in a range of ages; in these as well Edith noted similarities in attitude and background and trappings.

"My clients, they are important," declared Mr. Olivier. "Or they wish to seem so. Or, like my own countrymen, they were important in the past."

"I see," said Edith, nodding. "Yes, I see that."

She drifted further away from the man to stare harder at a series of canvases. She was in something of a muddle, she realized, dread spiraling through her. Because—she did not care for Mr. Olivier's style of portraiture—neither for the stiff, formal attitudes, nor for the ubiquitous piles of background rubble, as if each sitter had just survived the sack of Rome, nor for the pretensions to magnificence.

But she must find *something* complimentary to say! Here was this friend of Mr. Eldredge, being kind enough to invite her in and expressing himself willing to regard her own work—

Edith glanced at Margaret, but Margaret was cocking her head at a painting of Jean-André in a Charles II wig, his arm balanced on a broken column. More stiffness. More masonry.

"These are—dazzling, taken altogether," she managed at last. "An—embarrassment of riches. The colors are beautiful. And this drapery here—how well done it is." She pointed almost at random and then turned scarlet, seeing that she had indicated a painting of Jean-André, only half-draped and at his most Napoleonic.

"Yes, you have seen the Appiani painting?" demanded Mr. Olivier. "The *Apotheosis of Napoleon*?"

"Everyone has seen it," spoke up Margaret. "A version of it has been in all the papers." Of course, the English newspapers printed the engraving of Boney, enthroned and in Roman dress, as a joke, mocking his pretensions to empire, but she knew better than to say as much.

"My uncle was the Appiani of France," pronounced Jean-André, startling them, "but he cannot receive the recognition he deserves—here, as a lowly *emigré*."

"Jean-André," sighed his uncle deprecatingly.

"It is true," the nephew insisted, taking a few steps toward Edith and Margaret, as if they had challenged him. "But for my uncle's noble birth, he would never have had to flee France. Here, in England, however, they care only for their native painters. Bah!" He snapped his fingers, much as Mr. Olivier had. "My uncle, because he is not

English, cannot be elected to the Royal Academy of Art. Because he is not English, he cannot submit to their summer exhibitions!"

"That is unfortunate indeed," Edith said politely. "I know it was also a great disappointment to Mr. Eldredge not to be elected to the Royal Academy."

Her sympathy pleased the young man, and he gave her an approving nod, while Mr. Olivier began to bustle about, clearing a space on his worktable. "I have not been *un*fortunate, despite what Jean-André believes," he said. "Here in Bath I have been able to earn a modest living, between commissions and students and auctions. If you will be in town in March, some of my works will be featured in Mr. Evill's rooms, to be auctioned with other artists' offerings and sundry furnishings."

"Alas," said Margaret, "our lease will be up before then." She could not suppress a little glow when she said this, and Edith knew her sister was anticipating again her wedding to Dashiell and her wedding journey.

"*Tant pis, tant pis,*" Mr. Olivier dismissed this, oblivious. "It is too bad our acquaintance will be so brief. We must make the most of it. My dear Miss Edith, if you would be so kind as to show me what you have brought. Judah has written that you have much talent."

Blushing again, Edith unlaced the portfolio she had brought and again set out the items Dashiell admired the evening before.

She felt ashamed of how quickly she had surveyed Mr. Olivier's works, when she saw how carefully both he and his nephew scrutinized her own. Their minute examination lasted even longer than Mr. Eldredge's had, and they several times exchanged glances without speaking, making Margaret want to scream and Edith to sink into the earth. She could not imagine why both Mr. Eldredge and Mr. Olivier regretted not being able to exhibit their works with the Royal Academy—what torture that would be, if these private showings were any indication! And the more learned the viewers, the more torturous Edith found it. She was grateful for Margaret's hand at her elbow in silent encouragement.

At last, at very last, Jean-André thumped a finger down on one of the sketches. "This. Who is this?"

Edith followed his finger. "That's Lionel. My cousin. Those are our cousins, Lionel, Harriet, and Rosalie." She indicated each one. "Their father asked me to paint their portrait. It's funny—this sketch was the first thing Mr. Eldredge saw as well."

"Who has seen your works, besides ourselves and Judah and your family?" was Jean-André's unexpected question. "Anyone?"

Edith racked her brain. "Well, I suppose, the servants and a few neighbors of ours."

"They're very good, aren't they?" prodded Margaret, ignoring Edith's smothered gasp. The obtuseness of the Frenchmen tried her patience, and in her opinion this had gone on long enough. "Even though these are drafts. You should see the finished portraits. Quite remarkable."

"I believe you," said Jean-André dryly. "And, yes, they are." He turned again to Edith. "Perhaps you have ambitions of becoming a great artist? Of being invited to join the Royal Academy? Of exhibiting in London and painting the Prince?"

Edith straightened, forcing herself to meet his dark gaze. If she did not stand up for herself, she would end in being very intimidated by these Oliviers, and she could hardly return to Mr. Eldredge and confess that his kindly introductions had been sources of strain for her.

"Thank you, but no. My ambitions do not extend so far. I would, of course, like to be the best painter I can be, and to produce works that satisfy myself and which might, perhaps, bring pleasure to my friends and family, but, beyond that, I do not have higher aims."

"So fortunate," sighed Mr. Olivier. "*Ars gratia artis.* Art for art's sake."

"Oh!" breathed Edith, embarrassed anew. "I did not mean to imply any disrespect for those who have higher ambitions—"

"Or for those artists who must work and compromise to earn their bread," Jean-André put in coolly, "because they cannot afford merely to paint for pleasure."

"No—not them, either." Edith's voice caught. She had not meant to make anyone feel bad about anything! Beside her, she felt Margaret gathering herself, but before her sister could explode, Mr. Olivier beamed upon them genially once more, letting loose a volley of laughs and clapping his hands together. "Ho ho! Such a dear little earnest creature Judah has sent me. Such a dear little earnest, *gifted* creature. She wants to be the best painter she can be? Yes, and who should deny her? *Non!* She must be encouraged. She must be taught. She must blossom. She must not only draw—she must paint. We will begin lessons immediately."

"Dear me," said Edith, her head in a whirl from these mercurial transitions. "I thank you very much, but I am only here for a few weeks, and our family has much planned. I thank you very much, in any event."

Both uncle and nephew sagged under her refusal. "But you must let my uncle teach you," protested Jean-André. "What you have shown us is just—lines. Where is the color? You need color. Color provides *passion*, and that is what my uncle can teach you. If you want to be the best you can be!"

"Mr. Eldredge will teach me. We have spent many months on what you call 'lines,' but he assures me we will move on to more and more color."

"Judah Eldredge!" thundered Mr. Olivier, his Father-Christmas air vanishing again. "What does he know of color? A landscape artist! Are people brown and blue? Are people ochre and gris and celadon? Can the shades of a wood compare to the shades of a human countenance?"

"*Pas du tout*," agreed his nephew.

"Well, Mr. Eldredge's tuition must suffice," returned Edith loyally, though she felt doubt prick her. Rapidly, she began to gather her sketches, Margaret leaping to aid her, over the hand-wringing and protests of their hosts.

"You must stay for the tea!"

"You must not take everything—we should like to look longer!"

"You must come again, please."

It took effort and assurances that they would try to call again, but the sisters did manage to escape and find themselves once more in the street. They said not a word to each other until they had regained Westgate Street and were nearly to the White Hart. Then Margaret threw a glance over her shoulder and, seeing no Frenchmen in pursuit, she slowed their gasping pace. By the time the girls passed into Cheap Street, they were giggling and clutching at each other.

"What strange men," Margaret exclaimed. "I cannot say I think much of Mr. Eldredge's judgment in introducing them to you."

"That isn't fair!" objected Edith. "Mr. Liggett was perfectly amiable. And while the two Mr. Oliviers were certainly odd, it was very kind of them to take the time to look over my samples."

"When that Jean-André answered the door! I didn't know where to look."

"Well, they weren't expecting callers."

"Stop defending them, Edie! Is it because that Jean-André was handsome, in a dramatic, French sort of way? Don't tell me you liked them."

"I don't know about liking them, but I want to *try* to like them. And not because Mr. Jean-André looks like David's *Napoleon Crossing the Alps*. But rather because, after all, Mr. Eldredge must have had his reasons, to choose Mr. Liggett and Mr. Olivier."

Margaret made a scoffing sound. "I suspect his reason was that he had no one else to recommend you to. As you wrote me yourself, he must have reached the nadir of his career, to accept a drawing-master post far from anywhere important."

Edith sighed. "All the more reason, then, for me to try to appreciate them."

"At least that Jean-André person admitted you were good."

"When you forced him to, Margaret."

"Stuff. Who forced him? I only made him say what I suspect-ed. They were just keeping their own counsel because they envied you. Mr. Olivier might earn his living as an artist—and support his nephew as well, I suppose—but somehow I would rather look at one of your portraits than ten of his."

Here Edith only squeezed her sister's arm, and they were silent for a while. But when they had passed the Abbey yard, she ventured, "All the same, I am sorry I made them think I was boasting about not needing my art to keep me."

But Margaret had no patience for this, either. "For heaven's sake—as if men did not have everything their way to begin with! You, who cannot even have a lesson with Mr. Eldredge without a governess there to preserve the proprieties! And you are hardly a wealthy woman. Those men are the ones with the expensive ambi-tions. Even in Westgate Buildings they are still in Bath, and I imagine it requires £500 per annum at least to maintain them, where your annual keep at Bramleigh amounts to little more than £110 for Papa. Perhaps £120, with your art supplies."

Margaret would know, of course, as she loved to go over the Bramleigh account books.

"Do you suppose what Mr. Olivier said was true?" Edith pursued. "I mean, that Mr. Eldredge would not be the best teacher for color because portrait painting is so different from landscape painting?"

But here her sister was out of her element. "I don't know, dear. I haven't the least idea. Did it make you feel badly? I don't suppose it's something you could ask Mr. Eldredge, is it?"

Glumly, Edith shook her head. Nor could she imagine saying anything to her papa. After the dismal harvest that year, she did not want him to sack Mr. Eldredge and stretch what remained to afford a drawing master who specialized in portraits, for then what would become of either Mr. Eldredge or the family finances?

No, she would say nothing of the matter.

As if Margaret read her mind, she gave Edith's arm a swing. "Come on, you. That is enough food for thought for one day. We require food of another sort. Here is the Guildhall, where they have all manner of delicious eatables. Shall we surprise everyone with some sweets?"

CHAPTER NINE

**My son, if sinners entice thee, consent thou not.
—Proverbs 1:10, *The Authorized Version* (1611)**

"Lionel, explain to me, please, the letter I have had from Mr. Routh, President of Magdalen College, regarding disciplinary actions taken against you and Mr. Jason Clinkett shortly before the end of term." Bundled in greatcoats, caps, mufflers, and mittens, father and son trooped through Hyde Park beside the frozen Serpentine.

Hunching against both the cold and the tone of reproach, Lionel's eyes wandered enviously to the crowds of skaters and the booths pitched on the ice. "Sir, it was hardly worth troubling you. A mere matter of an uninvited guest—"

"Mr. Routh described the incident as a *girl* being found under one of the beds," Hugh continued inexorably.

"Well, indeed, the guest was a *she*..."

"A girl in your chambers *and* after hours, thus resulting in two violations."

"...Yes, sir."

Two of the skaters executed a series of complicated figures, while others formed an admiring semicircle around them. Hugh waited, to see if Lionel would be more forthcoming, but he was to be disappointed. After another minute, he asked, "Lionel, do you and Clinkett often invite girls to your room, against the rules of the college?"

"No, sir!" He was stout about this.

"Had you seen this particular one before?"

A hesitation. "Perhaps once."

Hugh repressed a sigh and wished for his wife. How to proceed? Lionel was a high-spirited boy—young man, rather. Much as Hugh himself had been, at his age. Girls, drink, gambling, and pranks were nothing to be wondered at, and, if Lionel had engaged in any (or all) of the other common vices, he had managed to escape detection. But youthful escapades could have adult consequences. Permanent consequences. Suppose Lionel were to be sent down?

It was too cold to stand long, and they resumed walking, back toward the inn, where they would later catch the Worthing coach to Crawley.

"Son," he began again, "I would prefer to discuss this and be done, before we rejoin your stepmother and sisters. I grieve that you cannot or will not explain the circumstances of the matter more fully..." (Once more he trailed off, only to be met with silence and a line appearing along his son's jaw.) "...But I hope you will consider our expectations of you and justify the pride we feel in you."

"Yes, sir. I intend to."

With that Hugh must be content, but he could not help adding, "It is not only your stepmother and I who would wish you to beware the various—er—temptations which school affords. Remember that your conduct serves as an example to your younger sisters and, indeed, I would say to your cousin Edith as well."

For the first time, his father's words appeared to penetrate Lionel's reserve, and he turned on him, alarmed. "Why need she—why need they hear of it? I mean, I am listening to you, sir, and I hope you will never live to be troubled by Mr. Routh again, regarding me. Therefore, why need the girls be told?"

Endeavoring to hide his surprise, Hugh replied, "They need not, they need not—on this particular occasion."

Relief washed over Lionel's face, but, once he had mastered himself, Hugh heard him mutter, "Hetty is sure to blab what is none of her business."

A rather unjust criticism, in Hugh's opinion, as if it were Hetty's fault Lionel misbehaved. But the father was too glad to have this sign of repentance—*any* sign of repentance, to prolong the subject, and they proceeded on their way.

The Hugh Hapgoods were a subdued party as they traveled to Crawley, but this was to be expected, as they shared the coach with strangers (Lionel gladly offering to take an outside seat). Hetty and Rosie were curious to see their cousin Caroline, though not eager to see their aunt and uncle Sidney, but Hugh viewed the visit altogether as a duty to be borne, as did Rosemary. And Rosemary felt an additional reluctance because she knew her husband would be occupied with the business of selling his former home, throwing her upon the Sidneys for company.

"How old is Caroline now?" asked Rosie in her sister's ear, when the coach was descending Ryegate Hill.

Hetty thought a moment. "Well, if Lionel is now seventeen, Caroline must be sixteen."

"I confess, I barely remember her," Rosie whispered. "She had hair so light it was almost white, though."

"Flaxen hair, and she wouldn't say boo to a goose. She was like Uncle Wellington in that way," Hetty continued. "Although that might have been because Aunt Lavinia is so overbearing." Hetty's stepmother must have guessed, with her usual acuity, that Hetty was saying something mischievous, because she raised one eyebrow her direction. But Hetty only grinned. Indeed—perhaps Aunt Lavinia shouldn't be discussed in front of strangers, but if their fellow passengers ever met Lavinia Sidney, they would learn soon enough that Hetty spoke no more than the truth.

"My, my, how you've grown," declared that same Aunt Lavinia, doing her best to enfold her nephew and both nieces in one awkward embrace. She was plumper than they all remembered, making the resemblance to their late mother less pronounced, but it was there. Stepping back, she inspected each closely. "How very long it has been—what—over four years? Lionel, your hair has grown darker, but I must say—you three are the image of my dear lost sister Harriet. I expect very long chats with each of you, because I will want to know all you have been doing in our time apart. Your father's letters are so dry and factual! But let that wait: you will hardly recognize your cousin Caroline now, I suspect, but here she is, your erstwhile playmate."

In fact, they did not recognize her. The whitish hair of her childhood had darkened to gold, and she had shed as well her childhood shyness, coming up to Lionel at once and accosting him playfully with, "Well, cousin? I suppose you remember how you once pinned my braid to the arm of a chair, so that, when I stood, both I and the chair tumbled over?"

"I remember you yowling like a cat held under the pump," he replied equably.

Caroline favored him with a roguish smile. "Ah, still incorrigible, then? I will be on my guard." And turning then to Hetty: "And you, miss. You were my friend whenever you and your brother were at odds, but when you weren't—why, I remember you took my new parasol and tied it to one of the village dogs, so that the poor beast tore down the street with it open and dragging and bouncing behind him. It was quite ruined."

"What delightful creatures we were," said Hetty. "You must have been quite anxious to meet us again."

"As a matter of fact, I have been. I hope we will find each other the best of friends and mutually improved. Except for Rosie, of course, for whom improvement was not so desperately needed. Rosie, you have been consistent. You began sweet and modest, and you continue so, I warrant."

As Rosie actually *was* sweet and modest, she could think of no possible reply. Nor was she certain what to make of this charming, bantering cousin who talked to her as if she were still six years old.

That first supper, Caroline was seated between Lionel and Hetty, with Aunt Lavinia on Lionel's other side, while Rosie found herself next to her silent uncle Wellington at the opposite end. Her uncle nodded at her and even once said, "You might like this soup," but that was the sum total of their conversation.

Instead the attention of all belonged to Lionel and Caroline. His cousin plied him with question after question about Oxford: would he read mathematics, philosophy, history, or classics? Had he many friends and what were they like? Did he like his tutors? Why were the end-of-term examinations called collections? Had he and Clinker and Clunker got up to any mischief?

"My dear," Lavinia broke in at this question, "the foolishness of young men may or may not be appropriate for discussion when young ladies are present."

That silenced Lionel, but, to the surprise of all, Wellington Sidney made his first contribution to the general discussion. "Hugh and I once exchanged our classmates' gowns, right before the Gaudy—do you remember, Hugh?"

His children were pleased to see their father's somber face crinkle in a grin. "I do. We hid all the gowns of the tallest fellows, the very morning of the Gaudy—the feast where those newly matriculated host the Old Members. There was scrambling and chaos, but it was either borrow a gown from a shorter lad or miss the feast altogether."

Wellington slapped the table, laughing silently. "Ormondsey—! Ormondsey was all of six-and-a-half feet tall, and the only gown he could find came to just below his knees!"

The picture this conjured made all of them laugh, with the exception of Lavinia, who gave her husband a quelling look.

"What a capital idea!" Lionel declared. "I will remember that one for the next formal hall." Catching his father's eye, he added, "That is, I will be sure to stow my own gown where no one may find it."

"Are there no ladies about at Magdalen?" asked Caroline, when the sweetmeats and cheeses were served. "All you have talked about are men—from the president, to the dean, to the tutors and fellows, to the pupils and porters and scouts!"

Lionel having glued his teeth together with a preserved plum, held up a finger to ask her patience. This time he avoided his father's gaze. "Well, there's Mrs. Routh, the president's wife. And the provost of The Queen's College has five daughters, but generally one must go into town to meet with womankind."

"How old are these five daughters of The Queen's College?"

"Oh, they range from perhaps four years of age to fifteen or so. But the fifteen-year-old and the next oldest board at school in town, to stay out of danger. The fifteen-year-old has already received six marriage proposals, they say."

Caroline sighed and shook her head at Hetty. "Imagine being one girl among so many young men! Should you like it?"

"If they were all like Lionel, I might be worn out before my time with rapping knuckles and punching midsections and checking my bed for spiders," answered Hetty dryly.

"I suppose matches *are* made in such a setting," Lavinia observed to Rosemary, "but the chaperonage of the various daughters and nieces associated with the university must be quite a chore. I do not envy those mamas."

"Our former governess met her husband at university," Hetty recalled suddenly. "Remember, Papa? Miss Parvill—or whatever her maiden name was—was the niece of a provost, was she not? And Mr. Parvill was a fellow. And they fell in love."

"I am not likely to forget it anytime soon," Hugh said, with a glance at his wife. "So perhaps there *is* something to be said for university matches."

"Well, Lionel," said his aunt, "I hope you will do better than to offer for some girl simply because she is underfoot."

To her puzzlement, Lionel flushed at this, though he only said, "No, madam. Have no fear." Then he jammed more sweetmeats in his mouth, in the hopes that she would drop the subject.

With an inward shrug, she rounded on her brother-in-law. "My dear brother, do you really mean to sell your cottage? I am sure, with a little effort, another tenant may be found. And supposing Lionel should choose to live in it, after he has taken his degree? Then you would be glad you kept it. We are so convenient to London, you know."

"Yes, I know," replied Hugh. "But as I do not intend to make any permanent return to Sussex, I would be glad to have done with it. If Lionel should choose to settle in or near London after he has taken his degree, other lodgings may easily be found."

"I'm going to live in Somerset," Lionel blurted. "To be near my family."

"Oh?" His aunt's response was more breath than question. She waved impatiently at the footman who tried to remove her plate. "Never mind that, Stephens. You may clear the table later." She gave a brittle laugh. "Lionel, my dear boy, I am certain I need not remind you that we are also your family."

"Yes, yes. Excuse me. By 'family' I meant my parents and sisters. And my Hapgood relations. I'm afraid I do rather prefer the country to town. I have missed Somerset."

It was Rosemary who helped the company past the awkward moment. "It makes sense that, after a few months of being walled up even in so pretty a town as Oxford, spending your time so much within doors, poring over books—that you should miss the countryside and the liberty your horse afforded you."

Hetty good-naturedly joined this chorus, supplying a description of Mannerly and telling an amusing story of how the squire's horse had developed a *tendre* for the filly. "If the squire is not already abroad on his morning ride when Rosie and I arrive for our lessons and Hal stables Mannerly, Bucephalus will shake his head and whicker and *literally* drag his feet. It frustrates Papa's cousin to no end, but the rest of us find it secretly delightful."

Lionel's lips parted, as if he would like to ask a dozen questions, but, catching his stepmother's eye, he shut them again and sat back in silence.

"A pleasant gathering, all in all," said Rosemary several hours later, when the Hapgoods had retired to the inn, and she and her husband were alone.

"As pleasant as things are ever likely to be, when Lavinia is present," he answered.

She was not the sort of woman to utter platitudes or pretend to a liking she did not feel, but she lay down her hairbrush and came to stand behind his armchair, placing her hands on his shoulders and resting her cheek against his hair. "Yes, that is what I meant."

"Come, sit with me," he said, tugging on her hand. "The room is a drafty one." When she was perched on his lap they were silent a while, watching the dwindling fire. "My talk with Lionel this morning was not successful."

"What do you mean?"

"I mean he was not forthcoming." Briefly he related the conversation by the Serpentine.

Rosemary considered this as she absently braided her hair. "So he would not say who the girl under the bed was?"

"He would not. And I gave him more than one opportunity."

"Yes. Nevertheless, I would not let it distress you overmuch, Hugh."

"No?" he asked hopefully.

"No. For I suspect the female guest was likely Mr. Jason Clinkett's doing. Lionel was merely reluctant to tell tales about his friend."

"But how can you know?"

"I don't know. I merely suspect. A suspicion which Lionel's comments at supper confirmed for me. You heard how he missed Somerset."

"What have Somerset and his horse to do with a girl under the bed?"

She smiled at him, tenderness lighting her eyes. "Remember when I told you Lionel was fond of his cousin Edith? He may not always continue so, but for the present I think it will prevent him from any serious entanglements with other young ladies."

Hugh stared. "You think he has not yet forgotten that? Has he said so to you? Does she know?"

"No, I don't think he's forgotten yet, but he hasn't said so to me. And she doesn't know. Because they are both so young, I advised Lionel to wait some time. Both that he may be sure of his feelings and that he may not involve his cousin's heart too soon. I can't help liking the idea, though, Hugh. It steadies him, and she really is a dear girl."

Thoughtfully, Hugh wound his wife's braid around his hand, sliding one finger through the plait. He remembered how Lionel had reacted, at the thought of Edith hearing of the girl under the bed.

"I suppose, if this little sweetness upon Edith keeps him from greater mischief, I should be grateful…"

"When a young man is like our Lionel," she returned, "with such high spirits and charm, one piddling letter from the college president does not seem so very high a price to pay."

Hugh did laugh then. "You are right, as always. Let us hope Edith's calming influence lasts—perhaps we should cut short our time in Sussex and rush him back to Somerset for another dose."

"Ha! That might please Lionel, but Lavinia would never speak to you again."

"You say that like it's a bad thing."

"Now, now…" Rosemary shifted her weight to spare his legs and snuggled against his side. "It did occur to me that Lavinia might have another match in mind for Lionel. I watched her during supper, and I could see her making the calculations."

"Good Lord! Do you mean between Lionel and Caroline?"

She nodded. "Hence her solicitude that Lionel might have a place to live in Crawley after he takes his degree."

"Well, even if Edith were not in the picture, bless Lavinia, if she thinks old Crawley and Caroline can compete with the wide open of Somerset and Richard Hapgood taking the boy hunting and riding and shooting."

"Love can make a man do just about anything," said Rosemary doubtfully. "And Caroline Sidney has grown into a pretty little thing. She looked at Lionel with admiration tonight. I think, if her mother does not plant the idea, Caroline may think of it herself. It would not be a *bad* match, I suppose. Especially from a financial perspective."

Hugh shuddered. "If it must be, it must be. Though, if Lionel were to marry Caroline, he may count on having Lavinia's full participation in any and all of his future plans and affairs. More punishment, I think, than even his sins deserve."

Chapter Ten

A few days after Margaret Hapgood's wedding to Mr. Dashiell Waite, Edith received a letter.

Dear Edie,

I know you all are still caught up in your whirl of gaiety there, but it seems an age since I received your one, solitary letter and ages more since we were last together. (I cannot reproach you, however, since—I am certain you are saying to yourself even as you read this—I did not write to you even the once! But it was because there was so much happening in London and Crawley. Trust me when I assure you that I thought of you a hundred times a day and wished you were with me.)

All the excitement is past now, and we are plunged into humdrumness again. Lionel has returned to Oxford, and Papa, Mama, Rosie, and I have now been home nearly a fortnight. Which means Rosie and I are at it again with Soppy and Mr. Eldredge (for whom I really must think up a nickname). Soppy is well, but my artwork seems to give Mr. E particular pain of late, so I am sure he would join me in wishing your hasty return. Not only that, but something must have happened between them while we were all away because Soppy is perfectly ice and granite *to him now. I have still caught him giving her sad puppy looks, but she positively ignores them and him, as much as manners will permit. Do you suppose he bared his heart and was spurned?*

But I hear your voice again: "Hetty, what a wretched letter! Stop gossiping about Blenkensop and Mr. Eldredge, and tell me at once what you mean by 'all the excitement is past.'"

Very well, very well, I will keep you in suspense no longer. There were several bits of excitement. Firstly, Lionel was nearly sent down *from Oxford because the* *college president wrote Papa to say <u>a girl was found under the bed in the room Lionel shares with Mr. Jason Clinkett!</u> (Did you just scream? I nearly screamed when I learned this fact, which no one knows I know.) I will confess only to you that I saw Papa receive the letter, change color, and leave the room. He said nothing about it, of course, and thus I was compelled to eavesdrop on him telling Mama the letter's contents. Then, when we met Lionel in London, Papa and Lionel went on a walk by themselves, although it was beastly cold out, and when they returned, neither Papa nor Lionel looked any better pleased. No more was said about it, and therefore I cannot tell you anything useful. Not who the girl was, nor how she came to be there, nor if such things are regular practices with Lionel and his friends. So frustrating!*

I can tell you more about the second bit of excitement, however. Which was, when we came to Crawley and saw our Aunt and Uncle Sidney and our cousin Caroline, our aunt and uncle were much as we remembered, but Caroline greatly improved. Improved in looks and manner, that is. She used to be pale as a wraith and small and insignificant and timid, but now she is nearly as tall as I, golden-haired and self-assured. She is your age or a little older. Somewhere between you and Lionel. And she told me she is to have a season in

London in two years, and didn't I want one when I was old enough? I told her I didn't particularly, thank you very much, although I have not decided yet if I was telling the truth. But I digress. Caroline's season is not the exciting bit. It is that I never before saw a girl set her cap for someone, but I vow Caroline was setting hers for Lionel! She talked to him the most and laughed an inordinate amount and insisted on lots of dancing, even though that meant I was usually partnered with Rosie. (Soppy would be proud of Rosie's and my performance—we were every inch as good as Caroline.) If Lionel happened not to be about, then Caroline would ply me with questions about him: what were his favorite foods? His favorite songs and books? What else did he like besides sport? Was he sweet on anyone that I knew of? (The devil in me dearly wanted to tell her about the mystery girl under the bed, but I valiantly forbore. Are you not proud of me?) And when she was not asking questions about Lionel, she was praising him, saying how she had remembered him as a pale, freckled, clamorous boy, but now he was tall and handsome and not freckled. To which I replied that surely she still found him clamorous, did she not? And she laughed archly and said, "What is objectionable in a boy often becomes admirable in a young man. Lionel's high spirits must make him the admiration of all." I suppose he is maturing—much as it pains me to admit it—for he is not nearly as clamorous as I remember. If anything, he is somewhat muted—to the point that I heard Mama ask him if he felt entirely well. But it very well might be something to do with the mystery of the girl under the bed!

My aunt Lavinia would like it very much if Lionel married Caroline, I think. She was after Papa not to sell our former home, in case Lionel should ever want it, but Papa pressed ahead with it anyway. I do not know yet if my own parents share Aunt Lavinia's wish, however. When I told Mama my observations and asked her opinion on the matter, she said only, "At Caroline's age, it is nice to have a cousin on which to practice." By which you see she wants me not to think it a serious matter. I am unconvinced by this seeming casualness. I think all the elders would agree on one point, though: if Lionel is to carry on with some girl—any girl—it had better be Caroline, rather than the girl under the bed. (NOT that Aunt Lavinia even knows of the existence of that mysterious young lady!)

What do you think? I could not help saying to Lionel myself that, if he must marry a cousin, I had far rather it be you, to which he rudely told me to shut my trap and mind my own business. Not for the last time do I tell you that brothers are useless and burdensome, and you are fortunate to be without one.

So much for my exciting news, and I dare you to do better. I only hope that Margaret's Mr. Waite has no younger brother or cousin to woo you in Bath, for I have a better idea for the both of us: when I am of age, I will ask Papa for a season. Not in order that I may find a husband, but rather as an excuse to take us to London, and you must come with us! For how will you be a great artist if you never see the British Institution or the Royal Academy?

Do come back to Bramleigh soon, Edith. I want to hear all about Bath and Margaret's wedding and what you thought of Mr. E's artist friends.

Your affectionate cousin,
Hetty

Carefully, once she had read it through several times, Edith folded the letter, glad that Margaret was married and gone and would not press her to share its contents. Gathering her knees to her chest, she sat tucked up in the window seat of her room in Henrietta Street, resting her temple against the glass. On the floor her trunk lay open and half-packed, papers and pencils scattered across the counterpane of the bed.

And to think she had received this letter so eagerly from Hudgins the footman, when he delivered it at breakfast! She had hurried upstairs and swept clothing off her favorite seat, not sparing a glance for the view over the little back garden, her fingers almost unsteady in her desire to devour the news as quickly as her eyes could take it in. How were her cousins? How was Lionel, and did he like university? Did being in Crawley again make them wish to return there permanently?

Well, she at least knew her cousins were in health, she supposed, but every other question remained unanswered or had an answer Edith did not care for. Hetty might speak of Edith's good fortune in not having a brother, but Edith couldn't help feeling Lionel was a brother in all but name, and, just as she had been anxious and sorry in times past to hear if one of her sisters was not behaving respectably, so did she feel anxious and sorry now. Who could the girl under the bed have been, and what did she mean to Lionel? Was the girl's presence indicative of a larger share of misdoings?

More difficult to analyze was her reaction to Caroline Sidney "setting her cap" for her cousin and Mrs. Sidney promoting the project. Edith did not like it and she knew she did not like it, but why? Was it that she wanted Lionel for herself?

The windowpane frosted with her breath, and Edith sat up straight again, using her fingertip to trace a mark of interrogation on the glass. Did she want to marry Lionel?

She was not yet sixteen, far too young (in her own opinion) even to be asking the question, and she could safely say she didn't want to marry anyone at present. Nor did her papa seem in any hurry to press the matter. With his three oldest daughters and both his spendthrift brothers-in-law off his hands, he was in no hurry at all! Indeed, after the wedding he had turned to her, saying, "So, my little love, only you remain. We must have a housekeeper at Bramleigh because you must finish your studies and have as much time as you please to devote to your painting. Should you like that?" And she had nodded eagerly and hugged him and thanked him, for the thought of who should keep house at Bramleigh had been weighing heavily on her. In Margaret's absence, the routines and systems instituted had gradually slackened or been forgotten or discarded altogether, until the household, like an unwound clock, ran less and less effectively and would soon cease to run altogether.

Edith had not forgotten Mr. Olivier's remarks or implications—that she was so very fortunate to pursue her love for art without regard to earning her living. She might paint what she liked and whom she liked, how she liked—she could not squander such an opportunity. No—any marriage—if she ever married—was a long way off.

So, if she did not like the idea of Lionel marrying his cousin, it was not because she wanted him herself. It was that he would, as his Aunt Lavinia schemed, settle in Crawley or London, and Edith would hardly ever see him again. And, even when she did see him again, it would not be the same, he having a wife and all.

She could not feel angry with the Sidneys, however, if they had such hopes. Everyone loved Lionel. Of course they would want him for themselves, and of course Edith must relinquish the idea of seeing him daily, or having him about in future to tease her or encourage her or dance with her or teach her to ride. It was sad, but it was part of growing up, she supposed. Even brothers and sisters who settled near each other, like Rosemary Hapgood and her brothers Roscoe and Norman DeWitt, grew to have their individual families and concerns, however close they were to each other.

Yes, it was just part of growing up.

But she sighed, nevertheless.

One final time she unfolded Hetty's letter and read it through. At least she would soon see Hetty and Rosie again, and she would have much to tell them, in turn. Tell them and show them. For, lying atop the tray insert of her open trunk was another letter, this one from Mr. Olivier and addressed to Richard Hapgood.

Hudgins had delivered this the very day after the wedding, placing it beside the squire's breakfast dish, and Edith's papa had scowled at it in puzzlement. "Mr. Alexandre Olivier?" he boomed, pronouncing it 'Alexander Oliveer.' "Who the dickens is Alexandre Olivier? Your mother better not have bought anything."

"No, Papa. He's one of the artists Mr. Eldredge introduced me to. Margaret and I went to see him at his studio."

He tossed her the letter. "Then you read it aloud to me."

Heart thumping, Edith set down her toast and obeyed:

> *45 Westgate Buildings*
> *Bath*
> *27 January 1813*
>
> *My dear Mr. Hapgood:*
> *Please pardon me immediately for addressing you,*
> *even though we are not introduced. I have had the plea-*

sure of meeting your daughters Miss Margaret and Miss Edith, who were so kind as to call at my studio, being mutual acquaintances of Mr. Judah Eldredge.

Permit me to say that I have known Judah many years, and after he left Bath to take up the instruction of your daughter and her cousins, he wrote me to say that his new position had given him unexpected joys. The first and foremost was to discover in your daughter extraordinary talent. You probably do not know, Mr. Hapgood, but it is the sad lot of a teacher to encounter at least three dozen boobies for every moderately gifted pupil. And to discover potential genius? Ah, that is so rare that many teachers never experience it! We believe your daughter is just such a person.

But even the rarest genius must be nurtured and shaped and encouraged. It is good that Miss Edith continues with her lessons from Judah. But he will be the first to admit that he is a landscape painter, and this is not where her interest lies. Mr. Hapgood, I am sure Judah would join with me in saying that, if Miss Edith is to flourish as a portrait artist, she would do better to study with an artist and teacher whose forte this is.

If you are ever again in Bath for any length of time, I

*here offer my services as your daughter's instructor, at
the usual rates.*

*Your humble servant,
Alexandre Olivier*

Edith did not read such a letter aloud without many stops and starts, her color coming and going. When she came to the sentence about her extraordinary talent, she attempted to pass it back to her father to finish, but the squire merely waved her off as he continued chewing.

"That's very kind of him to write," Edith said at last, when her father still said nothing, only staring out the window as he continued to chew, ruminatively. "And kind of Mr. Eldredge to—to so believe in me. But of course we are going home to Bramleigh now, and Mr. Eldredge will—will do very well. Why, only a short time ago I had no instructor at all! And it is not as if I am not perfectly happy and perfectly grateful to have the means and liberty to paint as much as I like, as it is. You know that, Papa, do you not?" she added anxiously.

"Mmph," was her father's response.

She thought of how he never balked at buying her more paint or pencils or paper and hoped he would not, by extension, think she now required a Bath establishment and more exalted instruction. Yes, to be sure, she felt the power of the flattery—felt it operating on her vanity—but she recognized it as such. How many times, after all, had she declared that she had no worldly ambition, where her painting was concerned? Would she now, as a result of a few compliments, get it into her head that she must be Great, no matter the cost?

No. Absolutely not.

I have been too much spoiled, she thought. *Always indulged and given what I wanted, even when Papa could ill afford it. Look at him hiring a housekeeper, so that I will not have to fill Margaret's place! I will not let Papa even consider a removal to Bath. How miserable he would be—he who loves to ride and be out of doors. And there is no one but me to look after his health now.*

Pushing back her chair, she came around the table to wrap her arms about her father's neck. "Never mind this letter, Papa. Tomorrow we will go home to Bramleigh and be content. So content! Why, Margaret and Dashiell have only been gone one day, and Bath already feels sadly flat. I must see if Mama needs help packing. I am nearly done myself."

She placed the letter beside his plate, only to have him slide it back to her. "Keep it," he grunted. "You may brag about its contents, in any event."

CHAPTER ELEVEN

**I hope, cousin, one may speak to one's own relations,
and not be to blame.
—Oliver Goldsmith, *She Stoops to Conquer*, II.38
(1773)**

Edith's world was a hopeful place in the late spring of 1813. Napoleon's ill-fated invasion of Russia the previous winter had cost his *Grand Armée* dearly, and, while the Coalition and Prusso-Russian armies had yet to score striking victories against even this diminished foe, there was a dawning sense of the tide beginning to turn. Margaret wrote that Dashiell believed Wellington's Peninsular Campaign drew closer and closer to prevailing, and Edith was interested, for their sake. Truth be told, however, Edith could not remember a time when Napoleon had not ruled France and marauded at will across the Continent, and England's newer war with the United States made the idea of peace even more difficult to imagine. War simply *was.*

She was at an age in life when nearer concerns naturally dominated. Concerns such as turning sixteen and, with the consent of her parents and Miss Blenkensop, being released from lessons with her cousins, apart from continuing sessions with Mr. Eldredge. As for Mr. Alexandre Olivier's letter, it was pushed to the back of her mind, and she had decided simply to become as good an artist as she possibly could, with the means and the instructor given to her.

Therefore, on this beautiful day in early June, she was to be found out of doors free as a bird, armed with her easel and sketchbook and campstool and pencils. She hummed like a bird as well, as she drew. Pillows of cloud dotted the enameled sky, and, whenever they happened to pass before the sun, Edith gladly removed her bonnet and let the breeze play in her curls.

She had just taken it off again when a bright head appeared at the top of the slope. She had not seen that head in months—oh, months and months!—yet she knew it immediately. Lionel!

Even as she thought it, his name burst from her, and she was on her feet waving. "Lionel! You've come back! Oh! Stop right there—on the stile—just for a moment—"

He complied, though she could both see and sense his fire of impatience. Complied and held still on the stile, a grin coming and going. She sketched as fast as she could, aware of a curious flutter inside her when she took one of her glances up. How university had changed him! He looked older—intent—his hair had darkened, and his lanky frame grown more solid. He was strange to her now; she felt…she felt shy. But she couldn't be shy of Lionel!

"What is it?" she asked, hurrying to finish her sketch. "You look as if you were ready to burst with something."

"I can't wait to spread the news that I am back in Somerset, having covered myself in glory at my first year of university."

This sounded like the old Lionel, at least (though even his voice was deeper), and she smiled, even as she made her final dashes at capturing the lines of his face. "That's not what your sister Hetty says. She said you were nearly sent down for your escapades."

"Sent down? I'll send her down! She's just envious. She says she doesn't see why she still has to have a governess when you no longer do."

Edith laughed at this, Hetty having made precisely that complaint to her as well. "Because my education is complete—apart from more lessons in drawing and painting. I'm afraid I now dance and play, read French and Italian, sew and work sums as well as I ever will."

"If your drawing and painting still need improvement, you had better let me see what a muddle you've made of me," he replied. "May I have a look?"

"One minute more…" She wondered if she would ever tell him about Mr. Olivier offering to teach her. She had resisted telling her sisters or Hetty, not wanting them to think her regretful or ungrateful. Roughing in the background rapidly, she said instead, "There. Behold—the Lion of Somerset! Hetty says that's the nickname you've been given, at any rate. Is it for your hair, which is so long? She calls the name ridiculous, but I think 'Lion' far better than your friends' names 'Clinker' and 'Clunker.'"

He didn't answer. He had leapt from the stile and was beside her in an instant—taller even than she remembered. And somehow more man than boy. If he had not seemed suddenly so big and strange and daunting, she would have hugged him. But the bigness and strangeness and daunting-ness won out, especially with him right *there*, and she shrunk from touching him. It was too bad he was only *like* a brother, and not truly her brother, because then she might have written him letters this whole time and avoided this awkwardness. Or perhaps not—Hetty had been vocal about what a haphazard correspondent Lionel was—but it would have been nice to write to him all the same. She would have liked to share with him her Bath adventures.

She gave herself a mental shake. This silly shyness must be thrown off, or he would notice and remark on it and make it ten times worse.

"Edith—"

"Oh, Lionel! What a delight to see you again. Did you ever get the picture of Mannerly I sent you?"

"Yes—"

"And how are you not on Mannerly today? I would have thought the very first thing you would do would be to saddle her up and make certain we had not spoiled her for you."

"I will. See to her, I mean. But I wanted to see—you all—first."

"Ah, yes! Papa will be eager to see you too." She glowed up at him. "I do hope you've done growing because I suspect I have, and, if you get any taller, looking up at you might cause permanent damage to my neck. You must tell Papa and me *everything*. We will be positively engrossed by your adventures, I promise." *As engrossed as Caroline Sidney*, she added in her head.

"Edith—"

"Yes. I'm sorry. I'm talking too much! It's just that I'm so very excited to see you." She made a motion to seal her lips, still smiling at him, as she began to gather her materials.

"No, wait—Edith. Wait a moment." Swiftly, his hand reached for her bare arm, just touching it, and all the pencils in her grasp dropped into the grass.

"Oh, dear."

That bought them a moment, as they both stooped to retrieve the scattered items.

"Thank you," she murmured.

"Here." Taking the pencils from her hands, he added them to his own and deposited them all in her basket. "Edith—before we go back to the house, there is something I would say."

"Yes?" Her heart seemed to be tripping at an alarming rate. It must be an odd sort of something, if he would rather not say it in the presence of Edith's father. Was she finally to learn the identity of the girl found under the bed? Or did he want to tell her he was now engaged to his cousin Caroline?

His blue eyes darkened as they searched hers, and Edith found her alarm increasing. She took a hesitant step back. The June day felt overpoweringly warm, of a sudden.

Lionel swallowed. Gathered himself. "You have grown," he said gruffly. "Not—in inches, so much, perhaps. But—grown up, I mean to say. I mean—you look more grown up."

"Thank you...?" she answered. "You as well." She could not recall him ever sounding so unsure of himself. He had always, always been at ease, teasing, superior, laughing.

"You are sixteen now, are you not?"

"Yes." She gave him a tentative smile. "Which means you are seventeen-and-a-half. I remember, from the very first time we met, your eighteen months' advantage."

He barely acknowledged this. Indeed, he seemed to be steeling himself.

"Edith, some girls are married at your age."

This shocked a laugh from her. "Not this girl!"

"No, of course not. And I am glad you are not. Because—because I hope one day—I—I hope one day you might care for me." This last came out with an effort, as if he had braced himself against a door to knock it down.

However the words emerged, they cast a powerful spell over the moment. The breeze ceased to blow, the birds to sing. There was not a rustle of grass or scratch of a cricket. There was not even movement, for both Lionel and Edith were holding their breath, their eyes fixed on each other.

What is happening? Edith thought. *Did I mishear him or misunderstand him? I must have. Or I have fallen asleep, and this is a funny little dream.* It felt like a dream, a vividly-colored dream. That enamel sky and green slope speckled with blue flowers. His bright auburn hair and her own bared black curls. Her chip bonnet with its wide red ribbon, discarded and lying in the grass.

Or, we are inside a painting, her mind rambled on. *A painting called* The Young man speaks *or* A Summer's surprise.

What nonsense she was thinking—of course they were not in a painting—for who was there to paint it but she herself? Therefore—one of her hands stole up, and she gave herself a hard pinch above her other elbow. *Ooh!* Nor was it a dream, apparently.

Her movement seemed to jog him from his own paralysis, and she found herself taken by the upper arms. "I know I've taken you by surprise, Edie. I didn't mean to speak—not yet—but I couldn't help myself. I came over that stile and there you were and you were so beautiful. Not that I am saying all this because you are beautiful! I mean—not that you aren't beautiful—because you are, as I just said—but that isn't why I feel the way I do—"

Edith only stared at him, her lips parted in astonishment.

Coloring deeply, he seemed to become aware of his hands gripping her (he might even have been guilty of shaking her gently, in emphasis), and he released her with an abruptness that caused her to lose her balance and stumble into her camp stool.

"Oh, Lord—Edith—I'm sorry. Please—let me—" He lunged for the collapsed stool just as she leaned to pick it up, and his head struck hers a blow that made her cry out. "Oh, dear God! Have I hurt you? What an idiot I am."

"I am all right," said Edith, though she seized the camp stool from him, opened it and sat down, lest she fall over in her dizziness. She shut her eyes and pressed her hands to them, thinking it wasn't only her head that felt topsy-turvy at present. She counted to twenty, trying to breathe evenly. Then she finally removed her hands and opened her eyes, relieved that her head raised no objections, only to discover Lionel had dropped to one knee in the grass.

"Whatever are you doing?"

"I'm trying this again. I've bungled this so badly that, if we weren't related to each other, however distantly, and if I didn't—love you, Edith—so desperately, I would run away to the Indies and never show my face here again—"

But Edith was shaking her head, her hand lifted and her face on fire. "Lionel—stop. Do stop. I cannot think why you are doing this—speaking to me like this, but I beg you to stop."

His face fell. "I can't. Please let me speak, Edith. I know I have gone about this in the clumsiest manner possible and caught you all unawares, but please only hear me out. You needn't answer me right away. In fact, I had rather you *not* answer me right away because I know we were neither one of us prepared for this moment. I only want to say that I love you and have loved you since I was twelve years old. Yes, it's true! I think you're the loveliest, sweetest, kindest, most talented girl in all England, and I burst with pride just to think of you. And if I could—hope—one day you might be my wife—not now of course, since you think sixteen too young, but I would wait forever—it would—I know the phrase is hackneyed, but your promise would make me the happiest of men. I—I just don't see how anyone could be as happy as I would be, Edith, if you loved me."

There.

It was said.

He let out a long, relieved breath, watching every flicker of expression that crossed her beloved countenance. For months he had been thrown back on the two pictures he had of her, pictures done by her own hand. And good as they were, nothing compared to her here, alive, present beside him. Even in the suspense, tinged with dread, of waiting for her answer, he was still conscious of his joy.

And what did she feel?

Edith hardly knew. She felt like a currant in a pudding—plunged into some opaque world she didn't recognize and uncertain which direction was up. Lionel thought he was in *love* with her? Lionel wanted to *marry* her? Why, they were still hardly more than children! And his declaration had been the very model of boyish bumbling—it did not require a woman's experience to judge it so. But neither did it require a woman's experience to recognize he was sincere.

And she loved him dearly, this almost-brother of hers. But to tell him so would encourage him, and it would not be fair to encourage him, would it?

"I—haven't thought of marriage," she faltered.

This answer seemed to hearten him. "I know. And that's good," he said. "I don't want you thinking of marriage if I'm not around. You aren't in love with anyone else, then?"

She could only shake her head, and this pleased him even more. "Good," he repeated. "Better and better. You at least like me, don't you, Edie? We've been very good friends and cousins."

A knot of anxiety began to form in her midsection. Lionel had never lacked for optimism and confidence. She could see that, if she let him, he would hastily build a substantial castle in the air from as few and as flawed bricks as she handed him, and that would never do.

She rose to her feet, glad to find she was steady now. "Lionel, I haven't thought of marriage, and I don't intend to think of it anytime soon. I want to be an artist, you know, and my training isn't done."

"I know." He stood up again himself. "I want you to be an artist, too. I would never take that from you. I would want you to draw and paint to your heart's content. I was your very first patron, re-member? Well—Hetty put her oar in, but you know what I mean."

"I know," she said quietly. "And I am grateful for your support. But I mean I haven't thought of marriage, and you mustn't either. At least, you mustn't with me."

The boy in him reappeared because his shoulders sagged and he gave a groan. "Oh, confound it. What a botch I've made of this. Look, Edith—won't you let me start over? Pretend you didn't hear any of that and that I didn't lay you flat as a flounder with my noggin—"

This almost drew a smile from her, but she couldn't help patting his sleeve to comfort him. "Lionel—you mustn't berate yourself. It's nothing to do with you or your—manner of delivery. It's only that I am too young and…too ambitious, I suppose. As I said, I'm not thinking of marriage and don't suppose I will for a long while."

"That must mean you don't think you love me."

She almost said, *Well, of course I love you!* but she managed to stop the words from flying out of her mouth because he meant one thing by the word *love* and she meant another. She forced herself to say in an even, deliberate voice, "I don't think I love you the way you are asking."

"But *could* you, Edith?" he pressed. "I don't mean this very instant—today. I mean could you not reject the idea of loving me out of hand, simply because you never thought of it before?" For all his talk of waiting forever for her and being content, as long as she didn't love anyone else, his eyes were shining, and Edith was horrified that it might be tears gathering there.

"It would be wrong to lead you a dance like that," insisted Edith. "It would be wrong to tie you to words you say now, when you are not yet eighteen and still—still a boy. Any number of things may happen! May already be happening. Have you...not met anyone at university?"

He shook his head with vehemence. "I'm not a boy! For all that I've acted like the stupidest hobbledehoy today. I already know exactly what I want and who I want and have for years."

"Every day might bring someone new or something new," Edith continued. "Why, a little bird once told me there was a girl found in your room at Magdalen, under the b—"

"A little bird named Hetty," growled Lionel. "That girl in my room had nothing to do with me. She was Clinker's...guest, I suppose you could call her. Not the first and not the last, I imagine. But if I love a girl like you, am I likely to transfer my affections to minxes who hide under furniture?"

"All right, then, not a girl like that," she conceded, "but that same Hetty bird thought you might make a match of it with your cousin Caroline—"

"I'll wring her neck!" he roared, kicking over the innocent camp stool. "Hetty's neck—not Caroline's. But only because Caroline's isn't worth wringing. Is this why you won't even consider me—because you think I've been gallanting with concealed trollops and whichever female cousin is nearest at hand?"

"No. No! I'm only saying that you are young, Lionel, and all the world lies before you, just like it lies before me. And you would be foolish to tie yourself down for a—a childhood affection you have not yet outgrown."

Instead of soothing him, her speech appeared to add fuel to the fire. Lionel clenched his fists, biting out each word of response through a tightened jaw. "Childhood—affection—I—have not—outgrown? Why are you speaking to me as if you were eighty and I was eight?"

"I'm not! I said the world lies before both of us—would I say that if I thought myself eighty?" she retorted.

With an effort, he managed to unclench his hands. He was panting, and so was she, she realized.

Slowly, as if he were now the octogenarian, he moved to pick up the camp stool and unfold it again. Then he sat on it and sighed deeply, running his fingers through his hair.

When he spoke again, his voice was calm.

"Apart from my supposed youth and my complete and total mishandling of this afternoon, including my bungled first attempt at a proposal and my show of temper just now, do you have any other objections to me?"

"Lionel—"

"Oh, and the fact that you don't love me. Let's not forget that one."

"Oh, Lionel," said Edith miserably.

"Do you find me repellent?"

"Of course not."

"Not repellent, then. Unattractive, maybe."

"No, not even that. You're very handsome, Lionel. More and more so."

"Stupid, perhaps? I know I'm probably not as clever as you."

"No. Not a bit stupid. You don't care for book-learning, perhaps, but you aren't the least bit unintelligent."

"You wish I were artistic, then. I am too humdrum, too workaday for you."

"Lionel, I don't believe anyone who has ever met you would call you humdrum or workaday."

"But you wish I were an artist."

"Why would I wish you were an artist?" she protested.

"So we might talk about lofty, arty things all the livelong day."

Indignation at this picture of herself banished some of her misery. "Is this what you think of me? That I'm insufferable and want to talk about lofty, arty things all day long? If that were so, I could just marry Mr. Eldredge and be done with it!"

"Would you, if he asked?" he pressed, rising to his feet in his agitation.

"Marry Mr. Eldredge!" It was Edith's turn to shout. "He's older than Papa! And *looks* old enough to be our mutual great-great-grandfather! Of course I wouldn't marry Mr. Eldredge!"

"Would you if he were twenty?"

"He *isn't* twenty!"

"But would you?"

"No! Not if he were twenty or forty or—or—or seventeen-and-a-half! Lionel Hapgood, you may be handsome and not overly stupid, and everyone may find you charming, but you do have an abominably thick head, if I must work so hard to make you understand that I don't have plans to marry *anybody*, and it's not at all to do with you. Everything in the world isn't all to do with you."

"You think I'm too preoccupied with myself, then."

Edith groaned, provoked beyond reason, and made to shove him out of her way so she could fetch her things and be done with it all. But no sooner did she lay her hands against his chest than he seized them in one of his own, flinging his other arm about her waist and drawing her against him.

"You beautiful, darling thing," he breathed. Then he ducked his head and kissed her.

For one immeasurable moment, shock froze her into utter stillness.

Then time jerked into motion again almost before she could register it, and the frozen shock was followed by a thaw. A precipitous thaw. A treacherous, treacherous thaw that was half panic, half—half *deliciousness*. A deliciousness that ran from her lips down the full length of her spine to the very tips of her toes and fingers.

"Yield," it whispered to her. "Oh, yield."

But the very deliciousness of the deliciousness increased her panic, and, without making any conscious decision she began to struggle and push and turn away.

Lionel released her instantly. His eyes were very dark and his breath short.

"Edith—"

"How could you?" she gasped. "Take such—advantage?"

He shook his head. "You must add 'lack of self-control' to my many shortcomings. I'm sorry. I meant no disrespect to you." The ghost of a grin flitted across his drawn face. "If you doubt my honorable intentions, we can go and see your father this minute."

"I think you had better go home, Lionel. And please don't speak of this again. I won't. We will—pretend it never happened."

"I can't pretend that," he said, so softly she wasn't sure she heard him aright.

But she wasn't trying to hear him. She was backing away, putting space between them, throwing her things in her basket.

Everything was ruined.

The day, their friendship, the summer she had looked forward to.

And something else: her certainty. What did she want from life? From her art? And why, *why* had her body betrayed her like that?

She had no answers to these questions. She had only the coward's way out, and she took it, fleeing both him and her questions, and leaving him standing alone on the slope.

Chapter Twelve

We beg leave to direct general attention, not only to the excellence displayed by the great painters in England, but to the promise...shewn by many young artists who have derived benefit from the Institution.
—Directors of the British Institution, *Visitors' Report to the Exhibition of 1813*

The greatest crowd gathered before the portrait of Mrs. Siddons as the Tragic Muse, but it was the painting of Kitty Fisher as Cleopatra that Edith kept returning to. In contrast to the grandness and even melodrama of the actress in her throne-like chair, flanked by Pity and Terror and eyes lifted tragically, the Kitty Fisher portrait was intimate, quiet.

"She doesn't look a thing like a courtesan," Edith's sister Margaret said, as if either of them had any idea what a courtesan looked like.

"Really, apart from being so elegantly dressed, she rather looks like Mama when she is listening to us read or play the piano, right before she dozes off."

"I suppose she *does* look rather sleepy," admitted Edith, running a thoughtful hand along the rail which held viewers at bay, "but that is rather what I like about the picture. She doesn't look grand. We aren't looking *up* to her as mere mortals, as we do with Mrs. Siddons. And even though she is supposed to be Cleopatra, she really just looks like herself. An ordinary person. If that is what she looked like, I mean."

"I can see why you prefer her, then. Whenever you draw the family as ourselves, we always look far less silly then when we are forced to be your classical figures."

"Silly?" repeated Edith, insulted. "You never told me you thought any of my pictures were silly!"

"I didn't say the *pictures* were silly, silly," Margaret answered. "I meant that we sometimes made ridiculous subjects. Papa as Zeus. Elfie as Aphrodite—well, to be truthful, Elfie never looked silly as a classical subject." She gave her still-frowning little sister a nudge. "What I am saying is that I can see why you like the less grandiose picture. It is your style. Shall you copy this one, then? I thought you were going to do one of the little Lady Gertrude Fitzpatrick."

"Elfie asked me to. For her nursery because she hopes her baby will be a baby Augusta."

"Who says her baby will be a girl?"

"Elfie says it will be a girl because Frederick wants a girl, and Frederick always gets whatever he wants." Edith leaned closer to squint at the brush strokes. "Well, if, for once, her Frederick does not get his way and they have another boy, there is always Alice's baby. If Alice's baby is a girl, she can have the painting."

"What would Alice and Joseph want with a painting of a little girl? I suspect they would rather hang pictures of frog spawn and birds' eggs."

The sisters fell to giggling at this, but soon Margaret was pinching her and hushing her—and Edith was pinching her back with a "*You* hush, Mrs. Waite!"—for both their surroundings at the British Institution in Pall Mall and their fellow exhibition-goers were very magnificent. It could hardly be otherwise, when the Prince Regent was a principal sponsor of the exhibit and hundreds of pounds had been poured into mounting it: more than 140 of Sir Joshua Reynolds' works, lent from everywhere in the kingdom, hung under special lighting, guarded by extra attendants, viewed by the public over extended hours, and, of course, protected by the three-foot-high rail which Edith now leaned against.

Margaret's invitation for Edith to join the Waites and the Arbuthnots in London could not have been more welcome. Where Edith had been looking forward to having Lionel back in Somerset for his long vacation, after their disastrous reunion she could not escape his company quickly enough. All their time seemed to be spent either in trying to avoid each other or in trying to pretend nothing had happened when circumstances thrust them together. As Edith was never a boisterous young lady, her quietness went unremarked, but Lionel chose the opposite tack. In Edith's presence he moved and talked relentlessly (just not to her); he bounced and bounded; he jested and danced and pranked; he waxed nostalgic for school and his friends. When he wasn't riding or shooting or playing cricket, he was talking of it. In fact he talked of anything now but Edith and art.

"To think I spent all this time wishing him home," Hetty complained. "Now I wish he could live with the Benfields again, but they have Colin and that new little boy Thomas. Both of whom worship Lionel as if he were the Second Coming. You don't know how fortunate you are to go up to town, Edie. The racket of London will be peace, compared to living with Lionel in close quarters."

The racket of London did indeed provide peace of mind, if not actual peace and quiet. Edith had not realized how tense she was until she was one hundred and fifty miles away from the source of her tension. She had not told a living soul about Lionel's offer and did not intend to, but Margaret greeted her in Bruton Street with a "My, but you're thin and pale. Does that new housekeeper not know how to manage Button?"

"Uncle Alwyn asked the same thing, when he fetched me from Bramleigh," replied Edith, "but then he decided after a few days that Button's cooking had *improved* under Macready."

Margaret sniffed at this, having taken much pride in her own running of the household before she married, but she listened grudgingly to her sister's reports of the housekeeper's success. "Well, I suppose I am glad Macready will make life smooth for Papa and Mama, if I cannot do it myself."

Edith nudged her sister affectionately. "Are you sorry not to have your own household to run? Do you and Dashiell like living here with Uncle Alwyn and Mrs. Arbuthnot?"

Margaret only shrugged, a mysterious smile playing about her lips. Then she had changed the subject. "Never mind me—here you are in London! I declare, when we were your age, Elfie and Alice and I never had such opportunities to gallivant around England as you do. There are a hundred things to show you. I have made a list of the best, but you may decide what you would like to see first."

"The Reynolds exhibition at the British Institute," Edith answered, before giving Margaret's list more than a cursory glance. "I have already read what I could about it and have been eaten with impatience to see it myself. And then the Royal Academy exhibit in New Somerset House, please, to see Wilkie's *Blind man's buff* and Dawe's rescue painting. And then—"

"Very well, very well," laughed Margaret, "art it is. The Tower and the theatre must wait. But if it is all to be paintings, don't expect Uncle Alwyn to accompany us."

"What about Dashiell? Will he come?"

"Hmm...we will see," Margaret said, with that mysterious smile. "He has much business to attend to."

If not for Margaret's and her uncle's presence, Edith would have found the Arbuthnots' home in Bruton Street a daunting place. The elegant little townhouse was six stories high, the ground floor faced in brick while the upper stories were white with dark green trim. It stood only steps from Berkeley Square and overlooked its own tidy yard. Inside, beautifully furnished rooms opened off the passages and a staff of servants double in number to Bramleigh's hastened up and down the back stairs to keep things running smoothly.

Edith was not used to having morning chocolate brought to her, much less waking to a maid asking when she would like Mrs. Arbuthnot's Floss to dress her hair. Nor was she used to having her wardrobe inspected, as Floss did with pursed lips, especially when unpacking Edith's charcoal-smudged and paint-bedaubed apron.

But though Mrs. Arbuthnot's servants might have talked amongst themselves about the mistress marrying a fortune hunter, and her handsome son Dashiell marrying the fortune hunter's equally penniless niece, both Alwyn and Margaret had so far proved inoffensive enough. (To be certain, Margaret's fondness for having a finger in every pie, when it came to household affairs, did require more patience than Alwyn's easygoing indifference.) It was only to be expected, however, the servants agreed, that all fortune hunters came encumbered with countless other poor relations, and they assumed Mrs. Waite's younger sister would be a grasping little thing, determined to catch a rich husband of her own.

Edith could not have been more of a surprise.

"That slatternly apron of hers is for her *work*," Floss reported at the servants' table. "She paints and draws."

"I heard Mrs. Waite asking her if she didn't want to go to an assembly to dance and meet some young men, and she said no, thank you, she didn't want to be up late because she wanted to make an early start on her copy of Cleopater," reported Binchin.

"Cle-o-pat-ra," intoned Floss.

"She can't be too bright, then," Walters the butler put in. "For here's her chance to make the most of herself at the least expense and trouble, and she's too dim to see it."

"Her dresses aren't half fine enough to fool anyone," Binchin said. "Mr. and Mrs. Waite'd have to put out a good deal of money there first."

"She's pretty, though," spoke up the under-footman, turning crimson beneath his freckles. "And polite."

"Ooh!" cried the two maids on either side of him, pinching and prodding him. "Jimmy admires Miss Edith, does he?"

"She's better looking and a sight nicer than you two," he retorted.

"Well, and if I hear she doesn't want to meet any fine gentlemen because she would rather run away with an under-footman, you'll be the first person I tell," one of the maids jeered.

"Mrs. Waite has her opinions, you know," interposed Binchin, to a chorus of agreement. (They were all familiar now with Margaret Waite's many opinions.) "And she said to Miss Edith that it was just as well she didn't want a husband now because she was too young to get married."

This met with puzzlement, it being the common understanding that fortune hunters were out for whatever they could get, that they should strike while the iron was hot, and so forth.

"What did Miss Edith say to that?" croaked Jimmy.

Binchin's brow furrowed. "She agreed with her—fast like. But she turned all red and acted busy with her pencil box."

"Ooh," nodded the jeering maid. "I can guess what that means. You can bet your buttons she doesn't want to meet anyone because she's already got a sweetheart, and one Mrs. Waite don't know about. Prob'ly poor as dirt, the chosen one, so she knows the family won't like it, not when Mrs. Waite and Mr. Arbuthnot've done so well for themselves."

Heads bobbed again in recognition of this general wisdom (Jimmy rather downcast by it), and then the soup was passed around and the business of eating got under way, lest the ring of a bell call them away from their meal.

"How fares your copy of Cleopatra?" Dashiell Waite asked her one night at supper, some days later.

"Yes—will we see it soon?" his mother Eliza Arbuthnot prompted. "I wish we all might accompany you to the Institute and look over your shoulder as you work."

"It is nearly finished," answered Edith. "And I fear my progress would be slower yet, with an audience." At least, she had no desire for Dashiell to hover over her shoulder. She was used to her family or her instructors watching her work, but that was all. She still found her sister's husband a little alarming at close quarters. He was kind enough, and Margaret doted on him, but he intimidated her nonetheless. *Lionel would not be an intimidating husband*, she thought. And then, as ever when she thought of him, she remembered their kiss and blushed painfully.

Thankfully Margaret interpreted this as her sister's reticence, and she was quick to proffer advice: "Edie, if you are to be a professional artist, you must not mind when people are curious about your work. Remember when we went to see Mr. Olivier? He was glad of our interest and not hampered by overmodesty."

"I remember," murmured Edith.

"You've had, what, four or five commissions now?" Alwyn guessed. He tapped his wine glass and Jimmy stepped forward to fill it. "Why, soon you'll be needing your own studio and hosting your own visitors."

"At Bramleigh I have my own studio," Edith reminded him. "And all the visitors I will ever want—my friends and family and an occasional neighbor."

"Everyone wants to put Edie forward except Edie herself," Margaret pronounced to the table at large. "I fear someone else will have to undertake to act as her agent, or she will never be known outside of one small corner of Somerset."

Her husband grinned at her. "Is this my cue? I mustn't miss it, then." Clearing his throat, he pronounced in a louder voice, "It sounds to me that you have grander ambitions for your sister, Margaret."

She bestowed a pleased smile on him and then gave a hop of excitement in her seat. "Oh, I cannot keep the secret any longer! Shall we tell them, Dashiell?"

"No need to ask him," drawled Alwyn. "It's plain you're going to tell us or burst with it, Mags."

"Very well." Beaming, she took a deep breath and reached for her husband's hand. "Dear uncle and aunt, Dashiell and I have taken a home in Johnson Street. Off Laura Place. In Bath."

"Dashiell!" breathed Mrs. Arbuthnot. "Is this true? You are leaving us?"

"We are, madam. Much as Margaret and I enjoy your company"—he nodded to include his father-in-law—"I fear London and the six stories of this house have been somewhat...trying on my injury."

"Of course, of course. I feared it would be," his mother sighed.

"If we return to Bath, Dashiell can take up his treatments again," Margaret rejoined eagerly.

"And you may have your own house to manage, Maggie," her uncle observed, chuckling, "which I know you delight in."

"I do." Her smile was apologetic. "Oh, madam, I hope you will not think us ungrateful. You have been so generous to have us with you so many months—"

"And you are welcome to return at any time, for any length of time," Mrs. Arbuthnot assured her.

"As you are welcome to come to us! We hope you will be our guests—our *second* guests." Here Margaret turned to Edith, almost clapping her hands with glee. "Because Edith will be our first! Won't you, Edie?"

"What?"

"It's the most wonderful idea I've ever had!"

"And that includes marrying me," Dashiell added humorously.

"Well, of course, marrying you," Margaret agreed, "or I wouldn't have a home to offer Edith. Because won't you come and live with us in Johnson Street, Edie? Papa and I both think it would be marvelous because then you could take those lessons with Mr. Olivier, as he proposed! *Portrait*-painting lessons, not landscape painting, don't you see? Papa told me all about Mr. Olivier's letter, and he and I have been *dying* ever since to bring it about somehow."

Stunned, Edith found no words.

Margaret rushed on. "You simply must come. We chose this home especially. Not just because it is so convenient to the baths, but also because you might have the entire third floor, with one room being your bedroom and the other *your studio*. Your studio, Edie! It has great big windows and a skylight, because the servants' garret is on the southern side. And then Mr. Olivier can come to Johnson Street to instruct you, and we can have a maid about when I am not there, and it will all be so very easy. Do say you'll come!"

Helplessly, Edith glanced at her new brother-in-law. She knew Margaret could be so managing—had he even agreed to this, or was Margaret forcing it all upon him?

Dashiell's face crinkled in amusement. "Have pity upon a defenseless brother, Edith. If you do not join us in Bath, she will have no one to badger but me, and I will be at your sister's mercy. Utterly defenseless, with no one to hide behind."

"You!" cried Margaret, tossing her napkin at him. "It was Dashiell who thought of finding a home with a room that could serve as a studio. I was dithering about whether it would be proper to send you with a maid to Mr. Olivier's home regularly, when you remember how that Jean-André—well—how he was."

Edith remembered.

She felt a tightness in her throat. "Oh—it's too, too kind of you. Of both of you. And Papa, too. How you all spoil me! Ever since Mr. Olivier sent that letter and talked about the difference between portrait painters and landscape painters, I wished I could learn from him. Only I didn't want everyone to feel badly about it, when you all have already done so much for me. It's too much!" The first tears were escaping now, and she dashed them away, laughing ruefully. "I promise I will not waste your generosity and the opportunity. I will learn everything I can from him. Thank you! Thank you!" Springing up from her seat, she circled the table to hug Margaret and kiss her, and even gave Dashiell a timid squeeze of the hand, and then they were all on their feet to embrace and congratulate her.

It was only much later, when the candle was blown out and she lay in bed, staring upward, that she whispered her other reason for gratitude.

"Now I need not see Lionel, and we need not avoid each other. By the time I return from Bath, he will be gone again to Oxford."

Chapter Thirteen

'Tis [colours] that give, as it were, Life and Soul to all that he does; without them, his Lines will be but Lines that are flat...'Tis they that must deceive the Eye, to the degree, to make Flesh appear warm and soft, and to give an Air of Life, so as his Picture may seem almost to Breath and Move.

—W. Aglionby, *Painting illustrated in three Diallogues* (1686)

"Mr. Alexandre Olivier and Mr. Jean-André Olivier," announced Church, stumbling over the foreign pronunciation.

"The nephew, too?" hissed Margaret. "Let us hope he is clothed today."

He was, but he was hardly less disturbing to Edith for all that. Even as she made her curtsey to the drawing master, she felt the bold sweep of Jean-André's black eyes, and she wanted to shrink into herself.

"*Madame et mademoiselle*," purred Mr. Olivier, making his bow. "Allow me to say how complete is my happiness that you have returned to Bath and that we may take up Miss Edith's instruction."

"We also look forward to it," Margaret replied, when it appeared Edith was still struggling to gather her courage. "And my husband and I thank you that you—er—you both—are willing to provide her lessons here in our home."

She hoped the reference to Jean-André would elicit an explanation of his presence—was that audacious-looking young man planning to accompany his uncle to every lesson? In such case, she might have to ask Dashiell to labor up the many stairs, that the Oliviers might know Edith had more protection than a flimsy maid or sister.

But the elder Mr. Olivier only bowed again, lower this time. "It is our honor and pleasure." When he straightened, he addressed his nephew brightly. "Jean-André, regard this beautiful studio! The air, the light! The skylight and the windows—they open, yes?"

"They do." Margaret moved to demonstrate unlatching and lifting the casement and started when she found Jean-André beside her, observing.

"Perfect, perfect. And Miss Edith, you have brought your most recent work, as I wrote Judah to tell you? The sketches and designs you have done since I have last seen you? All of them?"

Edith nodded and gestured at the portfolio that lay upon the worktable. "They are mostly pencil and charcoal and some ink. But there are a couple paintings. I fear that, after I met you, Mr. Eldredge seemed reluctant to have me color my portraits."

"Yes, I wrote him," Mr. Olivier answered complacently. He approached the table and spread his fingers upon it. "Before we look at these newest pieces, Miss Edith, Judah also tells me you have been in London and seen the Reynolds exhibit?"

"I have!" Her eagerness made her forget to be shy. "Marg—that is, Mrs. Waite and I—went several times, and I even made copies of some of the paintings, which you will see here. Oh, Mr. Olivier, they were wondrous!"

"You must have noted, then, Sir Joshua's use of color. He is famous for it. Rich, deep, gem-like color. The lecturer Benjamin Haydon compares him to Titian in his use of color."

Edith nodded again. She had read that in the catalogue but had never seen a single Titian to compare Reynolds with.

Mr. Olivier fixed her with a beady eye. "You know, Miss Edith, you cannot have such color without passion."

"Passion?" she repeated. "Do you mean suffering?"

"Suffering, yes!" he thumped the table for emphasis. "Suffering is a passion. Think of the passion of the Christ. But Hate is also a passion. Fear is a passion! Hope! Grief!"

"Love," interjected Jean-André from his station at the window. His arms were crossed over his chest. "Love is a passion. Love. Desire. Lust."

"*Mais bien sûr,*" agreed his uncle. "Love and its counterfeits. They are all passions. And it is passion that makes us live—that rules us. It is for passions we die!"

Edith swallowed. "Perhaps my color will be rather too mellow then, sir." This seemed an embarrassing admission, as if she were confessing to being a milksop sort of person who had better confine herself to browns and greys. Ought she to let her family spend such money on her, if all she would ever produce were passionless, colorless, trumpery rubbish?

Unbidden, she remembered Lionel asking if she wished he were an artist, that they might "talk about lofty, arty things all the livelong day." For some reason the memory comforted her. Surely this conversation fell into the category of a lofty, arty thing, and she mustn't feel bad for not being lofty or arty enough.

Before she could analyze this feeling further, she found Margaret beside her, fire in her hazel eyes. Clearly her sister thought this talk so much Gallic nonsense, and Margaret was always quick to resent slights to the family. "Mr. Olivier, this is all very well to speak of suffering and hate and fear and hope and such like, but you make it sound as if there will be nothing to teach my sister unless she be felled by some dreadful illness or—or made to beg in the streets." She did not even acknowledge Jean-André's contributions to the conversation, not from any prudishness but because, honestly, what could be done with such a person?

Unabashed, the painter made a clicking sound with his tongue. "Ah, we hope it will not come to that. Most people are passionate about something; they have only to discover what it is. Now, Miss Edith, may we open your portfolio?"

Stifling a sigh, Edith wondered if this moment ever got any easier. For someone who did not like to draw attention to herself, she had chosen an inconvenient profession.

She unlaced the portfolio with fingers that did not tremble noticeably and began to lay out the pieces from her summer in London: the painted copy of Reynolds' *Portrait of Kitty Fisher, as Cleopatra*; a study of his *Portrait of Lady Gertrude Fitzpatrick*; a sketch of Dawe's *A child rescued by its mother from an eagle's nest*; an impression of Turner's *Frosty morning*. To Edith's chagrin, Mr. Olivier regarded and disregarded these rapidly, emitting various, uninterpretable humphs and grunts. Then he turned to the remaining stack which she had not laid out. Taking them up, he retreated to the window, Jean-André at his side, to inspect these in the brightest light.

Margaret and Edith glanced at each other, Margaret giving a tiny shrug, as if to say, *Heaven only knows what Frenchmen think or do!*

These Frenchmen conferred in low voices, and not in English, Edith was certain. Jean-André pointed at one, his voice rising and falling, and Mr. Olivier nodded, passing it to him and selecting two others after further discussion.

At last the conference concluded. The autumn sun was higher in the sky now. In high summer Edith imagined it would grow too hot in the studio to work, with that skylight focusing the sun's heat like a magnifying glass. But it was comfortable enough in late September, and probably in the winter the sun would not even circle high enough to penetrate the skylight directly.

"Here." Mr. Olivier made a sweeping motion with one hand, and Jean-André swiftly gathered all of Edith's copies of other artists and replaced them in the portfolio, along with the rejected sketches. He then closed it and pushed it to the edge of the worktable.

"*Et voilà.*" With dramatic slowness Mr. Olivier placed the first of the three chosen sketches down. "These are where we will begin to learn color, Miss Edith. Because there is something in each of these, struggling to emerge. There is passion."

It was a quick drawing Edith had done in Bruton Street. Margaret sat at the pianoforte, her back to the viewer, while Dashiell leaned against the instrument, his mouth curled as he spoke to his wife. In the foreground, to one side, Alwyn and Mrs. Arbuthnot played a hand of cards.

Margaret made a little sound in her throat. "I didn't know you were drawing us, darling."

"The true artist is always drawing," declared Mr. Olivier, "whether or not he has a pencil in his hand." And Edith wondered if everything the man said must be trumpeted as a pronouncement.

He laid the next upon the table. This one depicted the servants in Bruton Street preparing the breakfast room: Walters folded back the shutters; Binchin was building the fire; Jimmy and another footman were placing teapot and dishes on the sideboard.

"Oh, dear, I suppose the passion in that one is suffering?" Margaret asked wryly.

Mr. Olivier clicked his tongue again and wagged a finger at her. "The passion comes from the artist, Mrs. Waite. Kindness can be a passion. Interest in our fellow human beings can be a passion."

"That's a relief to hear," muttered Margaret, and Edith silently agreed with her.

"This will be an excellent exercise for you, Miss Edith," he told her. "There is the fire—always tricky to capture—and the food in still life and the light that comes from the window. Color! And the subject itself, like a scene from Hogarth—only more respectable, of course, more appropriate for a young lady."

She nodded, feeling mounting excitement. Perhaps she would not be a colorless, passionless failure after all.

And then, his gaze fixed on her, Mr. Olivier placed the final sketch on the table.

It was Lionel.

Of course, it was Lionel. And Edith realized a portion of her dread was due to the thought of anyone seeing her record of that day at the stile. She herself had not dared to look at it since she hurried home that June afternoon and hid it away among sundry other pieces of paper. And when she arrived in Bath and found it in her portfolio, she thought briefly of destroying it, only she could not bring herself.

She could not.

Oh, heavens! What would they say? What would they think? Even Margaret was frowning at it.

"Tell me about this one," said Mr. Olivier.

Edith gripped the edge of the worktable, willing herself not to blush. *Act as if you were at the British Institute again*, she commanded herself. *Imagine someone else altogether drew this. Drew this picture of a perfect stranger.* She didn't know how successful she was in not blushing, but she did manage to say in a steady voice, "This is our cousin Lionel. He is—happy to be home from university for the long vacation."

"He is happy about *something*," muttered Jean-André.

"It was his first year away," explained Edith. "Away from the countryside, where we live, and away from his family, and away from his horse. That is why he is glad to be back."

"And you are happy to see him," said Mr. Olivier. "That is plain."

Now she did turn crimson. "Yes, I was happy to see him. I have three older sisters and two female cousins, so Lionel—because he is the only boy—is like a brother to me."

"A brother," repeated Jean-André blandly. Edith wanted to punch him.

"Has he really grown so much?" asked Margaret, who had not seen him in a year. "He looks altogether older—different. More like...a man, I suppose. How old is he now?"

"Nearly eighteen."

"As old as that! Why, the next thing you know, he will have taken his degree and be getting married. Did he say anything to you about any young ladies?"

"No," said Edith shortly.

"No? Well, you certainly must try painting this one, Edie, because he's quite handsome in it, and I'm sure when he does offer for someone, she will gladly take the portrait off your hands for a generous sum!" She blushed a little herself, ducking her chin. "Just like I might like to buy this one of Dashiell and me. I rather like the look upon his face."

"That is because he looks at you with love, Mrs. Waite." Mr. Olivier was still watching Edith. "I look at these sketches, and I see an artist wondering what it means to belong to the human race. What does it mean to love? What does it mean to live one's life? What does it mean to *be* alive? These are the things that Miss Edith must explore through her brush and through color. There are the questions in these sketches. I look at these and I know the artist has unfinished business. She has buried passion that must be brought to the surface. You will paint these ones, Miss Edith. You will make them live. And when they are alive, they will answer your questions."

She mustered a tentative smile, as if what he proposed didn't sound like a harrowing process.

Because there were some questions, Edith thought, that were probably better off left unanswered.

Chapter Fourteen

**It was supposed that serpents...
had also a power of charming.
—Oliver Goldsmith, *An history of the earth, and animated nature* (1774)**

Edith had not expected to see much more of Jean-André Olivier once her lessons began, but he accompanied his uncle regularly to Johnson Street, where his brooding presence and unreadable looks made her wish he would remain in Westgate Buildings. However, he spoke little to her beyond polite greetings and did not often train his dark eyes upon her, so it seemed unreasonable to her to complain.

Rather, Jean-André discussed business with his uncle, for it seemed modeling for the painter was only one of the young man's duties. He also acted as Mr. Olivier's agent and manager.

One morning, after Mr. Olivier and Edith discussed how she would transfer the sketch of Margaret, Dashiell, and the Arbuthnots to canvas (for the painting Mr. Olivier was already calling *The Players*), Edith began covering the back of her sketch with charcoal while the two Oliviers talked. Jean-André occupied what had become his preferred seat by the central window, and he had brought a lap desk, from which he retrieved a packet of correspondence. Mr. Olivier, who could never be still, stalked up and down the room as was his habit, arms crossed and a sharp eye kept on Edith's progress.

"Mr. Plura asks how many works you will submit to his auction in October."

"Who else will be represented there?"

Jean-André consulted the sheet in his hand. "Wynants, Wouvermans, Le Duc, Bergben, Polemberg, Griffier, Wilson, Smith of Chichester, Andersen, and Barker."

Mr. Olivier grunted. He tapped Edith's paper. "More charcoal here." Then he resumed pacing. "Bah! So many landscape artists. Tell Plura I will deliver five paintings."

"Very well. Which ones?" Here Jean-André opened the lid of his desk and plucked out another piece of paper, a list. "You have promised Mr. Evill's auction several already."

Another grunt. "I remember. Let me see then...If Plura has landscapes, it had better be the portraits with much background." He halted before one of the windows and peered out a minute before turning with a snap of his fingers. "The Napoleon enthroned. The Baptist in the wilderness. Christ disputing with the doctors (second version). Prometheus and the fire. Hannibal crossing the Alps."

Both he and Jean-André looked over sharply at hearing Edith giggle.

"Something is funny, Miss Edith?" asked Jean-André.

There was no one to save her, since Margaret was out and only the maid Filberts was at hand, working at the household's ironing by the fireplace. "Oh," she murmured. "Do forgive me. I only wondered if the younger Mr. Olivier served as the model for such a variety of famous subjects."

"He did," replied her teacher, a note of challenge perceptible.

"How—how marvelous," Edith said weakly. She turned to her workbox and shuffled its contents around, searching for her clamps.

"Perhaps Miss Edith thinks I am not very convincing when I play the hero," suggested Jean-André.

"Please—not at all! I think you have a very—er—very heroic form indeed." Mortified, she hoped he would assume that any inspection she had made of his form had been purely involuntary—an artist's habit. Jean-André was a well-proportioned, vigorous man, and she supposed many young ladies would call him handsome.

To her relief, her remark pleased him. His heroic chest swelled a few inches, and he rose, setting aside the laptop desk.

"But Miss Edith is correct in that those at the auction may think all my subjects are handsome young heroes," Mr. Olivier mused. "We will include the portrait of Sir Nightingale, Jean-André. Then they will know I paint middle-aged gentlemen whom few people have heard of, as well."

Edith concentrated on clamping her paper to the canvas as both uncle and nephew came to stand to either side of her.

"Be careful not to press," Mr. Olivier instructed, "or you will smear it. Have you a stylus to trace with?" When she shook her head, he called to Filberts: "You, miss. We require a teaspoon or other instrument. But the handle must be exactly right. Not too blunt or too pointed. Never mind—I will go with you to choose. Miss Edith, you wait for us, and do not press at all!"

Left alone with the younger man, Edith hoped he would return to the window and his lap desk, but he did not. Therefore she was compelled to move away, putting the table between them. She would sort the items in her workbox: group the pencils together and line up her brushes.

"Tell me again why you laughed," he said. He tapped the table with a fingertip and then rolled a pencil toward her. "If it isn't that my form is ridiculous."

"I should not have laughed. After all, I only draw and paint the same people over and over myself. It is not only a convenient practice, it is economical." And had she not once painted Elfrida, Frederick, and Margaret in the Judgment of Paris? What could be sillier than that?

"Then it must be the subjects that amused you," he persisted.

"Oh, Mr. Olivier—" Edith looked up at him helplessly. "I have already begged your pardon. I assure you it was not the subjects themselves, only the sheer—variety of them. You are—very versatile."

He nodded slowly. "You must please call me Jean-André. It is too confusing to have two Mr. Oliviers."

This request was not calculated to comfort her, and it did not help when he added in a mischievous tone, "I will ask my uncle—I am sure he will have you draw me as well. Then you may choose attitudes and subjects that do not make you laugh."

Before her mind supplied any appropriate response, Mr. Olivier was heard on the stairs and he led Filberts back into the studio, a teaspoon held high in triumph. "This one, Miss Edith. This is your stylus. You may now begin to trace."

Edith much preferred when Margaret sat through her lessons. It was not that her sister interposed herself any more than Filberts did with the ironing—it was just that her presence made Edith able to ignore Jean-André.

The tracing of *The Players* and of *Preparations for breakfast* were complete and the palette for each decided upon, and that left the sketch of Lionel. To be honest, Edith had left it—left him—for last, but she could not ignore him forever, and to make any fuss about it might lead to awkward questions.

As she applied the charcoal to the reverse of the paper, Margaret sewed, and Jean-André removed a paper from his lap desk to wave at his uncle. "Craven and Heath intend to apply to the Royal Academy again this year. Craven says he will submit his portrait of jugglers."

Mr. Olivier shrugged. "I have seen it."

"And Heath proposes to submit his *Mary Magdalene* and his *Christ in the house of Martha*."

"I would not be surprised if Heath is accepted. The English feel the lack of grandiosity in their native painters. Heath's paintings are too small for their subjects, but at least they have solemnity."

"Do the academicians prefer religious subjects, sir?" asked Edith.

"Some of them. The ones who want English painting to compete with Continental painting and Old Masters. For them, the grander the subject, the better. Christs, saints, mythological heroes, military figures."

"Why, that is exactly what you like to paint, Mr. Olivier!" she exclaimed. "Will you submit some of your work?"

He looked pained by her question, and Jean-André interjected reproachfully, "Miss Edith, only Englishmen may submit to the Royal Academy exhibit."

"Oh, yes, that's right—I forgot. Forgive me."

"Englishmen and English*women*," her teacher noted. "*You*, Miss Edith, might submit. Your talent is equal to many who will be seen there."

Edith's breath caught. She thought of her visit with Margaret to both the British Institution and the Royal Academy exhibits. She thought of the crowds gathered and the remarks overheard, both admiring and critical. She recalled the reviews in the newspapers and one paragraph in particular, which sniffed, "This writer has learned the artist F. Oakley is not a Mr. Frank Oakley or a Mr. Frederick Oakley, but rather a *Miss* Fernanda Oakley. While *Miss* Oakley's skill and execution show promise, may we advise her that she would do better in future to choose more ladylike subjects? It disturbs the viewer's mind to imagine a female artist painting nudes, however tasteful."

"Mr. Olivier, I am deeply appreciative that you would say so, but I am content without greater public scrutiny. Because—I don't suppose an artist may submit anonymously?"

"*Non!*" he declared decisively. "You may choose a false name, or you may choose only to state your first initial to hide your sex, but all paintings must be submitted under a name."

She thought again of Miss Fernanda Oakley and shook her head.

Margaret flung aside her sewing to come and give her sister an understanding squeeze of the shoulder. "Never mind all that, Edie. What is this you are tracing today?"

Reluctantly, Edith turned the sheet over to reveal Lionel on the stile, and she quickly made a business of finding her clamps and attaching the sheet to her canvas.

"Ah...the handsome cousin." This from Jean-André.

Edith ignored this. She set her jaw and picked up the teaspoon to begin the transfer.

"He *is* handsome, isn't he?" mused Margaret. "I never much noticed before. Our cousin Lionel is some years younger than I am," she explained to the Oliviers, "and he has always been something of the harum-scarum sort, which made him seem even younger." (She said this from the lofty age of twenty.)

"There is no doubt, from seeing this picture," responded Mr. Olivier, "that he has now become a young man. An adult. Miss Edith could see it."

"Could I?" asked Edith, the teaspoon slipping. She would have to brush off that smudge.

"Indeed. Whether you knew it or not."

"He is old enough for love," said Jean-André.

Seeing her little sister redden, Margaret's lips thinned. Trust these Frenchmen to speak such nonsense around a girl of sixteen! "That's as may be," Margaret said loudly. "He is at university now, and I expect carryings-on with young ladies are only to be expected at this stage."

Silence met this. Edith was determined to say nothing and to complete her task. She lifted the sheet, found the transfer complete, and removed the clamps. And there he was, Lionel, on the canvas.

"Tell me about the colors of that day, that moment," prompted Mr. Olivier. It was the same question he posed with *The Players* and *Preparations for breakfast*, but in neither of those cases had Edith felt such reluctance to remember and revisit.

"It was sunny," she murmured at last. "June. A flawless blue sky, like painted enamel. Everything was vivid: the grass, the wildflowers, the blue of his coat. His—his hair." *His eyes.* But she didn't say this.

"Lionel has very bright hair," supplied Margaret. "It used to be a light, reddish gold, but it has darkened a great deal."

"Yes," said Edith. "Now I would say it is nearly auburn."

"Mm-hm." Her teacher clicked his tongue thoughtfully. "And how did you feel when you sketched this?" Again, it was the same question he had asked with the other pieces, but again she struggled to answer. How clear it had been with the others! With *The Players* she had been filled with joy and curiosity (toward Margaret and Dashiell) and rueful affection (toward Uncle Alwyn—how *had* he managed to land such a wife?). With *Preparations for breakfast*, both curiosity and guilt stirred her. At Bramleigh, the few servants were so much a part of Edith's life and had been so put upon over the years that keeping them content was every Hapgood's duty. But in Bruton Street she saw with new eyes how most servants worked constantly and were expected to be largely invisible. She felt again how indulged she was by her family, that she was excused from household work, in order to be free to paint.

It was this recollection of her family's sacrifice for her and the lingering guilt about not having to work for her bread that brought honesty to her lips now. If so much had been given to her, was it not her duty to learn as much as she could? Which meant, if art required passion and self-revelation and truth, she could not—she must not—hold back.

Therefore: "I felt overwhelming joy to see him again," said Edith softly. "He is dear to me as any brother might be, and I missed him dreadfully when he was away."

Margaret blinked at this bald declaration in mixed company, before rousing herself and giving a matter-of-fact throat clearing. "Well, of course you feel strongly about him, Edie dear. We all do. We *all* feel strongly about our cousin."

"If you would excuse me, Miss Edith," began Jean-André, mild as milk, "judging from what I see before me, I daresay this cousin returns your feelings in equal measure."

She turned on him sharply, her normally serene grey eyes flashing as they met his dark ones. He merely held her gaze, raising his eyebrows as if he wondered at her vehemence. It did not take Edith long to run up against her limit to honesty, it seemed. Because it was no one's business but hers and Lionel's that he had offered for her, and it was no one's business but hers and Lionel's that he had kissed her. Or she him. Because she *had* returned his kiss, had she not? For that delicious instant?

It was Mr. Olivier who eased the tension. "Ah! So much affection!" he cried. "It warms the heart. This is what you must capture with your paint and your color, Miss Edith. This so-great, mutual affection. This brotherly love."

No more was said on the matter. Jean-André retreated to the window seat; Margaret took up her sewing again; and Mr. Olivier and Edith spent the remainder of the session discussing colors and how the paint must be mixed.

"You have much work to do before I see you again, Miss Edith, and we will leave you in peace to do it. Painting is a very personal matter. You must have privacy. We will not have another lesson for a week, perhaps."

"But we hope you will attend the auction at Mr. Plura's great room in John Street," added Jean-André at the door. "While you may not want to be a *famous* artist, it is worthwhile to see how the business is conducted."

"We will be there," Margaret assured him. "Mr. Waite and I have already decided upon it. Thank you. Huffman will show you out." She waited, listening for their footsteps to recede to the ground floor before marching over to Edith and demanding, "What on earth was that about?"

"What on earth was *what* about?" She gathered the darker shades first. She would begin with his coat.

"Put that down a moment, Edie," Margaret insisted, batting at the Prussian blue powder in her hand. "I want to talk to you. Come here. Sit with me."

Oh, dear.

Edith knew when she was pinned down. She set her palette knife and pigment aside and followed her sister to the sofa against the wall. Margaret took Edith's hands in her own.

"Dearest, may I ask you something?"

"If I said 'no,' I daresay you would still ask me."

"These painting lessons are a pretty kettle of fish, are they not? Mr. Olivier and his disturbing nephew are quite different creatures from Mr. Eldredge. I do not know why the nephew comes, but neither do I know how we might tell him to stay away." She patted Edith's hand absently. "What I mean to ask is, do you like them? Would you like to continue the lessons? Because, if you don't, I will get Dashiell to dismiss them. He will manage it better than we. Perhaps Mr. Liggett might agree to teach you."

"Mr. Liggett paints miniatures!"

"I know, I know. I suppose they are different?"

"Of course they are different. They are done on ivory and they are—miniature," Edith said lamely. "Nor has Mr. Liggett ever given any indication that he would like to teach. Or teach me."

"You prefer the Oliviers, then?"

"It isn't that I prefer the Oliviers, particularly, though the elder Mr. Olivier is pleasant enough," answered Edith. "It is that I feel there is much to learn from him. That he will challenge me. He has already."

"Yes." Margaret was silent a moment, her brow furrowing. "About that challenge. Edith—are you in love with Lionel?"

"What?" She was used to her sister's forthrightness, but this was too much! Whipping her hands away, she made to stand, but Margaret pulled her back down.

"It's a simple enough question, and who can you tell, if not me? You were uncomfortable when Mr. Olivier asked how you felt when you made the sketch. And that look on Lionel's face! Did you put it there, or was it there?"

"I don't know!" fretted Edith. "Mr. Eldredge said the artist always puts himself in the picture, whether he intends to or not. So if Lionel has a 'look' on his face, either it was there or I put it there without meaning to. What would you say the look is?"

"Why, that he loves you," Margaret said simply. "That he loves you, and not just as a brother."

Edith groaned and put her face in her hands.

"Ah-ha!" her sister triumphed. "You did not just put the look there, then, did you? He said something to you that day."

"He offered for me," Edith mumbled into her hands. But Margaret heard and understood.

"Offered for you? *Offered* for you? But that's—that's—how old is he, again?"

"Not yet eighteen."

"Oh! Well—I suppose it's not as astonishing as I thought. But you're only sixteen! Although, we have known him for years and years now." Margaret seemed unable to decide whether to find Lionel's offer shocking or a matter of course. "What did you say,

Edith? I assume you refused, unless you have been keeping a secret engagement."

"Of course I refused."

"Why 'of course'? I know you're only a baby—you probably haven't thought of such things yet."

Despite her discomfiture, Edith rolled her eyes. "I'm not a baby—although I had not in fact had any thoughts of marriage yet. I want to be an art—"

"Be an artist. Yes, yes," Margaret interrupted in her most maddening manner. "Well! Poor Lionel! Although I suppose he is hardly more than an infant himself. He will get over it, I imagine. Though he must have been thinking of it for some time, if he asked you directly after returning to Somerset. Does Hetty know?"

"Hetty? Certainly I didn't breathe a word to Hetty! You know how those two are always at each other. I can't tell Hetty about it. Lionel would never forgive me. And you must never say a word to them either, Margaret!"

"What do you take me for?" demanded her sister. "I can keep a secret." She continued to marvel. "Think of it—Lionel in love with you. What did he say that afternoon?"

But Edith had said enough. No young man should have to suffer his intimate words repeated—Edith would never think of asking Margaret what sorts of things Dashiell said when he proposed. It wasn't fair.

She shook her head. "That he cared for me, and could I care for him? But I told him I had no thoughts of marriage and wanted to pursue my art and my instruction at present."

"Poor, poor Lionel. And was he satisfied with that answer?"

"He *must* be satisfied," Edith insisted. "For that was the answer I gave."

"And are you still...glad that that was the answer you gave?" Margaret pressed.

"Yes. Yes, I am," she returned stoutly. "Though...I confess I miss him a great deal. I wish we might have gone on and on, always, as we were. Now I fear it's all ruined. All lost. At least, lost until he decides to be fond of someone else. Then perhaps we may be friends again."

Margaret gave a philosophical shrug. "You may tell yourself that, but whatever new girl he chooses may not like him to be jolly friends with a girl he used to love, even if she is his cousin of sorts. Nor may your future husband smile upon such a thing. Take, for instance, Jean-André. He does not appear the sort of man who would."

Edith gaped at her. "Then fortunate for me, perhaps, that Jean-André has nothing to do with anything. Nothing at all! Besides, he does not strike me as the smiling sort."

"I suppose not. He's more of the *moody*, Childe Harold type. A fellow who through 'Sin's Long Labyrinth' has run. Though he might still be wandering that labyrinth." (The Waites and Edith were reading *Childe Harold's Pilgrimage* in the evenings now, now that there was no disapproving Miss Blenkensop at hand.) "I must say, I don't particularly like how the younger Mr. Olivier looks at you."

"Oh, Margaret. He's a strange sort. I think he cannot help how intently he looks at people. We must try to ignore him."

"You don't think him handsome, then? Tall and dark and handsome?"

"He's handsome enough, from an artistic perspective," answered Edith primly.

Her sister gave her a long look. Then she gave a sigh and reached for her sewing. "All right, then. I agree that you are too young to think of marriage, and I am not sorry you refused Lionel (though I am very sorry for *him*), but do let me know if you change your mind about marriage. I feel responsible for you here, and Elfie and Alice would never forgive me if I let you form an unfortunate attachment. Not to mention what Papa would say—!"

By which Edith understood that Margaret would consider any attachment formed to Jean-André Olivier as "unfortunate." Very well, very well. She would get no disagreement from Edith.

"I will do my best not to fall in love with him, then," Edith grinned. "And his presence in Bath and at my lessons will be another of our little secrets, lest word get back to Papa and Papa feel obliged to come and drag me home."

Taking up her palette knife again, Edith drew it through the saucer of linseed oil and opened the jar of bone black pigment powder. She would layer first the darker shades, working her way toward the highlights. And she would begin with Lionel's coat because—well, because it could not look back at her.

Chapter Fifteen

Revealing day through every cranny spies,
And seems to point her out where she sits weeping.
—Shakespeare, *The Rape of Lucrece* (1594)

Angel Inn
Oxford
1 January 1814

Dear Edie,
Your letter dated 15 December has only just found me
because, as you will have already seen above, we are
not in Patterton! Yes, Papa has taken us to Oxford for
the Christmas season because Lionel actually put pen
to paper *to say he would not be returning to Somerset*

for his vacation, and, if the mountain will not come to Mahomet, Mahomet must go to the mountain. (And we were not the only Mahomets to go to the mountain—but more on that later.)

Before I share my news, I will treat with yours. By my calculations, your letter was ¾ about painting and ¼ about anything else. So, for the ¾: I am happy to learn of your progress with your lessons and to hear that Mr. Olivier sold three portraits at his last auction. If I were a serious artist as you are, I am certain I would find those bits captivating, but, as it is, I was far more entertained by the remaining ¼ of your letter: your account of the play you saw and your drive to Solsbury Hill and the Haworths coming for supper! I too am glad that Mr. Waite married Margaret, rather than his cousin Mrs. Haworth, not only for Margaret's sake but also because I find myself mistrustful of cousinly matches (again—more on that later). If you do not intend to return to Somerset anytime soon, would you greatly object to making your next letter only half *about painting and more about everything else? Suggested topics might include dancing at an assembly or two, taking the waters, attending a concert,* or anything else that ordinary people do in Bath, *Edith. Why, you don't even mention one single young man in the entire four pages! Unforgiveable. Don't you remember the letters*

Margaret used to write, when she was there last winter? How we devoured her accounts! Let me misconstrue Queen Gertrude from Hamlet *in asking, please, for "More matter, with less art."*

But enough of my complaints, or I fear you will not write to me again at all. On to my news, and I will teach you by example how to write interesting letters.

You will want to know if your father is well. With pleasure I report that he was in good health ten days ago. As were Blenkensop and Mr. E. Which brings me to my first exciting titbit, which you will never believe, but which I assure you is true because I have it on the very best authority. Dorcas was building the fire in the schoolroom and told me our housekeeper Bundish told your *housekeeper Macready that Soppy and Mr. E were seen walking outside Patterton, and that Mr. E* tried *to take Soppy's hand. Tried and failed! That is all I know, Edith. They both behave entirely as usual around us, but I think you must agree Mr. E must have been pressing his attentions on Soppy, only to be rebuffed (for the second time?). I wish you were here, so we could discuss this, although I know you would frown at me for encouraging gossip, but how else am I to learn anything?*

You will frown further when I record a dialogue between the two thwarted lovers which I freely admit I have composed myself (but I am positive it must have gone something like this):

Mr. E: Oh, love, love, my love, dearest love! [Tries to take her hand]

Soppy: [Wrenches her hand away] *You must not, Mr. Eldredge.*

Mr. E: How can I help myself, my darling, angular Penelope? I may call you Penelope, may I not?

Soppy: [Awfully] *I am Miss Blenkensop.*

Mr. E: But such a name as "Blenkensop" does not do justice to your loveliness! I would have you change your name. Perhaps to something like "Eldredge."

Soppy: How many times must I tell you, Mr. Eldredge? We can never afford to marry, even more so now that we have lost the tutelage of Miss Edith.

Mr. E: That is why I have taken on additional pupils in Taunton, four mornings a week. I only pray they are more talented than Miss Harriet and Miss Rosalie,

*whose work makes me want to poke my eyes out with
sharp pencils.*

[etc. etc. etc.]

*But, before you put my letter down in disgust, let me
share news I have been an eyewitness to. (Though I will
say the bit about new pupils for Mr. E in Taunton is
true.) As I said, Lionel informed us he would stay in
Oxford, and Papa must have known how dull I found
things, with both him and you gone, so he proposed this
trip. Edith, I am in love with Oxford. What I would
not give, to be a boy and go to university! We are putting
up at the Angel Inn, as Papa and Mama did before, a
bustling place just steps from Magdalen College. Magdalen is on the eastern end of town, bordering the river
Cherwell, and Lionel took us on a lovely tour, beginning with a beautiful chapel adorned with painted
glass, followed by a medieval hall where they take their
meals. The latter was full of dark wood and solemn
portraits hung high, and I said to Lionel that, if it were
up to me, I would take down Cardinal Wolsey and all
those dour benefactors, hang some of your portraits up,
and see if that didn't improve everyone's appetite! To
which he replied, "If you hung up Edith's paintings, I
doubt anyone would remember to eat at all." Which
was a very nice compliment to you, I thought, but when*

I told him I would pass on his remark, he only made a face as if he had a toothache.

We only looked at the Tower from the outside and then crossed the grassy quadrangle to the New Building to see Lionel's room. (There was no girl under the bed this time—I peeked and earned a scowl from my brother.) From there, we explored the extensive grounds, from the grove where deer graze to the water-walk. We must have spent three hours, altogether, and were quite ready for refreshment upon returning to the High Street. The shops and other eating and coffee houses and colleges we passed there must wait to be visited another time!

That day has been the best part of our stay here, however. For shortly afterward, my aunt and uncle Sidney and cousin Caroline arrived. Yes—remember what I said earlier about Mahomet and the mountain? Aunt Lavinia told Mama it was so delightful to see us last year at this time that she thought we should all make a tradition of it. By which I gather my Sidney relations continue to pin their faith upon Lionel marrying Caroline.

Caroline has further improved in looks, I am sorry to say. (You will think me an ungenerous cousin, but I would like her better if she would at least pretend *an interest in Rosie or me. But, no, she has eyes only for Lionel.) I suppose we may be grateful to her for drawing him out, for though he was not particularly talkative with us, manners required him to answer her thousand questions. By which we learned: yes, he is still good friends with Clinker and Clunker; no, he has decided against reading classics and has settled on mathematics because it involves less reading and writing; for amusement there was punting on the Cherwell or raiding the buttery or a violent match of foot-ball or equally violent cudgels; and no, neither Clinker nor Clunker has a dedicated sweetheart. You know as well as I, Edith, that Caroline asked this last question in a roundabout way to discover whether Lionel himself has a sweetheart, and I wanted to hug Lionel when he did not reward her deviousness. I daresay he saw through her too, but I cannot be certain. Each question and answer led to further questions and answers, you understand, but I am summarizing for you, or this letter would be thirteen pages long. As it is my hand is sore, and I must continue another time.*

4 January 1814

I did mean to send this by now but did not want to do so before I had occasion to tell you more. We return to Somerset tomorrow, and the town begins to fill up again with students returning for Hilary Term. Two of the students to return were Lionel's friends Clinker and Clunker, and I was glad of them, for they raised Lionel's spirits considerably. I do not mean to say he was downcast beforehand, only that he was not entirely himself. I heard Papa saying to Mama that he little expected it, when Lionel had been so boisterous this past summer. But Mama said, yes, he was, at first, but did Papa not recall how Lionel grew quieter as the vacation went on? She thought now that this was just a stage in his increasing maturity, although she would be sorry to think his liveliness something to be grown out of. And so would I, Edith, much as it surprises me to admit it! How sad it is to grow up, if it means no more teasing and pranks and gambols with one's sisters, and only the dull business of finding a dull wife!

Not that Caroline is dull, precisely. It is only that she is not interesting. Perhaps because she has no interests. One afternoon when Lionel was being fitted for new clothing (for he seems to have grown again), Caroline was thrown back upon Rosie and me for company. I thought this was our chance to become friends, and I attempted to pelt her with enough questions about herself that we could forestall talking about Lionel, but her answers were so brief and colorless that we ended up talking about Lionel!!! (Need I mention that Caroline

*asked Rosie and me not a single question about our-
selves, even after I despaired and launched into talking
about our life in Somerset as a broad hint that other
people besides my brother exist.) You will be pleased to
learn in one paragraph what took me two hours to discover. Caroline is seventeen. She had a governess until
last year. She doesn't think she has a favorite book and
doesn't remember the last one she read—something
about a girl in London who goes to Ranelagh Gardens.
She plays the pianoforte and the harp. Her favorite
color is blue and Aunt Lavinia has promised her a
gown in blue mull. A friend in Crawley likes pink,
but Caroline does not because, when she wears pink, she
looks like she has a head cold. She prefers quadrilles to
longways dances. No, she has never been to the country
and supposes it must be a rather dull place. (Are you
dozing yet? Wake up, wake up, my dear Edie! I have
not yet done.)*

*I think of Mr. Olivier, who told you that painting
required passion—any sort of passion. Suffering, grief,
hope, despair, compassion, curiosity, fear, hatred, love.
What do you suppose Caroline's paintings would look
like? Pale blue and dun-colored, would be my guess.
Maybe a dash of gold for Lionel.*

Ah well, if my brother and cousin marry, Lionel will

be lost to us, largely. Maybe that is why he is already fading? I had a wicked hope that Caroline might marry Clinker instead because she was pleased to have two more young men to "practice" upon. Since you have not met C & C, I will tell you they are twin brothers from Kent. Both weedy, both with brown hair, and both quite fond of Lionel and he of them. Clinker (Jason) is the mischievous one and Clunker (Edward) the poetical one. I think you would especially like Clunker because he tries his hand at painting. He and I managed a creditable discussion of art, for which I thank Mr. E's training. He did show me one of his sketches, though, and I'm afraid he isn't any better than I am. Alas. As for Clinker, he rattles on about anything, which I think Caroline liked. When Clinker rattled on at her, she cast many glances at Lionel, as if to say, "Do you see? Your friend pays me attention."

All I say with any certainty, Edith, is that I do not believe Caroline has yet succeeded in "bagging" Lionel (how Soppy would scold me for using such a vulgar term!). But I suspect she has made progress, since, as I mentioned, she does get him to speak, and as I have noticed him looking at her from time to time. But she must go home now as we must, and, unless she can bring him up to scratch within the next day, I think she must hope the seeds she planted will yet come to bear.

Perhaps my Sidney relations will inveigle a way to see him again during the long vacation. I have not invited them to visit, but Mama may not be able to avoid it.

I must conclude, if I am to post this before we leave. I did ask Lionel if he would like to add anything to my letter or at least send his regards, but he merely got his toothache look again and said, "Just include me in the general family greetings, Het."

Therefore, our general family greets you and hopes to see you at Bramleigh again shortly in this New Year.

Your own,
Hetty

Pallid winter sun threw oblique rectangles upon the floor of Edith's studio. Upon one easel, rich with browns and golds and cream stood *The Players*. She was pleased with it, even proud. She loved the way she had managed to capture Dashiell's attentive, wry affection for her sister and Margaret's response in the line of her back as she sat at the pianoforte. And Uncle Alwyn and Mrs. Arbuthnot in the foreground, cards in hand, of which only Aunt Eliza's were visible. She played what was probably a losing hand. And Alwyn? His face was half in shadow, his mouth twisting with what might be amusement or triumph.

Beside the easel, *Preparations for breakfast* lay on the worktable. It too was completed. Edith liked its composition, the placement of the figures in relation to the room, and she liked the palette of yellow and cream and black, with punctuations of orange and red in the fire and the bowl of fruit on the sideboard. But she was less pleased with the faces of the servants themselves. She didn't know them any better than when she sketched them, and it showed. They remained secret, hidden as good servants were, in plain sight. What they knew, they kept to themselves. She had not even captured possible relationships among them. Mr. Olivier liked the picture, but Edith didn't spare it a glance this morning.

No, she stood before the second easel, the one set just beyond the rectangles of sunlight. The one with Lionel's portrait upon it.

After reading Hetty's letter, Edith wanted to pour a bucket of tar over it.

"I must love him after all," she said to the empty room, "to want to do that."

Because it was a beautiful painting. Maybe—possibly—the best she had yet done. Jewel-bright. Vigorous. Personal. Alive. Although Edith's past subjects lacked neither charm nor personal attractions, the Lionel on this canvas was imbued with something more.

"One almost expects him to jump down from the stile into the room," had been Margaret's comment a few days earlier.

"You have outdone yourself, Edith," said Dashiell simply.

Mr. Olivier was beyond words. He hugged himself, nodding, alternately grimacing and beaming as he inspected the portrait from every possible perspective: from across the room to so close his nose was nearly touching the surface; in full sun and in shade; propped against the wall or flat on the worktable.

And Jean-André—he said nothing until he and his uncle were departing. Mr. Olivier was halfway down the stairs when the nephew ran back up, crossing the studio to collect his lap desk. At the door again he turned slightly and said over his shoulder, "A powerful love indeed—that of a sister for a brother."

When the door shut behind him, Edith found herself holding her paintbrush in a death grip; she had wanted to hurl it at his retreating back.

But now, now that she was alone with the painting and with Hetty's letter and with her own feelings, she admitted that she had only been angry with Jean-André because he spoke the truth, the truth she had not been willing yet to recognize. Jean-André only put into words what Mr. Olivier was too discreet to remark upon. That it was patent to him—if not to anyone else, including Edith herself—that she was in love with her subject. That *Portrait of a young gentleman* might more aptly be titled *Portrait of the secret the artist kept even from herself.*

Oh, how could this be? How could this have *come* to be? Just six short months ago—seven months ago, she had been so certain! So certain that she loved him only as a brother and that she had no thoughts of marriage. So certain that she would not even allow him to hope. And now...? Now she should hear again of his cousin Caroline's *tendre* for him and suddenly recognize her dismay as something uglier? As jealousy, perhaps? For what else could it be? She had gone from giggling over Hetty's imagined love scene between Mr.

Eldredge and Miss Blenkensop to bristling like a hedgehog when Caroline was mentioned.

A moan escaped her, the morning's plan to scumble the background trees with a darker glaze forgotten. She pushed her palette away. Wiped her brush absently. Walked away from the portrait but felt Lionel's eyes upon her.

If Caroline "bagged" him, according to Hetty, Lionel would be lost to them. But Edith feared that was already the case for her. Had they not been estranged the previous summer, after her refusal of him? Often in each other's company but not enjoying their former ease?

She wondered if he still cared for her. Hetty's claim that Lionel looked to have the toothache whenever Edith was mentioned might mean anything from lingering affection to distaste for an embarrassing incident he would sooner forget.

Edith would have to see him again, to determine where she stood in his heart, but when would that happen? The soonest would be the summer, she supposed, when—if—he returned to Somerset for his long vacation. She could not write to him. Young ladies did not write to young men, and, even if she defied the proprieties, what would she say? "Lionel, forgive me—I have decided I love you after all and would like to be engaged"? Some girls might be that bold, that immodest, but not she. In fact, she cringed at the thought of him receiving such a letter. She pictured him shrinking in horror as he recalled his boyish proposal, a proposal made before he had seen his cousin Caroline again and realized what true love was. Oh, it would be too dreadful! He would be kind to her, Edith—because Lionel was kind, and for the sake of their cousinship—but that kindness would be harder to bear than another person's rejection.

No, she could not write.

She would have to wait. Wait and hope.

But in the meantime—she turned back to face the portrait. "I was blind, Lionel," she whispered. "But it was the blindness of innocence, not caprice. Forgive me."

Quickly, with half a glance over her shoulder, as if anyone could come into the room without her hearing, she stole over to the painting. Giving a rueful laugh, she stood on the very tips of her toes and dropped on the canvas the lightest of kisses.

One thing at least she was sure of: if she could not have Lionel himself, she would never part with his likeness.

Chapter Sixteen

O Thieves! Thieves! I am robb'd.
—Daniel Defoe, *The Family Instructor* (1715)

Hardly had Edith vowed to herself that she would never be parted from Lionel's portrait than she was parted from Lionel's portrait.

"Miss Edith," Mr. Olivier said to her one morning in February, when he came to inspect the progress of her finishing touches, "I have momentous news for you."

For once he was not accompanied by Jean-André. Had Margaret been present, Edith could have trusted her to ask after the young man's whereabouts, but Margaret and Dashiell had gone for a drive to Bradford and Edith was accompanied only by Filberts the maid that morning. A useful chaperone but not a useful collector of information.

"I trust you have not changed your mind about submitting to the Royal Academy," he continued.

"I have not," said Edith.

"Yes. I understand that you are a quiet young lady who does not seek to draw attention to herself, Miss Edith, but it is a shame that the larger world cannot see your work."

She said nothing. They had had this discussion several times before.

"It is not in the hopes of fame or fortune, Miss Edith," her teacher went on. "I know fame holds no allure for you and you have been blessed with fortune sufficient for your needs. I tell you it is valuable—no, it is *essential*—to gather opinions and critiques of one's work. Opinions and critiques that do not come from family, friends of the family, or those in your family's pay."

This last made her catch her breath, as if he had surprised her with a dagger between her ribs. She turned alarmed eyes on him, but his usual Father-Christmas expression had given way to one that was bland and unreadable.

"Mr. Olivier, surely there is another way to gather...unbiased opinions of my work than exhibiting with the Royal Academy, if you think it absolutely necessary."

He gave a little bow. "There are. This is my momentous news for you. I have spoken with Mr. Plura, whose auction room you have visited in John Street, and he has agreed that you may hang your works in his February auction, where I also will be showing."

"Mr. Olivier!" gasped Edith.

"He will be coming by my studio in a few days to make his selections among my ready pieces, and I told him I would have your three paintings there as well."

She could only shake her head, backing away from him and sinking onto the little sofa. "I—I—"

"You have seen, Miss Edith, that many people attend these auctions. Not many make purchases, but many do attend. And everyone who looks at a painting has an opinion, and *these* are the jewels you must seek and collect. As you walk among the viewers, are they delighted? Puzzled? Disturbed? Saddened? Wistful? Do they ask, 'Who is this artist?' or do they snap their fingers and say, 'Bah! I do not care for this'? In Mr. Plura's great room you do not need to put your name forward. If he receives inquiries, he can speak with me, and I can speak with you. No one need know that the paintings have anything to do with you. You may wander the auction room invisible, as just another spectator."

The butterflies fluttering in her midsection were not all a result of dread, Edith realized. Some of them—some of them were butterflies of interest as she pictured the scene. It could work, she thought. She could pretend to be looking at the offerings herself, as she had when she attended Mr. Olivier's earlier auction. And he was right—every person present formed likes and dislikes and opinions, frequently expressing them to companions, as she had with Margaret. It was frightful to imagine eavesdropping on what perfect strangers thought of paintings she had worked so hard on, but she felt the lure of possibility. Would they agree with her own feelings about her work? If they did, their approbation would be all the more precious because, as Mr. Olivier pointed out, it would not spring from love or obligation or prejudice in her favor. It would be spontaneous. Genuine.

And if they disapproved? Well, that would hurt, but it would also teach her something.

"What are you thinking, Miss Edith?"

She raised her head. "I wouldn't want to sell them."

"And why not? If you were so fortunate to attract a buyer?" But he sensed her resistance giving way, and his genial Father-Christmas grin spread.

"Oh, perhaps I would sell *Preparations for breakfast,*" she conceded, "if anyone wanted it. But I already promised *The Players* to my sister Mrs. Waite, and *Portrait of a young gentleman—*" She broke off, her face suddenly hot.

"*Portrait of a young gentleman* you would like to keep," he said smoothly, holding up his palms as if this were so obvious it required no explanation.

"Er—yes." She was grateful beyond words that Jean-André was not there to make some insinuating remark about brotherly love.

Her teacher clapped his hands. "We are decided! Then you must let me take these home with me today or tomorrow, Miss Edith, and I will display them to advantage. You have signed them, yes? Yes—I see your tiny 'Ed. H' in the corner. For this auction of Mr. Plura's will not be landscape after landscape—no! I have convinced him that portraits must be the theme this time."

Though she felt sick at the thought of parting with her works so suddenly, she could think of no ready excuse for postponing the moment. They were complete, after all. She had already begun new studies for sketches she had made during her time in Bath: spectators in a box at the Theatre Royale; women gazing into the bow window of a shop in Bond Street; Margaret leaning on the balustrade in the Terrace Walk.

It was better this way, she told herself, when the paintings were wrapped and gone. Look how foolish she had already become about that portrait! She could already hear Hetty calling her a female Pygmalion, pining over her own daubs of paint. And if Lionel were ever to find out, there would be no living it down.

Edith may not have been prepared to crow about Mr. Plura's upcoming auction, but Margaret felt no need for reserve.

"Dashiell, darling," she said at breakfast, "I want to take Edith to the dressmaker. She must have a new dress and bonnet for the auction."

"But Margaret, it will be my paintings on display, not me," protested her sister.

"By all means," agreed Dashiell. "Although you are always so reluctant to spend any money on yourself, Margaret, that I am afraid I must add a condition to this proposal: not a single item may be purchased for Edith without an equivalent item being bought for yourself."

"Oh—please—I don't need anything," said Edith, but the Waites ignored her, wrangling playfully with each other.

"Are you saying I don't look smart enough for you, Dashiell?"

"I'm saying my reputation as a husband is at stake. When we were last at Bradford, I heard my cousin Charmaine say how she liked your gown—how she had *always* liked that gown, every *other* time you've worn it. Do you think a man can stand for that?"

"Oh, well, if it is a matter of your pride…"

"It is. Indulge me. I am as happy as you are to brag to all and sundry about Edith, but I'm rather proud of my wife, too, when she isn't stubborn."

With a laugh, Margaret blew him a kiss. "Very well. I yield. I will buy myself something new as well. But you're wrong to say I've bragged to all and sundry. I only have Charmaine to brag to here—oh, and I did say a little something to Sir Dodkins and Lady Hargate."

"What a falsehood!" he grinned. "You wrote a pile of bragging letters—to your father and your sisters and your uncle and Mrs. Hugh Hapgood. One would have thought you singly responsible for making Edith the artist she has become. I'm astonished you can still hold your head upright, it has got so big."

Much as she enjoyed seeing how fond her sister and brother-in-law were of each other, Edith couldn't help but say, "Oh, Margaret—I wish you hadn't written them all. It would have been soon enough to say something after the auction was over."

"Don't you fret, Edie. Dashiell exaggerates. I have indeed started letters to all our family, but I haven't yet posted a single one, for exactly that reason. I wanted to be able to add a final, triumphant paragraph summarizing how you were the toast of the event."

Edith made no reply and tried to look cheerful, despite her uneasiness. It was all very well for other people to brim with confidence and make light-hearted jokes—it wouldn't be their works hanging on the walls in John Street.

But, as it happened, Edith's worry was wasted. Not because she was the toast of the event, as Margaret predicted, but because she never participated at all.

She never participated because, two short days after her paintings were transported to Mr. Olivier's studio in Westgate Buildings, the Oliviers and another of their neighbors were burgled. Burgled before Mr. Plura even had the opportunity to lay eyes on the portraits. In one blow, Edith was robbed of her three best works, the approbation or criticism of the auction-goers, and even the opinion of Mr. Plura himself.

It was not Mr. Olivier who brought her news of the housebreaking. Perhaps the man was too distressed himself to come immediately. No, it was left to Dashiell to return to Johnson Street with a copy of the *Bath Chronicle* which he had read in a coffee house. His face heavy, he lay the paper beside Edith and said, "I'm sorry."

Her heart pounding and fingers trembling, she took up the newspaper and read of the thieves who, "using a ladder or long plank entered the studio of Mr. Alexandre Olivier at 45 Westgate Buildings using pick-lock keys. Some seven paintings were stolen from thence, and twenty to thirty French half-crowns from the neighboring home."

"Housekeepers, brokers and pawnbrokers are warned as to how they receive suspected goods," Margaret read over her shoulder, after Edith faltered. "Losses experienced by signatories - John Plura,

Alexandre Olivier, Armand Fanchet. A reward of thirty guineas is offered for information leading to a conviction."

When Edith could speak again, she ventured, "I am sorry for Mr. Olivier, to be sure. But he has many, many paintings in his studio. Even if seven were taken, there will be many left. And perhaps none of the seven were mine."

Dashiell shook his head grimly. "I am sorry, Edith," he said again. "When I saw this, I went to Westgate Buildings to learn more. The studio is in shambles and Mr. Olivier not much better. He was at a loss for words and could only sit with his head in his hands, groaning. I had to apply to his nephew for more information."

"Which one of hers did they take?" demanded Margaret, not caring a shred for Mr. Olivier's feelings at this point.

Her husband hesitated, and she read the answer in his eyes.

"All of them?" Margaret shrieked. "*All* of them? Out of seven paintings stolen, *three* were Edie's?"

"The younger Mr. Olivier, who was raging about, said that his uncle had displayed Edith's paintings prominently, in anticipation of Mr. Plura's visit. The thief or thieves chose Edith's three and the four of Mr. Olivier's works which were nearest at hand."

"Why, why, why?" moaned his wife. "Why steal paintings? Why steal *these* paintings? You cannot do anything with them—even the *Bath Chronicle* warns the art brokers and the pawnbrokers to be on their guard. If you cannot sell them, what use are they?"

Dashiell sighed. "Jean-André believes that thieves are sometimes in the pay of private collectors. Someone who is happy to have a painting and has no intention of selling it."

"It makes no sense, though," Margaret persisted. "No collector would have any idea of Edie's works, and—to be perfectly frank—I'm not certain any private collector would bother to steal Mr. Olivier's. They can be had at reasonable prices and are hardly worth the crime." Swooping down upon her younger sister, she gathered her in her arms. "Oh, Edie! I am so, so sorry! I am so terribly sorry this happened. I feel responsible. You're right—I shouldn't have written all those bragging letters. It was tempting fate."

"What utter gammon," Dashiell retorted, lashed into defending his wife from herself. "You are in no way responsible, Margaret. The only person responsible is the thief himself."

"Of course it's not your fault, Margaret," murmured Edith, who was inclined to think it was her own fault. Had Mr. Olivier not appealed to her own vanity, her three beautiful portraits would still be safe on the second floor.

Now no one would ever see them. Including her. She would never see them again.

She was too stunned to cry. Too stunned to do much besides sit utterly still, breathing shallowly.

But Margaret cried. Silently, miserably. And she punished herself by marching to her escritoire, gathering her stack of "bragging" letters, and hurling them in the fire. This was pain too deep to share. If it was ever told, it must be Edith's tale to tell.

Mr. Olivier and Jean-André did master themselves enough to call the following day, but Edith lay sick and listless in bed, and only Margaret descended to send them away. After this scene was repeated the next day, Mr. Olivier resorted to sending a note. Deeply regretful, apologetic, useless.

On the third day, Edith roused herself. She must put on a brave face, for Margaret's sake. And for Dashiell's, for he observed his pale and unhappy wife with anxiety of his own.

Therefore Edith rose and dressed and ate. She sewed and played the pianoforte and asked Margaret if they might walk in Sydney Gardens. After supper she asked if she might read to them the new book from the circulating library, and they heard two chapters. When she went to bed, she felt the slightest bit better and vowed that the morrow must be more of the same.

And it was.

But the effort was costly.

It was not only the three paintings that had been stolen from her, the three paintings and the five months of her life. No—it was more.

Though there was not a soul on earth she could tell, she knew that a share of her pain was having *Portrait of a young gentleman* taken from her. Foolish as it might be, it felt like losing Lionel all over again.

All that remained to Edith was a growing desire to leave Bath and seek pastures new. Her oldest sisters Elfie and Alice had repeatedly invited her to Buckinghamshire for a stay, and now she could see her nephew and new nieces. Four counties away no one would hound her about her artistic career. They had been pleased with her before she began all this becoming-an-artist business, and they would be absorbed in their domestic changes in any case. Maybe, if she thought she could bear to lift a pencil again, she might draw her new family members. And Margaret would see the sense in Edith going. It would be a relief to them all, to put this painful incident behind them.

Her stay in Bath held one final surprise, however. When Mr. Olivier and his nephew called to take leave of her (a most uncomfortable interview, with Mr. Olivier subdued and downcast), Jean-André lingered after his uncle made his bows.

"Miss Edith, if I might have one word with you."

He wanted to give further explanations, she supposed, or to defend his uncle or something. She didn't especially want or need to hear it, having decided Dashiell's verdict was just: the burglary was no one's fault but the thief's. But she nodded and, resuming her seat, gestured him toward an armchair.

He was looking less Napoleonic than usual, and she thought his uncharacteristic, hesitant air suited him better than when his bold dark eyes snapped at her, or when he tossed out those jeering little comments.

After one or two throat-clearings, he took a deep breath and plunged in. "Miss Edith, you must long have been aware of my feelings."

She stirred uneasily. This did not sound like the beginnings of an uncle's defense.

"You must have guessed. I came always to your lessons, though there was no need for my presence."

"I thought you came to keep Mr. Olivier company and to transact business," she uttered.

"Yes, and to see you."

Edith drew a sharp breath. Oh, dear—she didn't know how this was happening, but she knew she didn't want it to happen. But how to stop him?

"Since I have become my uncle's business manager, we have built steady sources of income—"

"The burglary must have hit you very hard," Edith interrupted. She glanced around the room, as if hoping to find someone who would rescue her.

"It—was a blow," Jean-André answered shortly. "But not one that cannot be overcome. There will be other auctions. I am sorry, again, for the loss of your works—"

"Yes, yes," she broke in again, her hands clutching each other in her lap. "Please—we have already discussed that and we must put it behind us."

"What I mean to say, Miss Edith, is that I am a good business manager and would be a good steward of your career as well."

Startled, she stared at him. Was this not, then, a marriage proposal? Thank heavens she had not committed herself in speech, or her assumption would have been mortifying!

But no sooner did she congratulate herself on her escape than Jean-André slid from his chair to one knee and reached for her hand. "Miss Edith—"

"What are you doing?" she cried, tugging to be released. Unlike Lionel in the same situation, Jean-André hung on.

"Miss Edith, please calm yourself. I want only to tell you that you are a beautiful young lady and an excellent painter, and I would be honored if you would become my wife."

"Oh!" With an almighty rip, she got her hand free and shot to her feet. "Mr. Olivier, I am afraid—I'm afraid I must stop you there. I have no thoughts of marriage at the present time. You do me a very great honor, but I'm afraid it is impossible." She had the dreadful feeling she was stringing together all manner of lines that ladies used in books. How horrible proposals were!

Slowly he rose, his dark eyes fixed on her. "I have been too sudden."

"That's not it. I am sorry to be so blunt. And I do thank you. But it is impossible."

"Because you do not love me."

"No. I mean, yes, that's it: I'm afraid I don't."

"You do not need to answer me right away. You can send word when you have had more time to think."

Her brows drew together, and she was about to snap, *What makes you think I don't know my own mind?* But the memory of her other proposal flashed before her and closed her lips on the words. She hadn't known her own mind when Lionel asked, and he had said much the same thing. Oh, if only she had accepted his offer to take more time on that occasion!

But this was different. Entirely so. She knew absolutely that she did not love Jean-André and could never love him, precisely because she had learned her own mind.

"Thank you," she said, her voice firm. "I will not require more time."

"You are very young, Miss Edith."

"My youth has nothing to do with this, in any event."

"You are very young," he repeated, drawing a step nearer, "but soon the time will come to let go of childish loves."

"What?" she nearly shrilled.

"Come now." He lay a hand on her upper arm, which she hastily shrugged off. "Come now. There is no need for pretense. I speak of your beloved brother-cousin whom you painted."

"That—he—none of that is any of your business and nothing to do with this!"

A lazy grin lifted one side of his mouth. "As they say on the stage, your secret is safe with me. If you like, I will not mention him again. But there is more to love, Miss Edith, than what you may feel for that boy." And then, before she knew what he was about, Jean-André took her by the shoulders and planted his mouth on hers.

For the second time in her life, Edith Hapgood found herself momentarily frozen by the shock of a kiss. But this time it was not deliciousness that thawed her—it was rage. With an impressive roar from so small a frame, she managed to raise her foot and stomp on his instep. She was neither a big nor a powerful girl, but her shoe did have a blocky wooden heel that made up for these deficiencies, and Jean-André spun and hopped apart with a roar of his own.

Abandoning manners, Edith fled, slamming the drawing room door behind her. Let him find his own way out, the rogue, and take his unwelcome advances with him!

But hours later, when she had calmed down somewhat, she realized that at least his unwelcome advances succeeded in banishing any guilt she felt for ending her lessons with his uncle.

Yes indeed.

She was fleeing Bath and shaking the dust of the place off her feet.

Chapter Seventeen

...From his Eyes the fleeting Fair Retir'd like subtile Smoke dissolv'd in Air.
—Dryden, Translation of Virgil's *Works* (1697)

As Hilary term of 1814 drew to a close, Lionel had no intention of returning to Somerset for the brief vacation before Trinity term. He had not seen Edith since the previous summer—the fateful summer—and congratulated himself that he was making progress in forgetting her. Nevertheless, it paid to be cautious, despite missing his horse and his rides with the squire and the fresh, open air of the country. He therefore wrote one of his vanishingly rare letters home to announce that they had better not expect him, for he thought of going into Kent with the Clinkett brothers.

Two developments changed his mind.

The first was that his stepmother wrote him back, expressing her great regret that they would not see him and (far more to the point), mentioning that his cousin Edith had "lately proceeded from Bath to Buckinghamshire for a stay of indefinite length." This news, combined with Lionel's own announced absence, left both Hetty and the squire "rather down in the mouth," they having hoped to see both Edith and Lionel home, after so many months away.

If Edith were guaranteed not to be at Bramleigh, Lionel began to think he might risk returning there. There would be no dark curls and bright eyes and soft voice and achingly tender mouth to torment him.

But it was the second development which made up his mind. He received another letter, this one from his aunt Lavinia. It seemed the Sidneys were planning a visit to Leamington Priors, accompanied by a friend of Caroline's, in order to see its new pump room and baths. As their journey would take them through Oxford, they proposed stopping to see him between terms. Instantly, Lionel took up his pen to reply.

"This must be something of an epistolary record for you," mused Clinker, as his chamber-fellow sanded and folded his second letter of the morning. "Both in number and in speed written."

"My hand was forced," Lionel answered, tossing both letters on the floor and kicking his boot-shod legs upon the desk. "If I did not reply immediately to my aunt Lavinia, she threatened to descend upon me over the vac, with Caroline and a friend in tow. I had to say, alas, I would not be here."

Clinker lay on his bed, a textbook open upon the crown of his head like a gable on a roof. "I rather liked your cousin Caroline. Dashing girl."

"Caroline isn't the problem, particularly. It's my aunt. She is not a favorite."

His friend went on as if he hadn't heard him. "And you know my weakness for yellow hair. *Our* weakness, I should say. Clunker was pretty taken with her, too. I think she inspired three perfectly horrible sonnets."

"Well, Clink, if Caroline Sidney were mine to give, I would bestow her upon you. Freely. As long as your intentions were honorable, of course, she being my cousin. Or I would bestow her upon the both of you, rather, and let you fight it out."

"Thank you, Lion. Exceedingly generous. But I believe she has already given you the preference." He sat up, letting the textbook slide off. "Some people like to marry their cousins. Keeps all that nice blood and nice money and nice property in one place. I don't see why you should kick against the goads."

"Lord, aren't you the one who is always hounding me to look at this girl or that girl, and now you tell me to marry Caroline?" There was a rueful twist to Lionel's smile as he proceeded to echo Edith's words: "Clink, I haven't thought of marriage, and I don't intend to think of it anytime soon." It was nearly the truth. Apart from his unsuccessful attempt to win Edith, he had no thoughts of marriage at all.

Clinker shrugged. "So be it. Does this mean you're coming to Kent with Clunker and me?"

"Afraid not. I think I'll go home after all. But maybe Kent in the long vac."

"I notice you have never yet invited us to Somerset. You must be hiding all manner of scandals and embarrassing relations there."

"No more than the usual," was Lionel's light reply. "One day I will invite you, but there's no space at present. My family are in lodgings."

"That's right," Clinker nodded, "hovering about, waiting to inherit."

Lionel's boots returned to the floor with a thump as he whirled to glare at his chamber-fellow. "If it were up to me, the squire might live forever. We don't need his money, and he allows me full run of the place. As for my father—what would he do with an estate? He's a banker."

Holding up his hands in surrender, Clinker gave a low whistle. "I've put my foot in it now! Come, Lion. Don't be so fearfully touchy. I repent of my distasteful remark in sackcloth and ashes."

Lionel pulled a face, already regretting his flash of temper. "Forget it, Clinker. I guess I am touchy."

"Say no more of the matter. Now what do you say we roust up Clunker and Bailey and have a hand of cards?"

A fortnight later, on a drizzly spring day, Lionel on Mannerly rode along the top of the slope that curved downward to Bramleigh. Spying the squire in the distance, he removed his hat to wave it and saw a hand raised in return. He clicked his tongue to his horse and set off to intercept him.

His first time home in months had been alternately restorative and painful. No more than he expected. Restorative, in the all the ways anticipated: long rides, country air, time with his family and the boys at the vicarage. And painful, for the things that reminded him of Edith—which was to say, nearly everything. It could hardly be otherwise, when he had lived there for years and seen her several times a week, throughout. He was safe from her memory neither within nor out of doors, though when he was on horseback he could at least ride out of the range in which she had habitually been found, perched on her camp stool sketching or standing at her easel. But when on these extended rides, he was frequently accompanied by his father or the squire. While Hugh Hapgood was not wont to mention Edith often, the same could not be said for Richard Hapgood, her father.

Lionel could never remember the squire talking so much of his daughters. He had always preferred topics like sport and dogs and weather and farming and rents and the general worthlessness of his brothers-in-law, but now, with all his girls flown, they seemed more on his mind than in times past.

"Edie sent me a picture the other day. The first one in a long time. Of Augusta and Charlotte. My two grand-daughters, you know."

"Yes, sir."

"Guess that would make them your third cousins, once re-moved."

"Oh?"

"I haven't seen them yet, but soon, I suppose. They're old enough to travel now. Babies look pretty much all alike to me: bald and red and squalling. Not Edith, mind you. She was a pretty baby. Dark hair and eyes and quiet as a mouse."

Lionel said nothing at all to this and kept his eyes trained on something in the distance while he cast about for a way to change the subject. Nothing came to mind.

"My only one left unmarried," sighed the squire after a few minutes. "Once I thought I'd have the devil's own time getting any of them off my hands. No dowries to speak of, no seasons in London for them, no gadding about with the gentry here, no help from their mother. And only see what has happened. The first three of them—snatched up!"

"They're all—pretty enough," Lionel said, after he swallowed some obstruction in his throat.

"Aye, pretty enough," the squire agreed, with a humorless laugh. "That's what ensnared me, after all. A pretty face. Much good it did me. Now look that way, boy—see where the trees lean and seem to prop each other up? That's where I want to do some draining..."

But the topic was taken up yet again the following day, as they rode in quite another direction: "Edie did a sketch of this perspective once. Did you ever see it?"

"No, I don't think so."

"She doesn't love landscapes or nature particularly, not like Alice, but it was a nice little thing. I will show it to you, if I remember."

"Mm."

"What ails you, my boy? Seems you haven't two words to say for yourself, and you always used to be rattling away. I suppose now that you've seen something of the world, you're bored talking about things like your little cousin."

"No! No—not at all." Lionel took a firmer grip on Mannerly's reins. "How—how is she—Edith? Is she enjoying her stay? Why, she's the one seeing the world."

The squire grimaced. "That she is. Mind you, I wanted her to go to Bath. See art. Get some lessons. I wanted it for her because I knew she wanted it but would never ask. And I suppose I understand her wanting to see her new nieces and little Frederick. But in my opinion, it's time she came home! *If* she comes home. What if that piffle-headed son-in-law of mine—Elfie's husband, you know—what if he introduces her to some other piffle-headed County Bucks neighbor, and the next thing I know she's married? Then she'll never come back!"

Lionel almost lost his seat and had to fumble for the pommel to steady himself. "What? Has Elfie or Alice or—or Edie said as much? That she is meeting young men?"

His companion made a scoffing sound. "Who can say? Am I not always the last to know? None of my girls told me a thing until that very thing was a *done* thing! Well, I suppose Margaret's Dashiell did ask my permission, but not until the very morning he proposed to her. No, no, I would not be surprised if the first I hear of Edie getting married is that the wedding came off nicely, thank you very much, and the groom looks forward to making my acquaintance!"

Lionel was finding it difficult to catch his breath, and Mannerly put her ears back, feeling his distress. With an effort, he managed to speak, his voice sounding strained and strange to his own ears.

"Surely not, sir. She's—too young to get married and has—has never shown much interest in it."

"What would you know? We neither of us have seen her in months and months. The girl is seventeen now, the same age Alice was, or thereabouts, when she married Joseph." He shook his head grimly.

But Lionel was taking hold of himself. *No*, if Edith were being courted by a County Bucks buck, Lionel would know, because Edith would have told Hetty, and Hetty would never have been able to keep that to herself. Though a disturbing comment of his sister's chose that moment to flit through his head: "Edie has become nearly as poor a correspondent as you, Lionel. She writes, but somehow says almost nothing, which is almost as bad as not writing at all! In Bath it was 'painting this' and 'painting that,' and at Stone Halt it's 'the babies this' and 'the babies that.'"

Would Edith have told Hetty? What if, even at that very moment, some stupid person Lionel didn't even know existed had noticed what a charming little beauty Frederick Tierney's sister-in-law was, and was laying plans to win her? What could be done about it? Could anything be done about it?

Lionel would have been much, much relieved if he had only known Edith was not, in fact, surrounded by swains in Buckinghamshire. Instead, she was just then riding in the Tierney family coach along the Aylesbury, Thame, Oxford & Shillingford turnpike with her brother-in-law Frederick, her sister Elfie, and their two children. But, as Lionel was not gifted with omniscience, he could not know this, and his anxiety was acute. Even the squire's detailed digression into the time he participated in a hunt some small distance from where his two older daughters now lived did not distract Lionel. It was on the tip of his tongue to make a full confession to the man, and if he had still been a stripling of fifteen, he probably would have done it.

But he was older now, for better or worse, and he forced himself to ask questions about the hunting anecdote until the urge passed. At the end of the ride, his secret remained his own.

The squire was not an inquisitive man, however. So Lionel's more impressive achievement was keeping Hetty in ignorance. His sister had first run into Lionel's wall of reticence during the Oxford visit, and her puzzlement was soon succeeded by regret. If Lionel showed no interest in Edith's doings, exciting as they were, it was because he was growing away from them. She said as much to her stepmother when they returned to Somerset, and Rosemary answered simply, "It is only natural, that a young man his age finds new interests and attachments."

"But he always liked Edith, Mama! And now, whenever I mention her, he makes a face or talks of something else, as if he couldn't be bothered."

Rosemary patted her stepdaughter's hand. "I think we had better let him be, at present. It's too much to ask, perhaps, that he be interested in his young cousin's development as an artist."

Hetty huffed. "I suppose because he's more occupied with his *own* development as the Great Lionel Hapgood. He never seemed to tire of *that* topic, when Cousin Caroline asked him question after question after question and made much of him. Well! It would serve him right if, after her painting lessons with Mr. Whatshisname in Bath, Edith were to become quite famous and too important to take any notice of Lionel, either!"

After the Oxford visit, Hetty hardly mentioned Edith at all, when Lionel came home. If he wanted to know the least little thing about what his cousin was doing, she decided, he would have to take the trouble to ask! But Lionel, of course, did not ask. Nor did his step-mother allude to her, and Lionel thought he would have been glad to have Rosemary speak of Edith to him, on balance. To his stepmother he might have confessed his disastrous proposal (she knowing so much already), but perhaps not, given that he had once promised her he would wait to speak.

For all these reasons, when Lionel once more climbed into the Taunton coach, bound for points east, he was not much wiser about his cousin's activities than when he came and had only the cold comfort of not having given way to his curiosity.

And it was merely curiosity, he assured himself. Yes, there had been danger of backsliding when the squire hypothesized suitors for Edith, but Lionel had overcome this. He was most definitely making progress toward complete and utter heart-wholeness. By the time he did see her again, possibly in June or July, he would be able to treat her with the same cousinly tolerance he showed Caroline. She would be to him again what he had always been to her: a well-liked, jolly, pseudo-sibling.

At Reading, Lionel climbed down and had ale and a chop at the inn. There was time enough before the Oxford coach departed to stretch his legs, and he chose to walk as far as the Abbey ruins. On this dank and foggy day he was the sole visitor, but he valiantly whistled "Sumer is icumen in" and tried to remember what he could of John of Gaunt, which was little enough.

With a shiver he turned back toward the inn, promising himself a hot cup of tea, and he arrived in the inn yard just as a private coach was departing, the liveried footman springing to the board behind, one hand reaching to tighten the strap securing the baggage.

The baggage.

Between two trunks, Lionel spied scarlet ribbons, trailing from a flat leathern portfolio, and his heart began to hammer. *He knew that portfolio!*

Before he thought, he was moving, beginning to run, and it was nearly his last action in life because he did not pause to look about him. The wagon that trundled across his path clipped his shoulder and sent him spinning. By the time he recovered and scrambled around it, the coach was in traffic, beginning the descent of Castle Hill along the Bath Road.

But he had managed one glimpse of the vehicle's interior, and that one glimpse had been enough. As if she had been illuminated by a dozen candles, he had seen her.

Edith.

Smiling—glowing—her bonnet off and a little boy who must have been her nephew Frederick climbing on her lap and pulling on one of her curls.

Lionel supposed the rest of the Frederick Tierney family accompanied them—his glance had been so brief there was neither time nor inclination to observe other details, other people. Only her.

"Oh, *hell*," muttered Lionel, his shoulders sagging. He became aware of a throbbing in one of them from its collision with the wagon. He turned and slowly retraced his steps to the inn, his desire for tea forgotten.

"*Hellfire and damnation.*" He wasn't normally given to swearing, but the circumstances seemed to warrant it.

For it appeared heart-wholeness was not as within reach as he thought. All his vaunted progress apparently depended on never seeing the girl again in his life.

Because seeing her—even for an instant—well—

Seeing her made him feel he was right back where he started.

PART TWO
1814

CHAPTER EIGHTEEN

And but one word with one of us? couple it with something; make it a word and a blow.
—Shakespeare, *Romeo and Juliet*, III.i.1537 (c.1595)

"Well, and what did you think of the painting?" asked Clinker. He sat with his brother and Lionel in a noisy public house, their meals before them. He and Clinker had thoroughly discussed the Tattersall offerings and how the horses for sale compared with the horses the young men owned at home, but Lionel had not contributed much. "Or did you not make it so far as the exhibition?"

"Oh, we saw it all right." Clinker swallowed a gristly bite of his roast. "And Lionel agreed it was himself to the life. Didn't you, Lion?"

"I mean to purchase the painting, at any rate," said Lionel. "If it's within our means."

Clinker groaned at this reminder of his debt of honor. "But I don't *want* a portrait of you, Lion! No offense meant, but I can see you any time I please at Magdalen, nine months of the year." Raising his empty beer-glass, he tried to attract the barmaid's attention.

"What if it isn't within your means?" asked Clunker. "I suppose I have a few pounds to contribute to the cause."

"If we can't afford it, I will steal it," declared Lionel.

"Oh, Lord!" cried Clinker. "That'll drive the nail home. Old Routh will send you down for sure, when you're clapped up in the Old Bailey. Our Lion, becoming a thief!"

"It won't matter if he's sent down then," his brother pointed out, "for I believe the punishment for thievery is transportation."

"Have you lost your mind, Lionel? Botany Bay—over a painting? Or are you having a laugh?"

Lionel sawed a hunk off his steak, speared it with the point of his knife, and popped it in his mouth. "I am in earnest. I will have that painting."

"But *why*?" demanded his chamber-fellow. When Lionel only continued to eat, Clinker set his beer-glass down with a thud. "Is this some kind of Narcissus thing? I barely passed my *Literae Humaniores* collections, but I remember he's the chap who fell in love with himself. Have you fallen in love with yourself, Lion?"

Lionel refused to dignify this with a response. He closed his eyes briefly, thinking. The barmaid refilled their glasses, lingering to see if the handsome auburn-haired young gentleman would look at her, and he did, but she could tell his thoughts were elsewhere. With a sniff, she stalked away.

"Look, both of you," he began. "You remember that my—my cousin Edith is an artist?"

"The one that did the picture of you and Mannerly that everyone made fun of when we were freshmen?"

"Yes. She."

"So what?"

"So—this is her...style."

Clunker, who had been tilting back on his chair, returned all four legs to the floor with a thunk. "You mean to say you think the young gentleman in the portrait doesn't just look like you, he *is* you?"

Thinking again of every secret that painting revealed to the world, Lionel hesitated. Then he gave a curt nod.

"But the catalogue said the artist was an A. J. Morris," Clunker pursued.

"I think A. J. Morris is an assumed name. Or else A. J. Morris is someone who submitted the painting to the Royal Academy on her behalf. She is rather shy about such things."

"If it's hers, then she's exceedingly good!" exclaimed Clunker.

"Well, why not just ask her if it is hers?" Clinker suggested practically. "There's no need to go tearing about, trying to buy the thing from your own cousin, and certainly no need to get shipped to New South Wales for attempting to steal it."

Lionel's face darkened. "We've—er—had a bit of a falling out, Edith and I. I don't care to talk about that now. Suffice to say, I must do this without consulting her. I mean to go to Jermyn Street tomorrow and find this A. J. Morris. At the very least I want an explanation of how this came about."

Hammering a fist on the board, Clinker bellowed, "A quest! We will accompany you, Lion."

Before the latter could protest, Clunker interposed. "We have to, Lionel. Supposing this A. J. Morris is not your cousin but some other person? You cannot march up to him, the very portrait come to life! No. We had better go with you, and you might want to adopt some sort of disguise."

The following afternoon found three gentlemen turning into Jermyn Street, two of them weedy and bearing a strong resemblance to each other—all eyes and long limbs and Adam's apples—and the third bespectacled, with hair a muddled shade of auburn and soot black.

63 Jermyn Street was a modest building set among more elegant ones. On the ground floor was a hosier and glover, and it was into this shop the young men repaired. Eagerly the shop boy came forward, only to be disappointed when one of the weedy gentlemen replied to him with, "Thank you, we are not seeking any hose or gloves today. We have come to see the artist A. J. Morris, if you could direct us."

The shop boy sighed. "He lodges above the shop. He's in great demand, that one."

"Ah. It is a *he*, then?" Clunker observed.

"Of course he's a he," frowned the boy. "Who should I say is calling if he's receiving today?"

"Mr. James Clinkett, Mr. Edward Clinkett and Mr. Lawrence Hillyard, to inquire after his painting at the Exhibition."

They waited as the boy slipped out and thundered up the staircase, Clinker idly examining the glove display. Lionel was too wrought up to notice his surroundings, every nerve straining for the appearance of A. J. Morris and the solution to the mystery.

"You're to come up," hollered the boy, as he thundered back down, re-entering the shop with a bound over the threshold.

Lionel's pulse began to race and perspiration to break out as he removed his hat and followed his friends up the cramped stairway. He must master himself, or the sweat would make his spectacles slide down his nose, and who knew what its effect might be on the soot with which Clunker had generously powdered his hair.

The door stood open to a small parlor sparsely furnished, with a window overlooking Jermyn Street and another door (now shut) leading to the rest of the suite. The walls were papered and wainscoted in gold stripes against a dark green background, and Clunker thought his eyes might begin to water, so at variance were the walls with the several canvases standing on easels or leaning against them. And such canvases! An array of heroes and messiahs and classical figures, standing amidst ruins or bestriding stallions or blessing crowds or stabbing or poisoning themselves or each other.

Amidst this crowd of painted demigods stood, presumably, Mr. A. J. Morris, a handsome, well-built young man with thick dark hair, dark eyes, and a bold air.

"Good afternoon," said Clunker, the designated spokesman. "Thank you for seeing us. I am Mr. Edward Clinkett, this is my brother Mr. James Clinkett, and our friend Mr. Lawrence Hillyard."

"A. J. Morris," replied the other, as they made their bows.

"Ah, so then, you *are* A. J. Morris?" fumbled Clunker. "Not, that is, a—er—a representative of A. J. Morris? Or—uh—delegated by an A. J. Morris?"

"As you see."

"Oh! Well, isn't that something. Because, you know, Mr. Morris, when one finds only initials in an exhibition catalogue, one can't be quite sure what to expect: man, woman, giraffe, banana—"

"A. J. Morris," said A. J. Morris in a chilly tone. "Alexander John Morris. Now, to what do I owe the pleasure?"

Clunker would have liked to say, "To your magnificent works, of course!" but somehow the words stuck in his throat, surrounded as he was by so many paintings completely unlike the one he admired. He darted a look at Lionel, who seemed to be clenching both his jaw and his fists. All right, then. They had ruled out the possibility of A. J. Morris being a pseudonym for his cousin Edith, so Clunker's next task was to ferret out if Mr. Morris had submitted the portrait on that young lady's behalf.

He gave a discreet little cough and murmured, "I was so fortunate to see your submission at Somerset House—the *Portrait of a young gentleman*, and I thought, I must meet that A. J. Morris and tell him or her how I admire it!"

Mr. Morris regarded Clunker, likely to determine if this second reference to his ambiguous initials was another hit at him. Dismissing this, he shrugged and bowed in acknowledgement. "I thank you. Its acceptance has been a great honor. Please—I invite you to look around at some of my other pieces."

Dutifully, the three young men made a show of inspecting the informal gallery. Clinker was suppressing a grin (though he rather liked the stabbed Marat, with a strapping Charlotte Corday hulking over him), Clunker appeared to be fighting indigestion, and Lionel in his impatience could hardly pretend interest. He nudged Clunker: *Get on with it*.

"Astounding, sir," piped Clunker. "Your—uh—success seems assured. It so happens, I myself would like to add one of your works to my collection."

Mr. Morris grimaced in that day's closest approximation of a smile. "Ah, I am flattered. Honored. May I ask which one you are interested in?"

"To be sure: the very one that brought me here. *Portrait of a young gentleman*. What can you tell me about it? Uh...I mean, as to the subject and the setting? It is marvelous—the lifelikeness, the colors, the—er—the charms—ahem!—of your sitter."

"It is a recent work. You observe that my predilection to this point has been to paint in a grander vein. This was an informal portrait and setting."

"I do observe that, sir." Clunker steeled himself, hoping his next remark wouldn't earn him a punch in the face. "It is not only that the subject matter and setting are a new direction for you as an artist, but the style of the paintings I see here is so very, very different from the style of the portrait in the exhibit. In *Portrait of a young gentle-*

man, there is a certain lightness. Liveliness. Dare I say, humor? And here—" He gestured feebly around him. "One might almost—one might almost suppose they were done by an entirely different hand."

There was neither lightness, liveliness nor humor in Mr. Morris' face, that was plain. His mouth worked for a moment. He seemed to consider one response, only to discard it. Then he bit out, "Thank you. But I do assure you, they were all done by my hand. These *and* the Exhibition portrait."

"It's a lie!" blurted Lionel.

Mr. Morris whirled on him. "I—beg—your—pardon?"

"He said, 'It's alive!'" declared Clinker, flinging himself in front of his friend and stabbing a finger toward the window.

"What is alive?" hissed Morris.

"That skylark," said Clinker.

"That goldfinch," said Clunker.

The brothers looked at each other, and Clinker added, "That—bird—which just flew away. Its wing was—er—"

But Lionel pushed his friends aside, shaking his head at them, to confront the supposed artist. "I said, Mr. Morris, that I do not believe you. I do not believe you were the painter of *Portrait of a young gentleman.*"

"How dare you? How dare you say such a thing?" Morris paled, even as Lionel reddened.

"Just tell me," Lionel went on. "Have you submitted this painting to the Academy on someone else's behalf? If—this other person—authorized it, I will not challenge you further."

For a long, long minute the men measured each other, Morris calculating.

"I do not owe you a reply," the artist said slowly. "But I will tell you it is my painting and mine alone. I cannot think what basis you have for these insinuations. And now I must ask you to leave. You have no right to invade my home and question me, nor to deliver these wild accusations."

Lionel stood his ground. "I do have a right to ask and a right to know," he replied. With deliberation, he set his hat down on a nearby chair. Reaching up, he removed his spectacles and set them alongside. Never taking his eyes off Morris, he took both hands and drew them through his hair, holding his palms up afterward to show the smudges of soot. Then he gave a great shake, sheepdog-like, sending additional ash flying.

"Who—who do you think you are?" demanded Morris, enraged, sweeping soot off his sleeve.

"No, Mr. Morris," rejoined Lionel, "the question is, who do *you* think I am?"

Both his companions inhaled sharply, but he held them still with an outstretched hand.

In the silence that fell, the room was so quiet they could hear a vehicle trundling down Jermyn Street and the jingle of the shop-door bell below.

Clunker thought Morris looked like a fish on land, gulping spasmodically. The aspiring poet's fingers flexed, and he resisted the urge to pull out his notebook. "Fish gasp," he muttered under his breath.

"With fish-like gasp he was flecked with ash. With fish-like gulp, he gasped, '*Mea culpa.*'"

"I am Lionel Hapgood of Somerset," Lionel said at last. "At home I have a cousin who is an artist and painter of portraits. Last summer—a year ago—that cousin sketched me on a stile, just as the young gentleman is, in the portrait hanging at the summer exhibition. I must ask you again, Mr. Morris: were you the painter of that portrait, or was it my cousin?"

"I have already answered that question."

"Then how came you by that exact subject and attitude and setting?"

Morris' lip curled. "If you are so certain I am a fraud, my self-righteous young man, why do you not simply ask your cousin?"

Lionel said nothing. His jaw tightened so hard it appeared cemented shut, and a portion of his fury was directed at himself, for he hated to admit Morris' question was valid. If he, Lionel, had not been such a fool the previous summer—such an impulsive, blundering fool, burning with impatience—he would have held his tongue with Edith! And had he done so, they would not now be estranged, and Lionel would have no need of asking this infuriating stranger these obvious questions. He would already have known what became of the sketch she made of him and how it came to be painted. He would already have known whether she decided to submit it to the Royal Academy and under what auspices. But as it was, he himself had erected the barrier of silence between them. And then, cutting off his nose to revenge his face, his own pride had forbidden him asking his family for news of her.

"I can only assume," Morris continued in that supercilious voice, "that you are not in a position to ask your cousin these things. Which means you have no grounds for your conclusions. While you are a very agreeable-looking young man, Mr. *Hapgood,* I have seen many faces such as yours and many stiles in the country to sit upon, and I suspect I will see still more. It is a frequent occurrence that spectators will trace imagined resemblances between works of art and people they know. For this reason, I will pass over what was said here, but I'm afraid I must ask you again to leave."

Smarting under this treatment, Lionel's chest was heaving, and his friends each took a step nearer, in the event they might have to restrain him.

"I will go now," said Lionel. He picked up his hat and spectacles, though he did not bother to put the glasses on again. "But this is not the end of the matter."

Morris waved a lazy hand. "It is, as far as I am concerned." He turned to Clunker again. "I presume, Mr. Clinkett, that you no longer wish to purchase the painting, since your companion here so doubts its provenance?"

"Er—" He cast Lionel a questioning look and saw his infinitesimal nod. "Uh—well, even if the portrait isn't actually of Mr. Hillyard—that is, Hapgood—the remarkable likeness still pleases me. What are you asking for it, if I may be so bold to ask?"

"I'm afraid that isn't how it works, Mr. Clinkett," said Morris coolly. "You are not the only one interested in purchasing the piece. What were you inclined to offer?"

Clunker did some hasty arithmetic, but his brother knew Edward had no talent for bargaining, so he interceded. "What would you say to fifty pounds, Mr. Morris?"

"Hmm. I'm afraid I would have to refuse. I have been offered more for it."

"Seventy-five, then."

"Again, my regrets."

Clunker thought of his own funds and blurted, "A hundred pounds!" His brother glared at him, attempting through wordless communication to say, *We haven't got a hundred pounds in ready money, even if we all pooled our resources together, you numbskull!*

Morris appeared to consider. "Ah—a hundred pounds. Why, that's a respectable amount. How soon would you be able to pay that over? I intended the portrait to hang until the end of the exhibit, but I could draw up a bill of sale."

The three young men came swiftly together, muttering and murmuring, Lionel making all sorts of vows and promises *sotto voce*. After a minute of this, they broke apart, all of them rather white about the gills.

"We could pay you half by this afternoon," announced Clunker faintly. "And the other half perhaps within the week." They had no experience with moneylenders, and there would surely be hell to pay with the Clinkett *paterfamilias*, but never let it be said the Clinketts did not stand by their friends.

"Ah!" Morris put his fingers to his forehead as if a thought had just struck him. "Wait a moment, young gentlemen. It seems I must refuse your generous proposal after all. I have just now recalled another collector who spoke with me, who would also like to purchase the portrait."

"Indeed?" snapped Clinker, losing patience. "And what did this collector you just happened to recall propose to pay?"

Morris put his hands together, taking a deep, satisfied breath. "You will not credit me when I tell you," he chuckled, "but the man offered one *thousand* pounds."

"You lie!" roared Lionel for the second time, and on this occasion, there was no feigning he had said something else, for he simultaneously rushed at Morris, flinging aside his hat and butting him in the midriff with his still-sooty head.

His arms grappled the man to the carpet before anyone could react, and there followed a whirlwind of grunts and fists and kicks and bellows and curses as attacker and attacked rolled about, each struggling for the upper hand.

"Lionel! Lionel!" yelled Clinker and Clunker, as they scrambled to avoid the wheeling fists and boots.

Morris was older and more muscular, but Lionel was taller and had longer arms. They were equally angry, however, and ended up being well matched.

"Tell—the—truth—you—blackguard!" commanded Lionel, as well as he could while being tumbled about and socked in the face.

They crashed against furniture, knocked down two of the easels, and somebody's boot kicked a hole through a Saint Sebastian stuck full of arrows. By this point Clinker and Clunker were leaping up and down, crying, "At him! Get him, Lion! You show him!"

In all the tumult, no one heard the shop boy thundering once more up the staircase, but when he threw open the door, Morris howled through a swelling lip, "Con—constable! Call—the—constable! *Now!*"

Speechless with amazement and alarm, the boy gawped at the brawl, only recovering himself when Morris and Lionel hurtled against the worktable, sending pots of paint, brushes and other tools of the trade raining down upon them. Then the boy spun on his heel and fled.

For Lionel, all was a cyclone of flying limbs and surging pulse. He was aware of a ceaseless flood of sound coming from him—snarls, groans, curses, and breaths forcibly expelled when his enemy's fist or knee or foot connected with him. Blood flowed freely into one eye, and he had drawn blood himself. Sweat poured. He felt his strength waning, but Morris was weakening too. He must make...one...last...effort—

With one terrific roar worthy of his Magdalen sobriquet, Lionel heaved Morris off him and rolled atop, pinning him to the floor with a knee on his right arm and a palm and widespread fingers holding his head down.

"His other arm!" warned Clinker, even as Clunker yelled, "The left! The left! Watch for it, Lion!"

And then there was a sharp, stabbing, piercing pain in his side that made everything go red and then white and then blank.

Chapter Nineteen

Ill News is wing'd with Fate, and flies apace.
—Dryden, *Threnodia Augustalis*, ii. 3 (1685)

Wellington Sidney entered the modest confines of his club, signaling the waiter for coffee and a paper and retreating to his favorite armchair. Though he found himself in town several times a year, he was not wont to visit the place often, and his wife Lavinia had more than once asked why he considered it necessary to retain a subscription. But on this particular stay, Wellington had been found at the club for some portion of nearly every day, the simple explanation being that, on this trip, Lavinia and his daughter Caroline accompanied him to London. Here in this men's retreat, he found shelter from all manner of troubling things: demands, complaints, idle chatter, summaries of shopping completed or shopping planned. He did not seek male conversation per se, but rather a surcease of conversation in all its forms.

"The *Times*, sir," droned the waiter, depositing it and a cup of coffee on his table.

Nodding his thanks, he gave a sigh of pleasure and unfolded the paper. It was full of the Allied sovereigns' visit (the hubbub of which made the capital even noisier and more crowded)—the races attended by them at Ascot, the honorary degrees bestowed at Oxford, the reception at the Royal Arsenal, the upcoming Guild-hall banquet. Lavinia and Caroline had clamored to witness the parades and illuminations, and he had yielded to them, grumbling inwardly when he noted the inflated prices charged by enterprising merchants, hoteliers, and restaurateurs.

An article or two on the American war followed, the *Times* in its triumphant mood calling for the upstart former colonists to be put down in the same manner as the French. And then, when he was on his second cup of coffee, he came to the local news, his eye falling on a headline: "Royal Academy Art Exhibition Artist Attacked." There followed a breathless paragraph on how Mr. A. J. Morris of 63 Jermyn Street, was ruthlessly assaulted in his own home, by youths posing as art dealers. "Mr. Morris was compelled to fight back with the only weapon at hand, his palette knife, with which he stabbed the main assailant, who then fainted away. The arrival of the con-stable ended the altercation, and the suspects, Mr. Lionel Hapgood, Mr. James Clinkett, and Mr. Edward Clinkett, were apprehended and taken to the watch-house, where they remain."

"Waiter! Waiter!" called Wellington Sidney, springing up and heedless of the coffee cup he knocked to the floor. "My hat. At once."

The next day, Hugh Hapgood received the following letter:

16 Devonshire Street
London

14 June 1814
Dear Brother,
You will see from the address that we are in town, and you must prepare yourself, for I have grave news.

I am certain you are aware that your son Lionel is also in London, having journeyed here with his friends Mr. James and Mr. Edward Clinkett at the beginning of their vacation. We ourselves did not know of our nephew's presence until Mr. Sidney chanced to read in the Times *of an incident between a Royal Academy artist and the young men. They are accused by a Mr. Morris of entering his home to commit assault! In the tussle that took place, damage was also done to some of his paintings and furnishings. Mr. Morris claims Lionel was the chief assailant and, in order to defend himself from your son, Morris was compelled to take up a palette knife and wound the boy. The paper reports that the victim intends to bring an action against all of them, and Lionel in particular!*

Upon learning this, Mr. Sidney went at once to the watch-house where the young men were being held and, by dint of vouching for Lionel and paying a fine, he was released to Mr. Sidney's custody. (The Clinketts remained behind because their father's arrival from Kent was imminent.) Lionel lost a great deal of blood and has not been altogether coherent. Mr. Sidney fears infection of the wound may set in. You may be assured we sent for a doctor, who has bled him twice and applied white lead plaster but the man says we must wait and see. Please tell us we may expect you immediately!

Yours very faithfully,
Lavinia Sidney

Before he finished his first reading or even half understood what the letter contained, Hugh was on his feet, rushing through the house and calling for his wife.

"What can it all mean?" wondered Rosemary, after she scanned the contents. "Lavinia leaves out as much as she puts in. Why on earth would Lionel have attacked this person? And was he so incoherent when Wellington found him that he could not give an explanation himself? Or the Clinkett boys could not? Lavinia does not say whether James or Edward was injured."

Hugh was tossing things in a trunk. "I wish I could tell you. But I promise I will write as soon as I know more."

"And why does she not say where he was injured? Is infection the sole threat, or—or must we fear both infection and some other horror?" Her husband had no answer to these questions any more than the others, and Rosemary was left to fret, even as she helped and handed him things. "Lionel is not the sort of young man who goes around beating people! If the Sidneys did not positively say here that Lionel was detained in the watch-house and released to their custody, I would not believe a word of it!"

"A word of what?"

The distraught parents startled, upon finding Hetty in the doorway, Edith peering around her shoulder.

"What has Lionel done?" demanded Hetty.

"Is he all right?" asked Edith faintly.

"What are you two doing here?" asked Hugh.

"Soppy sent us to copy some sheet music from Miss Benfield. Never mind that. Where are you going? What is happening? Tell me, Papa."

He sighed heavily and resumed packing his trunk. "Your brother has got into some sort of trouble in town, Harriet, and has sustained an injury. We hardly know more than that."

"But he will be all right?" repeated Edith.

"I will write as soon as I know more."

"I'm coming with you, Papa," Hetty announced. And then, when he appeared on the point of objecting, she did something she had not in years: she threw herself at him, clutching him around the waist. "Please—*please*—Papa! If I don't see him myself, I will think all manner of things until I go mad. *Please*. I won't trouble anyone and I will be so, so, so good for Aunt Lavinia, and I will look after you, Papa. Only please let me."

"You had better," murmured Rosemary. "It might cheer him to see her."

Hugh gave a short nod. "You must pack, then, Hetty. We leave on the afternoon coach."

And then, while Hetty was still shouting her thanks, Edith astonished them all (including herself) by bursting into tears.

"Edith!" cried Rosemary.

"I—I am sorry. I do apologize," sobbed Edith. "I don't mean to add to your distress at such a time. I—I only wish I might ride with you in the coach! I would not burden you in London—I could stay with my uncle Alwyn and his wife—only—only may I please come? I haven't seen Lionel in a year, and I know my father will be terribly upset, too! Oh, what will I do? Papa mustn't be upset with his heart condition, Mr. Lewis says—" She was crying against Hetty's shoulder now and trying, trying to master her feelings.

"Oh, please, Papa! May Edith also come with us?" Hetty pleaded, reaching again to grasp her father's forearm.

"Hetty, darling," remonstrated Rosemary. "Your father has much on his mind."

"I am sorry," gasped Edith again. She dashed away the tears still streaming down her cheeks, already horrified at her own outburst but unable to stop altogether. Of course she could not ask Hugh Hapgood to take her to London. She could hardly believe she had. After all, what was she to Lionel but a paltry third cousin? She ought to beg their pardon and leave them alone and go home to Bramleigh, but—oh—she could not!

"We can send Olcott to Bramleigh with a note," Hetty suggested, "to tell Dorcas to pack for you and have Hal bring it over. And you could write a line to your father—if you said only that Lionel had been arrested by the constable, and Papa goes to scold him and repay my uncle, that wouldn't excite Mr. Hapgood at all. He would just think it was good fun."

"Yes, yes, that's true," Edith panted. "How quick you are, Hetty."

Both girls turned at once to see what Hugh thought of the plan, and the poor harassed man only threw up his hands, just wanting to be on his way.

"Send who you will, where you will, with what you will," he declared. "I am going on the afternoon coach. And whoever is with me, is with me."

CHAPTER TWENTY

By and by thy bosom shall partake
The secrets of my heart.
—Shakespeare, *Julius Caesar,* II.i.931 (1599)

In gratitude for the Hugh Hapgoods allowing her to accompany them, Edith made every effort to be silent and invisible, forbearing to initiate conversation or to draw attention to herself, and only replying when one of them (usually Hetty) addressed her. They were all exhausted and drawn by their anxiety, in any event; nor was there any privacy to be had in the mail coach.

She remembered little of their arrival in the metropolis, apart from the riot and dust and noise of the Bolt in Tun in Fleet Street where they descended. To her very great relief, no sooner had Hugh handed her out than he said to her, "Edith, I hope you will not mind if we proceed directly to the Sidneys' in Devonshire Street. We will likely secure lodgings as near them as possible, and you are welcome to join us, or we can see you to your uncle's afterward."

Afraid to trust her voice, she nodded. If she might have her way, she would never go anywhere. She would sit in a chair beside Lionel's bed, praying, until he was out of danger. Oh, what if they were already too late?

Hugh secured a hackney coach and saw to the luggage, and then they were off, jolting and lurching through the London streets, all of them simultaneously fighting sleep and yearning to slice through the Gordian knot of town traffic.

At last they arrived. 16 Devonshire Street was a graceful, four-story townhome faced with cream stone, adorned by carvings and lacy railings bluish-green in their patina. An austere butler answered their summons, and Hugh impatiently pushed past, with a growl for the man to see to the bags and trunks.

Appearing at the top of the wide stairs leading up from the *piano nobile*, Lavinia Sidney clasped her hands together, crying, "Brother!"

Hugh took the steps two at a time, chased by Hetty and Edith. "How is he?"

"Feverish, brother, feverish. Mr. White has bled him for a third time and says he approaches a crisis. One of us sits with him constantly. Come." Only when Edith reached the top of the stairs did Lavinia notice her. "Why—you're not Rosie," she accused.

"This is my cousin Richard's youngest daughter, Miss Edith Hapgood," rumbled Hugh impatiently. "Edith, Mrs. Sidney. Lavinia—I entreat you—take us to him."

Lavinia raised inquiring brows but obeyed, marching ahead of them along the passage.

Edith found herself in a stifling chamber, dim from drawn curtains of scarlet velvet. Several chairs lined the outer wall, with people she did not know disposed in them, but she had no eyes for them at first. Her gaze went immediately to the narrow bed in the center of the room, upon which Lionel lay, only a sheet across him in his nightshirt and his auburn hair loose across the pillow. His eyes were shut and she could see perspiration on his brow, even in the gloom. Through his parted, dry lips came shallow breathing. Beside the bed stood the doctor, a bald and burly man with a flourishing mustache. He held a finger to the pulse at Lionel's wrist, a frown upon his lined face.

"Mr. White, this is the young man's father Mr. Hapgood," murmured Lavinia.

The doctor nodded, still counting, presumably, but presently he looked over and made his bow.

"I am afraid, sir, that the instrument with which your son was wounded was none too clean," Mr. White said in a surprisingly gentle voice. "There is infection, which his body tries to fight with fever. I have bled him—multiple times over the past two days—and we attempt to keep him cool and calm. I think things will soon come to a crisis."

"Are you—are you hopeful?" Hugh asked, having to clear his throat.

"He is young and otherwise healthy, but I would hesitate to offer any guarantees. He has been sleeping, which is good, but when he is conscious, he is not coherent. I would feel better if he were to take a little broth."

"We have tried, Brother," Lavinia spoke up, a defensive note discernible. "But he mutters and tosses and knocks away the spoon."

"I will try again," said Hugh, "when he is next awake."

"And I can try too," Hetty insisted. "Please, Papa."

"You must all be very weary with the journey," Hugh addressed the girls. "I will sit with him now. Alone." Seeing Hetty about to protest, he added, "Lavinia, the girls are very tired from our travels. Might I ask you to offer them refreshment and perhaps a place to rest? I will seek for lodgings soon, but I beg a little patience from you."

"Of course."

Hetty threw him an anguished glance, and Hugh sighed. "Hetty, you and Edith rest. If you like, you may sit with him in a few hours."

They had no choice but to follow Mrs. Sidney from the room, Edith wishing for the thousandth time that she had the rights of a sister, that she might also beg to remain. But she was, in fact, very tired. So tired that she could muster only the barest curiosity when Hetty introduced her to her uncle Mr. Sidney and her cousin Caroline. Caroline, who was as pretty and golden-haired as Hetty had described.

"I will take care of Hetty and Miss Edith," Caroline announced, dismissing the maid with a flick of her fingers. "Come, you two."

She led them up another flight of stairs into what was clearly her own chamber, a feminine space papered in pink and silver, with gilded armchairs beside the fireplace and a charming escritoire against the window. Gesturing toward her bed, laid invitingly with a pink silk coverlet, she claimed one of the armchairs. "What brought *you* to town, Miss Hapgood?" she asked Edith, cocking her head like an inquisitive canary.

Edith was too weary to dissemble. She sank onto the bed, where Hetty had thrown herself, head toward the foot. "I was concerned to hear that Lionel was in danger."

"Ah."

Hetty gave a loud yawn, kicking off her slippers. "Edie has been like a third sister to him."

"Fancy that," said Caroline. "When Papa brought Lionel home, I was beside myself with concern. He was so dreadfully pale because he hadn't a fever yet to give him color. I have sat with him and read him poetry and even sung a little, but he is either asleep or fretful. I do so hope he recovers."

"Thank you for helping care for him," Hetty said.

"I cannot imagine how he came to be in this situation," Caroline rattled on. "*Attacking* someone! I was most exasperated with Papa for how few details he got out of those Clinkett brothers, but he was distracted with Lionel all blood-stained and faint, of course, and the Clinketts were being held separately, and now they are gone back to Kent, I suppose, because their father was coming for them. But they will have to come back at some point because you will have heard that the victim intends to bring an action against them."

Sitting up abruptly, Hetty snapped, "Don't call that person the 'victim.' We haven't heard Lionel's explanation yet, and it is Lionel who has come away injured and in danger of his life."

Caroline's Wedgwood-blue eyes widened in mild surprise. "Well, I won't, if it upsets you. But I did wonder—has Lionel a history of attacking people?"

Edith saw Hetty's hand crumple the silk coverlet as she threw herself down again. "He hasn't, unless you count attacking *me*, and I always gave him a Roland for his Oliver."

"Oh!" Caroline gave a charming little titter. "I'm sure you jest, Hetty. It must have been delightful to grow up with Lionel."

Hetty shut her eyes.

Turning her bright smile on Edith, Caroline said, "Surely Lionel never attacked *you*, Miss Edith, even though you are like a third sister to him?"

"He never has. Though perhaps that is where the 'like' a third sister comes in. And won't you call me Edith?"

"Thank you, if you will call me Caroline. Hetty has told me you draw and paint."

"I sometimes do. I haven't for a while," she demurred.

But Hetty flung a loyal arm over her. "Edie is a painting genius."

"Then did you ever hear of this Mr. Morris before? No? Nor have I, but I do not know much about art, I'm afraid. I wonder what he can have done, that Lionel and Clinker and Clunker should storm his home! And I wonder what sort of man he was—young or old, ugly or handsome. The *Times* said that the crowds at the Academy's summer exhibit grew so much after the altercation that Mr. Morris' paintings have been taken down! It is too bad—I should have liked to see them now, but, you know, we have stayed at home to sit with Lionel. He has lost at least a stone already, Mr. White says, because of not eating and—er—perspiring so much. I suppose the blood-letting, too. And what funny things he mutters when he is delirious! Horses and dogs and eating and something about mathematics and then more about eating. I thought he must be hungry, with all the talk of eating, but, like Mama said, no one could get him to take anything."

Caroline Sidney chattered on in this fashion until both Hetty and Edith dropped asleep, despite their interest in the subject and their desire to stay alert, in case they were called to Lionel's side.

When Edith awoke, Caroline was gone. "I must have slept for hours," Edith murmured, observing the light from the windows was growing dusky. Hetty was curled in a ball, her hair tumbled down and her breathing deep.

Quietly, Edith slipped from beneath the blanket someone had placed on her and glided to the door. In the passage the sconces were lit. Peering over the railing to the staircase, she saw footmen moving below on the first floor, carrying covered dishes and trays. A door opened and the hum of conversation rose to her. The family was at supper.

For a moment she thought of returning to Caroline's room and waking Hetty because she was too shy to go down by herself, but then she remembered Hugh Hapgood must still be keeping vigil at Lionel's bedside. How tired he must be! She would go and relieve him.

It was not altruism alone that moved her, she knew. Now that she was rested, all her fears for Lionel flooded back, and she wanted to see him closely for herself. She had hung back earlier, with the chamber so full of strangers, but she would not be so timid if only Hugh were there.

Creeping down the stairs, she scratched at the door as lightly as a mouse skittering along the floorboards. There was no response. When she opened it and peeped inside she knew why—Hugh still sat in the chair nearest Lionel, but he was fast asleep, slumped, with his head fallen back against the wall. He was lost to the world, despite Lionel tossing in the bed, muttering.

Edith shut the door behind her and flew to her cousin's side. He was bathed in perspiration, his auburn hair dark where it clung to his forehead and the pillow. For a moment she hesitated, her outstretched hand trembling above him. Then she withdrew it and backed away a step.

The sickroom was hotter than ever. How could this help his fever? It might earn her a reprimand, but she went to the window, tying one side of the curtains back, and struggling with the stiff latch. When it yielded to her efforts, she heaved up on the sash, thankful it didn't squeak or rattle or scrape, and admitted a warm but fresh breath of air.

At the washstand she poured water into the basin and took up the washcloth beside it. Saturating it and wringing it out, Edith returned to the bed to lay it gently across Lionel's burning forehead.

He turned at her touch and his eyes opened. They were glassy, and she didn't know if he saw her, but she thought of his cousin Caroline reading him poetry and singing to him, and she wanted to give him something as well.

His lips moved, but no sound emerged. Remembering how Mr. White said Lionel must take broth, Edith glanced about but saw none. Should she ring for the servant? Had he already taken some?

She leaned closer to him and whispered, "Lionel, will you drink some water? I can help you."

"W-water." It was hardly louder than the breeze at the window, but Edith heard him. She flew to fill the cup on the washstand, but he could hardly drink from it lying down. Setting the cup on the bedside table, she put her arms about him—how hot he was!—and *heaved*, pulling him against her as she scrabbled for another pillow to push behind him. It was like holding a burning brand, and he was heavy and ungainly for a small person like herself to maneuver, especially when he was too weak to assist her. And when she hoisted him past the halfway point, he fell forward against her, nearly knocking her back on the bed, the washcloth sliding off his face and one of his arms flopping against her side. Panting now, Edith had almost to kick the other pillows into position, before she thrust him back against them. He slumped back limply, his hand somehow in her hair and taking her with him.

"Good heavens!" she hissed, floundering up on her knees on the bed and attempting to disentangle herself. But tugging on his hand only made it close on a hank of her hair. "Let go!" she whispered urgently. "Lionel, you must let go!"

His parched, cracked lips twisted. The feverish fool was grinning at her!

Mustering as stern an expression as she could, she shook a finger at him. "Release me this instant, Lionel Hapgood. I insist." To her amazement, he obeyed, his grin widening.

"Angel," he croaked faintly. "Where is your trumpet?"

"What nonsense," murmured Edith, climbing off the bed and straightening her rumpled dress. She was deeply grateful that Hugh slept on and that Lionel was delirious, so there was no one to see how hard she was blushing. Taking up the cup and maintaining her frowning look, she held it to his lips, tilting his head back a little with her other hand, her fingers as tangled in his hair as his had been in hers.

He drank the entire cup. And a second. By the third he broke off and began to sing, half rasping and half inaudible:

> "Where have you been all the day, my boy Willie?
> Where have you been all the day,
> Willie, won't you tell me now?
>
> I have been all the day
> Courtin' of a lady gay.
> But she is too young to be
> Taken from her mother!"

In vain did Edith bid him hush. His father stirred. Blinked, even. But then his head rolled the other direction, and he was out again.

Lifting one hand languorously, as if he would conduct a drunken choir, Lionel croaked another verse:

"Can she make a feather bed, my boy Willie?
Can she make a feather bed,
Willie, won't you tell me now?

She can make a feather bed
And put pillows at the head.
But she is too young to be
Taken from her mother!"

Turning his head from the fourth cup of water she offered him, he shut his eyes. Edith smiled then, shaking her head. She replaced the cup on the washstand, retrieved the washcloth and wet it again. Before she lay it across his brow once more, she lightly pressed the back of her hand to his forehead. *Please, dear Lord, let his fever break!*

She knew she might never have the nursing of him all to herself again. Nor ever an opportunity like this to tell him what she had learned of her feelings.

If he did not recover—she could not think of that. She would not think of that.

But if he did not recover? Edith wrapped her arms around herself.

If he did not recover, she could not bear the thought of never telling him.

His breathing was even. He slept again, his expression peaceful. But her own pulse was flying.

Edith carried one of the chairs closer to his bed. Throwing Hugh a look, she saw his eyelids twitching. He would wake soon.

"It must be now or never," she whispered.

Then let it be now.

Her decision made, she smoothed Lionel's hair from his eyes with the barest touch and then leaned over him to say softly, so softly, at his ear, "My dearest, you must try to get well. For I love you with my whole heart and don't believe for an instant that you can have done anything wrong. Even if you no longer love me, you must try—try your very hardest, my love, to live."

CHAPTER TWENTY-ONE

And what's a fever but a fit of madness?
—Shakespeare, *The Comedy of Errors*, V.i.1499 (1594)

When Edith made her bedside confession, hope sprung in her breast uninvited. For who knew what Lionel might have heard or understood in his heart of hearts, feverish or unconscious as he had been? She went to bed that night, unable to stop herself from hoping that her words would work magic. Love is a fever of its own, and Edith's imagination ran away with her, not heeding any calls to be rational. She pictured Lionel's fever breaking, upon which some inner urging would prompt him to ask for her. She would fly to his side, where once more he would declare his feelings, and she would confess with joy how her own heart had changed. What mattered after that hardly concerned her. She did not care if they had a long engagement while he finished his university course, or if they married at once, before he was transported to Australia. So long as he lived and loved her.

But by the time she awoke, late the following morning, it would be to rather different circumstances.

The doctor Mr. White called early before beginning his rounds, finding Lavinia and Caroline keeping vigil by the patient.

"Hmm," he grunted, after having felt Lionel's forehead and taken his pulse. "Still elevated. Perhaps slightly less so, but I fear the permanent effects of so long a fever, if he survives this."

"Oh, Mr. White!" cried Lavinia. "What can be done? Will you let his blood again?"

"No, I think not. If three times has not remedied the imbalance in his humors, I must look elsewhere. I think a dose a laudanum is in order, if I can get him to swallow it. If nothing else, it will give him more restful sleep." Mr. White took up a little brown bottle from his bag and a dropper. "Mrs. Sidney, will you assist me by holding your nephew's head up?"

Having administered the dose, the doctor took his leave, assuring them he would call again at the end of his rounds.

"Let us hope for the best," said Lavinia grimly. "While Lionel is as dear to me as any son could be, it is rather trying to have the nursing of him, not to mention three additional houseguests. If his fever breaks, I am sure Mr. Hapgood and Hetty and the other one will feel comfortable removing to their own lodgings."

"I do not know why the other one came, Mama," wondered Caroline. "Hetty said it is because she considers herself like a sister to Lionel, but if Rosie did not come, who *is* a sister, I find it odd an honorary sister would think it necessary."

"Oh, probably she is in love with him," shrugged her mother. "He's a winning young man. I must meet with the housekeeper, my dear, but I will send in Reddy to sit with you. Shall she bring you a cup of tea?"

Caroline had no idea if the medicine helped her cousin's fever, but it did make him quiet. A half-hour later, she was stitching content-edly on a fine seat-cushion (a bouquet of purple hydrangea blooms against a moss-green background), while the maid Reddy held a pile of rougher sewing in her lap.

"E-Edie," sighed Lionel.

"Oh!" Caroline exclaimed. "What was that?"

"The young man," the maid answered composedly, licking the end of the thread to make it pass through her needle more easily.

"Edie."

"You see?" Caroline asked of Reddy. "He often talks of eating when he is delirious."

"I would too," replied Reddy, "if I 'adn't 'ad naught but a little broth in three days. Should I fetch 'im some more, miss?"

"Yes, do."

When Reddy returned some minutes later, bearing a steaming mug on a tray, Caroline was seated against the bed, her hand in Lionel's. "Look at this, Reddy! I went to pat his hand to soothe him, and he grabbed mine! Positively grabbed it. It must comfort him." She gave a gentle tug, but he only gripped her the harder.

"Lionel, just let go for a second. I have broth for you."

"I love you," he muttered, frowning.

"Oh!" Caroline raised her eyebrows drolly at the maid. "Good heavens! One must make allowances for his condition, I suppose. Er—I love you too, cousin."

"Marry me. Edie. Marry me."

This made Caroline laugh. "Well, this is a most unconventional proposal. Do you think he is in earnest?"

"S'pose so. But 'e still wants to eat, sounds like." Taking up two pillows and plumping them, Reddy rammed them behind Lionel, causing his head to loll forward. Then she carried a spoonful of broth to him and waved it under his nose. "Lookee, young master. Nice warm broth for 'e. Open up, sir. Miss, can you tilt 'is 'ead back? Don't want it to run down his chin."

With her free hand, Caroline pressed his head back against the pillow, and his eyes flickered open, glassy. Reddy rushed in with the spoon, but Lionel grimaced and turned his head, spilling the broth all down his neck. His eyes shut again.

"Gracious me," said Caroline, as Reddy grumbled and mopped at the patient. "What a trial!"

"Marry me," Lionel groaned. "Waited. Marry."

"Just say yes, miss," advised Reddy. "It may calm 'im down. Unless you don't want to marry 'im, of course. Never know what 'e might 'old you to, when 'e's in 'is right mind again."

Caroline considered. "Well, it so happens that I *would* like to marry him. If he lives. I didn't think it would happen like this, but he's a playful young man, besides being handsome and lively—when he's not sick, I mean. He is rather pale and sweaty at the moment, but I suppose he can't help it." She carried Lionel's hand to her lips and then clasped it with her other.

"Cousin," she declared, "be easy. I will marry you."

Whether it was the furious blood-letting or the dose of laudanum or his cousin's assurance or merely the course of the illness, Lionel's fever broke within the hour.

He came to, still bleary from the drug, to find himself in a stuffy, shaded room, lying in a rumpled hot bed, under scrutiny by his uncle Wellington and aunt Lavinia, and holding hands with his cousin Caroline. This last, in particular, made him ill at ease, and he feigned unconsciousness again to think it over. Meanwhile, there was an ache in his side and he felt sticky and stale.

With a rush, the events of the past few days flooded his memory: *Portrait of a young gentleman.* Clinker and Clunker. 63 Jermyn Street. The insufferable, lying A. J. Morris.

The mere thought of Morris provoked a growl from him.

"He's waking up," came Caroline's voice. She squeezed his hand. "Darling!"

Darling?

There was the sound of the door opening, and he recognized his father's tread. "How is he?"

"His fever has broken!" sang Caroline.

"Thank God."

"And the first thing he did, Uncle Hugh, was ask me to marry him."

Lionel's eyes flew open.

"Didn't he, Reddy?"

"That 'e did," vouched the maid. She was a solid, stolid woman, with neat hair, and Lionel did not think she looked given to excitement or exaggeration. Good heavens—what had he done?

"We can speak of that later," Lavinia interposed. "Look—Lionel, can you hear us?"

He licked his lips. Gave his voice a try and found it rusty but operational. "Yes. W-water."

"I'll get it, my love," Caroline insisted. She released his hand (which he hastily pulled back under the sheet) and scurried to the washstand. When she leaned over him, tenderly passing an arm behind his head, and placed the cup to his lips, he suddenly recalled a dream he had had, where a girl had given him water. Not just any girl. No...it was Edith in his dream.

He tried to hold the remembrance, but, like all dreams, it receded like a wave from the shore. But he had no leisure for feeling bereft. Muttering his thanks, he tried to struggle to a sitting position, dismayed to discover how much effort it required. "May I—have something to eat?"

Caroline's laugh rang out. "I am so glad you *can* eat now, Lionel! Heaven knows you talked about eating the whole time you were delirious, but we could hardly get you to take anything."

"Talked about eating...?" he faltered, feeling his face grow warm.

"Yes! Even when you asked me to marry you, you mentioned eating."

Wellington Sidney rose from his chair by the curtained window. "The boy is probably tired. Lavinia, Caroline, let us leave him with his father in peace for a little while. There will be time enough for other things."

His wife and daughter were caught off guard by the authoritative note in his voice and submitted to it before they knew what they were about, leaving Lionel and his father alone. Hugh went first to the window, pulling open the curtains as Edith had the previous night and throwing up the sash. "Now that we know you are going to live, we may as well have some air to breathe."

"How long have I been here, Father?"

"This is the third day. Your uncle read about your fracas in the paper and fetched you from the watch-house. You were already muddle-headed from your injury and quickly developed a high fever. Your aunt wrote, and we came as soon as we heard."

"And Clink—I mean, and the Clinkett brothers?"

"They have purportedly gone into Kent, brought there by their father."

"This was my doing, Father, not theirs," declared Lionel.

"I wouldn't be surprised," Hugh said dryly. "If you have the strength, I would appreciate an explanation."

"Yes, sir."

There was a knock, and Reddy came back in with a heaping tray, which lifted Lionel's spirits in spite of everything. His father watched him eat steadily, leaving him in peace as he put away six slices of toast, four boiled eggs, cold meat, cheese, and coffee.

"That's better," sighed Lionel. "Now if I might only have a bath and clean clothing."

"Soon."

With food in him, he felt courageous enough for the matter at hand, and it only remained to decide what exactly he might tell without revealing too much. That is, without revealing his feelings for Edith.

"Er—well, sir, you know how Clunker likes poetry and art and such?" His father nodded, and Lionel brushed crumbs off the sheet. "He—uh—saw a painting at the Royal Academy's summer exhibition that he swore looked like me, so I went with him to see it."

"Is this where Mr. Morris comes in?"

"Yes, sir. The painting was called *Portrait of a young gentleman* and was ascribed to this A. J. Morris."

Hugh nodded again. "And wherein lay the offense?"

Lionel sat up straighter. "Sir, I recognized the painting. That is—not the painting, but the design of the painting. I mean, it was a sketch that I had seen before because it was a sketch my cousin Edith did of me last June. You see, the painting hanging at the exhibition, I could have sworn Edith did it because it was exactly the sketch and her style and everything!"

Hugh held very still. Then he raised a hand and rubbed his jaw thoughtfully. "Go on."

"So I thought 'A. J. Morris' must be an assumed name for Edith herself, or this person was exhibiting on her behalf (because she is so shy about these things, you know), so I got Clinker and Clunker to go with me to Jermyn Street, where the catalogue said he lived. And A. J. Morris turned out to be some fraud of a young man who claimed he painted it entirely himself and who resented me suggesting otherwise. Clunker then offered to purchase the painting from him, and he seemed willing, working at us until he had us up to one hundred pounds, though we didn't know how we would manage that, sir, even with our money pooled, and then the blackguard went and told us never mind, he had already accepted an offer for a *thousand* pounds! That was when I lost my temper entirely, sir, and went for him." This long tale took all his breath and effort, and he fell back against the pillows exhausted.

"Then stabbing you with the palette knife truly was in self-defense."

"Is that what he got me with?" Lionel winced. "I guess you might say so, though he was defending himself respectably with his fists, and I would never have attacked him to begin with, if he not been such an insolent liar."

"Can anyone back your story? I don't imagine the Clinketts saw the original sketch."

Coloring, Lionel swallowed. "I don't know that anyone besides me saw that sketch, except for Edith herself."

"Did you not think to ask her about it, before you went and accosted this Morris person?"

"I—how could I? You know I don't even write to you all as I should. I have never written her. And, I'm afraid, I was hot-headed and impulsive."

"Indeed. Mr. Morris intends to bring an action against you and the Clinketts," Hugh told him. "For assault and property damage."

Lionel groaned. "Then—well, then, I must make my own case, sir. If Edith could see the painting, she could counter this villain. She could—produce the sketch and let the truth be known."

Slowly, Hugh shook his head. "I'm afraid, in all the fuss, the Royal Academy apparently saw fit to remove Mr. Morris' works from the exhibit. We may need to retain legal counsel—perhaps Morris could be made to produce the painting, for your cousin to examine."

"Yes! Yes, that would do it," Lionel insisted. "Sir—I am terribly sorry to have caused my family anxiety and shame, and to now require your financial assistance in the matter, but if she could only see it, all would be vindicated! If some impostor is masquerading as a great artist by using her work, he must be stopped and made to pay."

"Indeed."

"I must say, sir, you are taking this all very well."

"Mm. Well, you did almost die," his father grinned. "Which inclines me to listen with more sympathy than you apparently deserve or expected. We must indeed get to the bottom of this portrait's mysterious origin and ensure justice for your little cousin. You have my word. But let us speak now of your other cousin."

"Which one? Is Margaret all right?"

"As far as I know, Margaret is well. No, Lionel. Of course I refer to your cousin Caroline Sidney. Is it true you have offered for her?"

Lionel gave a terrific groan, falling back once more against his pillows and covering his eyes briefly. When he faced his father again, his eyes were pleading. "I can't have, sir! I must have been delirious and ranting. I never would have, in my right mind. Never."

"And yet the maid Reddy confirms that you did."

Lionel only held up his palms helplessly. "You must believe me, sir. I don't know how it came about. I woke to find her holding my hand and fawning on me. Whatever I might have said—I don't want to marry Caroline. Good Lord! And, worse yet, she seems keen as mustard on the idea."

"That she does," agreed Hugh. "Do you remember nothing? I hope you took no...liberties with her."

"Oh, sir. If I did, I don't remember that either. But surely not! Surely, surely not. I hope. Please—Papa—is there any way out of it? Out of the engagement? I mean, without insulting her horribly and being a scoundrel myself? Not to mention, Aunt Lavinia would probably *murder* me if I jilted Caroline."

His father grimaced. He knew well enough the burden and pain of an unwanted engagement, as well as the burden and pain of displeasing Lavinia Sidney. "I don't know. I must think about it. And consult your stepmother. In the meantime, you must be as polite as you can to Caroline and not give her further encouragement."

"'Further' encouragement? That's rough, since I don't recall giving her *any*. Oh, I'll give her no encouragement—have no fear," Lionel assured him. "Short of relapsing and losing my senses again, I'll be as encouraging as a wooden block!"

"That must do for now. I'll ring to have a bath drawn for you, and then Hetty and Edith will be most eager to see you, I'm certain."

"Wh-what?"

"Did I not mention? They accompanied me to town. You gave everyone quite a scare, son."

Lionel might have said that his father had now returned the favor. Edith was *here*? The sudden racing of his heart had nothing to do with his recent illness. Life could not be this unfair, this cruel—being stabbed by that worthless counterfeit artist was nothing, compared to seeing Edith again, finally, after an endless year of estrangement, only to have her think he was engaged to his cousin Caroline!

"How is he, Hetty?" asked Edith, coming down the stairs to see her cousin with her ear pressed to Lionel's door.

Hetty jumped, and her stricken face when she turned sent chills through Edith.

"No," gasped Edith, her breath stopping and her hands flying to her throat. "Is he—is he gone?"

With a violent shake of her head, Hetty tiptoed over to her. "No—not gone," she hissed. "But nearly as bad, Edie."

"Nothing could be as bad!" Edith scolded, breathing again.

Hetty only looked skeptical.

"This could: Lionel and my cousin Caroline are engaged."

CHAPTER TWENTY-TWO

**I must dissemble, and speak a language
foreign to my heart.
—J. Addison, *Cato*, I.ii (1719)**

Something like a trap door opened beneath Edith, when Hetty told her of Lionel's engagement. For she felt, all at once, as if the ground had given way, and she was falling, plummeting.

I must not faint, she thought.

She must not faint.

What had she expected, after all? That someone like Lionel, loving and loveable, would never have feelings for another person, after she herself refused him? That, after so summary a rejection, he would still pine for her, an entire year later?

Edith was aware of Hetty watching her, and of the concerned expression on her cousin's face. Therefore, with an effort, Edith folded up her heartbreak in a neat square like a handkerchief and tucked it away. It must wait until she was alone to be removed, examined, cried into.

He is going to live, at least. And that is not nothing.

It would have to be enough for her.

"Shall we see if breakfast has been removed yet?" she murmured.

With Lionel out of danger, the Sidneys and Hapgoods all gathered in the breakfast room, and the talk at the table could not have been more delicate or freighted with significance than the Treaty of Fontainebleau, which had been negotiated that April in Paris.

Hugh began it, saying, "Wellington, Lavinia, I cannot thank you enough for your assistance these last few days. I shrink to imagine what would have been the result of Lionel's fever, had he remained in the watch-house until I could reach London. Nay—Sidney, if you had not seen the article in the *Times*—"

Wellington Sidney only shook his head and waved away his brother-in-law's thanks, but Lavinia declared, "Brother, I thank Providence we were in town and not in Crawley. But his recovery is reward enough for us. He is our nephew, after all, and soon to be dearer still." She cast an eye along the table to see if Hugh would like to make the Great Announcement, but when he was silent, it was Caroline who bounced in her chair, clapping her hands.

"Lionel and I are going to be married, Hetty—and Edith! He asked me this morning, as Reddy and I sat with him. I thought surely it was the fever talking, or the laudanum Mr. White gave him, but Reddy confirmed that it was clear as day, and, when Lionel woke again later, he did not deny it." She made happy fists. "An unconventional proposal, to be sure, but when has Lionel ever been like every other young man?"

"We congratulate you," said Hetty stiffly, while Edith managed a murmur of agreement.

"So Hetty, we will be both cousins and sisters! Is it not delightful? If you would pass me the marmalade, please, Edith."

"Delightful," agreed Hetty.

Edith passed the marmalade.

Hugh cleared his throat. "Ah, Lavinia, I did think I would see about lodgings for us today. I think we must stay in town until this dispute with Morris is cleared up."

"Of course you must stay in town! But why would you not stay with us? I do not think Lionel should be moved."

"The four of us make something of a squeeze for you, Lavinia."

"Oh, but..." (her eyes flicked over to Edith) "I thought Miss Edith had an uncle in Bruton Street, so it would only be three of you."

"Edith will be staying with us, for the present," rejoined Hugh, "therefore we would rather not inconvenience you." Seeing Edith preparing to speak, he added, "Lionel will explain to you, Edith, but it seems he will require your assistance to deal with Mr. Morris' forthcoming action against him."

Wondering what he could mean, she nodded. There was no purpose in saying she would do anything to help Lionel—it would only make her throat tighten further.

Lavinia's lips pressed into a line and she blinked several times. "Very well, then. Four of you. Nevertheless, we can make room for you here, so please do not speak any more of seeking lodgings."

Thus it was decided: for as long as it took to settle Lionel's matter with Mr. Morris, the Hapgoods would remain with the Sidneys. And because Edith's mysterious assistance was required, she could not retreat to Bramleigh, now that Lionel was on the mend. A bittersweet determination, blending the joy of being near her cousin with the daily pain of seeing him lost to her, and Edith did not know whether the joy or pain would prevail.

As Hugh announced his intention of spending the rest of the morning writing letters ("And I will include a note to your father, Edith"), Caroline persuaded Hetty and Edith to walk with her in the Regent's Park. "There is a fearful amount of construction going on there, and Papa says it will take decades for all the villas they propose to be completed, but there is nevertheless a lovely promenade beside the water."

Indeed, the girls passed a great deal of digging, excavating, and building as they proceeded from Portland Crescent into the grounds, where they followed the gravel path beside the water.

"I am most desperately eager to hear more of Lionel's incident," Caroline chattered, as they walked the long tail of the lake, her arm through Hetty's and Hetty's determinedly through Edith's. "I wanted to ask your papa, but he can look so fearfully stern, can he not?"

"He can."

"I do hope that, by the time we return, Lionel is strong enough to come down and sit with us. Otherwise, I will go up and sit with him again, though perhaps an invalid who is conscious does not require watching? But now that we are engaged, surely it wouldn't be improper for me to sit with him. Nor for me to ask him why he attacked that man. He will *want* to tell me, I am sure. I believe a husband and wife should have full confidence in each other and be boon companions—what do you think?"

Fortunately, neither Hetty nor Edith were required to think anything, for Caroline did not wait long for a reply.

"I suppose we will be married in Crawley, though I am content for it to be in Somerset as well. It's just that I've never been to Somerset, but I will have to see it now, shan't I? And I will have to learn to ride. Do you ride, Miss Edith?"

Startled at this direct address, Edith said, "Yes."

"Lionel taught us," Hetty told her. "Me and Edith and Rosie. He taught us all to ride his horse Mannerly, even though teaching us meant he had first to teach himself to ride aside."

Caroline laughed uncertainly. "Lionel on a side-saddle! Only think!"

And so on.

By the time the girls returned, the day had grown warm, and, between the heat and Caroline Sidney's prattle, Edith felt the beginnings of a headache. But when she saw Lionel in the drawing room, placed on a sofa and fending off his aunt's fussing, her feet locked and refused to carry her upstairs.

"Lionel!" cried Hetty, pushing past even Caroline to greet him. "How much better you look! Clean, for one thing." She threw her arms around him in so uncharacteristic a manner that he was too surprised to avoid it. "Budge over. I want to sit beside you."

"Dearest!" breathed Caroline, not to be outdone. While she did not hurl herself at him, she came forward with hand extended, and he was forced awkwardly to take it and give it a squeeze. She then claimed the third seat on the sofa, dropping demurely down on his other side. Only her skirts touched him, but she let her hand fall into the open space, as if by chance, should he wish to take it.

He did not take it. He was looking to the doorway, where Edith hesitated.

"Won't you greet me, Edith?" he asked quietly.

Her feet seemed to have become a permanent part of the floor. Clasping her hands together, she forced a smile and said, "I am so glad you are feeling better."

It was Hugh who helped her. "Come in, come in, my dear. There is much to discuss." As he spoke, he placed a chair for her and beckoned, and she found she could move again.

"Are *you* feeling quite the thing?" asked Lionel.

She nodded, but he looked at her a moment longer and said, "Aunt Lavinia, might we have some lemonade? I think the girls had a tiring walk."

"*So* thoughtful," sighed Caroline.

Edith would have liked to say the same. As it was, his consideration threatened to silence her altogether. Although—possibly he was only thirsty himself.

Hugh waited for the lemonade to be served, while Caroline supplied all the talk. And then, when the footmen were dismissed, he turned to his son. "Lionel, if you are prepared, you can explain to your family the recent events which resulted in your injury and illness."

"Yes, sir."

They were all seated now: the three on the sofa and the rest scattered on chairs facing him. Caroline leaned forward, as if prepared to catch every word that dropped from him, as the gentle rain of heaven upon the place beneath, but Edith sat with her hands folded in her lap and her eyes lowered.

"It is not a terribly long story," said Lionel. He glanced at his father. "It so happened that Clunker—that is, my friend Edward—and I were at the Royal Academy of Art's exhibition in Somerset House, where a painting hung that struck me as—as very like something I had seen before." He stopped. Swallowed. "I decided I would speak to the artist about it, to ask about the remarkable likeness."

"What was the subject of the painting, Lionel?" asked his aunt.

"Er—the subject—it was called *Portrait of a young gentleman*, and the young gentleman in question looked—well—looked very much like me."

Caroline gasped. "Oh! I should like to see it, then."

"You mean you wanted to speak to the artist to find out who the model was, who looked so much like you?" Hetty prompted.

"No. Not precisely. I mean I wanted to speak to the artist to find out who he was. Because—because the subject didn't just look like me. He *was* me. I remembered being sketched thus. I thought the artist might be—might be *you*, Edith."

Her eyes flew to his face.

"It was the sketch you did by the stile last June—you remember?"

Remember? Of course, she remembered! As if either one of them could possibly forget that day! Edith felt herself turning a brilliant red.

But then the greater implication of what he was saying penetrated her embarrassment, and her lips parted. "Are you saying it was a painting based on the sketch by the stile?"

"That is precisely what I'm saying." His gaze held hers. "Did you ever make a painting from that sketch, Edith?"

She did not know which was worse: to admit that she had, and have him know how she had labored over and loved this portrait of him; or to say she hadn't, and let the thief of her work go unpunished. Both choices seemed intolerable. But, faced with such a dilemma, she chose the truth.

"I did make a painting," she admitted. "When I was in Bath, my instructor Mr. Olivier chose three of my sketches for me to turn into oil paintings. That—was one of them. Later, my three paintings were all stolen from Mr. Olivier's studio, as he was holding them for an auction. I never discovered what became of them." Nor had she touched a brush since. Though she was glad to find that, after the passing of several months, she could speak of the affair calmly.

Not that everyone could receive it calmly—general uproar followed her revelation (as well as reproachful looks from Hetty for having kept this secret), but when all the questions were asked and explanations given, Lionel pounded a fist on his leg. "I knew it! I knew it was yours, Edith. But the catalogue said the artist was an A. J. Morris. I didn't know your paintings had been stolen, I just thought you were being shy and calling yourself A. J. Morris, or else you asked this person to enter your painting under his own name. In any case, I took the Clinketts with me and called on him, determined to know the truth."

"And...?" Edith almost forgot to breathe. "What did this person look like, and what did he say?" Whatever the answer was, she knew Lionel hadn't liked it, or he wouldn't have attacked the man.

"He said *he* was the artist! I put the question to him repeatedly, and always he insisted the work was his. That was why I lost my temper. For him to lie to my face without the least sign of remorse. One had only to look at the other canvases littering his home to know he had no more painted *Portrait of a young gentleman* than I had!"

"What were the other ones like, Lionel?" asked Hetty. "Were they landscapes?"

"No—they were pompous, overblown exercises in grandiloquence—Christs and saints and generals and Hercules and I know not what. And all of them standing in rubble like every last building on earth had been blown to atoms. No person in the world would ascribe *Portrait of a young gentleman* to that artist's hack."

Edith's heart was beating so loudly she could hear it. She set down her empty lemonade glass, lest it fall from her suddenly nerveless fingers. It could not be. It was absurd even to think it. After all, Mr. Olivier was not the only painter fond of posturing heroes and suffering saints.

"Edith." Lionel's voice sounded very far away. "Edith, are you all right?"

"What did A. J. Morris look like?" she asked again. Or perhaps she mouthed it. "He didn't happen to look like Father Christmas, did he?"

"Father Christmas?" he echoed. "No...he wasn't that old, to begin with. Nor did he have white hair or a beard or cherry cheeks. He was possibly in his twenties...? And he looked...foreign. He didn't sound foreign—just looked it. You know—dark hair and eyes and an insolent manner. He was not as tall as I, but he was strong. We thrashed each other pretty well, without either one of us beating the other hollow. Not till he grabbed hold of that palette knife and did his best to puncture me. Why do you ask if he looked like Father Christmas? Do you have an idea who it might be?"

Her mouth moved, but no sound emerged, and her eyes had been growing wider and wider as he spoke. Moreover, she was turning scarlet again.

"You do know," said Lionel, feeling his own temperature rise. Why was she blushing? *Why was she blushing?*

"I—I think—" Edith floundered. "Mr. Olivier—he has a nephew. The—the—the person you describe sounds—something like Jean—that is, something like Mr. Jean-André—I mean, the younger Mr. Olivier. And the other paintings you saw—well, they sound like the sort I saw in Mr. Olivier's studio. The elder Mr. Olivier, that is. Who looks like Father Christmas. But it can't be them, of course. They would have no reason to—to pretend my paintings were stolen from their home."

"No reason?" Lionel's voice was stony. "*Your* painting got A. J. Morris into the exhibition. *Your* painting is the one he claimed a collector offered one thousand pounds for!" Sitting forward on the sofa, he appeared on the point of paying A. J. Morris a second visit.

Now Edith really did stare, and Hetty breathed, "Edith! A thousand pounds!"

Hugh held up a hand to calm his son. "Let us take this carefully. We do not know that A. J. Morris and this Jean-André Olivier are one and the same. There are many dark-haired, dark-eyed, insolent young men in London, I daresay, as well as many painters of classical and religious subjects—"

"I will go see the painting," Edith interrupted (a sign of her agitation). "And, if it is mine, I will call on Mr. Morris."

"You will do no such thing!" declared Lionel, slapping the sofa and causing Caroline to squeak in alarm. "I will accompany you."

"Lionel, the man already had you arrested and is bringing an action against you," his sister pointed out. "You can hardly go marching in there again. Someone else had better go with her. Me, or Papa. Or both."

Groaning in frustration, Lionel crossed his arms over his breast, only to wince and uncross them, touching his bandaged side.

"Edith, you cannot see the painting, at any rate," said Hugh, "for the Academy has removed it. Too much uproar, I'm afraid."

"That's right. Caroline said so. I had forgotten."

"However," Hugh resumed, "you and I can call on this Mr. Morris. As soon as tomorrow."

But here Edith shook her head. "I beg your pardon, sir, but I think you had better not accompany me. If Mr. Morris is indeed the younger Mr. Olivier, I do not think he will admit anyone by the name of Hapgood but myself."

"You cannot go by yourself," Lionel insisted, remembering the rogue's bold eyes and Edith's telltale blush.

She raised her chin and gave him a steady look. "I will ask my uncle Alwyn to go with me. The name Alwyn Arbuthnot means nothing to—to him. Let me send a note to Bruton Street now."

"But you'll stay here with us, won't you Edith?" Hetty pressed. "Because your uncle and Mrs. Arbuthnot will surely ask you to stay in Bruton Street."

In the instant she had to decide, Edith weighed Mrs. Sidney wishing her gone against being near Lionel. Or, rather, against being near Lionel with Caroline always on hand. And Lionel won.

"I will stay with you, if I may," she said quietly. And then added, for Mrs. Sidney's sake, "Wherever you might happen to be."

"And we will be here," finished Hugh. "All is decided, then. Edith, you had better let your uncle know."

Chapter Twenty-Three

O Traitors fel, which in your hartes could fynde
Like frendes of hel, the guiltles to betraye.
—Wm. Baldwin, *The last parte of the Mirour for mag-
istrates* (1578)

The exertions of explaining himself to his family, bearing Caroline's attentions, and wishing everyone would fall in a pit so he could just talk to Edith, quite finished Lionel for the day, and he retreated to his room to sleep another twelve hours. He had a memory of Mr. White returning and threatening more laudanum, but Lionel roused himself long enough to refuse.

The following morning found him improved, though still easily tired. After devouring the breakfast Reddy brought up, he dressed himself slowly, that he might make his way down and collapse upon the sofa. If he could not accompany Edith to Jermyn Street, he was at least determined to see her before she went.

For one all-too-brief moment, Fortune favored him, for when he entered the drawing room, he saw Edith alone, at the window overlooking the street, her back to him.

He paused before greeting her, seizing the chance to look at her without her being aware. She was seventeen now. Still small, but with a light, pleasing figure, glorious curling hair, and a face that had borne out its promise of beauty, and Lionel wondered how long it would take, exactly, for him to feel nothing when he saw her.

"Good morning, Edith."

She started. Blushed. "Oh, good morning. You're awake early. Are you feeling any better?"

"Much." He tried not to sound out of breath from merely descending the stairs. With what nonchalance he could muster, he sauntered to the sofa and leaned against the back of it. "Perhaps I might go along with you and your uncle? I would wait in the carriage. Lie low, you know."

Noting how he had paled, she hastily took a seat, so that he might rest on the sofa. "I don't think you'd better, Lionel. I wrote Uncle Alwyn and told him it might be a long day."

Having expected this refusal, he gave a brief nod. He wanted to ask what that Jean-André person was to her, that she should blush when mentioning him, but he couldn't think of a way to go about it. Instead he said, "When you return, you'll tell me everything that happened, won't you?"

"Of c—" She broke off abruptly, thinking of the last time she saw Jean-André. If this Morris turned out to be an altogether different person, she could tell Lionel everything; but if Morris really were who she thought he was, there likely would be plenty she would rather keep to herself. "I will certainly tell you everything relevant," she amended.

This was not a promise phrased to give him peace of mind, and he frowned, but she did not notice because she was working up the courage to say something she had wanted to, since hearing the details of his scrape.

Placing her hands in her lap, as she had the day before, she said in a very soft voice, "Lionel, I mayn't have time or privacy to say this later, but I wanted to thank you for your...zeal in trying to find out about my painting. It was very noble of you. And brave. And loyal. And I will always count it as a very great act of friendship."

And there Fortune abandoned him, for, before he could do more than register the melting sensation spreading through him, or think that—yes—he would throw himself at her feet once more (Caroline or no Caroline), a carriage pulled up outside and the voices and footfalls of his family were heard on the staircase.

Then everyone was in the drawing room: the Sidneys, Hugh and Hetty, Alwyn Arbuthnot, a scattering of servants. Lionel was pelted with questions and fussed over; Alwyn was bowing and booming and sweeping up his niece; Hugh was consulting on the day's plan of attack, with suggestions from Hetty, who also begged to go along and wait in the carriage (and was also refused). And then Edith was bustled out by her uncle, and Lionel was left at the mercy of Caroline, with only the comfort of a second breakfast.

There was not much to be learned at Somerset House about *Portrait of a young gentleman*. As she had been warned, the painting was gone, its space filled in, and the simple note "Removed" added to the catalogue. But a quick perusal of the exhibition catalogue was enough to confirm Edith in her suspicions. A. J. Morris was Jean-André Olivier. Because how else could Morris also be the contributor of *Portrait of Sir C. Nightingale, Bart*, a painting Edith had seen with her own eyes in Mr. Olivier's studio? *Portrait of Sir C. Nightingale, Bart* had also been taken down, but it must be the very same work, unless Sir C. Nightingale was so vain he needed multiple artists rendering multiple portraits of him.

A year earlier, when she and Margaret had visited the British Institute's Reynolds exhibit, Edith had taken hours to have her fill. But now she hurried Alwyn away from the portrait of Byron.

"To think, your painting hung among those ones, Edie," crowed Alwyn, when they were in the carriage again.

"No one knows it was mine."

"That doesn't matter a jot, since you prefer anonymity and penury to fame and fortune."

This made her smile. "I am hardly poverty-stricken, Uncle."

"Well, you're hardly as rich as you might be, anyhow," he returned. "Imagine! One thousand pounds! Would you be very angry with me, if I commissioned something from you and then turned right round and sold it?"

"But it wouldn't sell for so much because of my anonymity," she reminded him.

"Oh, right. Then, would you be very angry with me, if I commissioned something from you and then submitted it to the Academy under 'E. B. Hapgood' and *then* sold it for a thousand pounds?"

"I think I wouldn't be happy with you. After all, you have no need of fortune, now that you have married your dear Mrs. Arbuthnot."

"True, true," he sighed. "And my Eliza is priceless for her own sake. Did I tell you, Edie, that we are thinking of going abroad, now that the peace has come? Why, you should join us! Every artist ought to see Paris and Rome."

"Paris and Rome," breathed Edith. The faintest flicker of excitement passed through her. Supposing she were able to rescue Lionel from his predicament—repay his friendship with friendship—then he would be free to marry his cousin Caroline, and she, Edith, would be free to go very, very far away. Perhaps in the shadow of the Pantheon or in the *allées* of the Luxembourg Gardens she could draw and paint again and forget all about how much she loved him.

She gave herself a shake. "I confess I would like that, Uncle. But first we must deal with this Mr. Morris."

Pounding one fist into his open palm, Alwyn vowed, "He must be made to admit he stole your painting and profited by it."

Edith eyed the gesture doubtfully. "There must be no more attacking or wrestling the man. Unless he tries to flee, I suppose. We cannot have Jean-André bringing actions against still more family members. Please, Uncle Alwyn, let me do the talking. I am more concerned with persuading him to leave Lionel and the Clinkett brothers alone, than I am in vindicating any artistic cause of mine."

"Very well, very well," he conceded with poor grace. "Though I don't imagine his case would go very far, once the world knew what he had done. But I will do my best merely to hulk in threatening silence."

But when the landaulette turned into Jermyn Street, Edith and her uncle were dismayed to see a half-full remover's wagon outside number 63.

"We must hurry," she urged, climbing down before he could assist her.

They entered the hosier and glover's shop, Edith not waiting for the shop boy to bow in welcome before she blurted, "Please—we are come to call on Mr. A. J. Morris. Do you know if he is here?"

"Well, they're still bringing his things down and loading the wagon, so he's here all right. But he hasn't been receiving visitors. Not since the Incident. Even employs a guard nowadays." This last he said with a jerk of his chin toward the stairwell, where a heavyset man leaned against the rail.

"I am an old acquaintance of Mr. Morris," she answered firmly. "We will announce ourselves."

"Oh!" cried the boy, darting in front of her. "He'll have my hide if I let you up there! He said nobody, miss. Nobody was to come up."

The burly man looked up in interest, raising a brow at Alwyn.

Edith smiled her sweetest smile at both men and managed to inject shy hesitation into it, when she really intended to go up there, and nothing was going to stop her. "Please—he will want to see me.

And I promise you, if he does not, I will explain how it was all my fault."

The shop boy crumbled at her entreaty, though he made one last effort, pointing to Alwyn. "What about him? Is he an acquaintance of Mr. Morris, too?"

"He's my uncle," explained Edith. "A young lady can't go about on her own, you know. He is only with me today in the role of chaperone and has no business with Mr. Morris."

With another smile for the shop boy and a shy duck of the head to the guard, Edith moved past them, followed closely by Alwyn.

The door to Mr. Morris' apartment stood open, and when she was halfway up the staircase Edith heard a familiar voice: "No—be careful with that one, you oaf." She paused, her hand tightening on the railing. So it was indeed Jean-André, whom she had hoped never to see again in her life.

If it were only a matter of her painting— But, no, there was Lionel.

She went on.

If Edith thought the younger Mr. Olivier would be shocked to see her, she was disappointed. There was no element of surprise. When she appeared in the doorway, he looked over and made a clicking sound with his tongue. "Ah. So you have found me, my little beauty." His gaze moving to Alwyn over her shoulder, he added, "And you have brought a bodyguard."

"You have one yourself, I saw," she countered.

"Yes. You must have heard by now of the dangers posed to me."

Without acknowledging this, she said, "This is my uncle, Mr. Alwyn Arbuthnot. Uncle Alwyn, this is Mr. Jean-André Olivier. Or should I say Mr. A. J. Morris?"

Jean-André made a mocking bow and gestured them in. "Maurice is my own uncle's middle name. Alexandre Maurice Olivier and Jean-André Olivier. I thought John Andrew Morris a happy compromise and very English-sounding."

He didn't sound at all embarrassed by his admission, and Edith was vexed to hear her own voice tremble. "Mr. Olivier, if you were expecting me, you must know what I am going to say."

"That does not mean I want to lose the pleasure of hearing you say it," he replied. "It has been—what—four months since we have met? I would offer you a seat, but, alas—they have already taken my chairs."

His airy tone further provoked her. Neither embarrassment nor remorse troubled him, then.

"Mr. Olivier, I come to ask you two things—"

"Ah," he interrupted, holding up a finger to stop her. He nodded at the two removers: "Come back in an hour."

The door shut. Edith crossed her arms, taking hold of her elbows for courage. "I come to ask you two things," she began again. "Firstly, were you in any way involved in the theft of my three paintings from Westgate Buildings? And secondly, did you submit one of them—the portrait of my cousin Mr. Lionel Hapgood—to the Royal Academy under your made-up name?"

He gave a deep sigh. "I see we will have no preliminary pleasantries. What a shame it is, that such a pleasing form hides such a suspicious nature! Your questions insult my honor, just as your cousin's visit insulted my honor. I hope you have no plans to attack me as he did."

"If you would please answer my questions, sir, insulting though you might find them. I personally see no need for you to take umbrage, when you have already confessed to falsifying your name, and, by extension, your nationality. As your uncle Mr. Olivier told me more than once, only Englishmen may submit to the Academy."

"A silly rule. For I've lived in England longer than ever I lived in France."

"Silly or not, you do not meet the submission requirements, and I suspect the Royal Academy has no notion of the deception practiced on them."

"Are you threatening to expose me, little Miss Edith?"

"Here now," interposed Alwyn, taking an early dislike to this puffed-up secret Frenchman who spoke to his niece with so little respect. But Edith placed a warning hand on her uncle's arm, and he reluctantly subsided into silence.

"I am merely stating a fact. Please answer my two questions, Mr. Olivier."

He shrugged. "Very well. The answer is *no*, I had nothing to do with the burglary of my uncle's studio in Bath, from which he also suffered losses, if you recall. And, secondly, *no*, we did not submit your portrait of Mr. Lionel Hapgood to the Academy for consideration. We submitted a copy. A painting done from memory. Heaven knows my uncle and I saw every stage of development of your work, from pencil sketch to finished piece. There was not a brushstroke we did not witness. It was a pleasing painting. We thought it would have the best chance of being accepted, and we were right. But, Miss Edith, it was only your painting in terms of subject. Which is to say, it was not your painting at all. If any one artist were to say, you cannot paint a Madonna and Child or a Crucifixion or an Ascension because I have already painted one, what would become of all the works of the Great Masters? There is no copyright on *subjects*."

With quickened breath and flushed face, Edith said, "I am aware, sir. But I know every brushstroke of my painting, too. Let me see this copy."

Another maddening shrug. "I am sorry, Miss Edith. It is gone. *Poof*." He made the gesture with his hand. "I told you it was a nice painting. I have sold it and the buyer has taken it."

This was a stab, and she faltered briefly. "Was it—was it for the thousand pounds you taunted my cousin with?"

He winked at her. "Miss Edith, this was a business matter. I can only tell you that the buyer was part of Prince Metternich's train and that he was very satisfied. It will hang in some *schloss* in Austria, no doubt."

She gasped. Could he be telling the truth? Or did he invent someone so exalted and remote from her world simply to thwart further inquiry?

Jean-André was watching her closely.

"The...the Allies are still here, are they not?" she wondered. "Perhaps I might discover more of this person and—and—"

"Oh, Miss Edith. Do you not read the newspapers? The visit is nearly ended. I believe they embark for the Continent again shortly.

This is why the gentleman was so anxious to come to an agreement. They are no longer even in London, having gone to Portsmouth to see a naval review before they embark."

Lowering her gaze so he could not read it, Edith tried to gather her thoughts. She would never learn the truth from this horrible man. And to think, the elder Mr. Olivier had come on dear Mr. Eldredge's recommendation! Perhaps Mr. Eldredge had not known what a viper Mr. Olivier nursed to his bosom, in the form of the nephew. But—was the elder Mr. Olivier not guilty as well? Whether he had copied Edith's painting or whether he merely assented to the schemes of Jean-André, his conduct was far, far from blameless.

Very well.

Her painting was lost and its fate unknown. But that had been the case before she set foot in Jermyn Street. She must put that aside to be dwelt on and mourned later. For the present, there was still the matter of Lionel, and, to save him, Edith was willing to go further than she would for herself. For him she could be brave.

Her chin rose. "You have behaved badly, Mr. Olivier. Whether you only copied my painting or whether you did more than that, I must leave that matter in God's hands. But I would ask you to let drop your charges against my cousin."

"Oh? And why should I do that, when he is most definitely guilty of assaulting me and damaging valuable property?"

"It seems a fair exchange. You suffered no lasting harm, and you have done harm yourself."

"And the painting which was destroyed? It was a Saint Stephen."

"Did you have a purchaser for it?"

Grudgingly he shook his head.

"Then supposing I offered you twenty pounds, to pay for the materials and the fictional A. J. Morris' time? Would you then let drop the charges?" Edith persisted.

"How cheaply you must think I hold myself, Miss Edith. And if I were to refuse your offer?"

Hearing her uncle make a growling sound behind her, Edith said sternly, "Then—then I will be compelled to inform the membership of the Royal Academy of your deceptive practices."

He chuckled. "My, my, how terrible that would be. We would never be allowed to submit again—oh—wait—Frenchmen aren't allowed to submit in any event. Oh, Miss Edith, even if you revealed A. J. Morris' true heritage, that would be the extent of the damage, for you have no proof of anything else. And how your name would become notorious as well! The papers would write of the jealous little vindictive failed artist..."

"Now, see here!" bellowed Alwyn, unable to take any more of this. Thrusting his niece aside, he seized Jean-André by the lapels of his bottle-green frock coat and shook him like a hound worrying its helpless prey. "I don't know what kind of rotten—lying—slippery—impudent—unscrupulous *rascal* you are, but you may not address my niece thus!"

Jean-André's teeth were clacking together as his head lolled about, but Edith was still able to discern that he was cursing volubly in French, even as she tugged on her uncle. "Uncle Alwyn—stop! You must not! Stop!"

With another bellow, Alwyn hurled his victim across the room, where he crashed into a stack of folded easels and slid to the floor, each easel giving him an additional rap on the head as it clattered down atop him.

Jean-André leapt to his feet, only to stagger around dizzily in a manner that would have made Edith giggle, if the circumstances hadn't been so dire. He raised an accusing finger. "Another assault from another of your family members, Miss Edith! You, sir, will be arrested as well! Arrested and charged. Guard! Guard!"

"Perhaps you'd like to stab me with a palette knife first," Alwyn taunted him, clenching his fists and lunging for him again. But Edith managed to throw herself between them, her hands pushing on her uncle, even as the heavyset man burst through the door.

"Uncle Alwyn, what did I say? You *must* calm yourself."

"I'll see your entire family transported!" cried Jean-André, quite red in the face. "Every last cousin, uncle, brother, father—"

"Don't forget her infant nieces," smirked Alwyn. "You know what a menace they are."

"Grab him, Benoit," ordered Jean-André. "This man attacked me."

"Uncle Alwyn," Edith interceded, as Benoit moved toward her uncle, "please go with this man and wait below."

"On no account, my dear—"

"Please—the door will be open, and I promise I won't be long."

"Your father would never forgive me—"

"He will never know!"

Reluctantly Alwyn retreated with the guard, not without cracking his fingers in a threatening manner and glowering at Jean-André, who sneered, "Beware, Mr. Arbuthnot. It is easy enough to send for the officer of the peace."

Jean-André and Edith watched each other steadily as they caught their breath and listened to the tread of the men receding.

What Edith could offer him next she did not know. She only thought that, perhaps with no one else there to lunge at him, Jean-André might see reason.

Alwyn's departure did seem to be settling him. But as his furious expression gave way to a calculating look, Edith found herself equally uneasy.

She took a long breath, clasping her hands in front of her. "Mr. Olivier, we once were friends. Please—I hope we can settle this matter without more unpleasantness. I ask you to forgive my cousin and my uncle. They are both protective of me, as you see, and as I hope you too would be of any young female relation you might have..."

He did not answer immediately, instead walking over to the fallen easels. One by one he picked them up, propping them back against the wall. Then he turned and crossed his arms over his chest. "I have no young female relations. I did once ask you if *we* might be more than friends, Miss Edith, if you recall."

"I do," she said. "And I gave you my answer."

"Yes. But had you said yes to me then, you would have found that I could protect you even more fiercely than your belligerent relations."

Her grey eyes narrowed. He dared to make such a claim, when he was the very one threatening her and those she loved? "Yes, well—if it pleases you to think so."

Straightening, he sauntered around the edges of the room before stopping beside her. "It does please me to think so. Have you thought more of it, Miss Edith? See here: I promoted and sold a painting that looked like yours for—a goodly amount of money. If you married me, we might continue in such a fashion."

"You must be joking."

He pretended to consider. "No, I think not. After all, had we been engaged, none of this would have happened."

"Well, Mr. Olivier, we are *not* engaged, and all this *has* happened." And was all his fault, she might have added.

He wandered again, stopping this time between her and the open door. "But I am saying, Miss Edith, that if we were engaged now, all might still be remedied. I might entirely forget my grievance against your cousin and your uncle."

She retreated a step, still too incredulous to be upset. "Mr. Olivier," she said, striving for a jesting tone, "if I went back to my uncle and my cousin and told them you and I were engaged, they might finish you altogether."

"Ah," he purred, "is that another threat from tiny little you?"

"Please do not speak to me like that."

"Like what?"

When she said nothing, he tapped his chin. "I think you do not want to marry me, Miss Edith."

"I think you are right."

"I can give you two days to decide—"

"I don't need two days, sir!" she protested. "I have already given you your answer."

"Then you would rather leave your uncle and your cousin to the mercy of the courts?"

She threw up her hands. "No—not at all. But can we not find another solution than me marrying you? For I assure you, it is quite out of the question."

Suddenly his eyes were hard. "Of course. Do not think I have forgotten that this violent cousin of yours seems to have a hold on your heart."

"He does n—"

"But a lady should always have a choice," Jean-André cut her off, "and here is yours: you may either see that silly boy you love and your uncle prosecuted to the full extent of the law, or you may marry me and have them generously forgiven. It is that simple. Either way you will not see the cousin again. I will forbid it if you marry me, and if you refuse, both he and your uncle will likely be imprisoned or transported. "

"Why should you do this?" asked Edith, fighting back angry tears. "If I do not love you, the marriage cannot be a happy one—"

"It can nevertheless be a profitable one. And you may yet learn to forget your cousin and care for me." Stepping back, he allowed her free passage to the door. "I will give you two days to decide. You may leave word with the shop below. Two days, Miss Edith. Or I will have your overzealous relations arrested and seek my solace in revenge."

CHAPTER TWENTY-FOUR

...Sollitude best fits my cheereles mood.
—Thomas Kyd, *The Spanish Tragedy*, I.sig.B4 (1592)

"What did you say to him, my dear, and he to you?" demanded Alwyn, when Edith stumbled down the stairs to him, her face pale and her whole person trembling. "Did that villain insult you again? Why, I will pound him into a pulp!"

"No!" She seized his sleeve. "Don't go up again. He has threatened to call the constable, as he did on Lionel, but I persuaded him to wait and see if he didn't change his mind later." It was a lie, but she knew if Alwyn learned what Jean-André had actually said, her feeble strength would not be enough to restrain him. She must think—she must have time to think. "Let us go back to Bruton Street, Uncle Alwyn."

"But shouldn't we return to Devonshire Street first?" he asked as the footman handed her up. "Your father's cousin was quite anxious about how this interview would go."

"I think we may safely say the interview went as poorly as it possibly could, and I must give the matter some thought. We can send a note over, saying Mr. Morris was out until later. It is a lie, but a tiny one."

"Bruton Street it is, then."

Lionel was feigning sleep again. He found that if he did not, he was in danger of spending the entire day with his cousin Caroline affixed to his side. Had he been in love with her, her indefatigable fascination with all things *him* would have been flattering, but as it was...

Hetty, wanting very much to have a private conversation with her brother, tried several times to get rid of the girl, even reading aloud from Bowles' guidebook to London, which made Caroline pat a yawn from her mouth prettily. But when Hetty finally succeeded in sending her cousin in search of more amusing books to entertain Lionel, Aunt Lavinia plumped herself down, sewing in hand. The siblings were left to communicate in true sibling fashion, through a silent series of raised eyebrows and unobtrusive pantomime and mouthed words, which was how Lionel finally rose, stretched exaggeratedly, and announced he was in need of a nap. Hetty followed shortly, making some excuse about writing her stepmother.

"Shouldn't they be back by now?" Lionel demanded. He lay head to foot on his bed, staring upward at the coved ceiling, his stockinged feet propped up on his pillows.

"You know Edie," answered his sister. "If they were going first to the exhibition, she is probably still standing in front of the portrait of Byron."

"I should have insisted I go along. That A. J. Morris or whoever he is, is capable of anything."

But Hetty scotched this right away. "If you had gone you would surely have made it worse. We must suffer the torture of waiting for news. But in the meantime, how did you come to decide you wanted to marry Caroline, of all people?"

It was just like Lionel that Hetty's scathing tone made him perversely mischievous. "Why? What's wrong with Caroline?"

"Nothing at all, if your tastes run to adoring sycophants."

"What a kindly cousin you are, Het. What if I just happen to *be* adorable? Isn't she pretty enough and amiable enough to suit you? Why do you always go about thinking you're better than everyone else?"

"Do I? Just because I don't care to flatter people. But don't dodge me—how long have you been harboring this secret passion? Did you even consult Papa first?"

Groaning, he folded his arms behind his head. "What an idiot you are. Of course I didn't consult him because of course I don't harbor any secret passion for her—because, only just yesterday morning if you will recall, I was *delirious* with fever, and not in my right mind."

"What are you saying?"

"I'm saying that I have no memory of proposing to our cousin, but I must have said something to that effect while I was working off the last of that infection, for I woke to find her holding my hand and considering the matter all settled."

Hetty was on him in an instant, darting up from her chair to sit beside him on the bed. "You mean it, Lionel? That's really what happened?"

"Why would I make up such a ridiculous story? That's really what happened—from my perspective. Though Lord only knows what happened when I hadn't any perspective to speak of."

"Then you don't actually want to marry her?"

"Of course I don't want to marry her!" He spoke with more vehemence than he intended. "Haven't I just said so? And I've explained it all to Papa, but he says we must take each crisis as it comes and first resolve the matter of whether I am to be tried in the courts or worse."

"True. If you are to be transported, Caroline doesn't seem the sort to want to come along. You might do better to choose some pretty pickpocket off your prison ship. If they hang you, however, we will all be sure to stand in the crowd and weep for you."

"Do be serious."

"You be serious! This is a dreadful business. I almost think I'd rather be shipped to Botany Bay than marry Caroline. Do you think Papa means to have it out with Aunt Lavinia? He could tell her that you never meant to propose, and Aunt Lavinia could tell Caroline."

"How should I know? I don't really care at present." Sitting up, he flung off the bed and went to peer out the window. "Why do you suppose Edith hasn't returned? Hadn't we better call in Bruton Street? Mrs. Arbuthnot might have news."

"We have not even been introduced to Mrs. Arbuthnot, Lionel."

"Since when were you such a slave to propriety?"

"I would have thought you noticed by now that propriety is rather a binding thing, whether one is enslaved to it or not."

"I won't be bound by it," muttered her brother, his fist clenching. He winced and gave his healing wound a furtive touch.

"Good gracious—don't injure yourself about it. I suppose Papa will take us to call in Bruton Street if you feel so strongly."

"I don't mean Bruton Street." He turned on her, wincing again. Trying to make his movements appear casual, he returned to lie down on his bed. "I mean it's silly that a fellow has to marry some girl just because he said something raving in his sleep—something he has no memory of saying. I won't do it. No matter what happens at my trial."

His paleness did not escape his sister's observation, and she felt a twinge for badgering him. Rising, she moved toward the door. "You're right. You shouldn't have to do it, even if you aren't sentenced to years of hard labor. I do wonder though..."

When she paused, trailing off, he cast her a suspicious look. "Wonder what?"

Hetty dragged her toe along the edge of the carpet and then kicked a couple times absently at the door frame in an unladylike way which would surely have earned her a reprimand from Miss Blenkensop. "I wonder if you would mind so much if it was Edie you proposed to, when you were delirious," she ventured at last.

Lionel turned positively crimson. Crimson and sputtering, which was answer enough for her. "Of—of course I would mind! A man should always be conscious for such things, no matter—no matter—"

"I don't mean the consciousness part," she replied with maddening patience. "I meant the person applied to, consciously or unconsciously. I have thought for some time that you were rather sweet upon Edith than otherwise."

Here her brother was overmastered, and he snatched a pillow to cover his face. "You—you—keep your trap shut!" came his muffled outrage. "You—interfering—mind your own—go away!"

She went, unmoved by his agonies of embarrassment. But the thoughtful look was still on her face. Opening Bowles' London guidebook again (she had held her place by creasing the corner of the page—another bad habit Miss Blenkensop had yet to break her of) and reading once more the interesting bit about the dome of St. Paul's, she began to form a plan.

CHAPTER TWENTY-FIVE

Bad is the match where neither party wone.
—Michael Drayton, *Englands heroicall epistles,* v.I
(1599)

Edith's retreat to Bruton Street resulted in a small flurry of correspondence. First, she dashed off a paragraph to her father at Bramleigh, claiming they were still trying to understand the scope of Lionel's scrape, but that he was otherwise well. "A partial lie," she muttered, folding the sheet. Second, she wrote her father's cousin Hugh Hapgood in Devonshire Street, saying that Mr. Morris was not in when they called but would be visited again the following day. "A thorough lie," she sighed. To avoid having to repeat the falsehood to their faces, Edith added that she would be staying a night or two in Bruton Street with the Arbuthnots. Untruthful as those two missives were, they were the easiest. Her response to Jean-André still remained to be written.

Sitting in Margaret's former dressing room, Edith tucked her legs beneath her and ran her finger up and down the barbs of her goose-feather quill. She wished her sisters Elfrida or Margaret were with her—they were both so practical they might be able to penetrate the murk surrounding her.

"I must put on my practical hat," Edith told herself. "Pretend I'm Margaret."

She did not doubt that what she told Jean-André was true: even if she could bring herself to accept his proposal, Lionel and her uncle would probably wind up right back in the watch-house when they heard, charged with a second assault. Nor would she be able to lie convincingly to her family and say that she married Jean-André for love. The ensuing uproar might even bring on the fatal apoplectic fit they always dreaded would finish off her father.

No. Agreeing to marry Jean-André was impossible and would solve nothing.

"He doesn't even love me," she murmured. "He only wants to triumph over me and profit by me."

Profit.

Her thoughts snagged on the word.

He wanted to profit by her. He had said as much.

What if she could offer him an opportunity to profit, without having to marry him? Would he then release his grudge against Lionel and her uncle?

Edith laid a hand to her chest, feeling it rise and fall with her quickened breath. Could she do it? She did not know if she could. But she had to try, with so much at stake.

Tossing the quill pen aside, Edith rose from her seat and went in search of her uncle.

The Arbuthnots and Edith dispensed with a carriage the next morning, choosing to walk from Bruton Street to Jermyn Street, Edith explaining, "It would be better not to give forewarning to Mr. Olivier, should he still happen to be there."

Alwyn had forbidden Edith to call on the "filthy blackguard" again, but she wore him down, promising that it would be her last attempt to persuade him toward forgiveness. His wife Eliza, having had the matter explained to her, thought it would be well for her to join them, and Edith acceded to this, thinking Jean-André might behave more agreeably with another (older) woman nearby.

"He may already be gone, however," Edith pointed out. "In which case we can only leave word that we would like to see him at his convenience." She said this half in hope and half in dread, but when they entered the hosier and glover shop once more, the shop boy blurted, "There's more and more of you each time! And his guard Mr. Benoit isn't even about at the moment."

"If you would let Mr. Morris know I am here again," Edith said, "and that my aunt and uncle will wait below for me?"

The boy nodded and darted away, hammering up and down the stairs before returning and hollering, "He says to go on up, Miss, if it's just you."

With a glance at her relations, who assumed their post at the base of the staircase, Mrs. Arbuthnot's hand on her husband's sleeve, Edith took a deep breath and started up.

The room was even emptier than the day before—the easels had been packed up, so there was no danger of Jean-André being thrown against them today. The man himself stood contrapposto by the window, one elbow up on the sash and his head turned toward his shoulder to watch her enter, and Edith thought wryly it was much the same attitude Michelangelo chose for his David. Did that make her Goliath?

"Miss Edith, welcome."

"Mr. Olivier."

He gestured at the only seat remaining in the room—a wooden stool beside the empty worktable. "You come sooner than I expected with your answer."

Ignoring his offer to seat herself, she nodded.

"And what have you decided? Shall you be my bride and watch your family live, happy and unpersecuted? Or un*prosecuted*, at least."

Edith held her palms up in appeal. "Jean-André, let me begin by saying that I do not believe you want to marry me anymore than I want to marry you."

Hearing her bald pronouncement, he abandoned his David attitude, turning to face her in full, hands on his hips. "Ah, Miss Edith. I see you have decided to refuse me. Come what may. Is this because I wound your vanity? I do not make love to you properly? Perhaps you would like me to swear that I would die without you."

"Not a bit of it," she snapped. "And had you bothered to say such things, I would not have believed you."

"Not have believed me?" he echoed with mock incredulity. "And why not? You think perhaps you know what *true* love looks like?"

"At any rate, I can spot its unauthorized copies," countered Edith, reddening. "No man who claimed to love would threaten and manipulate and deceive his beloved, as you have me." Seeing the fire in his eyes, she turned away, struggling to control her resentment. Why, she would grow as sharp-tongued as Margaret—he was so provoking! And what good would it do her? It would only harden him against her.

"Please, Jean-André—I have another proposal for you," she began again. Clasping her hands before her, she made an unsuccessful attempt to smile. "Yesterday you mentioned how a match between us could be...profitable. Suppose—suppose there were a different way you might profit from me."

His dark eyes gleamed. "My dear Miss Edith—are you soliciting me?"

"I—beg your pardon?" Without knowing precisely what he meant, she didn't like the look or sound of it.

"Are you offering yourself to me—for a price?" he purred, the corner of his mouth twisting.

The empty room wavered in her vision and small red spots appeared at the fringes. For a moment she thought she might faint. Or explode. And all of a sudden, she understood Lionel and her uncle's violent bursts of rage at this man. She thought she might lunge at him herself. The line of her jaw appeared through her soft cheek, and, had any of the Hapgoods been there to notice, they would have remarked how Edith's resemblance to her rumbustious father really was there, after all.

She should call Alwyn up. But, no—he would likely defend his niece by hurling Jean-André from the window, and then the rogue's dying corpse would sue for attempted murder.

Moving unsteadily, she made her way to the worktable and groped for the stool. She knew she should stand, but she did not think she would be able to, and at least if she sat upon the stool she could not fling it as a missile at his head.

"That is not what I meant at all," she managed to say after another minute, her voice quiet and hard. "As I'm certain you must know. There is no need for such insults, Mr. Olivier. My male relations might have dealt hardly with you, but I do not recall having done or said anything myself to warrant your hostility."

He smirked. "Does it not warrant my hostility that you come in here and accuse me of stealing your paintings and deceiving the Royal Academy?"

But you very well might have done the former and you certainly *did the latter!* she thought furiously. Edith was beginning to wonder if she herself was in danger of apoplexy.

There was a silence, and she knew she must rally and speak again, or Alwyn would become anxious and investigate. But while she was still trying to regain her composure, Jean-André's curiosity won out.

"Shall we declare a temporary truce, Miss Edith?" he suggested. "Long enough for you to explain how we might still profit together?"

She nodded. "Yes. Thank you." Trusting she was steady enough to stand again, she rose. "What I meant to propose, Mr. Olivier, was that, as you were so successful in promoting and selling a painting that—that looked like one I had done—perhaps we might come to an arrangement. I could offer you two paintings, say, and you might promote and sell those ones—under the name of A. J. Morris or even Alexandre Olivier—in return for dropping the charges against my relations."

While he did not answer immediately, nor did he look away fast enough to hide the spark in his eyes, and she felt her pulse speed. *This might work. This might work!*

Affecting nonchalance, he strolled to the window again and looked into the street. Then he turned and glanced back, drawling, "What sort of paintings?"

"Well—what sort would sell?"

"Have you some ready?"

Regretfully, she shook her head. The weakness in her plan. "I'm afraid not. Only some portraits that I've already given to other people—" (And unless he wanted to stage additional break-ins at her relations' homes, she didn't see how he could get them even if he wanted to.) "But I could—I could begin work on them immediately—and this way you might choose the subjects." She hoped there was no bitterness in her voice. The night before, as she lay in bed, she found herself wondering what had become of *The Players* and *Preparations for breakfast*. Had those also been sold? If they had not, they represented just that much more money in his pocket.

Jean-André had recovered his self-possession. He tapped one of the windowpanes idly and shrugged. "It's a tempting plan, but the next sessions sit in less than a month, and you know your cousin and his companions were only released because their relatives paid a fine. Otherwise they would be in Newgate, waiting to be tried for their offence against the peace. Not to mention your uncle. I need only go to Bow Street to get a warrant against him."

Edith swallowed. "I could finish the paintings in a month."

"Indeed?" He raised skeptical brows, and she hardly blamed him. Not only had she taken a few months to finish her stolen paintings, but she had worked on her art constantly at the time. And now—now she had not even sketched for so long...!

"Yes. I could—I could have sketches for you within a few days and begin painting as soon as you chose. Perhaps you might—you might even write to the person who bought *Portrait of a young gentleman* and interest him in them."

She must have hit on his very thoughts because he jerked away again. "It's an idea," he said, with the same affected carelessness.

"Will you consider it?"

He said nothing, his gaze fixed again on the street. Edith tried not to twitch with the torture of it. She knew he was making calculations, weighing odds. If she was guaranteed not to expose him, he might either sell her paintings right away or submit them to the Academy for the 1815 exhibition. A nomination to the Academy might follow, and then A. J. Morris' career might benefit for several years, even if he were only to produce lesser, inferior works thereafter.

"Edith?" a voice called up from below. "Is all well? Shall I come up?"

She hurried to the doorway. "Thank you, Aunt Eliza. I think our discussion will conclude soon. You need not trouble yourself." Looking back at Jean-André, Edith added more quietly, "Shall I give you more time to consider? I could return again tomorrow."

"No." He had made his decision, for a smile that made her uneasy spread across his face. "No, that won't be necessary. Say you were to return within four days with your sketches? I will require at least five of them to choose from. And if I can find two that please me, we will move forward. If I cannot..." He shrugged and made the clicking sound with his tongue. "*Tant pis.*"

"Very well," she answered, around the lump in her throat. "Have you any preference as to subject?"

"I do." His smile widened. He was enjoying this. "I would like more sketches of your beloved, brother-like, criminal cousin. Other people may figure in the scene, if you like, but he always must. Imagine a series with him. Instead of Hogarth's *The Rake's Progress*, we have Morris' *The Felon's Progress*. There is already the promising young gentleman on the stile. There must follow his introduction to the iniquitous den of London. It is too bad he is *not* being held in Newgate, for it would make a charming picture. Perhaps he has a sweetheart? I would very much like one of the sketches to be the young gentleman with his sweetheart in London. Would that involve a self-portrait, Miss Edith?"

Hating him, she said only, "It will not. But I can sketch something of the sort."

"Perfect! And who can say what the last scene will be? The young gentleman receiving his pardon and marrying the sweetheart, or the young gentleman waving his farewells from the deck of the convict ship? Alas—his fate is in your hands, Miss Edith. It is entirely up to you and the skill of your pencils and brush."

CHAPTER TWENTY-SIX

The signes of two opinions contradictory one to another, namely, Affirmation and Negation of the same thing, is called Controversie.
—Thomas Hobbes, *Humane Nature* (1650)

Lionel awoke toward evening, bolting upright when he heard the murmur of voices. He rubbed his healing injury ruefully as he eased open his door.

He had heard right. Edith had returned.

After splashing water on his face and dragging fingers through his long, unruly hair, he hurried below, to find his family in the drawing room, dressed for supper. In the center of them sat Edith, her sketchbook on her lap and her pencil moving busily.

"You've come back," he croaked lamely.

"Lionel!" cried Caroline, flying to take his arm. "How long you slept! Do you feel any better? Mama says we should summon Mr. White again to check your progress. And we stayed supper, hoping you would wake." Tugging on him, she pulled him back to the sofa where she had been sitting. "Are you hot? Cold? Hungry?"

Her fussing made him frantic, especially when he saw that, apart from one glance at him when he appeared, Edith kept her eyes on her work.

"I'm fine," he muttered, tacking on a "thank you" when he saw his aunt look up from her sewing and frown. On the pretense of straightening his neckcloth he managed to extricate his arm from Caroline's clutch.

"Edith—what happened?"

"Edith is drawing my picture!" Caroline exclaimed. "And she will draw yours! We are to go all over town tomorrow—if you feel well enough—that she might sketch us!"

He shook his head, like a horse troubled by a particularly persistent fly, and said again, "Edith, what happened? Did you see him?"

"She did," answered Caroline promptly. "And you will never guess, Lionel, but there is hope that the man will relent against you and the Clinketts—not to mention Mr. Arbuthnot—"

"Caroline," Hetty interjected, "you had better let Edith answer, or Lionel might burst with impatience."

"Oh, very well," her cousin agreed, giving a little bounce upon the sofa and taking Lionel's arm again. "You tell it, Edith."

But to his frustration, Edith seemed as reticent as Caroline was eager. Instead of meeting his eyes, she looked toward his father. "I've told it all to you, Cousin Hugh. Perhaps you would rather explain it?"

"It had better be you, Edith. I'm sure Lionel will have numerous questions, and it would be more expedient not to talk in circles."

She nodded, setting her pencil aside and shutting her sketchbook to hold it in her lap, her hands folded across its cover. If not for her heightened color, Lionel would have thought she were about to recite a lesson.

"As I told your father when I returned," she began (in exactly the voice she would have used to recite a lesson, having carefully memorized and practiced her story), "my uncle Alwyn and I called on Mr. Morris the first day and found him out. We returned the following morning—"

"Was it that Jean-André person?" interrupted Lionel. "Posing as A. J. Morris?"

Edith took a deep breath. She had debated this point but decided she must admit it, lest Alwyn undermine her story. "Yes. It was," she replied calmly. "And you guessed rightly, Lionel, when you supposed the painting entered in the exhibition was based on the sketch from last summer."

"It was *your* painting," he insisted, not taking his eyes off her.

Her hands tightened. "Well—as you never saw my painting, and as Mr. Olivier has sold it to a foreign buyer, and *I* cannot see it, we cannot be certain...He told me that it was his uncle's copy of my painting, done from memory."

"Utter falsehood! A black-hearted lie!" Lionel half rose, but Caroline dragged on him like an anchor, and he sank back.

"Really, Lionel," reproved his aunt Lavinia. "You must remain calm or you will surely relapse."

He swallowed his retort with an effort, but then tried to make his voice steadier so his Sidney relations would leave him alone. "Edith, you saw the man's other work, surely—nothing like your style. Nothing, nothing like. This painting—the one I saw—wasn't stiff and formal and ponderous. It was alive and—and real—and truthful. The color—the *vividness* of it! Why, no buyer on earth would pay one thousand pounds for any of the stupid works I saw in Jermyn Street—no, they would be lucky to get ten pounds for the lot—"

Edith's color deepened. His vehemence and every word he spoke poured joy and warmth into her. She could live off it forever. She might have to.

But it would do no one any good—and him least of all—for him to champion her further.

"It can never be known for certain," she repeated. "But I thank you for your—good opinion."

His *good opinion*? Lionel wanted to kick over the furniture, hearing his feelings described in such milksop fashion. Kick over the furniture and push Caroline off the end of the sofa. Why couldn't everyone go away and give him five minutes—five *little* minutes—alone with her?

"Tell him about your agreement with Mr. Olivier," Hetty prompted Edith, reading her brother's vexation.

That only irked Lionel further. What sort of agreement could she have with such a man?

Edith noted his fists and hastened to deliver the rest of her rote speech. "Yes, indeed. You see, Lionel, I explained to him—Mr. Olivier, that is—that you grew overexcited out of your loyalty to me—"

"My loyalty, and the fact that he's a lying, insolent, unrepentant fraud," he grumbled.

"Yes—he has a trying manner, at times. My uncle also took offense at Mr. Olivier's—er—comportment," Edith admitted. "But I asked Mr. Olivier if he might be willing to forgive and forget, if we also forgave and forgot that he misrepresented himself as an Englishman when he submitted the portrait to the Academy. And he said he might be persuaded of it."

She paused, as Lionel uttered another expression of his disgust. The falsest part of her falsehood lay ahead, and she braced herself for it.

"Mr. Olivier was very pleased by the price the portrait garnered, and—and he thought that, if I were to produce another painting or two, and he were to sell them, we might...share the proceeds, and he would then drop all charges against you and the Clinketts."

The last of this speech she delivered in a rush, but Lionel was already protesting before she finished.

"Absolutely not! Why should you—cooperate—with such a villain, merely to make him do what he ought in conscience to do?"

"Because he hasn't any conscience, clearly," said Hetty.

"Lionel," interposed his father, "I did speak to your cousin and tried to persuade her not to compound the injustice this person has already done her, but..." He held up his palms.

"As Mr. Olivier pointed out," Edith resumed, maintaining her placid tone with effort, "no artist has a sole right to a subject. If I cannot prove that the painting the Oliviers exhibited was the one which came from my brush, then nor can I prove that they have done me an injustice."

"Does he propose to sell these paintings as yours?" demanded Lionel.

Hugh Hapgood had asked her the same thing, and it had been no easier to answer him.

"He...does not," she confessed.

Then Lionel did spring to his feet with such force that the sofa rocked, Caroline and all. "No, Edith," he said, his voice low and dangerous. "No."

She bit her lip, her façade threatening to crumble. "It is my decision."

"You can't let that—you wouldn't let that—that untalented, scheming, artist's *model* use even more of your works, to pose as a great artist himself? Is it not bad enough that, as A. J. Morris, he peddles his uncle's second-rate pieces? Don't do it, Edith."

"Now, now, Lionel, you are overexcited again," admonished Lavinia. "I will ring to let them know we are ready for supper. A little food will settle you."

"We told Edith as much," Hetty insisted, both she and her brother ignoring their aunt, "but she won't be moved."

"She must. You must, Edith. Why should you make these concessions to this man?"

Edith rose to her feet because six feet of Lionel glowering down at her was too much to bear. "I already told you: if I strike this bargain with him, he will tear up the warrant he has against you and the Clinketts."

"I would rather rot in Newgate than have you do this!"

"And I would rather do this than have you rot in Newgate!" Frustration choked her. "If Newgate is all that might happen to you—it might be seven years' transportation, Lionel—or—or worse! It is not only assaulting him, as if that weren't bad enough! But you also kicked in that painting of Saint Sebastian. People are sent away for far less than that. People have been transported for so little damage as twenty shillings! Why won't you see reason?"

"Because—confound it!—excuse me, Aunt—why should you have to sacrifice in any way for something I myself did?"

Oh, my dearest, she wanted to cry, *I would give up far, far more than this, to save you.*

The footmen entered with ceremony, and then Lavinia was taking Hugh's arm and Mr. Sidney led Hetty. Caroline was hanging from Lionel before he knew what she was about, but he offered his other arm to Edith. Laying her fingers so lightly on his sleeve he could scarcely feel them, she murmured, "You *must* listen to me, Lionel. Don't you see? He tells me he managed to sell the portrait of you to someone in Prince Metternich's entourage. And, if he had two companion paintings to offer that person, that person would of course want them to be done by the same artist. By A. J. Morris."

He said nothing, but Clinker and Clunker would have recognized the cemented-shut appearance of his clenched jaw.

"I, for one, cannot understand the fuss," Lavinia Sidney began, after the soup was served. "Lionel, you are a young man with your education and your future to think of. I think your cousin Edith has hit upon a very neat solution. After all, whatever your talents, Miss Edith, you are *not* a famous artist, and if this unscrupulous person has found a means to profit by using your work, there is something to be said for his skills there."

Her nephew set his spoon down and regarded Edith. "Exactly what proportion of these profits does he propose to share with you, Edith, if not any credit for the works?"

Edith set her own spoon down, clearing her throat quietly. She had decided beforehand that her family would prove immoveable if she gave away both her paintings *and* the profits gained, so she managed to reply with seeming sincerity, "If he can sell the paintings, Mr. Olivier has assured me ten per cent of the purchase price." With her limited pin money, Edith did not dare to vouch for a greater amount. In which case, she probably should not have mentioned the Austrian buyer, but she comforted herself that no one but Jean-André would ever know the final prices.

"You see?" asked Lavinia. "Lionel, you and your friends are excused, and Miss Edith possibly sees some profit. You are young, Miss Edith. You have all your life to paint many works and receive *all* the credit and profit for them. When I see your sketches, Mr. Sidney and I may very well commission a portrait of dear Caroline from you, in honor of her engagement."

"Thank you." It was nearly a whisper and was drowned out, in any event, by Caroline's excited squeak.

"Oh, Mama! I can't tell you how I should love to be painted! I *do* hope you like Miss Edith's style. I know Lionel does, and he has excellent taste." Caroline beamed at her intended. "Lionel, Edith says the two proposed paintings will possibly form a series, to go with the portrait of you on the stile. That was the young gentleman in the country, and these will be the young gentleman in town. And there will be one of us together because I am to be the young gentleman's sweetheart! Only imagine!"

"I have not yet consented to be painted, or sketched," said Lionel through gritted teeth.

But Edith had had enough of his stubbornness. "Then I'm afraid I will have to sketch you without your consent. You never minded before."

"I never minded when they were for your own practice and pleasure."

"We will go to St. Paul's," struck in Hetty. "I was reading in Bowles' guidebook about the wonders of the cathedral, and I have never been. Wouldn't it make a marvelous background, Edie?"

"Marvelous."

Lionel remained obstinate and silent during the remainder of the meal, though Caroline easily filled the space. He saw Hetty watching him fixedly, and when he finally glared at her to make her stop, she spread her hands and mouthed, *Wait. I have a plan. Trust me.*

He grimaced. Hetty and her plans.

Well, he had plans of his own.

He was going to talk to Edith alone, without every Hapgood and Sidney in London hanging about, even if he had to lock every last one of them in the Tower of London to do it.

Chapter Twenty-Seven

Then go above the Gallery of the Cupola…where lean-ing your head against the Wall, you may easily hear all that is said, tho' it be whisper'd ever so low and at the most distant Place from you in the same Gallery.
—T. Bowles, *A New Guide to London* (1726)

What did it feel like, to draw the new beloved of the one you loved? As her pencil moved swiftly over her paper, Edith was aware of a curious mixture of relief and pain. Relief, that she could still take a likeness, after months of refusing even to take tools in hand, and pain that—well, that was obvious.

It should have been a day of lifting spirits. The young people were abroad on their own, with no Lavinia to cluck at them, and the possible solution to Lionel's troubles lay within Edith's control. But it was only Caroline Sidney who bubbled with enthusiasm. Lionel was silent and surly; Hetty fidgeted with impatience because Caroline insisted on going to Regent's Park again, before proceeding to St. Paul's; and Edith—Edith was quiet as Lionel, apart from giving little instructions to her models.

"Lean out a little way, Lionel," she told him. "With your elbows on the railing of the bridge. And turn your head to look at Caroline. Caroline, you be looking at the water, while he studies your face."

Lionel obeyed, but not before favoring Edith herself with a long glare, to which her only acknowledgement was a murmured, "You needn't smile, but it would help if you didn't appear cross."

"Oh, I don't know," said Hetty over Edith's shoulder. "The course of true love never did run smooth. Perhaps the young gentleman is fretting over obstacles in his path."

"Well, he had better not fret quite so much because we can't have his sweetheart smiling in bliss while he scowls in vexation."

His sister's jokes did not improve Lionel's mood, but he mustered a more neutral expression for the bridge sketch. And a neutral expression as he and Caroline admired swans from the gravel walk. And a neutral expression even for the pose by the willows, where Edith had him take Caroline's hand. Nevertheless, when Hetty fell into step beside him, he hissed at her, "Is this all part of your supposed plan?"

"No, but St. Paul's is," she muttered. "When we get there, we'll climb up to the dome. I'll get Caroline to come ahead with me, and you will get your chance to talk to Edith."

Hetty's plan proved easier said than done. For, while Lionel and Edith were willing enough to let Hetty direct their outing, Caroline had ideas of her own. As the hackney coach bumped and rattled down Tottenham Court Road and turned into Holborn, she cried, "Who wants to see old St. Paul's anyway? I would rather go to Hyde Park and St. James. Wouldn't those make better settings, Edith?" She fluttered her lashes Lionel-ward. "Or St. George's, Hanover Square. Perhaps one of the sketches of the young gentleman should be his wedding day."

"St. Paul's," said Hetty inexorably.

And then, when Caroline peered from the clouded coach windows, she gasped, "The Old Bailey! And Newgate Street! I had no idea they were so near to St. Paul's. Oh, Lionel, I shiver for you."

Peering out onto the fortress-like solidity of the Sessions House, its connection to the prison hidden behind brick walls, Lionel was perfectly capable of shivering for himself. He paled and darted a glance at Edith, whose eyes met his briefly, her lips trembling.

"Dreadful," pronounced Caroline. "I don't want to be anywhere near such places. I don't even wish to be reminded that they exist. Hetty, let us tell the coachman to take us to Westminster Abbey, instead. Won't that do, if you want a scene in a church?"

"Don't be silly," said Hetty, though she looked unsettled herself. She forced a jesting tone. "We are already here. And if we get brave enough, perhaps Edith might sketch Lionel outside the Old Bailey: *Portrait of a young gentleman turned convict.* Or, *His doom is sealed.*"

It was a silent group that descended from the coach in the churchyard.

Lionel paid the fare and Edith drew out her sketchbook, Hetty hustling them to inspect the church's exterior. She read to them from her Bowles' guidebook as Edith shaded in the porticos and columns of the three doors, but Caroline did not bother to conceal her boredom and declared the conversion of St. Paul depicted in the pediment too blackened and distant to interest.

More to her taste was the interior of the cathedral, with its soaring space, its elaborate carvings and patterned floor. As for Sir James Thornhill's painted cycle of incidents from the apostle's life, Caroline said, "I do not see why they always put the paintings up where no one can see them clearly. They ought all to be at ground level, if they expect anyone to learn from them."

"But that's just it," Hetty replied eagerly. "Bowles recommends we climb up to the gallery, where we will see the paintings much better, as well as have a view downward. And, after we have seen the gallery, we may climb still further to the outside of the dome and look out upon the city."

Edith's eyes shone. "Yes, let's! At least climb to the inner gallery. I should very much like a closer look at the art."

Caroline shrugged. "If you like, but I will wait here below. You need not hurry. I will be quite content."

"No!" exclaimed Hetty. "You *must* come, Caroline."

"Whatever for? I don't particularly care for art or views."

"You just said the art ought all to be at ground level where you might see it," her cousin pointed out in exasperation. "Besides, you—you can't remain down here by yourself. You know your mother would not approve."

"Mama is not here." But she tilted her head and smiled at Lionel. "Though perhaps you might wait with me? Hetty and Edith can go up."

"I'm going up as well," he said.

She pouted becomingly. "Wouldn't you rather sit a while and have a quiet coze?"

Hetty's elbow jabbed Edith, and Edith blurted, "But Caroline—if I do any sketches up there, I would certainly need you. Imagine—imagine *The young gentleman and his sweetheart, with the world at their feet.*"

This appeal to her vanity overcame her fear of fatigue. "Oh! I didn't think of that. Very well, then," Caroline agreed. "Lionel, may I take your arm?"

"Take mine," urged Hetty, seizing Caroline's hand. "Lionel will have to carry Edith's sketchbook and tools—he won't have a limb free." With that, she practically dragged her cousin away, ignoring her surprised protest.

With a deprecating shrug, Edith handed her sketchbook and pencil box to Lionel, who took them as eagerly as Hetty might wish, and they followed.

Their tuppences paid, they climbed the narrow stairs, Edith conscious of him on her heels. The idea of Lionel watching her—backside and all—almost made her forget how to put one foot in front of the other. She wished he had gone ahead, that she might observe *him* to her heart's content. At one point she slowed and could almost feel his breath when he asked, "Are you tired?" Shaking her head, she went on.

For his part, Lionel's gaze did indeed keep returning to the tantalizing glimpses of Edith's ankles, appearing and disappearing in the movement of her skirts, and his quickened breath was not altogether attributable to the many steps. What would happen if he caught hold of her now? One tug on her slender arm and she would tumble backward against him. Would she be angry? Would she cry out? He imagined silencing her cry by pressing his lips to hers, and the vision made him pause. He leaned against the staircase railing. *Easy, there.*

They emerged into the railed gallery of the dome, some hundred feet above the floor below. Clapping her hands, Edith forgot her embarrassment and ran to the iron rail to marvel at the patterns of the cathedral floor far beneath, then twirled to gaze upward at Thornhill's *grisaille* scenes from the life of St. Paul. "Wonderful! Wonderful," she breathed. Her face turned to him, alight. "They truly look solid, like carved stone. Do they not? Caroline is right—the *trompe l'œil* is even more effective at this distance. And how powerful the figures are! Like the prints Mr. Eldredge showed me of Michelangelo's prophets in the Sistine Chapel. Did I tell you Uncle Alwyn and Aunt Eliza may go to Paris and Rome, now that the peace has come? And they said I may go with them, if I like."

No sooner did the words escape her than she remembered her beloved cousin might be rotting in a prison hulk or laboring under a blazing New South Wales sun while she frolicked on the Continent, and she blushed. "Oh, forgive me, Lionel. I certainly wouldn't consider going anywhere until these two paintings are done."

She needn't have felt bad—being sentenced for assault was the furthest thing from his mind at the moment. He saw in a glance that

Hetty had somehow inveigled Caroline halfway around the dome already and was pointing up at one of the statues in the niches. As if feeling his look, his sister jerked her head to meet his gaze. Swiftly she motioned to him, pointing to the gallery wall and then moving her hand to indicate talking. Again, she pointed to him and then the wall, and then made the talking motion.

Lionel had no idea what she was flapping about, but he didn't care, because he intended to make the most of this opportunity to speak to Edith, whom he stepped to block when she made to follow the others.

"Edith—wait."

On the opposite side of the dome, Caroline straightened in surprise and looked about her. "Did you hear that, Hetty? It sounded like Lionel, but he is all the way over there."

Hetty put a finger to her lips. Pulling her cousin nearer, she cupped a hand and whispered in her ear. "It's a secret. I didn't tell you all. But, if we stand close to the wall and are very quiet, we can eavesdrop on Lionel and Edith. It said so in the guidebook."

She was relieved that Caroline made no protestations of propriety—rather her eyes lit up, and, nodding and wiggling with glee, she crept closer to the wall. Cupping her own hand, she hissed back in Hetty's ear, "I do hope he says something about me! If he does, I will not be able to resist answering. He would be able to hear me as well, wouldn't he?"

Nodding, Hetty again put a finger to her lips. Caroline mirrored her nod, and they leaned in.

"Edith, you must tell me," Lionel was saying. Though his voice was pitched low, Hetty and Caroline heard him distinctly. For privacy, he and Edith had turned naturally to the wall on their side of the dome.

"What must I tell you?"

"Why are you doing this? Why are you so willing to give this villainous man your work?"

"You know why—I've already said—if he accepts them, he will forgive you." She was flustered, speaking quickly.

"I can defend myself," he declared. "If I must appear in court, I must, and I have no qualms about exposing him. I may have attacked him first, but he was the one who stabbed me."

"In self-defense," she murmured. "He will say he had to, in self-defense."

Lionel muttered something his sister and Caroline couldn't catch, but Hetty guessed it was a curse directed at his antagonist. Then he said, "But, Edith, I must know—is there more to it? Do you cooperate with him for another reason?"

"What other reason could there be?"

"What I mean to say is—I need to know—does—does this person mean something to you?"

There was a silence. Both girls peeped and saw Edith shaking her head with vehemence. "No. No, he does not. He is the nephew of my former teacher. That and nothing more."

"Then why did he—why do you suppose he...*jeered* at me when the Clinketts and I called? Tried to antagonize me?"

"That is just the sort of person he is. He has always had a scornful manner. And, as you described it, you *did* make him angry by questioning the provenance of the portrait."

Lionel batted this away, leaning closer to her. "Tell me the truth, Edith—does that man care for you?"

"Care for me? What—what nonsense. Why should he care for me?"

"Because you are so beautiful," came his unwilling but earnest response. "Beautiful inside and out. Like a star—"

She gasped softly. The two girls ventured another peek and saw her back away from him a step, holding up her hands as if she would ward him off. "It's—it's—it's very kind of you to say so. But you must not seek reasons to resent Mr. Olivier any more than you already do. I assure you, he cares only for himself and for profit!"

"Then he never—made advances to you?"

Again she was silenced. They saw her retreat another step. But she did not deny it. She did not shake her head.

"I knew it!" he declared, so loudly that the girls had no need of cunning acoustics to hear him. They turned back to the wall nonetheless, afraid he would look over and see them listening. "He pretends to care for you and treats you thus? Of all the slimy, presumptuous, iniquitous, insolent, pernicious, *fraudulent*, lying, thieving, bandy-legged—"

"Shhhhh...." Edith tried in vain to quiet him and finally had to clutch the lapels of his blue frock coat and give him a little shake. "Hush, Lionel," she murmured. "I am not defending his character. I only want him to leave you alone and be gone. Vanish forever.

You were very good to take my part. I am everlastingly grateful that you did. But the price you will pay is too high. What do a couple paintings matter? What does it matter, if he should profit by them? I only want to repay your kindness with kindness of my own. I only want to leave you free to live your life. To go back to university and finish your degree. To marry, when you like—"

He took hold of her hands, clinging on when she tried to pull them away. "But I'll never marry, Edith," he said. "Not ever. Are you listening to me? I'll—never—marry. Not unless I can marry you."

This declaration drew simultaneous gasps from both sides of the dome, one of them much louder and from right beside Hetty. She saw that Caroline's eyes were round as saucers and that she gazed blankly at the gallery wall, as if the astonishing revelation she had just received were carved in stone upon its face.

There, thought Lionel. It was said. Or said again, rather. And this time the confession was made under far worse circumstances than the previous summer. It was almost laughable. While he had managed not to smash her on the head this time, he made up for it by having a criminal charge looming over him and a betrothed hanging 'round his neck, not altogether figuratively. Worse yet, Edith thought she had to save him. Save him, when he had meant to save her!

She pulled her hands free, and he pressed a fist against the wall of the dome.

"If you were mine," he said, "I would never let you do what you're trying to do. I want to sacrifice for you, not you for me."

Her beautiful grey eyes searched his.

Wondered.

Doubted.

"How can you be saying these things?" she whispered.

He held up his palms, helpless. "How can I not?"

"But—if this is how you feel—why—why did you propose to Caroline?"

"I didn't, Edith! Not consciously! I mean, I wasn't conscious, when I said whatever it was I might have said. I was feverish. Or drugged with laudanum. Or both! I simply woke up to find myself engaged. Convicted on the testimony of two witnesses, apparently." He reached for her again, and she was so dazed and fluttered that she left her hand in his. "You must believe me, Edie. Edie—precious Edie."

"He said 'Edie,'" peeped Caroline, putting her own hand against the wall to steady herself. It slid down.

"Of course he did," Hetty hissed beside her ear, wanting to clap a hand over the girl's mouth. "It's her name, after all."

"But I thought—I thought he wanted to eat." With that, she fainted, collapsing against Hetty, who staggered under her cousin's limp body and struggled to maneuver it onto the stone bench lining the gallery's perimeter.

"But what will you do?" breathed Edith, oblivious to the drama across the wide space of the dome. "Caroline adores you! You cannot mean to jilt her? Your aunt might very well kill you."

He gave her a bleak smile. "Perhaps I will embrace my sentence of transportation. Hetty says she doesn't think Caroline is the sort to follow me to Botany Bay, and waiting seven years or more for my return might stretch even *her* devotion."

It wouldn't stretch mine, Edith nearly said. But she succeeded in checking this confession. Because she had to keep her head clear. She *had* to. To think for both of them.

Hadn't he troubles enough? If she were to throw herself at him now and say she had begun to return his feelings, what would happen? He would assert his rights over her—he had said as much. He would forbid her to "sacrifice" herself, and by doing so he would seal his own doom. He would have to abide by whatever punishment lay in store. On top of that, he would throw over Caroline for certain, causing a rift in his family, and adding immeasurably to the distress of the situation—and likely be happy about it. Off he would go to New South Wales, heedless of the consequences to all.

Against all this, would it not be better, then—wiser—to continue with her own plan? To buy his freedom from Jean-André by her own efforts, and then to leave to time and chance a possible end to his engagement with Caroline?

Yes. It would.

She made up her mind in that instant. There would be no confessions, no embraces, and no distractions. No kisses of utter, unforgettable deliciousness. She would paint her paintings as she planned. She would work for his freedom as she planned. And, if somehow things played out as she hoped, perhaps he might drag out his engagement to his cousin until Caroline's adoration faded or she met someone else. They were young—all of them. Lionel not yet nineteen, Caroline eighteen, and Edith seventeen. Anything might happen.

For one moment more she left her hand in his; and then she freed herself.

"But I hope you will never face transportation," she said, "if I can help it. And, as I am *not* yours, I'm afraid it is not your place to tell me what I may or may not do with my works."

"Edith—don't pull away. You must tell me—may I hope? Do you still feel exactly as you did last June? Because when I saw the painting—your painting—I thought perhaps you might have begun to care for me, even if only a little. That maybe I succeeded in opening your eyes."

Temptation raised its head again. How she longed to tell him that he had indeed succeeded! That what he had seen in his portrait anyone with eyes could have seen—did see. Jean-André had known it at once. That she loved her subject. Dearly. Oh, would she play this moment out again and again over the years, wishing she chose differently?

One more lie, she told herself. *But it will be the last.*

"Lionel," Edith said softly. "I have told you. You are dear to me—dearer—than any brother could be. But that is all. It would not be fair to tell you otherwise. It would not be wise for you to believe otherwise. I think—yes—I think—"

"You think I had better not hope," he finished for her dully.

"...Yes."

He turned from her then, looking anywhere but at her, going to lean against the railing. "Dear God," he said, "Caroline's swooned or something. We had better take her back to Devonshire Street."

"All right." She felt her throat close as he withdrew from her. Even if he came through it all unharmed—and even if he somehow managed to shed his unwanted engagement—would too much damage have been done? Would she have hurt him too many times?

I am hurting him to help *him. Being cruel to be kind.*

He picked up her sketchbook and pencil box from the bench. "I wonder what would happen if I just dropped these over the railing."

"You'd kill someone, I imagine," Edith managed. "And then we might as well leave you at Newgate while the rest of us return to the Sidneys'. Besides, I don't want them dropped over the railing. I need them."

"Not for my sake you don't," he said shortly, beckoning across the dome for his sister and cousin to join them.

"And why is that?"

"Because I'll have nothing more to do with these two paintings you propose."

"But, Lionel—"

"I won't trouble you again with my attentions," he said bitterly, stabbing her to the heart, "but I'll be *horsewhipped* if I lift a finger to help that man profit by you. If you insist on carrying out your plan against my wishes, you must do so with no more assistance from me."

Chapter Twenty-Eight

The longer Men live in Sin, the more Unwilling they are to think of a Judgement-Day.

—E. Maynard, *Sermon preach'd before the University of Oxford* (1722)

Edith set her brush down, frowning at the painting on the easel before her. It was the scene from the bridge in Regent's Park, which she already titled in her mind *Portrait of a young gentleman in a dreadful mess*. As a piece of art, the portrait was something of a dreadful mess itself.

With a heavy heart, she had gone to meet Jean-André again, accompanied by her uncle's wife Mrs. Arbuthnot, who could be trusted not to assault the man if he was provoking. Edith had exactly five sketches to present to him, for, after the debacle at St. Paul's, Lionel had been good as his word and refused to pose for her anymore. More surprising was Caroline's lack of protest at his decision. She was subdued and possibly cross, but Edith was too upset herself to be curious.

"This is it?" Jean-André demanded, laying out the drawings. Three were from their time in the park. The fourth was a combination of Edith's sketch of St. Paul's exterior, with Lionel and Caroline added from other occasions. And the last was a pure figment of Edith's imagination: the couple in profile, standing before the Old Bailey at their parting. She had copied the building's front from an engraving in the newspaper and attempted the lovers entirely from memory, and she could not say it was very successful, but she suspected Jean-André would like the idea of it, and he did.

"It is a simple story," said Edith. "In *Portrait of a young gentleman* we met him fresh from the country, with his future before him. In the second painting, he meets his true love. And in the third, they must separate because he has got into some sort of trouble and will soon be imprisoned or transported—"

"Or hanged," Jean-André supplied cheerfully. He tapped his finger on the table, considering. "Yes, this could work."

"It could?"

"*Could*, not *will*, Miss Edith."

"But if I agree to paint two of these scenes for you, you will indeed drop your action?"

He took a long time to answer, but she knew he wanted to torment her with suspense, so she held her tongue. She would not plead or argue, for it would only add to his satisfaction.

At last he said, "I had better see how the paintings develop, before I make a decision. They will be somewhat rushed affairs, you know."

"I know. The sessions are coming up, however. I would not wish to begin painting if it is all for naught."

"You might keep them yourself, if it is 'all for naught,'" he suggested. "And, if you could sell them, you might use that money to purchase passage to visit your dear cousin."

Edith's mouth thinned. "Have you at least written your buyer?"

From the way his gaze flicked away she knew that he had, but he shrugged. "I have not yet heard a response. I suppose the letter must chase him back to Austria." To change the subject, he placed his hands flat on the table. "I had better make my selections so that I may describe them to him. Hmm...let it be this one and...this." He drew aside Lionel and Caroline on the bridge in Regent's Park and the two of them parting before the Old Bailey.

"Get started, and I will call on you in a week to see your progress. I suppose you can arrange it that I need not encounter your violent cousin when I come?"

"You need not," she agreed coolly, "for it happens I am now staying with my violent uncle. But I will ensure he will not trouble you either. His wife, my aunt, will leave a card with their address."

And now the week was gone, and Edith was beside herself.

The figures were passable, she supposed. Stiff, but passable. But the faces! The faces of her young gentleman and his sweetheart were

so impossible that she had painted them over in the bridge picture—only empty moons stared, where their countenances should
be. And in the Old Bailey piece she had abandoned the entire plan
of depicting them in profile and begged her uncle Alwyn and aunt
Eliza to model for her, so she could sketch them from behind, looking not at each other but both toward the brick wall. Wretched,
wretched. She was certain Jean-André would reject it and insist on
them being shown in profile, and then what would she do?

It was as if Lionel's disapprobation cursed her fingers. Knowing
if she remained in Devonshire Street, defying him, she would not
be able to paint a single stroke, she had fled to the Arbuthnots in
Bruton Street. But the spirit of Lionel pursued her. And here, in
an upstairs bedroom with the best morning light, she had produced
these...failures.

"What will I do?" she murmured, wringing her hands. "Is it
because I secretly *want* Lionel to be transported for seven years, so
that Caroline will dissolve their engagement? Or is it because I have
always been tutored and coddled and petted and praised for my art,
and now that I am alone and forced to paint a subject who is angry
with me, to suit a patron who hates me, to please a buyer I'll never
know, everything falls to ruin?"

And if she failed—if Jean-André refused to accept these clumsy,
unbeautiful works, would Lionel be not only lost to them all, but
go away thinking she didn't care? That she had not tried?

"But you told me not to paint these!" she argued with the invisible
Lionel. "So you should not be able, then, to accuse me of not trying,

when you did not want me to try! Oh, but the worst thing is that I *am* trying."

Not only trying, but spending a good deal of money as well, since she had left all her brushes and pigment powders and linseed oil and spirit of turpentine in Somerset and had to buy them anew in town.

There was a scratch at the door, and one of the Arbuthnots' maids appeared. "Miss, a Mr. Jean-André Olivier is here and asking to come up. He says you are expecting him."

"Yes, I am expecting him, Binchin," sighed Edith. "But before you send him up, will you let Mrs. Arbuthnot know he is come? And please remind my uncle that he had better keep to his study, if he insists on remaining home."

Despondently she removed her apron and went to stand beside her painting, mustering an approximation of a smile when her Mrs. Arbuthnot appeared, sewing in hand. "Thank you, my dear aunt."

Eliza winked at her. "Alwyn says I am to ring for Binchin, if the man so much as looks at you sideways, my dear. But I fear it will not be Binchin who comes bursting in."

"I hope that will not be necessary, Aunt."

A minute later, they heard Binchin's tread again, followed by the heavier footsteps of the young man.

"Mr. Olivier, miss. Ma'am." With a curtsy, she withdrew.

"Ah! Let me see this," cried Jean-André, nodding at each of the ladies before striding across the room. But he halted as if he had walked into the brick wall of the Old Bailey itself when he caught sight of the bridge portrait's blank faces. "What is this?" He peered more closely. "You began their faces, but then you painted over them!"

"They weren't right," said Edith.

"But they will be, will they not? Of course you cannot have a faceless painting."

She swallowed. "I will continue to work on them. The question is, do you think my progress is satisfactory?"

He whirled to stare at her, his expression suspicious, repellent. "I cannot say yet. Where is the other one? *The Parting*? Don't tell me this is all you have done in a week! You must not be very anxious about your beloved cousin."

Edith's squared her shoulders. Stepping around where her aunt sat uncertainly on a pink sofa with a curving back, she retrieved the canvas which leaned against the wall and returned to lay it on the worktable. "The paint is not yet dry."

But Jean-André was already clicking his tongue and shaking his head. "No. What is this? Why am I looking at their backs? Why are they not looking at each other? This is not how it was in your sketch. This is not what we agreed to, Miss Edith."

"They are contemplating his grim future," she said, nervousness making her voice hard. "He is going to prison or into exile, and it will be a sentence for both of them, being apart. That is why they are looking at the wall."

"No!" He rapped his knuckles on the table. "No, this is not what I described to him."

Her mouth fell open slightly, and then she snapped it shut. "Mr. Olivier, do you mean you have heard from your potential buyer in the past week? Is it the Austrian?"

He drew back, a mask of blandness falling over his face. "I may have a buyer," he replied in an offhand way. "But I described the sketches clearly, and it was those precise descriptions that he is considering. Therefore, you cannot paint something else entirely."

"I'm *not* painting something else entirely," she objected. "It's a different interpretation of the scene."

"Blank moon faces?" He jabbed a finger toward the bridge portrait, his voice rising. "People staring at a brick wall? No! No, no, no! You must do exactly as I say—"

"Or you will not honor your part of the bargain?"

"There was no bargain yet," he reminded her. "There was only the chance of a bargain, depending on what you did this week. The court session draws nearer, when the matter will be taken entirely out of both our hands, Miss Edith."

Mrs. Arbuthnot had not listened to all this impassively, and she had come to stand beside her niece. "Edith—shall I ring for Binchin?"

"No!" blurted Edith. All she needed now, on top of everything else, was Uncle Alwyn hurtling in, hurtling at Jean-André, and sending Jean-André hurtling in turn to Bow Street for another warrant! "No, please, Aunt Eliza. Mr. Olivier and I can settle this matter."

"There would be nothing to settle if you were not trying to change the terms of the agreement!" snapped Jean-André.

"And I say that 'change' is too strong a word! You want faces on the bridge picture? Very well, there will be faces. Of *course* there will be faces. And as for *The Parting*, perhaps we might compromise with them facing the wall at three-quarters position, so that one quarter of their face is visible—"

"Pro-file! Pro-file! Pro-file!" he bellowed, pounding a fist on the worktable with each syllable.

In all the rumpus, no one heard Binchin's scratch at the door, so when she opened it, three surprised faces turned toward her.

"Er—a Miss Blenkensop to see Miss Edith. Should I tell her to come back later?"

"I *cannot* come back later!" declared a familiar voice, calling up the stairs.

"*Soppy?*" breathed Edith, astonished into using her cousins' rude nickname for the woman. "What on earth...?"

Miss Blenkensop's familiar voice was soon followed by Miss Blenkensop's familiar shape in the doorway. "Edith!" She rushed at her former charge, scaffolding her in her bony arms. "Edith, forgive me arriving without warning. I had to see you at once, for I must make a terrible confession to you!"

"A confession?" echoed Edith.

But her unexpected visitor was taking in the others present at their conference. Mrs. Arbuthnot received a brief curtsey, but one long look at Jean-André resulted in all Miss Blenkensop's secret pudding softness being covered with a cloth and put back in the cabinet. "Sir?" she accosted him loftily. "I have not the honor of your acquaintance."

"Miss—dear Miss Blenkensop," began Edith, "this is Mr. Jean-André Olivier, an acquaintance of mine from my time in Bath. His uncle is a friend of our Mr. Eldredge. Mr. Olivier, this is my former governess Miss Blenkensop."

Edith's former governess drew herself to her full height and apparently put on her full armor, for she announced in a voice of iron: "I have heard of this young man."

Somehow it seemed Jean-André had heard of Miss Blenkensop as well, for his color drained away, and Edith could swear he shrunk some inches before their very eyes.

Doubtfully, she looked from on to the other. "What brings you to London, Miss Blenkensop? Mr. Olivier and I were conducting some business, but it will not take much longer, if you are able to wait below for me—"

"My business in coming to London will likely be *of great interest* to the business you are conducting with Mr. Olivier," Miss Blenkensop replied ominously. She watched Jean-André as if he would sneak from the room if she took her eyes off him. "And I would recommend he stay to hear my business, if he knows what is good for him."

"Ah...won't you sit down, then?" invited Mrs. Arbuthnot, indicating the pink-padded armchair opposite the sofa.

Miss Blenkensop looked askance at the deep cushions and instead removed Edith's palette from the stool on which she had placed it, set it on the worktable, and then perched herself on the stool. "Thank you."

Edith took a seat beside her aunt on the sofa, leaving Jean-André to drift to the padded armchair like a sleepwalker and collapse onto it. All eyes turned to the rigid older woman, and, for the first time, she hesitated. Withdrawing a handkerchief from her reticule, she blew her nose in it, dabbed once at each eye (fiercely), and then replaced it.

"Miss Edith. I regret to say I have news of an alarming nature. No, no—it is nothing to do with your father or family. I left them all in perfect health. Rather—it is to do with Mr. Eldredge." His name emerged with something of a squeak, and she resorted once more to the handkerchief.

"Is Mr. Eldredge also in good health?" faltered Edith. "My former drawing master," she added, for her aunt's understanding.

Miss Blenkensop sniffed. "I hate to say it, but Mr. Eldredge has—has—perpetrated a crime of the most reprehensible nature. So reprehensible that I felt—felt called upon—to—to report it—to you, Miss Edith—his primary v-victim!" Here, to Edith's utter amazement, the woman burst into racking sobs, swiftly reducing the handkerchief to a sodden ball.

"Miss Blenkensop!" cried Edith, springing up to put an arm about her heaving shoulders, while Mrs. Arbuthnot dug a remnant of fabric from her workbasket for the governess to bury her face in. "Miss Blenkensop, please—I beg you to be calm and explain yourself. Mr. Eldredge has never done me any wrong, so there has been a misapprehension of some sort—"

"Stop!" shrieked the woman, pointing a terrible finger at Jean-André, who had risen unnoticed from the pink armchair and crept toward the door.

He did stop, for a bare instant, flinging her a panicked look, but then he turned and lunged for the door handle, nearly breaking it in his eagerness to escape the room.

"He's getting away!" Miss Blenkensop screamed, throwing off Edith's arm and shoving aside Mrs. Arbuthnot as she leapt after the fleeing man.

But Jean-André was a good fifteen years younger than his pursuer, and he was slamming through the door and vaulting down the staircase before she even reached the threshold. "Stop him! Somebody stop him!"

By the time Edith and Mrs. Arbuthnot reached the door and Miss Blenkensop the top of the stairs, there came a series of tumbling thuds, followed by a world-ending crash and then, as a postscript, the tinkly shattering of a favorite Doccia-Ginori porcelain bowl Mrs. Arbuthnot kept by the first-floor landing. When Edith scrambled to her former governess' side, she joined her in looking down at her uncle and Jean-André engaged in another grappling match, rolling and sliding on the polished wood floor as they punched and wrestled and kicked.

"Alwyn!" gasped his wife, pushing past them. "Trenton! Smollett! Come quickly and help your master!"

The footmen (who had already been drawn by the noise of the row) materialized as the women descended, but before anyone could intervene, Jean-André scrambled to his feet, a long, wicked shard of the Doccia-Ginori bowl in his hand. He waved it in a wild semicircle at them, shouting, "Get back! Get back, all of you!" Both his lip and his hand were bleeding, his lip from a lucky punch of Alwyn's and his hand from the sharp porcelain he held. "Nobody touch me," he growled, backing slowly.

"This man is a thief, a fence, and a deceiver!" pronounced Miss Blenkensop direfully, her eyes ablaze with vengeful justice. "I declare this on the confession of his accomplices, who have all benefited greatly, share and share alike, and those wronged by him will prosecute to the full extent of the law."

"Not if you can't find me!" Jean-André countered. Swinging the shard at them again, he suddenly clenched his fist even more tightly around it, bent his elbow at a right angle and slapped his upper arm with his left hand. Edith had no idea what this gesture meant, but that it was rude and defiant was obvious even before Alwyn gave another roar. When her uncle dove for the young man again, however, his arms closed on empty air, for Jean-André had thrown himself down the first-floor staircase, half flying, half sliding down the banister on his midsection. The front door was open in a flash and slammed behind the absconding villain with such force that Mrs. Arbuthnot's Meissen Harlequin vibrated right off the mantel, to land unharmed in the thick turkey carpet.

"Well, then," said Miss Blenkensop, a little breathlessly into the ringing silence, "I suppose that's that."

Chapter Twenty-Nine

**One misfortune frequently becomes
a consolation for another.
—J. Smeaton, *A narrative of the building and a description of the construction of the Edystone Lighthouse* (1793)**

If Edith passed a wretched week, Lionel's was no better. No sooner had she decamped for her Arbuthnot relatives than he wished he had not taken so implacable a stance with her. If she had stayed in Devonshire Street, he might have ensured that little work went forward on the objectionable sketches and possibly even have prevented her going to present them to that scoundrel Jean-André. Would it not have been better, to persuade her gently to yield, out of her sisterly love for him?

Her sisterly love.

He grimaced each time he thought of it. What a fool he had been. Over and over. It seemed if she were near, he could not help himself—he must speak. And if he divorced himself from her, avoided her and all mention of her entirely, as he had for the previous year, that proved no better guarantee of wisdom.

Clearly, she did not want him defending her. While she claimed to appreciate the sentiment behind his impulsive attack on that villain, now she viewed Lionel's predicament as an account to be balanced, by making a gesture and sacrifice of her own. She would never believe him if he told her that he hardly cared, now, what became of him. Prison. Transportation. Marriage to his vapid cousin. It was all one. Because what did any of it matter, if she wouldn't have him? If she didn't want him?

Had Lionel not been so absorbed in his unhappiness and in berating himself, he might have noticed that his "vapid" cousin Caroline was deep in thought herself, and had been since the visit to St. Paul's. Hetty noticed, of course, but Hetty was on the lookout for signs. Caroline no longer hung on her cousin. She no longer teased and pouted and questioned him. Instead she worked at her sewing when he was present, a frown coming and going on her pretty face. Or she played songs on the pianoforte, which she had earlier learned from quizzing Hetty and Edith that he enjoyed. She listened when he spoke with others and waited to see if he would address her, but Lionel did no more than the minimum. With her or with anyone. Hetty observed as well that, if her brother noticed Caroline's withdrawal, the only feeling it evoked was incurious relief.

He won't be able to hold out much longer, Hetty thought. *And then he will give in and go to Edith. But how long before Caroline surrenders?*

Before there were any new developments, a letter came for Lionel from the Clinkett brothers. It had been written days and days prior but had first gone from the Clinkett home in Kent to Somerset before being forwarded to London by Rosemary. As Clinker and Clunker were no better correspondents than Lionel himself, the receipt of a letter was novel enough to rouse him temporarily from his lowness, and he hurried to his room to read it privately.

Lion—

I have good news and bad news for you, if you survived your stab wound.

The bad news is, our paterfamilias *responded to our little scrape exactly as we might have expected. There has been talk of disinheritance, the evils of keeping bad company (viz., you), the sad state of education at Magdalen (because we have surely brought disgrace on Mr. Routh and our entire college with this), and finally, threatened reductions in our quarterly allowance to reimburse Father the fine he paid to set us at liberty. The good news is that the next sessions approach, when we will be obligated to return to town and appear at the Old Bailey, if only to see you hanged or locked up or exiled. (Father thinks, since Clunker and I only stood by and watched you pummel the victim while we failed to try to separate you, we will escape with just time in the pillory. In my opinion, having mobs pelt one with rotten fruit, rocks, and execration sounds little better than hanging.) What I have not yet shared with my sire is that Clunker and I have decided, if you are sentenced to transportation, we will likely join you on our own, because what a lark that would be! So chin up, Lion. You will not be sent to the underside of the earth without companions.*

I enclose a hideous sonnet by Clunker commemorating our adventure, which I suspect he would like to mail to the Times. *He assures me that, if not for the brevity sonnets require, he would have mentioned* our *part in it, but I suspect Father's harangues contributed to our erasure. It makes you look more heroic, in any event. If your stab wound has not finished you, this very well might.*

Clinker

Both comforted and bemused, Lionel unfolded the second sheet and read:

The Stolen Likeness" by E. Clinkett (1814)

"Justice!" cried the youth, with visage gris.
One summer day his cousin took up pen
And chalk, his likeness for to apprehend.

But of the final painting she was fleeced.

A theft unsolved, but when all searching ceased

The purloined portrait showed its face again

In exhibition hung for praise of men

Within Academy walls of Somerset Place.

The thief, false Morris, all credit assumed as well.

"Confess, foul villain, lest I beat you fast to pulp,"

Urged youth with upper hand, till he impaled

By Morris with palette knife did groan, "Oh, hell."

"Ne'er will I," vowed the blackguard, "cry mea culpa,

While you your life in exile will bewail."

Lionel rather liked the poem, but he suspected neither his own father nor Edith would welcome it being published in the *Times*. It heartened him that his two friends offered to join him in exile, although if he were sentenced to forced labor it didn't sound like such a lark, and he doubted they would come. (He had a brief vision of himself, chained to other convicts, swinging a pick under a roiling sun, and shuddered.) But perhaps it wouldn't come to that. He was a first-time offender, after all, from a good family with money enough—not of the "criminal class," as it were. The judge would have to exact *some* sort of punishment, to be certain, but it need not be the legendary seven years' transportation. This was minimal comfort, however, for even if his sentence was shorter, the voyage itself was so long that he would surely be gone from England at least a couple years.

There was a knock at his door, followed by his sister's entrance. "Anything of interest in the letter?"

Wordlessly he handed it to her, while he lay back upon his bed, arms folded behind his head, staring up at the canopy.

Hetty chuckled, and Lionel said dryly, "I'm glad my sad fate gives you pleasure."

"Well, you won't get pity from me," she returned, "when you refuse to participate in your salvation." Plumping herself on the side of the bed, she regarded him. "Are you going to tell Edith you will accept her help after all?"

He made the same face he had been making the last several days. "Not her help—her *self-sacrifice*. She gives up recognition and fortune to rescue me, and she must go wheedling and groveling to the person who has already defrauded her."

"It was her idea, Lionel. She was willing."

"Somehow that makes it worse," he muttered. "But, I suppose, knowing Edith, she will pursue her plan with or without my help."

"Most assuredly," agreed Hetty. "She loves you dearly and has no more desire to see you buried in prison or sent 'round the world for years than you have to go."

When she said the word "love," he rolled away, putting his back to her. "*Your* plan didn't work, Het."

"Of course my plan worked. I said you would get an opportunity to talk to Edith and you did. It's not my fault you drove her away."

She waited for him to answer, but when he didn't she went on. "But that was just the part of my plan you knew about. And though you did your best to bungle your portion, you didn't succeed because, as we just said, she is likely still trying to save you."

"So what was your part of the plan, which I didn't manage to bungle?" he asked with feigned crossness. In actuality, he felt a faint shiver of optimism.

"Why, getting Caroline to break her engagement with you, you blockhead."

Abruptly, he flipped over again to face her. "What do you mean? That was your plan? It didn't work one bit. She hasn't broken the engagement."

"Oh, but I think she will. She has merely been trying to accustom herself to the idea and giving you a chance to change your mind."

"What makes you think this, Het?"

"Just something a little bird told me," she replied. "Or perhaps a big bird. You're more of a cassowary than a canary, you know, especially in your blue frock coat." But she was too pleased with herself to be mysterious or teasing for long. "All right, I'll tell you. Because you'll never guess, Lionel. It was when we were in the dome of St. Paul's—up in the gallery, you remember—you and Edith were talking on one side of the gallery while Caroline and I were on the other."

"So?"

"So, you didn't know, but Caroline and I overheard nearly everything you said to Edith, including how you loved her and wanted to marry only her! That was why Caroline fainted—she heard your confession and realized it wasn't her you loved."

"*What?*"

Embarrassment warred with incredulity and hope. Sitting up, Lionel didn't know whether to kiss Hetty or box her ears. He took refuge in physics. "But what do you mean you overheard me? How could you have?"

"I got the idea from Bowles' guidebook! It said that if you leaned into the wall of the dome in the gallery and spoke, you could be heard all the way on the other side, and it was true! I had to keep Caroline quiet, because if you had heard us as well, you would have realized how it worked, and all would have been lost."

For the first time in a week, Lionel broke into a grin. He even gave a bark of a laugh and slapped the coverlet. "*That* was your plan? Giving me a chance to talk to Edith and then eavesdropping on the result?"

"Well, why not?" she said smugly. "It isn't as if I haven't known you my entire life. I knew that, given the chance, you would never be able to keep your feelings to yourself, so if there were just some way Caroline could be a fly on the wall, as it were, you would be able to ask for your release without directly asking for your release. See?"

"But—how did you know I cared for Edith?" he demanded, coloring.

"I didn't, until you began acting as if you *didn't* care for Edith. When you no longer liked to talk about her and never asked after her, and always seemed taken with the toothache when I mentioned her. And when I actually asked you outright...well, then enlightenment began to dawn on me."

"Ah." He rubbed the coverlet between his fingers, pressing a crease into it and then smoothing it out again. "Edith doesn't care for me, however—in that way. You must have heard her tell me so."

"Honestly, Lionel!" Hetty groaned. "What else could she say? You're in the world's biggest muddle *and* you are engaged to someone else. Under those circumstances, what would be the use of telling you she loved you?"

"What are you saying? That—that you think she actually might?"

His sister only rolled her eyes. "I am saying it cannot be ruled out. I make no promises because Edith doesn't exactly babble about these things. And where's your spirit? If she says she loves you like a brother, it's a good place to begin, isn't it?"

Lionel did kiss her then (which made her squeal in surprise)—kissed her and then leapt off the bed, fighting the urge to cut a caper. "Oh, Het—if Caroline would only jilt me and Edith say she perhaps could love me one day, I would go happily to the Antipodes, for however long I was sent."

"I imagine you would, and if Edith loved you, she's probably silly enough to wait for you." Rising, she gave him a push. "But come on then. If you don't place yourself where Caroline can find you, how is she to renounce you? And, for heaven's sake, when she does, try not to look too gleeful about it."

As it happened, Hetty arranged that moment as well, insisting upon another afternoon walk to Regent's Park, where she left the two of them safely on the bridge and wandered some distance away to watch the proceedings.

She saw Caroline remove her bonnet and let it dangle by its ribbons, as if to give her cousin one last opportunity to admire and fall in love with her, but when he hardly glanced at her, Caroline nerved herself and spoke.

Lionel's surprised reaction was a little overdone, as was his remorseful one, and Hetty half feared Caroline would be persuaded to retract her retraction. But then he began to rock on his heels in an attempt to disguise his relief, leaving his sister to fret that his delight would wound their cousin.

But at last it was done. Neither Lionel nor Caroline spoke a word of it when she rejoined them, but that evening their aunt Lavinia was icy in her demeanor and made no demurral when Hugh Hapgood mentioned again a possible removal to lodgings.

"Yes," Hetty told herself as she dropped off to sleep that night, "it's been a good week's work."

Chapter Thirty

**Is the revelation of secrets the
greatest expression of friendship?
—James Harrington, *Horæ Consecratæ* (1682)**

A mile lay between the Arbuthnots' elegant home in Bruton Street and the Sidneys' newer construction in Devonshire Street, but Edith thought she could fly between them, she was so bursting with news. Her aunt and uncle's insistence that Miss Blenkensop, their unforeseen dame in shining armor, must take ample refreshment and enjoy ample leisure before she stirred again made Edith want to scream with impatience. Joyous, painful impatience.

She could not bear to send a note to her Hapgood relations; she must tell them the good news herself. She must *see* Lionel's face, when he learned he was delivered! Edith herself could hardly sit still when Miss Blenkensop told her story— "I will give you just the brief version, my dear, for I find myself faint, now that the crisis is past." Which meant that Edith could not ask the hundred questions she wanted to ask and must bite her cheek and fidget and encourage Miss Blenkensop to, please, take more tea, and agree that, yes, it would be just the right thing, if she were to lie down for an hour and recover.

But she could be patient now, she counseled herself, if it meant the sword of Damocles no longer hung over Lionel. Well—not the larger sword, at any rate. There was still the matter of his cousin Caroline, "but now I know how dearly I must love him," Edith whispered, as she paced back and forth before the drawing room window, "if I can so rejoice at his rescue, even if it means nothing can prevent Caroline now from insisting on an early wedding."

If Edith could pretend patience, her cousin Hetty could not. While Miss Blenkensop was still resting, a note came from Devonshire Street.

> *Edie—*
>
> *What can you mean, staying away from us so long? It has been a week, and I must see you! I have such news for you, and I do not know if you will take it the way I want you to. What are you doing over there? I know you and Lionel had a disagreement (about which His Surliness would not speak until I compelled him), but I believe you will find him coming around. Please, please, I must know how your paintings are coming, or if the sketches even passed muster with that swindler!*

Send word at once. *Either write or come, but I must hear from you.*

In violent impatience,

Hetty

Upon reading this, Edith flew off in search of her aunt and uncle, only to have her whirling plans forestalled by their own.

"My dear," Eliza Arbuthnot said, taking Edith by the hands and leading her to a seat, which Edith could scarcely keep in her excitement, "when I showed Miss Blenkensop to her room, she asked that the sharing of her confidences be kept to a minimum. It is a very private matter which nearly concerns her, of course."

"Of course. But—surely we may tell the Hugh Hapgoods," urged Edith. "Apart from myself, they are the primary people affected by her news."

"Yes," agreed Alwyn, "but not their Sidney relations." Seeing the protests bubbling to her lips, he held up a hand. "Have no fear, Edie. Eliza and I have decided we will invite the Hugh Hapgoods to supper tonight. As we are not acquainted with the Sidneys, they can take no offense at not being included."

Eagerly she nodded. "Oh, yes, I see the sense in that. In all of that. May we please send the invitation at once?"

They could, but only after Eliza Arbuthnot summoned the cook for a quick conference—was there fish, or did the Hapgoods prefer duck? What vegetables were in the market? What cheeses? At last, at last, the note was sent, but Hetty must have been waiting as restlessly as Edith, for it was soon accepted.

Edith took especial care with her hair and dress that evening, choosing a rose silk mull with matching bandeau, above which her black curls were wound and hanging down. But then, as the hour drew nearer, she feared her accelerating pulse would make her skin as pink as the dress, and she would have the overall appearance of a slice of ham. There was not time enough, however, to change, even if she had the courage to summon her aunt's maid again.

At precisely eight, the sound of a carriage was heard. Edith kept her seat, clinging to her embroidery hoop, the eagerness which possessed her all day giving way to agitation. If she had any sympathy for her former governess, she might have seen that Miss Blenkensop's color was equally high at the thought of sharing her story again, but Edith was too engrossed in her own feelings to spare any.

"Mr. Hugh Hapgood, Mr. Lionel Hapgood, Miss Harriet Hapgood," announced Binchin.

Barely were the required bows and curtsies made than Hetty shrieked, "Miss Blenkensop! You are in London!"

"I am," smiled Miss Blenkensop, some of her starchiness wilting at the sight of two of her favorite people. "And why I am I will presently explain."

Though Edith could not lift her eyes higher than Lionel's kneecaps, she heard her uncle say, "Young man, I hear you are to be congratulated."

"Er—" said Lionel.

"Oh, I do not refer to the charges against you or your looming court date, to be sure," Alwyn chuckled, "I mean your engagement."

"My dear husband," murmured his wife, "the Hapgoods will think you heartless to speak of the younger Mr. Hapgood's situation so lightly."

"That's as much as they know," he grinned, nudging her roguishly. "But, hey there, Edie tells me she's a pretty little thing, your cousin Miss Sidney."

"Er—" said Lionel.

"Caroline has thrown him over!" announced Hetty. "Just yesterday. And won't you please call us Lionel and Hetty?"

But Edith didn't hear a word of what her aunt and uncle pleased to call them, so loud was the sudden roar of blood in her ears. Her eyes flew up and sought Lionel's. The very corner of one side of his mouth lifted.

Then it was...true?

Moving in a daze, the next thing she was aware of, they were all seated at supper, Lionel as far from her as a table for seven could place him. Miss Blenkensop held the very center, that everyone might hear what she had to say, and Mrs. Arbuthnot mercifully told the footmen to deliver all the courses to the table at once, that they might be quit of them.

When the servants had removed at least to the other side of the dining room door, Hetty could bear it no longer. "Please, Miss Blenkensop, take pity on me and tell us your news. What brought you here to London?"

"Yes. My news. Very well." Precisely the woman lay down her soup spoon. Precisely she reached for her glass and took a silent sip of wine. "My dear Harriet, what I say may come as a shock to you. It did certainly to Edith. And I am heartily ashamed of my involvement, however tangential. Moreover, Mr. Hapgood—" (addressing Hugh) "—I am aware that, after you hear what I say, you may no longer wish me in your employ, because—because—"

"Papa is always just," Hetty said hastily, when she saw Miss Blenkensop draw a handkerchief from her sleeve. She wondered what on earth her proper, upright, blameless governess could possibly have done, to warrant such hemming and hawing, but thought, at this rate, she might well have to shake it out of her.

"This is difficult for me," the woman continued in an unsteady voice, "though I have already told an abridged version of this to the Arbuthnots and Edith. However, to begin: you will recall, of course, that—the drawing master—Mr. Eldredge—was quick to recognize the talent of our Edith..." Her listeners nodded (apart from Edith, who looked at her bowl of soup). "He was the one who recommended she visit her sister Mrs. Waite in Bath, where she might receive instruction from an artist friend of his, Mr. Alexandre Olivier.

"The life of an artist is a difficult one—I make no excuses for anyone, I simply state a fact. Judah—that is, Mr. Eldredge—had long pursued a career as a landscape painter, with limited success. Mr. Olivier was still hoping to make a job of it but gladly accepted Edith as a pupil because most artists are in dire need of income."

She paused, taking another sip of wine. The others hardly touched their food, not wanting to miss a word, with the exception of Alwyn, who forged ahead, having no desire to eat cold fish.

"So far, all was well and to everyone's satisfaction. It was only when—when Mr. Eldredge found himself wishing to increase his income that the trouble began."

Hugh frowned at this. "He did not feel the tuition paid by the squire and myself was a fair one?"

"No—that is to say, Mr. Hapgood, he thought it perfectly adequate until—until his plans changed." The handkerchief reappeared, but only to be waved at Miss Blenkensop's suddenly heated cheeks. "You see—Mr. Eldredge thought he might like to marry. But—er—the woman applied to felt it impractical, if not impossible, even on their combined wages, and she refused him."

There was no need to ask the identity of the woman applied to, but Hetty and Edith exchanged a glance, Hetty's rather mischievous.

In recollecting the evening later, Miss Blenkensop must have thought that, never before in her experience had she held the complete and unwavering attention of an entire party as she did at that supper. Certainly it had never been her experience as a teacher. If the circumstances to be related had not been so sensitive, so embarrassing, she might have enjoyed it.

"Mr. Eldredge wrote Mr. Olivier about the sad state of his fortunes," she went on, "and—well—Mr. Eldredge claims, that Mr. Olivier claims, that it was the *younger* Mr. Olivier who...contrived...a scheme to remedy matters. This nephew person had often pressed his uncle to make more effort to become known, that his paintings might sell better. And when Edith entered the uncle's sphere, the nephew recognized both her tremendous gift, as well as the use it might be put to. In short, he proposed passing off Edith's paintings as his uncle's."

"I knew it!" said Lionel, banging his fist on the table so that the salt cellar tumbled over. He replaced it with an apologetic look at Mrs. Arbuthnot, but then leaned far over the table to meet Edith's eye. "I *knew* that was your painting at the exhibition."

"Hush, Lionel," his sister urged. "I want to hear how it came to be there."

Miss Blenkensop raised teacherly eyebrows and waited for silence before resuming. "The uncle objected—weakly—to this proposal before giving in, and so the nephew arranged for Edith's paintings to be 'stolen' from the Olivier home. In reality, the younger Mr. Olivier staged the break-in himself, hiding away the stolen goods. He knew he could not sell them for some little while—not while every art dealer and buyer in Bath knew of the crime, but he thought he could pass them off later in London. And then, on second thought, the nephew realized that if the paintings were passed off under an altogether assumed name—an assumed *English* name—they would then also be eligible to be submitted to the Royal Academy. I need not tell you what an honor this is to any artist, Mr. Eldredge once having the very great fortune of a canvas being accepted, but it also brings wider exposure. That is, an artist who has exhibited with the Academy may always boast about it later and perhaps garner higher purchase prices. By submitting one of Edith's paintings, the Oliviers might kill two birds with one stone. They might become famous and they might make money. And so they did."

"Pardon me, Miss Blenkensop," Edith spoke up for the first time, "but if it was indeed the portrait of Lionel on the stile that was submitted, do you know what became of the other two paintings?"

"My dear, I cannot say exactly," Miss Blenkensop admitted, "but I do know that, altogether, the younger Mr. Olivier managed to sell all three of your paintings, and that the total came to nearly twelve hundred pounds!"

Gasps issued from both sides of the table, and Edith, too, felt overpowered by amazement, while at the same time she was aware of a pang. Ah, then the painting she wanted to give Margaret and Dashiell was lost forever. As lost as her portrait of Lionel.

When her attention returned to her former governess, she saw Miss Blenkensop putting the handkerchief to work again, this time patting at her eyes. "I know it was that much because, I am ashamed to say, Mr. Eldredge applied once more to that—certain woman. He told her he had come into an unexpected inheritance of four hundred pounds, and would that not be enough to provide some security? She yielded and engaged herself, all unknowingly."

"She cannot be blamed," Edith murmured, all too aware of Lionel's visibly clenched fists along the table. "For who possibly could have guessed where or how such a sum was come by, especially when told by a person she trusted?"

"But how did you learn the truth?" pressed Hetty.

This drew a long sigh. "Mr. Eldredge was not himself. His conscience smote him, making him silent and nervous in what should have been a happy time. But I do not know when the truth would have emerged, had news not reached Somerset of Lionel's—incident. At nearly the same moment, Mr. Eldredge received the elder Mr. Olivier's account of it, Mr. Olivier also suffering qualms and regrets. The moment Judah—Mr. Eldredge, rather—made a full confession, I—er—the engagement was ended and I hastened to town." Her long chin lifted, and she met their gaze fully. "With Mr. Eldredge's agreement, I am fully prepared to submit a statement to the court, though now it may no longer be necessary."

"Why not?" prompted Hugh. "It would be greatly appreciated."

"Because when Miss B came to see Edith," Alwyn burst in, "that conniving Jean-André happened to be present—"

"Conferring with me over the progress of the paintings I had agreed to do," Edith interposed swiftly, seeing the jerk of Lionel's surprise.

"And Miss Blenkensop confronted him like a fury," Mrs. Arbuthnot added, "throwing his deeds in his face!"

"Did he admit his guilt?" demanded Lionel.

"His actions did. He attempted to flee—"

"But Alwyn fastened upon him—"

"And would have prevailed, but the villain happened to break one of my wife's favorite porcelain bowls, and he wielded a piece of the pottery at me like a dagger."

"It is my opinion he intended not only to flee the house but also the country," Miss Blenkensop concluded with satisfaction. "For the elder Mr. Olivier had spoken of the two of them taking the

Olivier share of the 'earnings' and returning to their native France, now that the peace has come."

Lionel turned to his father. "What will happen now? Will the Clinketts and I still have to appear at the sessions?"

"You will appear," Hugh answered slowly. "Because, even if he has fled, I doubt this Olivier stopped at the Old Bailey to withdraw his charges."

"He would be too fearful of being locked up himself!" declared Alwyn.

"But, when Olivier fails to show," Hugh continued, "and if Miss Blenkensop will be so kind as to submit her written testimony beforehand—"

"I have it," she nodded. "And signed by Judah Eldredge."

"—I imagine the case will easily be dismissed. You and the Clinketts will be cleared."

Lionel and Hetty erupted in whoops, Hetty beating on the table in a most unladylike manner, which did not even draw a frowning look from her governess. "Three cheers for Blenkensop!" Hetty hollered, and, to the woman's blushing pleasure, the entire party complied. "Hip hip, hurrah! Hip hip, hurrah! Hip hip, hurrah!"

By the time the excitement died down, the food was stone cold, but not a person complained, not even Alwyn, and they all fell to with renewed and hearty appetite.

CHAPTER THIRTY-ONE

Here didst thou dwell, in this enchanted cover,
Egeria! thy all heavenly bosom beating
For the far footsteps of thy mortal lover."
—Byron, *Childe Harold's Pilgrimage* (1812)

July, with its long, mild, sunlit days, was come to Bramleigh. Blue skies above, flecked with cheerful clouds, and below every shade of green, as the eye moved from slope to field to pasture to hedgerow to copse. And the wildflowers! Buttercups, clover, red valerian, and chamomile begged to be gathered in straggling little posies or captured in Edith's sketchbook.

And she had indeed been sketching, until she drifted off beneath a spreading oak, having taken shelter from the warmth of the day. Nearby, Mannerly cropped the luxuriant grass, reins trailing beside her. Edith's drowsiness was no great surprise because she had hardly slept the two nights before, waiting for news from London as Lionel's court date came and went. It was cruel of them not to send an express, she thought, a sentiment echoed by Rosemary, whom she had called upon. But was the silence good or bad?

When her eyes flickered open, she saw the very person she had been thinking of ceaselessly: Lionel, coatless, reclining in the grass beside her, propped up on one elbow. The sunlight which made its way through the leaves and branches of the oak tree glinted off his auburn hair, and he was chewing idly on a straw, watching his horse.

"Are you real?" asked Edith.

His head turned, and he grinned at her. "No. I'm a ghost. I was hanged yesterday."

"You wretch!" she laughed. But she touched the edge of his sleeve, just to be certain. When he proved to be altogether material, she rolled to a sitting position and said, "You deserve hanging, to make a joke like that, when your stepmother and I have been on tenterhooks."

Reaching up, he picked a blade of grass from her curls. "Were you really worried?"

"Yes. After all, there's many a slip 'twixt cup and lip. Supposing Jean-André returned to accuse you? And Miss Blenkensop, unknown to you all, had been run down by a hackney coach?"

"And the testimony she submitted beforehand to the court?"

"Had been lost," suggested Edith, "because the clerk who took it was thinking about the lamb chop he would have for supper, so he left it on his desk, where it blew off when he shut the door behind him at the end of the day, and then the following morning the servant tore it in strips and used it for spills to light the fire."

"Good heavens. Perhaps you ought to write novels, instead of drawing pictures."

"Oh, Lionel, do tell me what happened!"

He sat up, wrapping his long arms about his knees. "Pretty much what Papa predicted. The court was called to order by a dusty, fusty bewigged judge who favored the Clinketts and me with a disapproving look, but what could he do? The person who ordered the warrant on us did not even trouble himself to show up. Worse yet, there was a testimony on file and witnesses at the ready to say the missing man was more sinning than sinned against. So, even though a goodly number of spectators had paid their shilling to watch the proceedings, the amiable judge had no choice but to dismiss the case, much as he would have liked to load us on the next convict ship weighing anchor."

"Oh, Lionel," she said again. "I am so very, very glad."

They fell silent, and the summer air between them seemed to thicken with fragrance and warmth. Edith wanted to say more—so much more—but she didn't know how to begin.

As for Lionel, well—he found himself in a familiar place. It was the same old story, where she was concerned, and he had a suspicion it might always be.

He had gone in search of her as soon as the coach arrived in Patterton and he had a chance to change his clothing and wash the dust from his face. He meant to ride Mannerly to Bramleigh this time, but the stable lad was quick to say Miss Hapgood had required the mare, oh, maybe an hour or two ago.

But even though he had to walk, he knew Edith's favorite haunts, and it had not been difficult to find her, especially when he spotted his horse grazing.

To come upon Edith, like the sleeping beauty in the wood, her head pillowed on her arm, bonnet cast to the side, and her pretty limbs outlined by the draping of her light summer frock, robbed him of breath and volition for a minute. He sank down in the grass beside her, understanding why whoever wrote that story had the prince awaken the princess with a kiss—Lionel could think of nothing he would rather do. But she slept on, and he mastered himself enough to sound merely friendly when she awoke. Friendly. Brotherly. Because what if Hetty was wrong, and Edith's sisterly affections never grew into anything more?

The silence stretched.

Fearing he would read her mind, the longer she said nothing, Edith sought shelter in discussing others. "Do you know I wrote Miss Blenkensop that she ought to marry Mr. Eldredge anyway? He may have given in and condoned what he ought not, but he repented in time. He isn't a wicked man—he was just a desperate one."

Knowing a thing or two about desperation, Lionel didn't reply right away.

"And I said—I said, to keep the four hundred pounds. What's done is done," she added hastily. "It's ironic, isn't it, that if Jean-André had never stolen my paintings, I never would have received a penny for them. Because they were studies. They were for myself. Not meant to be sold."

"And now you never will receive a penny for them, if you told Soppy and Eldredge that," he observed. "I suppose the Oliviers haven't offered to return any of their ill-gotten gains?"

"Miss Blenkensop wrote back, enclosing a letter the elder Mr. Olivier sent Mr. Eldredge. It was all in French, which is just like her, to make me practice my French at the same time that she is imparting information."

"And what did it say?"

"That they are living under the name Maurice, in a little apartment on the Rue du Richelieu, where they have a studio on the topmost floor and propose to start again and live as honest men."

"Using your money as the means to start again," Lionel muttered.

"Yes, I suppose. But would you believe me, Lionel, if I said all that money (that I never had in the first place) doesn't seem like too much to pay, just to be rid of them?"

He smiled ruefully. "I might. Soon come, soon gone. Still—knowing all I know now, I wish I'd got a few more punches in."

She gave him a teasing shove, that made him lose his balance and topple onto his back. "Well, I'm glad you didn't. Because here you are, at liberty and still alive and in England, and that seems to me all that one could wish for."

"Hm." Not meeting her eyes, he rolled up on his elbow again, pressing a hand over the grass to flatten it. Then he grasped a handful of the blades and tugged, uprooting them.

"It turns out…" he said in a low voice, "I can still think of one more thing to wish for."

"Oh?" She felt a painful blush wash over her and her heart began to thump like a drum. Abruptly she climbed to her feet, afraid he would be able to hear her unruly organ if she remained too near him.

Lionel gave a sigh and shut his eyes briefly. Because he was going to do it again, Lord help him. He was going to tell her still one more time that he loved her, even after vowing in the gallery at St. Paul's that he never would trouble her again with his attentions.

If she rebuffed him this time—after all that had happened and after Hetty's hints that she cared for him—well, there would be an end of it, wouldn't it? He couldn't keep asking and asking and asking. He really would have to wander to the ends of the earth, somewhere far away, where he would never see her again or hear her mentioned—after giving Hetty a good shake, of course, for raising his hopes.

Slowly, he stood.

"Edith."

A shiver ran through her, despite the warmth of the afternoon. "Yes? Oh, I—I meant to ask you—how is your wound? Is it all healed?"

"The one from the palette knife is."

"Is—there another?"

"You know there is."

She shook like a leaf now and had wild ideas of running away. Or vaulting onto Mannerly and galloping away. Only, she still didn't know how to gallop, and she still couldn't climb onto Mannerly without assistance or a handy stump.

He hoped she would encourage him—ask him what the other wound was—but Edith was inwardly frantic with panic and at a loss to remember her own name.

Fortunately for both of them, and for their children and grand-children, she swayed then on her feet, undone by her shallow breathing. And Lionel, of course, caught her by the upper arms to steady her. When her head fell back, her eyes wide and bottomless, her lips parting, he didn't hesitate. Without thinking, Lionel accepted their wordless invitation.

Birds sang; bees buzzed; breeze blew. Or maybe it was all in their minds, as they embraced.

Delicious, thought Edith, when she could think at all. He loved her still! Could there be any greater joy than being loved by the person dearer to you than anyone in the world? If there was, she could not imagine it.

It was only some minutes later, when Lionel felt a tugging on his neckcloth and whickering breaths on his cheek that did not sound like Edith or come from Edith, that they broke apart, to find Mannerly had joined their blissful rapprochement.

"Blasted horse," grumbled Lionel, pushing the mare away, while Edith giggled.

"Oh, don't, Lionel—she loves you too."

That drew his gaze back to her in a flash. "Too? Do you mean—Edie—that you—?"

Edith only laughed harder. "Well, of course I do! Do you think I kiss young gentlemen that I do *not* love in such a fashion?"

"You'd better not be kissing *any* young gentlemen besides me in such a fashion."

"Very well," she agreed solemnly. "From now on, I won't." Then she shrieked as he seized her and tossed her over his shoulder, spinning in a circle until she was pounding him on the back with her little fists. "Put me down, Lionel! What if someone sees us?"

"You think they would mind a little horseplay, if they didn't mind the kissing?" But he obeyed, setting her down, and they both promptly fell over dizzily into the grass.

"When will you marry me?" he asked, after a time. "Do you think seventeen is old enough?"

"No, I don't," was her unexpected reply. So unexpected that he sat up again.

"What do you mean?" he demanded. "Aren't you going to marry me?"

She raised herself to a sitting position as well and took his hands. "Yes, if you'll have me. But not quite yet. Seventeen is hardly better than sixteen."

"It's an entire year better!" protested Lionel. "Why is it still too soon?"

"There are two reasons. In the first place, you haven't taken your university degree yet."

"Confound my university degree!"

"Confounded or not, why couldn't we wait until next summer? I should be eighteen then, and you nineteen-and-a-half *and* an Oxford graduate." Seeing his unpersuaded glower, she added, "And secondly, if we wait until next summer, I might gain a little more experience and scope as an artist."

Then he was on his feet again. "Oh, no—wait a moment—don't tell me Eldredge has some other slippery, dishonest thief he wants you to study under! Another criminal to steal your work, while his nephew makes love to you? Absolutely not!"

Edith's laugh rang out again. "Honestly, Lionel. Why would I want that either? No. I mean that, while you finish your studies, I will finish mine, by accompanying my uncle Alwyn and aunt Eliza abroad. I should very much like to see the art and artists at Paris and Rome."

"Of course you would, and you should!" he agreed, pulling her up beside him. "But why shouldn't we do it together? We might marry and go to the Continent for our honeymoon."

"Oh, Lionel. There is still the matter of your mathematics degree, and I suspect I would neither learn as much nor spend as much time working if you were with me and we were married."

His eyes drifted over her beloved face, lingering on her eyes and mouth, and he kept them off her person only with an effort. Yes, she was probably right.

Seeing him begin to yield, she murmured, "I told the Arbuthnots I would come, before I knew all would be well with you. I thought you might be in New South Wales or Newgate or—or married to your cousin Caroline. But now I see it would be a lovely use of my time, while you finish your own tasks. Especially since you fall so short as a correspondent."

"I would write to *you*," he insisted. At her skeptical expression, he added, "More than I wrote my family, I mean."

"Even so," said Edith. She slid her arms about his waist. "Wouldn't you be willing to wait for me a little, Lionel? I am so happy today, I feel I could live off it forever."

"That's because you've only loved me for a few minutes, and I've been loving you the last six years."

"A few minutes!" She squeezed him reprovingly and dropped a light kiss on his jaw. "I know you hate the Oliviers, but it was they who opened my eyes a year ago. They no sooner saw my sketch of you at the stile than they as much as told me I was in love with you. And it turned out I was!"

"You've loved me for the last year?"

"At least. It must be longer than that, though, or I would not have painted you with love."

"Then why did you not tell me?" he pressed. "Why did you not write to me instantly and say you had changed your mind?"

"Oh, Lionel, I thought about it—of course I did—but I didn't know how to go about it. And what if *you* had changed your mind? Hetty wrote me soon enough about Caroline and her interest in you and how pretty she was."

He gave her a playful shake. "Surely when you met Caroline for yourself, you couldn't think I would choose her after you."

"Oh, couldn't I?" she countered. "It was very shortly after I met Caroline for myself that I learned you were engaged. I knew she liked you, and I knew she was pretty—yes—but your engagement still caught me by surprise."

"That made two of us."

They laughed, and he pulled her against him again, rubbing his cheek against her curls. "Tell me, Edith—why did you lie to me in the gallery at St. Paul's, when I told you again that I loved you and that I wanted to be rid of her?"

"Because you would have stopped me from trying to save you, if I gave you any right to."

He didn't argue with this, only hugged her harder. "I may still hire an assassin to visit your dear Olivier friends in the Rue de Richelieu."

Edith smiled to herself and decided she had better not tell Lionel that Jean-André never meant to share the profits from the bridge portrait and *The Parting*.

Resting her head against him she said, "Try to forget all about them. They can't spoil our happiness now, and, if not for them, we would not have learned how much I love you, nor how much someone besides myself would be willing to pay for pictures of you!"

"That's something, I suppose," he mused. "Worth losing your dowry of twelve hundred pounds to them."

"You!"

"To support us, I will have to put you to work, churning out portrait after portrait of me, to tempt that Austrian fellow," he teased. "*Portrait of a young gentleman on his wedding day. Portrait of a young gentleman reading the newspaper. Portrait of a young gentleman with his favorite rifle. Portrait of a young gentleman looking left. Portrait of a young gentleman looking right—*"

"*Portrait of a young gentleman being ridiculous*," she chided. "And you haven't answered my question about waiting a year."

He heaved a sigh. "Of course I'll wait. Have I any choice? What's one more year, after all? I've only spent a third of my life waiting. But we're engaged as of this moment—or the second I speak to your father—so that no one will be alarmed if they find me kissing you, like this. Or like this. Did you know, while I was ill I had a lovely dream of you?"

"You did?" she startled. "And what happened in this lovely dream?"

"You appeared like an angel. My Edith angel. I was so hot and so thirsty, and you gave me cool, cool water and held me in your arms and told me you loved me. But when I awoke, you weren't there, and the dream became a nightmare because I woke to find Caroline holding my hand and saying we were engaged!"

Trying not to smile, Edith wondered if it had been her own actions—nursing him and confessing her love while he was delirious—that led to his abortive engagement.

"Poor Caroline. She did adore you, you know."

"She was nicer to me than you were, at any rate," he agreed. "Quite clung to me. Had no interests apart from me. Would never abandon me to go to Paris or Rome."

"Perhaps you are already regretting your second engagement?" returned Edith mildly. "If you are, you might ask Hetty to get you out of this one, too."

"Unfortunately, I must make the best of it." He kissed her again, feeling a thrill run his whole length because he was permitted to. Welcome to.

She was his, at last.

Or would be, in one short, short, endless year.

"Gather your things, Edie," Lionel said, reaching to catch at one of Mannerly's trailing reins. "And let's go find your father."

The adventures of the Hapgood family continue with Hetty's story in *A Fickle Fortune.*

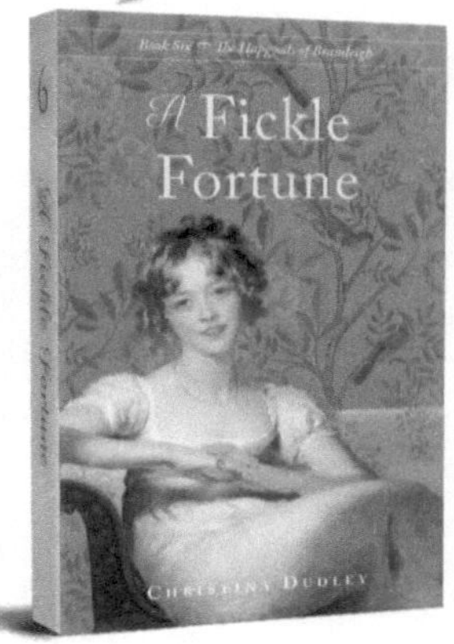

THE HAPGOODS OF BRAMLEIGH

The Naturalist
A Very Plain Young Man
School for Love
Matchless Margaret
The Purloined Portrait
A Fickle Fortune

THE ELLSWORTH ASSORTMENT

Tempted by Folly
The Belle of Winchester
Minta in Spite of Herself
A Scholarly Pursuit
Miranda at Heart
A Capital Arrangement

PRIDE AND PRESTON LIN

www.christinadudley.com